Kraven

VLG – Book Two

Vampires, Lycans, Gargoyles

By Laurann Dohner

Kraven by Laurann Dohner

Batina Dawson wants two things most in her life. She's determined to become a partner at her law firm and secure her younger sister's financial future. That's why she talked Dusti into flying to Alaska, to mend fences with their terminally ill, rich grandfather. It seemed to be a perfect plan—until things go wrong.

The plane crashes and their lives are saved by two large, muscled brothers. Kraven is a spiked-haired menace with a handsome face and a killer body. He also believes she's in danger from her own grandfather, and that Vampires and Lycans once bred, making him a VampLycan. He even claims her mother was one too. He may have kidnapped Bat, but his misguided hero complex is almost sweet. She knows exactly what defense she'll use if he becomes one of her clients. Insanity.

Kraven is frustrated. Bat refuses to stop arguing with him at every opportunity. She's stubborn, mouthy, and oh so sexy. She might be right when she accuses him of being crazy—she's driving him nuts. But she's in danger and he'll stop at nothing to keep her safe.

Author Note: VLG stands for Vampires, Lycans, Gargoyles...and breeds in between. Living in Alaska's harsh, pristine territories, these creatures live and love fiercely. These are their stories.

Dedication

Always and forever, my thanks to my wonderful husband. He's more than a partner and a lover, he's my best friend. This year marks twenty years of marriage, twenty-five years of cuddling with you in our sleep. Where did the time go? It seems like only yesterday when you stole my heart and changed my world for the better.

I'd also like to thank Kelli Collins. She ROCKS as an editor. Thank you for taking me on.

Kele Moon - You're my sounding board and the person who always keeps me sane and laughing over the trials of writing. I cherish your friendship. You are AWESOME!!!

VLG Series List

Drantos

Kraven

Kraven

Copyright © January 2016

Editor: Kelli Collins

Cover Art: Dar Albert

ISBN: 978-1-944526-03-0

Table of Contents

Kraven - VLG – Book Two

By Laurann Dohner

Chapter One

Guilt and regret were two things Batina had experienced most of her adult life. She'd talked her baby sister into this trip to visit their dying grandfather. She'd believed it would be for the best if they made peace with their only remaining relative.

Bat's greedy need to also persuade him to leave them money in his will was about to get them killed.

The tight squeeze on her hand drew Bat from her self-loathing. She turned her head to meet a nearly identical gaze to the one she faced in the mirror every morning. Dusti's blue eyes were wide open, terrified, and she'd paled with alarm.

The small charter plane's pilot had informed them they were going to crash. Vibrations shook their seats, the overhead compartments rattled loudly, and no amount of regret would save them.

"Fire in engine two," a panicked pilot shouted. "Shit! The system is offline. It's not responding. We're only twenty miles out but we're not going to make it to the airfield."

"Dump the fuel," the second pilot demanded harshly.

"Got it." The pilot cursed. "Do you see anything? Do you?"

"It's just trees. We're going down hard. Why the hell aren't they answering? I know it's a tiny airport but Jesus. Where are they? Maybe we lost communications and they aren't getting our mayday."

"Damn cheap bastards for not giving us a backup system," the other man hissed. "Fuck. We're going down. Seventeen hundred feet and falling." He paused. "Sixteen hundred." He paused again for several long seconds. "Fifteen hundred. Shit!"

"It's been good knowing you, Mike."

"You too, Tim. Drop the landing gear but I don't know why we should bother. When we hit those trees we're going to come apart." There was a pause. "Shit. Cut the mic!"

The attorney inside Bat grimaced. If anyone survived, they'd probably attempt to sue the small airline for that screwup alone, never mind the crash. The pilots had obviously lost their professionalism but she could hardly blame them. They were going to crash, and one glance out the window beyond Dusti confirmed there wouldn't be a safe place to land. In law school, she'd studied suits filed by families of the deceased enough times to know the end result of plane versus wooded area.

Bodies—dead ones.

Her grasp tightened on Dusti. They were born two years apart but had been as close as two people could possibly be growing up. It had fallen upon Bat at the tender age of eighteen to raise her younger sister, still in high school when their parents had died tragically. She'd had to make tough choices...selling the family home they both loved, moving them into a cheap apartment. She'd entered law school to make a better life for them both.

What did it get me?

Her frantic mind paused on that thought. She'd just earned a huge promotion by nearly killing herself, putting in massive amounts of overtime. She'd accepted nightmare cases no one else in her firm would touch with a ten-foot pole. No amount of soap would ever clean away the filth she called clients. Most had been guilty of crimes she'd secretly hoped would send them to prison, but losing on purpose hadn't been an option.

I hate my life, hate what I've become, and now I'm going to take my sister out with me because I thought our grandfather would leave us his damn money.

Movement from the right tore her from her thoughts. Two burly thugs were making their way toward the cockpit along the narrow, downward-sloping aisle. They had to grip seats to avoid being pitched forward when the entire fuselage quaked.

Terrific, she thought. *They're probably going to storm the cockpit, thinking they can do better than the pilots. Who gives a shit at this point? We're going down either way.*

The guy in the lead suddenly paused next to her seat. His jean-clad thigh rubbed her arm before nearly crushing it against the armrest. She jerked it away—and then gasped when he lifted a leg to step over hers. He wedged his big body between Dusti and the seat in front of her.

Something brushed her leg, again from the aisle, and her mouth dropped open completely when the second thug put a boot between her high heels. He nearly stepped on her foot. Both men faced Bat and her sister.

Astonishment muted her when he planted the second boot between her feet and shoved her legs apart until her knee breached the aisle. She gaped at the front of his tight, faded jeans directly in front of her face. He had a skull on his belt buckle, and her gaze lifted to take in a flat stomach covered in a black tank top, a leather biker jacket, all the way up to his tanned face and spiked black hair.

He didn't look at Bat, but instead glanced at the man in front of her sister.

Dusti gasped. "What—"

"Good luck, Kraven. Love you."

The guy wedged between Bat's thighs replied, "Love you too, bro." He sighed, a look of grim resignation on his ruggedly handsome features.

Ask them what the hell they think they're doing! she ordered her mouth, but it refused to work.

The one in front of Dusti spoke. "I'm Drantos."

He needs a haircut in the worst way. He also needs a personal shopper to pick out clothes that don't make him look like a biker, she determined. *Wait a minute. I'm losing my mind! What the hell am I thinking?*

Oblivious to her inner crazy-talk, the man continued, "We're hopefully going to save your asses by protecting you with our bodies. We might survive this if we don't blow up or get ripped apart on impact like the pilot thinks. I'm hoping he's wrong about that."

The spiked-headed hulk in front of her dropped to his knees and put his hands on her before she could do more than gasp. Her knees were

11

shoved up roughly, pinned under his leather jacket and tight to his sides, nearly in his armpits, his thick biceps trapping them in that position. Her mouth parted to scream but his body slammed roughly against hers with enough force to knock the air from her lungs.

Shock kept her from fighting him off when he unfastened her seat belt. An arm encircled her ass and jerked her against something metal that painfully pressed into her pelvic bone. The scent of leather and male filled her nose when he adjusted enough for her to pant in air again.

The hard press of something against her panties finally made her struggle, but the guy had a death grip on her. He wiggled his hips in a suggestive manner that had her crying out. Whatever was digging in to her rubbed when he adjusted again, and she wondered if this was the beginning of a sexual assault. One last nasty thrill for him before the plane went down.

It wouldn't surprise her; not after the guy she'd defended two years ago who had been into necrophilia. Of course, Bat wasn't dead yet, so it was probably considered a bonus to the psycho to rape her both before and after she died.

"Let her go!" Dusti shouted.

Bat would have turned to check on her sister but the asshole assaulting her squeezed her in a bear hug that threatened to crush her rib cage. She clawed at him as best she could with her hands, her nails digging into his thin cotton top, and she could feel hard flesh under her fingers. He snarled next to her ear, gripped her wrists, and shoved them down his body between his thighs. They clamped around her hands so tightly she winced.

What in the hell? What does he think he's doing? Her stunned mind remembered what the long-haired guy in need of a haircut had said. *They think they're going to protect us with their bodies? They have to be on drugs.* She ceased her struggles, knowing no matter how hard she fought, she couldn't win against a possibly amped-up drug addict.

Screams erupted inside the small fuselage and Bat grabbed hold of the guy's thigh just for something solid to cling to. The other passengers could see what she couldn't, what with her face buried against a black top and most of her head tucked inside his thick jacket. She moaned softly, knew with certainty they were about to slam into the ground, and she actually pressed firmer against the stranger.

We're going to die, he's holding me, I'm not alone. I love you, Dusti. I'm so sorry I—

A violent impact with something threw the guy holding her backward, her body slamming hard into his, and the sick sensation of her stomach being shoved up into her throat kept her from screaming along with the other passengers. Strong blasts of air whipped her and the plane slammed into something else, hard enough that she heard metal screech in protest.

One vicious jolt sent her and the man cradling her into the air, and she momentarily knew pure terror. Memories of a childhood trampoline flashed at the weightless feeling of being tossed, and then they landed brutally. She came down on top of the man, his body cushioning the impact. He made a horrible hissing grunt and while his hold on her didn't loosen, his hands did slide a little on her body. The arm under her ass

13

ended up around her lower back, and the one protecting her shoulders was now pressed firmly against the back of her head.

Something slammed into her, the press of perhaps another body falling on top of hers. She couldn't breathe, sandwiched between the stranger's torso and the pressure against back. Then an explosion sent a sharp stab of pain directly into her brain through her ears from the loud blast, and they rolled into something hard, unforgiving, before agony shot up her rib cage.

The back of her head bounced painfully against the floor, which vibrated with an intense shudder before everything came to a grinding halt that rolled their bodies once more.

The sudden stillness was eerie. Then everything she could hear became proof of life.

The guy sprawled over her had a heartbeat that pounded erratically where her ear remained crushed securely against his chest. Bat lay there pinned until he suddenly yanked his arms out from under her body. She gasped in a lungful of air when the guy lifted up enough to separate their torsos. She opened her eyes to stare at him but remained too traumatized to speak.

She took note that some of the spiked-up hair on top of his head had been flattened during the crash, giving him a dazed, somewhat boyish appearance.

On closer inspection of his ruggedly masculine features, she ditched that opinion.

A grim man in his early thirties regarded her with an air of danger that couldn't be considered boyish or innocent by any standards. He blinked a few times, drawing her attention to thick, lush eyelashes the same color as his jet-black hair. The light blue shade of his eyes made them appear intense, as if he could peer straight into her soul or read her mind.

He growled in a manner that reminded her of a guard dog about to attack. Bat startled.

"Let go." He was the owner of the deepest baritone she'd ever heard.

Her confused brain struggled to make sense of anything at that point. She continued to stare up at him until one thought surfaced. *We're not dead.*

"KRAVEN?" It was the other man's voice, from somewhere nearby.

"Fuck," the guy on top of Bat snarled. "We're alive. Did yours make it?"

"She's alive."

Bat prayed the stranger referred to Dusti. But she needed to see her sister herself, make certain she wasn't hurt. Her mouth opened but the huge guy on top of her continued talking to the other man.

"I hate flying." He grimaced. "I mentioned that, right?"

"Several times, but we're not flying anymore, are we? I don't mind flying but I hated the crashing part. I bet you wish you were still in the air right now. Quit bitching and let's see how bad the situation is. We survived. That's all that counts in the end."

They're joking? Seriously? Rage quickly replaced the numbness from the disaster they'd just endured. "Get off me. You're crushing me!"

15

The guy frowned but didn't move. Bat tried to move her hands but they were still trapped between their bodies, his weight locking them in place at her pelvic area, and frustration rose quickly.

"Bat?" Dusti's voice quivered. "Are you okay?" She sounded close.

Bat twisted her head, trying to peer around the man on top of her, but couldn't see anything in the aisle but the sides of seats next to them in the narrow space. "Dusti! Thank goodness you're alive! Are you all right? Get *off* me, asshole! You weigh a thousand pounds. I need to check on my sister!"

A soft growl came from the man—Kraven—and his blue gaze narrowed to give her a murderous look. "Maybe I *would* get off you if you weren't gripping my dick. That's not my thigh you've been clutching in terror, woman," he snarled. "Let. *Go!*"

Bat's fingers unclenched slowly, hesitantly, until she confirmed *exactly* what she'd gripped in her left hand. Her eyes widened when, as if on its own, her hand gave a gentle squeeze around flesh too small to be his thigh, but still a handful.

She tried to yank her hand away but it had nowhere to go, since he still pinned her. Her only option was to leave the fingers wide open to avoid gripping him again.

"Ewww!" She hated that the squeal escaped her, as if she were a little girl. "Get off me, asshole! My hand is trapped there, damn it."

"My name isn't asshole," he hissed through clenched teeth. "And I'd move if I weren't still in pain."

Bat blushed. She heard her sister and that Drantos guy speaking softly, though she couldn't make out the conversation. She wiggled under

16

the asshole sprawled over her but he didn't budge. If anything, he seemed to enjoy it when she tried to get out from under him, judging by his sadistic expression.

Movement out of the corner of her eye had her turning her head to see Drantos rising to his feet from behind the seats where she and Dusti had been sitting. His long hair looked even wilder and messed up than it had before the crash. His dark blue gaze met Bat's before he fixed his full attention on the guy crushing her.

"Are you going to just lay there on top of her or are you going to get up? It's no time to take a nap, Kraven."

"Go to hell. I think she crushed something vital when she squeezed my dick. I'm trying to recover. She's got nothing on a cock ring, that's for sure."

Drantos shook his head with a chuckle. "You're going to give her a bad impression if you don't watch your mouth."

"Like I give a damn what she thinks," Kraven grunted before climbing to his feet.

Bat took a deep breath, shifted her body gingerly to make sure everything worked, and then glared up at Kraven while she frantically shoved at her skirt to lower it over her thighs. She knew he'd gotten a good view of them since he didn't bother to hide where his focus lay. Anger ignited hotter inside her.

"Stay there, woman. I'll put you back on your ass if you get up—and you keep those iron hands to yourself. What are you? A masseuse?" His chin lifted and he shot Drantos a dirty look. "The bitch has strong hands. I swear she injured my dick."

17

Bat ignored him, struggling to her feet. She glowered at the man, who gave her an angry look right back. "Why did you grab me like that? What the hell is your problem?"

"I was *protecting* you. I'm Kraven. You can thank me later, by the way."

"Thank you?" She was outraged. "You'll be lucky if I don't have your ass arrested for sexual assault, battery, and...hell, bad hair! Move out of my way. I need to check on my sister."

He curled his full lips to sneer at her. Bat responded by shoving him. He stumbled back a foot, until he hit the side of one of the seats, and she tucked in her shirt that had pulled from the waist of her skirt. "Pervert," she hissed.

"Bitch," he retorted when she glared at him.

Her emotions all over the place, the urge to slap him made Bat's fingers itch. *Nobody calls me that—and he's done it twice.* She flipped him off. He softly growled. *Damn animal,* she thought. *Overgrown idiot.*

She reached for the back of her head, suddenly noticing the throbbing sensation there, and hoped she wasn't bleeding. Her hair pins were gone, the bun torn down into a tangled mass of a ponytail, and she found a painful lump on her head. She bit back a curse but was grateful it didn't feel wet.

She needed to check on Dusti. Bat tried to get around Kraven but he shot a hand out and pushed her back, hard enough to make her stumble, his palm squarely hitting her breast.

His brother was talking but she didn't hear the words; she was far too angry.

18

Kraven gave a jerk of his head. "I have the women."

"Have *this*, you jerk," Batina spat.

She lifted her leg, tore off her shoe, and threw it as hard as she could at his face.

Her aim ended up being off. The shoe struck his chest, then bounced to the ground. But he *did* stagger back with a stupefied look on his features, which gave her a little satisfaction. It also let her reach Dusti when he staggered back a step.

Pure joy filled her at seeing her sister safe. She hugged her instantly, relieved. Worry came next. She frantically studied Dusti for injuries but didn't see any visible ones.

"It's okay, Bat. I'm okay. Are you hurt?"

Bat eased her hold on her a little. "Nothing a good drink won't fix. I'm so glad you're okay."

Dusti nodded before turning away. Bat didn't miss the way her sister's delicate features twisted in horror, her skin changing from pale to absolute white before she swayed on her feet.

Bat followed her gaze to witness the horrendous sight where the side of the plane used to be.

The opposite wall had been torn open during the crash. A corpse with a missing arm remained strapped into his seat, soaked in bright red blood, and it made her knees weaken. She'd seen worse in photos from crime scenes, even in video evidence, but the real thing looked a hundred times more horrific.

Dusti gagged and the sound jerked Bat out of her stupor. She latched on to her, spun her until their gazes locked, and prayed she could hold her sister together by appearing calm. She was far from it on the inside, but she'd become a pro at hiding her emotions.

"Look at *me* and not that."

The tears that filled Dusti's eyes broke Bat's heart. She'd always tried to protect her sister, but nothing could shield her from reality at that moment.

"Oh God," Dusti moaned.

"I know." Bat nodded. "We survived though." *Give her a bright side; rally her to stay strong*, she thought, caressing her cheek. "We're Dawsons. We're tough, remember?" Bat inhaled sharply. " Just take deep breaths. In and out. Remain calm. It'll be fine. We both made it. We're okay."

"Sit down," Kraven ordered, his tone irritated. "And I'll spank you if you hit me with another shoe, you little hellion."

What an insufferable ass, she seethed. Bat was trying to help Dusti and this prick picks *now* to fuck with her again? She released her sister and spun, her middle finger going up. She was pissed enough to nearly make her see red. "Take a hint and get away from me, you perverted bastard. You should have picked another woman to molest."

He leaned closer, his anger clear. "I saved your life," the jackass spat. "I covered your body with my own to *protect* you, Cat."

I'm going to kill him, Bat silently swore. *No jury will convict me. I deal with guys who know where to hide a damn body. My clients owe me big time for keeping their vicious, murdering asses out of jail.*

20

"It's *Bat*, you moron. B.A.T. Back off, asshole. I refuse to deal with you right now. Can't you see my sister is freaked-out? I'm trying to calm her down."

"Crazy as a bat or bat-shit crazy. It fits."

She would have slapped the rude bastard but Dusti's shaky, frightened voice stopped her cold.

"Let it go. Let's help the injured."

Right. Calm down. Dusti's seen enough bloodshed. She shot a dirty look at Kraven, her furious gaze promising retribution later, before she pulled herself together enough to address her sister. "He's irritating me and he felt me up!"

"That's the least of our worries."

Bat was chagrined. She needed to keep Dusti's mind occupied to distract them both from the nightmare they were living at that moment, and being bitchy and combative wouldn't help.

"You're right. I'll ignore the big ape just for you this one time because I'm in shock too. I hope I'm not as pale as you look. You're doing a hell of a ghost impression." Bat cringed. "I shouldn't have said that, considering the circumstances. Sorry." She took a deep breath. "Let's help out. People are hurt. Just breathe and focus on that, okay?"

She released Dusti to smooth down her jacket and her fingers touched something small and hard. *My cell phone! I can call for help! I can get us back home!*

Excitement at the idea made her heart race. She'd gotten her sister into this mess by using guilt to make her travel to Alaska to visit their grandfather, but now she would fix it. She pulled the phone out and inspected the slim case that fully enclosed it, which looked perfect. Her hands shook badly; she hesitated before checking the phone itself until she got her nerves under control.

Dusti peered at her with a hopeful look. "Do you think you're going to get a cell phone signal out here?"

Bat knew there were cell towers all over most of the United States, but she didn't know about Alaska. She hoped there'd be a signal. She didn't even want to consider the alternative, because she needed to rescue her sister. She couldn't live with the guilt otherwise. She'd taken enough from Dusti already when she'd put her career first.

"I hope so."

Fumbling the case open, she got a glimpse inside—and the phone had been crushed into a mess despite the protective shell. The glass screen had cracked in too numerous fractures to count, and it didn't even light up to indicate the battery worked.

No! Bat silently screamed. *This can't be happening. I put her on this plane with me and I can't let her down now.*

A snort from Kraven made her head slowly rise until she met his gaze. The bastard looked amused.

Her grip on her tenuous control snapped. She knew it has happening, understood why, but the situation was too much. "You broke my phone with your gorilla-sized body!" She waved the phone in his face. As she did, the screen completely came apart, pieces of it falling to the floor.

She froze inside and tried to say something, anything, when the implications of not being able to call for help slammed into her brain. "You owe me a new one! Give me yours."

Did I really just say that?

I did, she acknowledged, wincing at how lame and petty she sounded, and took a calming breath. *Get a grip*, she ordered her brain.

"It's in my bag." He pointed up to where the overhead cabinets had once been. "Wherever that is now."

Bat stared at the destruction of the plane, taking in the fact that some of the cabinets had been sucked away at some point. It was a miracle they'd survived.

She knew she was in shock. Focusing on the ridiculous—including the annoying man—was keeping her from freaking out. It was a basic human reaction. *Avoidance.*

"Oh God."

Damn! Bat winced. *So much for avoiding.* "I know! I can't dial 9-1-1."

"Shut up, Bat," Dusti snapped. "*Look.* Oh my God."

Bat stepped up next to Dusti in the narrow aisle to see what her sister gaped at in the back of the plane.

It wasn't there anymore.

It had been torn away entirely, and the sight of forest where the bathrooms had once been made Bat fight to keep bile from rising. Whoever had been in the last few rows of seats were just gone too. Debris, broken trees, and one lone seat were scattered in the path of destruction caused by the plane's crash and long slide along the ground.

Blood covered what used to be a human being, still strapped into the seat. Bat realized she'd grabbed hold of her sister's hand.

The long-haired biker guy, Drantos, suddenly stepped into the aisle farther down, busy helping a fellow passenger. His big frame blocked most of Bat's view of the path of horror. She hoped Dusti couldn't see it anymore either. The man's dark blue eyes appeared haunted when he lifted a hand to run fingers through his shaggy, wild hair. He slowly approached them.

"There are ten survivors besides us in the cabin. Most of them will make it but I'm doubtful about a few. One of us should go hunt up the back of the plane to see if any of those people made it. We also need to check on the pilots."

"Fuck," Kraven sighed from behind Bat. "What a damn mess. I'll go search for the tail section of the plane." He paused. "You watch the bitches. The one in the dress suit is a terror, so don't turn your back on her."

Bat wanted to scream. People had died, they had no way to contact help, and guilt over bringing Dusti along on the trip nearly overwhelmed her. Dusti hadn't wanted to come, but she'd practically made her.

On top of everything, this Kraven guy seemed determined to piss her off. She knew how to deal with anger. She spun on him.

"I'm going to rip off your nuts if you call me a bitch one more time."

Dusti tugged hard on her hand. "Batina Marie Dawson, enough!" Tears shone in her eyes when Bat glanced at her. "I know bitchiness is your defense mechanism when you're scared or mad but please *stop*! I can't deal with it right now."

Then alarm struck Bat fast when Dusti started to collapse.

Her features paled to a chalky white, her legs giving way beneath her, and Bat lunged to grab her around the waist to try to prevent her from keeling over. She took Dusti's weight but knew they were both going down, even as she continued struggling to keep them upright.

That long-haired guy came to their rescue. Bat released her when his thick, beefy arms took her sister's weight, and allowed him to cradle Dusti, which he did seemingly without effort. The guy looked as if he were a bodybuilder.

She panicked when she realized what had to be wrong with her sister.

"Where's my purse?" Bat realized she was yelling but she didn't care. "It's black. I need it!"

"I'm okay," Dusti muttered, her voice too weak to believe. "It's just a dizzy spell."

My ass, Bat silently protested. Dusti needed one of her shots. Bat wanted to kick her own butt for not realizing sooner how the trauma of the accident would affect her sister's frail health. She frantically tried to get around Kraven to search the area by their seats but he blocked her path.

"My purse, you big gorilla! Move out of my way. My sister needs her medication." She shoved him hard, not caring about anything but finding it, and managed to squeeze around him.

Bat located their seats quickly, dropped to her knees, and searched the floor.

Her purse wasn't there.

She wanted to burst into tears. Without the shot, Dusti could go into shock. Her body would start to shut down, she'd start to slur her words, and eventually she could die.

A sob caught in her throat. She may have killed her sister regardless of them surviving the crash. Their parents had trusted Bat to care for Dusti when they'd left her guardianship in their will. They'd roll in their graves if they knew how badly she'd screwed it all up.

She suddenly caught a glimpse of a black strap, and shoved her arm under the seat in front of her—dragging her purse out. She furiously blinked back tears, her hands trembling, but she spotted the case inside the folds of her purse, where she kept a few of Dusti's shots in case of emergency. She hadn't fucked up.

Her fingers curling around her purse, she shoved her body up and turned.

"I found it!" She elbowed Kraven aside again to reach her sister as she tore out the case. "Hang on, Dusti! I have some of your shots. Here it is. They aren't broken."

She'd save Dusti after all. At least in one way. It was a start.

Chapter Two

Worry ate at Bat as she glanced for at least the hundredth time at her sister sitting on the ground. The long-haired biker guy might be a thug but he had taken really good care of Dusti. He'd located a blanket to put on the forest floor, stretched her sister over it, and had even removed his jacket, wrapping it around her to keep her warm while she recovered. Bat felt gratitude toward him for everything he'd done.

A hand brushed her arm to draw her attention.

Kraven's light blue eyes were narrowed as he glared down at her. "You're not injured, so follow me. We need to find firewood before the sun goes down. It may be late spring but it still gets pretty cold at night. The injured passengers could die without a fire to help keep their systems from going into shock."

She clenched her teeth. He'd pissed her off since the moment they'd met. "What did I ever do to you?"

"Excuse me?"

"You're always so rude. You could say please."

"*You* could—" His generous lips pressed together in a tight line and he growled low in his throat.

"Yeah. I wouldn't finish that sentence either. I'm not afraid to remove my shoes again to beat you with them."

"Follow me," he barked.

It was the last thing she wanted to do but freezing after dark seemed even less appealing. She glanced at Dusti once more, then at the biker guy who'd helped injured passengers from the plane to the clearing next to it. She figured it would be okay to leave her sister. Drantos may be scary looking but he seemed to have a hero complex. It wasn't a bad thing in this day and age.

She trudged into the woods after the spiked-headed jerk.

"Too bad you aren't more like your brother," she muttered.

Kraven turned. "What did you say?"

"Your brother seems nice. I guess none of that rubbed off on you, huh?"

"You're one to talk. Your sister is pleasant. You, on the other hand, are obviously more of a bitch in every sense of the word."

This jerk is unbelievable! "I told you not to call me that name again," she fumed as her gaze lowered to the front of his pants to further make her point. "You want to keep your nuts, right?"

He moved faster than she'd ever thought possible. Fear gripped her hard that he'd strike her, but he'd just closed the distance until only a foot separated them.

"Keep it up and I'm going to put you over my knee."

The threat hung in the air and she studied his eyes. She hadn't expected him to say that. She'd been threatened by a lot of people over the years but that particular one was new. He looked angry, but not crazy or mean. She'd become a pretty good judge of character, dealing with her clients. "You wouldn't dare."

28

"I would." He clamped his hand on her upper arm but it didn't hurt. "I'll redden your damn ass with my bare palm if you mention my nuts again. I'm not someone you want to piss off. Do you understand me?"

A shiver ran down her spine at his cold tone. He seemed to mean it. "Let me go."

"Don't make threats."

She swallowed hard and nodded. "I understand. Please let me go."

"Be useful and collect some firewood. We need to return to camp fast." His voice still held a gruff tone that affected her. He let go of her arm as quickly as he'd grabbed it, spinning away.

She blew out a relieved breath as soon as the tense moment passed. He hadn't hurt her. That was the important part. They'd been in a plane crash, were stuck in the woods, and rescue teams hadn't arrived yet. The sun was nearly down. It meant spending the night in the woods. He would know the dangers they faced more so they she would.

She glanced over her shoulder at him; he'd bent to reveal a nice ass. He had a meaty one encased in snug denim. He grabbed broken branches from the ground.

Bat could silently admit she had a weakness for aggressive, dangerous bad-boy types. They were kind of sexy. He hadn't threatened to punch or kill her. Instead his mind had gone straight to spanking her ass.

Her mind went there too, imagining him putting her over his knee. He probably knew how to turn a woman on, considering his looks and the size of him. She wouldn't like him striking her in any way, but the thought of him caressing her skin didn't exactly disturb her. It had the opposite effect.

What the hell is wrong with me?

Oh yeah. I probably have a concussion. That's got to be it.

She glanced around, located some broken branches, and moved toward them. *He'd better be a great fuck with that shitty personality of his. Otherwise he'll never get laid,* she decided. One more glance and she was certain women probably flocked to him in droves. *If he keeps his mouth shut. Otherwise all bets are off.*

Bat noticed her sister looked a lot better when they returned to camp five minutes later. Bat dumped her heavy load of dirty branches to the ground. Drantos had already started a fire. The sun lowered quickly, a chilly wind picking up, and Bat spent her time helping some of the passengers get more comfortable.

Her heart went out to an elderly married couple. The woman had a head injury and didn't look so good. Her husband had a broken wrist. Bat helped him make a sling for his arm with a jacket, wishing she knew more about first aid.

"Thank you, young lady." The man reached out and took his wife's hand. "It's going to be okay, Mary. I'm right here with you."

"Simon," the older woman whispered.

"Yes, my love. I'm here." He scooted closer, snuggling up to his wife. "Help is going to come soon. You just hang in there for me. We're going to celebrate fifty years of marriage next week. Remember?"

"I do." Mary smiled. "You're still the most handsome man I ever met."

"And you are the most beautiful woman I ever laid eyes on. Remember when Simon Junior was being born and I almost lost you? You swore you'd let me die first because I can't live without you. Don't break your promise to me. We've been through worse."

"I'm going to be okay." Mary's voice came out stronger. "You just hold my hand like you did in the hospital. We're going to go see our grandchildren."

"Yes, we are." Simon leaned closer and brushed a kiss on her forehead.

Tears filled Bat's eyes and she had to turn away before the couple noticed. Their love was strong. She couldn't imagine spending that length of time with someone but it had once been a dream. They reminded her of her parents. They'd had that kind of close connection. It was something she'd always longed for but had given up on finding. Her luck with men turned out to be shit.

She walked away from the fire toward the hulking, dark shape of the crashed plane to compose herself. She didn't want Dusti to see her fall apart. Her sister knew her too well and would worry. It was important to keep a positive attitude until they were rescued.

A hand clamped down on her shoulder and caused her to gasp.

"Where are you going?" Kraven didn't sound happy. "It's dark out there."

She wasn't about to admit the truth. She was emotionally drained and just wanted to escape to get herself together. "I saw some cushions on some of the seats in the front of the plane. When you and your brother were helping everyone out, I took some time to do a bit of searching around. It's not much but it's better than nothing. That elderly couple needs to be made as comfortable as possible. I'm also going to see if I can find some discarded jackets or clothing. It will help keep people warm."

"Hell," he sighed. "That's a good idea. Take my hand. I'm used to maneuvering in the dark. I'll lead you there, you wait, and I'll search the plane. I don't want you climbing around blind. You could get hurt."

It surprised her that he'd be so thoughtful. "Thank you." She reached out and his warm fingers brushed hers. A jolt went up her spine at the contact when he gripped her firmly. He had big hands. A saying drifted through her mind. *Big hands, big feet...wonder if everything is big?*

She grinned, amused. It beat being depressed.

He stopped minutes later. "Can you see anything?"

"Not really."

"There's a tree a few feet to your left. The plane is in front of us. Just stay put and I'll bring things to you."

"How can you see so well? It's so dark." The shapes of the tree and plane, and his big form, were barely distinguishable.

"Just stay put." He sounded almost...disgusted, for some reason.

She actually missed Kraven's warm touch when he let her go. She shivered in the cold as she waited. It didn't take him long to return. He placed something on the ground near her.

"Those are two intact suitcases. Hopefully something in them will be useful. They don't weigh much. You carry those and I'll get the cushions and blankets I piled up. I also found your sister's purse. I'll be right back."

She blindly bent and fumbled for the handles of both cases and lifted them when her fingers located the plastic. Kraven hadn't lied. They weren't heavy. He returned and she followed his moving shadow back to the camp. The firelight was more than a welcome sight.

One glance at Dusti had her worried again. Her sister looked nervous and a bit pale. She abandoned the suitcases to head in that direction to check on her. She forced a smile she didn't feel to put on a brave front.

The quick conversation with her sister eased some of her fears. Dusti seemed to be okay, albeit a bit anxious. It was reasonable under the circumstances. She refused to take another shot and swore she felt better. There were enough to last them for a few days if it took the rescue teams that long to find them. She really hoped they'd be located early the next day.

Bat watched Drantos and Dusti while they seemed to have a staring contest. The sense of something being wrong nagged at her but she dismissed it. It may just be her guilt over bringing her sister to Alaska, the exhaustion, the stress of their situation, or all of the above. She'd feel better once they were back in civilization.

Bat zoned out, answering a few questions from Drantos with her thoughts elsewhere. Her head hurt worse than ever but she didn't complain about the pain. The earlier dull throbbing of a beginning headache had turned into a loud pounding, but she was pretty certain she didn't have a concussion. Her vision wasn't blurry and she didn't feel as if she would throw up. It was just stress and probably lack of caffeine.

Kraven joined them. Bat silently studied him—and found herself annoyed that he looked so good. She felt like shit, yet he seemed at ease with the great outdoors. And she didn't want to be attracted to the big ape. He was annoying but hot, the type of guy she loathed most. His brother seemed so polite. It amazed her that they came from the same family.

He announced he was going to go hunt for fresh meat, then flashed her yet another dark look. It was the last straw.

"What are you going to use to hunt with? Your bad manners? Maybe you can just talk to the animals and they'll commit suicide."

The enraged glare he directed at her made her feel a little satisfied. "I told you to shut up. We have an agreement, remember? I don't whip your ass if you keep your lips sealed together." He turned his head, regarding his brother. "I'll be back soon. I'm going to scout while I'm out there to see just how fucked things are."

"I'm sure rescue crews will be searching for the plane at first light. They're going to have to fly out of Anchorage. The smaller airport won't have helicopters. And with no place to land, the best the planes will be able to do is help with the air-spotting." Drantos sighed. "The question is, do we leave on our own or wait for help?" He looked at the survivors near the fire. "They're helpless if we walk out of here on our own. I'm afraid they won't be found and will die from exposure. Not one of them has survival skills. I asked."

"We'll worry about it later." Kraven glared at Bat. "I'll be back." He turned on his heel to march out into the darkness.

She seethed inside at his response, especially when he said it in front of her baby sister. And he meant every word. She could easily see that, and she'd just managed to curb a rude response. Though she'd been tempted to point out that he'd said he'd spank her if she mentioned his nuts, which she hadn't. It was almost a relief when Kraven disappeared from sight.

Then she immediately felt worry. What if he was hurt out there?

Bat got Drantos's attention. "Are you sure it's safe for him to be traipsing around the woods at night? We didn't find a flashlight, or anything to use as a weapon. Aren't there wild animals around here that we should be worried about? The fire is here, not out there. He won't be able to see them but I'm sure the same can't be said for anything that might attack him."

"We live in Alaska and were raised not too far from here. We know what we're doing. It's not unusual for us to hunt at night and nothing out there can hurt Kraven. Trust me on that one. He'll be back within the hour and have something for us to eat."

"I couldn't even find a real knife, just plastic ones." Bat carefully sat down on a cushion and tucked her skirt neatly around her legs. "How will he skin it? I guess he could try to tear off part of the plane. Some of it is pretty jagged and sharp."

Drantos pulled a knife from his boot. "He's got one of these."

"But those are illegal to take on planes," Bat sputtered. Though seeing the weapon *did* help her worry less about the big jerk who'd just

35

foolishly strolled into the dark woods. Only an idiot would do that, in her opinion. "How did you get that past security to smuggle it onboard?"

"We have our ways, and the smaller airports are more lax about rules up here. It's common to carry weapons when you're flying in and out of smaller airports. It's life in Alaska. Don't worry about it." He shoved the knife back inside his boot. "He'll be fine. He's going to bring back something tasty to eat and then we'll all get some shuteye."

Bat wasn't entirely convinced, but she still wanted to assure Dusti that everything would be alright. "Help will find us tomorrow. I bet they're already putting together a huge search party to look for us as soon as the sun rises. We'll be rescued in no time and will arrive at our grandfather's house by tomorrow night."

As the minutes passed, the pain at the base of Bat's skull grew worse. Her sister spoke softly to Drantos. Dusti brought up their grandfather, explaining why she disliked the man. Bat tried to interject; she loathed for strangers to think they had a dysfunctional family. Her sister was certain their grandfather was some kind of pervert, though Bat hadn't ever gotten those vibes off him. He was an asshole, sure, but she'd dealt with a lot of real sickos in her line of work. She wasn't about to point out to Dusti that he'd have liked her a little too much if he were into young girls.

Decker Filmore had visited them a few times when they'd been kids. For some reason, he'd taken an instant disliking to Dusti. It might have been that he just wasn't comfortable with really young kids. Some adults weren't good with them. Though that didn't explain why he'd offered Bat a home after their parents had died, but denied the same courtesy to Dusti. They'd been teenagers at that point.

Bat's opinion of Filmore wasn't high, but she could forgive him for being an ass in their youth if he left them money in his will. She wanted to make sure her baby sister was well taken care of.

She studied Drantos as he interacted with her sister, relieved to find the uneasy feeling from earlier had dissipated. She must have imagined the tension between the two of them. Bat chalked it up to her naturally suspicious attorney disposition.

Her focus lowered to her skirt, wincing at the damaged, torn material, and wasted dollar signs flashed in her head. The outfit was one of her favorites, and she'd worn it to court often to intimidate a jury. The idea of someone very tailored and well-groomed defending a suspected murderer made some people doubt the prosecution. Most juries assumed violent offenders were poor, couldn't afford expensive attorneys. They associated wealth with financial crimes, such as fraud or money laundering.

"Your suit is ruined. You can try to smooth out that skirt until your hands fall off but it's toast. Were you able to find our suitcases?"

Bat looked at her sister. "No. The belly of the plane ripped open so the bags were scattered all over the place. It was too dark to widen the search. We only brought back those few suitcases so people could use whatever clothes were in them to help keep warm tonight. I'll look again in the morning. Until then, I'm stuck wearing this. I refuse to put on some stranger's outfits." Bat buttoned her jacket to ward off some of the cold then smoothed her skirt once more.

"Give it up," Dusti urged.

"I'm trying to do something, anything. I'm not used to just sitting around, and I'm hungry."

Drantos stood. "Kraven forgot to pass out the food you salvaged from the plane before he went hunting. I'll do that now so you can eat something while we wait. Just say my name if you need anything. I have *very* good hearing."

"Weird guys, huh?" Bat watched the big man walk to the pile of stuff brought from the plane. "I'm totally getting 'future client' vibes off both of them but they don't have dead eyes, so I think we're safe." Kraven probably had crossed over some legal line a long time ago, but she wasn't about to admit that suspicion to Dusti. He likely already *did* need her services, or would in the near future.

"It scares me that you can say shit like that. Dead eyes?"

"You'd know if you saw them. Trust me."

"Bat, we need to get out of here and away from them."

"Fuck that! Those guys were raised in Alaska, and look at what they've done so far. They handled setting up a camp and built a fire. There's no way I'm going to go walking into the woods to get lost searching for a cabin or a house that might have a working phone. It would be like finding a needle in a haystack. Our best hope of being rescued is to stay beside the crash site. I'm sure there're plenty of signs from above that we went down, where the plane took out those trees. It will probably resemble a path from way up there when the search planes fly over. Like it or not, we're stuck with these guys, and trust me, I'm not happy with that concept. Kraven is a lunatic."

38

She lowered her voice to a whisper, her gaze locking with Dusti's. "But he's *hot*." Distracting her sister from worrying was her priority—and she knew admitting her attraction to Kraven would do it.

Sure enough, Dusti's mouth dropped open. "You're attracted to Kraven? Do you have a concussion? I realize you were thrown out of your seat and hit your head. You still have a mark on the side of your temple. He's not your type, Bat. A briefcase isn't surgically attached to his hand and he doesn't have news anchor helmet-head hair."

"I did hit my head, but nothing's wrong with my eyesight. I see the way Biker Bear there has his eye on *you*, and how you keep watching him when you think he's not looking." Bat climbed to her feet. "I have to pee. I'll be back."

"But—"

Bat fled before Dusti could protest. She needed a few minutes alone, she really had to go to the bathroom, and, most of all, she wasn't sure how long she'd be able to put up a strong front for her little sister.

It also shook her up that she was attracted to Kraven. Maybe telling Dusti wasn't her best idea after all. How was she supposed to explain something to her sister that she couldn't understand herself?

Kraven was an asshole but it had been a long time since she'd even wanted a man. The fact that she might want *him* made her walk faster into the cold, dark night.

Maybe she had hit her head too hard. It would account for the headache from hell and how distracted she seemed to be.

* * * * *

39

Kraven just wanted the night to end. He'd brought a deer back to the camp that would feed the survivors well. His brother had also sought him out with everything he'd learned from the sisters while he'd been hunting. The news wasn't what he wanted to hear. The only thing he and Drantos currently agreed upon was what Decker Filmore most likely wanted to do with his granddaughters.

Aveoth, the powerful GarLycan clan leader, had recently lost his lover, which meant he'd be seeking a new one. And rumor had it that Aveoth was addicted to a particular bloodline—the one the sisters carried in their veins.

By using Dusti or Bat, Decker Filmore could secure Aveoth's help in his bid to take over the VampLycan clans.

Drantos believed the sisters were ignorant to their grandfather's plans. Worse, his brother was convinced the sisters didn't know VampLycans even existed.

That's where they'd disagreed.

How in the hell is that possible?

Kraven wasn't buying it. He refused. The sisters had been captured by him and Drantos, VampLycans from another clan, who they'd consider enemies if they were in league with Decker. They were lying.

His brother might be older, but that didn't make him wiser. He also seemed to be attracted to Dusti. It had to have affected his judgment.

Kraven needed to be the vigilant one.

As he'd cooked the deer and passed it out to the passengers, his gaze kept drifting to Drantos. He was spending too much time with the younger sister. He wouldn't take it well if the sisters turned out to be onboard with Decker's plans.

His mood darkened as the night wore on. One of the survivors was becoming a pain in his ass. The human seemed determined to panic the others. Kraven finally pulled him aside.

"Knock your shit off. These people have been through enough without you telling them animals will eat them while they sleep and no one is going to find the downed plane."

"I can say whatever the hell I want. Fuck off, man."

Kraven grabbed him by the front of his shirt and yanked him off balance. "You didn't get too hurt in the crash." He lowered his voice. "I can fix that. Do you understand me? Don't fuck with these people. Shut the hell up or I'll break your jaw. Try talking shit then."

"You can't threaten me!"

"I just did. You're one of those assholes who love to instill fear in others. It probably makes you feel like a big, important man. It actually just makes you an asshole I want to deck. *Stop.* This is the only warning you're going to get." Kraven lifted him off his feet to make a point, but quickly lowered him, aware that others might witness what was going on.

Instead, he let down his guard and allowed his true nature to show in his eyes. He wasn't going to waste any more time arguing with the moron. "Go sit your ass down and don't talk to the others until after you're rescued. You're allowed to nod and shake your head to answer anyone who asks questions. That's it. Am I clear?"

The guy nodded.

Kraven felt no guilt as the guy stumbled away and found a place to sit. He didn't speak to the others, the command set in his mind.

Kraven spun away and went to clean up a little before bed. He really wanted to leave the crash site *now*. They needed to get Bat and Dusti to Howl, their clan's village, and especially to their father, Velder, the clan leader. But Drantos was determined to get a fresh start in the morning.

And on top of that, Drantos ordered him to keep Bat warm, claiming she couldn't regulate her own body heat. That meant he'd have to hold the little hellion in his arms and trust that she wouldn't attempt to slit his throat while he slept.

He might have to take orders from his older brother, but that didn't mean he had to like it.

Returning, he dropped some sleeping gear next to Bat and crouched.

She gasped. "What are you doing?"

She wasn't about to just agree to sleeping with him, so he didn't give her a choice, attacking before she could react.

He grabbed Bat after settling next to her and pinned her down. "Shut up," he hissed.

"Fuck off, asshole. Get off me," she ground out.

Kraven let her know who was in charge by making her look deeply into his eyes. He knew the second she noticed their color change. Fear widened her gaze...

A curious thing happened then, though. She went lax under him, just staring.

He frowned, watching her.

The silence was broken by his brother and Dusti speaking softly, but he ignored their conversation. "Bat?"

She said nothing.

It sank in slowly that she was affected by his eyes. Kraven slowly shifted his hold on her and grabbed her breast, figuring that would piss her off enough to react.

She remained still beneath him, her expression blank.

Son of a bitch. What the hell? She's acting completely human. It can't be... He'd been under the impression when he'd learned of the sisters that they knew exactly who and what their grandfather was. Their mother had obviously mated with a human, for them to smell the way they did, but they should know their heritage.

He released her breast and trailed his hand lower, over her hip, and shoved his fingers under her ass, firmly gripping.

She didn't even blink and her breathing remained shallow. She was totally under his control.

How is this possible?

Was Drantos right? Had the sisters inherited so little of their mother's VampLycan blood that they were literally helpless? All the possibilities filled his mind. Decker Filmore could easily control Bat and take away her will.

That didn't sit well with him.

Kraven released her ass and adjusted his body a little, getting more comfortable. Bat continued to gaze up at him, completely docile—and suddenly he didn't like seeing her that way. It felt wrong, somehow. She

43

wasn't totally human so she shouldn't be responding like one. He cupped her cheek, leaning in closer to stare deeply into her eyes.

"Are you attracted to me? Answer."

"Yes."

He scowled. The Bat he was coming to know wouldn't admit that so easily. But he still felt distrustful. "I'm going to ask you some questions and you are going to answer them all honestly. Do you understand?"

"Yes."

A faint smell filled his nose, and he felt both satisfaction and astonishment. She *wasn't* faking it. The little hellion was getting turned-on. A few more breaths, though, and he realized the scent wasn't coming from the woman under him—but the sister a few feet away.

He turned his head and saw his brother was on top of Dusti. He sniffed deeply again and cursed, looking back at Bat.

"Sleep," he whispered. "Forget everything from the moment I laid down until you wake in the morning. Do you understand?"

She gave a slight nod of her head and closed her eyes.

Kraven released her and rolled away, going after Drantos before he fucked Dusti in front of the remaining survivors.

His brother had clearly lost his damn mind. Kraven had to pull him off and physically restrain him from trying to get back to Dusti.

Kraven tried to make light of the situation. Of course Drantos wanted to fuck the woman. The blonde sisters were attractive. He was even guilty of wanting to nail Bat. He was just too smart to actually do it.

It came as a huge shock when Drantos declared Dusti was his mate.

Oh, hell no. This shit can't be happening. It's a nightmare. It has to be.

They'd leave first thing in the morning and take both sisters to their father. He'd know what to do. Decker couldn't get his hands on either of them.

Chapter Three

Bat opened her eyes to bright sunlight. The headache was less severe but still present. She frowned, blinked a few times, before she realized Kraven was crouched in front of her. He looked concerned.

She was immediately alarmed. The last thing she remembered clearly was going to the bathroom the night before and sitting back down near her sister. There were a few brief flashes of talking to her sister this morning but it was mostly a blur. The pain in her head had been pretty bad but it alarmed her that her memory was fuzzy.

"Did I pass out?"

He leaned in closer. "No. You've been sleeping."

"I had the weirdest dream. I was in the circus." She'd been upside down, swaying on a swing, and there had been bears waiting for her to fall. They'd wanted to eat her. She blinked a few times to clear her head.

"Are you all right?" His concern was evident and a bit touching.

"Yes. It wasn't a nightmare or anything," she lied. Her attention finally turned to their surroundings.

They weren't in the clearing anymore.

Woods totally surrounded them, the plane was gone, and no survivors were spread out around a campfire. Bat currently sat on a rock with a blanket wrapped around her. "Where are we?"

Kraven suddenly gripped her jaw with a warm, firm hand, drawing her focus. "You were exhausted. You slept so long I actually worried about you."

Bat shrugged. "I work a lot of hours. I've had one high-profile case after another for the past few months. I've gotten behind on my sleep. I guess it must have all caught up with me." Bat gripped his hand. "Why are you touching me?" She tried pushing it away. "Let go."

Kraven released her and stood. "My mistake."

"Where is Dusti?" She was warm so she let the blanket drop off her shoulders, pooling behind her.

He bit his lower lip, staring at her. "What's the last thing you remember?"

Fear was instant. "Is she okay?" She jerked to her feet but it was a mistake, as she immediately swayed on her feet. It also made her aware that her shoes were gone. Her bare feet were planted on dirt. She turned her head, again taking in their surroundings. Nothing was familiar.

He curved his two big hands around her hips. She wanted to push Kraven away but she needed his support while the world still spun a little. "You were utterly worn down to the point of exhaustion. I should have seen it last night but I was too angry to take notice. I'm sorry."

She lifted her chin, staring at him with confusion. "For what? *Where* is the plane? The other survivors? Most importantly, my sister?"

He hesitated.

"Oh my God. Is Dusti okay?" Full panic set in.

"She's fine." His tone softened. "She's with Drantos."

47

"Why aren't we at the crash site?" It had been years since she'd sleepwalked. And out here, it was a daunting concept. "Did I take off in my sleep?" It would account for a lot, including the loss of her shoes.

"What's the last thing you remember?" he asked again.

"I was sitting next to Dusti and you came up to us. I think we were getting ready to go to sleep."

"I carried you out here."

Her mouth dropped open. A new fear crept in. "Why? I'll fight if you're thinking what I hope you're not. I'll totally press charges if you sexually assault me."

He slowly shook his head, a look of pure disgust on his face. "Give me a break. I wouldn't have to force you to do anything. You're too easy."

"I'm not easy!" she snapped, completely insulted. "Did you just imply I'm a slut?"

"No." He carefully released her and took a cautious step back, as if making sure she wouldn't sink to her knees.

Her legs held her up and the dizzy spell passed. "Where the hell is my sister?" That was her priority. She'd worry about his motives for getting her alone later and why he'd obviously kidnapped her from the crash site. She must have been really out of it if he had carried her. She was usually a light sleeper.

"My brother and Dusti are nearby. Will you please sit back down? There are some things I need to tell you."

"I'll stand."

"You're wobbling on your damn legs," he snapped. "Sit!"

48

The harsh, deep command startled her enough that she actually sat. It was that or fall. It stunned her that he sounded so vicious. The rock dug into her ass a little but it was better than collapsing. Kraven crouched before her again.

"You're in danger."

She studied him, her heart racing. She hoped that wasn't a threat. He was a big guy and she missed her security detail all the sudden. Her law firm assigned guards to pick her up in the mornings to go to work and take her home every evening.

"From you?"

"No." He scowled. "From your grandfather."

"Okay." She tried to remain calm. "He's a frail old man who's dying." Maybe Kraven wasn't functioning on all levels.

"He's not ill. He's devious and cruel."

She stared into his eyes. Years of dealing with her clients had made her aware of certain tells when someone told her lies. Kraven didn't seem to be. "How would you know that? Have you met him?"

"Yes, and that bastard is pure evil."

A sick feeling settled into her stomach. And it wasn't just rumblings from the hunger she'd suddenly become aware of. Her grandfather was rich. Maybe he'd made an enemy of Kraven and she was his payback.

"You know who he is…" She paled. "Did you do something to bring the plane down?"

"Are you out of your mind? I hate flying, and crashing was even worse."

He looked sincere. She believed him. "So what's your angle? Why did you bring me out here? Do you want some kind of reward for saving my life? You obviously aren't a fan of my grandfather's. What do you want from me?"

"I'm trying to tell you why we're in the woods, miles from the crash site. We couldn't stick around there. His men will be looking for you and I can't allow you to be found."

He was a nutcase. Terror seized her body. "Where is my sister, you son of a bitch?! What have you done with her? What is your brother doing to her?"

"Calm," Kraven demanded just as loudly. His hands wrapped around her upper arms. "He's not going to hurt her. We need to talk."

"Talk to the hand, asshole. Get away from me! I swear I'm going to kill you. Make your long-haired biker brother bring my sister back!"

"I said calm down," he hissed, leaning in close.

"I want my sister." She glared at him and struggled but couldn't break free of his hold on her arms. "I'll see you both in prison if he so much as touches a hair on her head."

His hold eased but he didn't stop touching her. "I'm attempting to tell you the truth." His deep voice turned gruff. "I'm not having a good day...hell, a good year. You don't want to push me with your threats. I don't fight women but for you, I'd make an exception. I'm not like other men, as you might have guessed. Perhaps you weren't raised around ones as wild as me but I won't be pushed too hard. I'm an enforcer."

"Yeah. You're different all right." She knew what his job title meant. He beat the shit out of people for a living. She wished he wasn't wearing a jacket. She bet he sported prison tattoos. She'd love to get a look at them. It would tell her more about his past. "How long did you serve?"

He frowned. "All my life, of course."

She winced. Most guys like that had gone into the system as young offenders, then were transferred into prison at the age of eighteen straight from a juvenile detention center. His crimes as a minor must have been pretty heinous to get that kind of sentence.

"Did you get early parole or did you serve your time? What did you go down for? Murder? Armed robbery?" It would help her determine how dangerous he could be.

He frowned. "What in the hell are you talking about?"

He's dense, she decided. "How long were you locked up and what for? Is that clear enough? Are you on parole still or did they just cut you loose? I'm a defense attorney, remember? You'd be surprised at how familiar I am with guys like you."

Shock widened his eyes. "I'm not a criminal! I'm an enforcer *of the law*."

Bat barely suppressed a groan. "Great. You're a cop. My day just got worse. I guess now I know why you're such a dick to me. Let me assure you that every defendant deserves an adequate defense. It's their constitutional right to have counsel." She gave him a quick once-over. "Undercover narcotics? You're pretty good. I never would have pegged you for being vice. Is my grandfather a drug dealer or something? Do you expect me to turn state's evidence against him? I hate to break it to you but I don't know shit about the man."

He continued to gawk at her. He looked mean with the spiked hair, had the body of a weightlifter, and dangerous vibes radiated off him in droves. Criminals would accept him into their lives with ease. Someone would have to be insane to accuse him of being a cop. Career criminals would assume he'd kick their asses for the implied insult if they ever doubted what side of the law he lived on.

"Let's not make it personal. We survived a horrific experience and we're stuck in the wilderness until help arrives. We should be adults about this."

He continued to stare at her until his lips slowly curved downward. "You really don't know, do you?"

"Know what?"

He leaned closer, invaded her personal space, and inhaled deeply through his nose. "Damn. It's weak. I thought you were playing my brother. He said you were clueless, but I was certain it was an act."

"What is?" Bat stood slowly.

"When I call you a bitch, you think I mean a nasty-mouthed woman, don't you?"

She blinked a few times, trying to figure out where his mind had gone. But she quickly gave up. He'd obviously spent way too many years working vice. It got to some men, made them antisocial, and in some cases, outright nuts. The criminal lifestyle rubbed off on them, changed them. Some of them were forced to do drugs to fit in when it came to do-or-die situations; it couldn't be helped. The unfortunate ones became addicted. Lines blurred for them until they became the very thing they'd wanted to arrest.

"I don't like being called that, okay?" She tried to be nice about it. "It's insulting. I'm a strong woman who says what I mean. That's not a bad thing. I stand up for myself. Again, not a bad trait. I know I'm a bit too blunt but you have to admit you haven't exactly been undeserving of some of the shit I've said."

He straightened and spun away, ran his fingers through the jet-black spikes and softly cursed. "Unbelievable. How can she not know?"

"Know *what*?"

He slowly faced her again. He kept a good five feet between them and cocked his head to stare at her curiously. "Tell me about your parents."

Left field, she thought. *Where the hell had that question come from?* "Okay, I'll play the game. My parents were wonderful people. They were killed in an accident when I had just turned eighteen. My sister is two years younger and I raised her to keep her out of the foster care system. My parents had left me guardianship over her. We're from Los Angeles."

"What about other family?"

"Just the grandfather you know about. He contacted me after he discovered he's dying. We were traveling to him when the plane crashed."

He hesitated. "How much do you know about your grandfather?"

"Not much. He's rich, a recluse, and my mom left home at a young age. They didn't get along. She moved to Los Angeles. That's where she met my father and they married. She was a teacher and he worked construction."

"What kind of accident killed her?"

53

Bat winced. "That's rude."

"Answer me."

"No. That's none of your business."

The guy lunged forward and grabbed Bat. She gasped when her feet left the ground. He'd lifted her body a good foot until they were nose to nose with each other.

"Answer me now. Details."

Fear overrode everything inside Bat. He'd looked strong but he didn't even appear strained by holding her full weight. She swallowed hard. "They were killed in an auto accident. A semi ran a red light. It had been raining and the truck came down a hill towing a trailer. The driver couldn't stop and it struck the car so hard it ripped in half. Both of my parents were instantly killed."

He eased her back to her feet, let go of her arms, and backed away. "That would do it."

Outrage burned. *That would do it?* We're discussing my mom and dad, you callous son of a bitch. Losing them destroyed my life. Do you *get* that? I was barely eighteen, scared shitless, and had a sister who depended on me. I had to make choices I'm going to regret for the rest of my life but I did the best I could."

"That's not what I meant. I'm sorry for your loss. What do you regret?" His tone and facial expression softened slightly.

"I'd been accepted to law school but I had to sell our house to afford it. I spent most of my college money on burying my parents, and then fleeing when the state tried to come in and take my sister away from me.

They didn't feel an eighteen-year-old could care for her sixteen-year-old sister. Times were pretty tough though. The housing market wasn't that strong and we struggled. I think my sister still has resentment but I just thought once I finished law school we'd be set."

"Why didn't you go to your grandfather for help?"

Heat warmed her cheeks. "I tried. He doesn't like Dusti and she doesn't like him. We only met him a couple times when we were kids but for whatever reason, they didn't get along. He offered *me* a home, but not her. I told him to kiss my ass when he said he didn't want me bring her." She snorted. "As if I'd dump her into a foster home just so he'd put a roof over my head and pay for my schooling." Her shoulders straightened. "I may regret some things, but never that. My sister is everything to me."

"Why go see him now if he was such an ass?"

She hated to admit the truth, but at least it easier with Kraven being a stranger. "He's rich and dying. I make good money but Los Angeles is expensive. My lifestyle isn't cheap. I thought if I talked Dusti into coming with me that she could make peace with the tough old bastard and he'd leave us some money in his will. She won't live with me, and I don't push the issue because in my line of work, it's really better if she doesn't. I help when she allows it but she rarely takes a dime from me. You should see where she lives." Bat grimaced. "It's not the best neighborhood. I'm always terrified I'm going to get a call saying she was mugged, raped, or murdered. The money is for her."

His gaze drifted over her tailored suit dress. "Maybe if you didn't waste money on your expensive clothes you could help your sister out more."

His sneer wasn't missed and Bat found him totally offensive. "For your information, I have an image to uphold. My fashion expense is a necessary evil of my job. Besides, it's the *living* expenses that kill me every month. I've made enemies in my line of work, and I have to live in a high-rise building that costs a small fortune. Security is tight there. Thankfully my law firm supplies bodyguards for me when I leave home."

That made Kraven's jaw drop. "You really have bodyguards?"

She sighed, resenting having to explain it to him. "People like someone to blame when a court case doesn't go the way they wanted it to. Win or lose, someone isn't happy. Either the family of someone a client allegedly harmed in some way, or even my clients themselves. Some families view me as helping to free someone they feel deserved to go to prison, and on the flip side, my clients aren't thrilled if they get sentenced. See where I'm going with this? I have a target on my back either way."

"Why would you *do* that job?"

She wondered that often too but refused to admit it. "I made a really good impression this year with the partners and I've made a name for myself."

"It sounds as if you're an egotistical person looking to suck up as much fame and fortune as you can." He pointedly glared at her fingers. "I'm surprised you're not wearing some expensive rock, married to some rich asshole."

"I don't like you," she snapped. "I earn my own way in life. I don't need someone to do that for me, and I'm not for sale."

"Sounds like you are...to anyone with enough cash to pay you to get them off."

"I'm not a prostitute." She choked on rage. "Listen, you little prick. I'm an attorney. That's totally different."

He lunged again. She tensed when his hands gripped her. He didn't jerk her off her feet this time, but spun her around in his arms. His body bent forward, one arm locked around her waist, his weight forcing her to bend. His groin pressed hard against her ass.

"Be prepared for me to prove you wrong if you call me a name like that one again."

She clawed at his hand, her nails digging into his skin, but he didn't let her go. His hot breath fanned across her neck when he chuckled.

"Let me go, you buffoon!"

"You should know I'm not small, despite you crushing my dick in the crash while you were clinging to it. Need a reminder? I'm willing to prove I'm not a *little prick*."

"I'll scream."

"Go ahead. Who's going to save you?" His other hand released her arm to grip her jaw, forcing her to look at him. Their lips nearly touched. "This is the last warning you're going to get, you little hellion. Keep insulting me and I'm going to get even."

Her heart raced. His voice did things to her when he spoke in that gruff, rough tone. His eyes were so blue and intense that she couldn't look away from them. They had to be the most fascinating things she'd ever seen. They nearly glowed from the blueness of them.

"I bet you earned a lot of spankings as a kid." He licked his lips, his tongue slowly sliding across the full bottom one more so than the top. "Maybe you need another one. I'm not your father though. I won't leave your clothes on and it won't have the same effect if I put my hands on your ass."

For once, Bat was speechless.

"Here's what's going to happen. You are going to stop insulting me. I'm getting fed up with it. It's starting to piss me off, between you threatening to rip my nuts off and implying I'm dickless. You don't want that. I'm not one of those pathetic men who will allow you to continue to lash out with that vicious little tongue of yours—unless you're on your knees and my pants are open."

She couldn't believe he'd said that to her. She found her voice. "I'd bite it off."

His expression tightened. "I believe you would. Now believe *me* when I tell you I'm going to whip your ass with my palm until you beg me to stop if you don't learn some manners. Are we clear?"

Bat heard the sincerity in his threat. She swallowed hard. The guy would really spank her. *Literally* spank her. It was a scary concept.

His features softened. "Easy." He inhaled and softly cursed. "I'm making you afraid of me." He lifted up until they were both straightened but he kept his arm locked around her waist to hold her in place. "A little fear of me is good but I don't want you terrified. I'd never really hurt you, but don't think I won't redden your ass. Do you want to know what I'd do then?"

She shook her head. "No. Let me go."

58

"I'd kiss it and make it better." The color of his eyes seemed to turn a little lighter and brighter, shimmery. "And I'd want to kiss other things once I started at your ass." He released her chin, ran his palm down the front of her shirt, through the valley of her breasts, and hesitated just over her waist. His hand was heavy and hot against her thin skirt at her lower stomach. "Do you understand? Don't bait me, because we'll fight or fuck. That's how I deal with aggression. Only one of those two you'd enjoy." He suddenly released her. "Don't push me."

Bat stumbled away, trembled from head to toe. She refused to look at him while she tried to regain control of emotions that ranged from fear to arousal. It was the guy's sexy voice—and the fact that she now had a mental image of him kissing where he'd implied.

She hadn't gotten laid in over a year. The last one-night stand she'd had left her feeling cold and disgusted. She suspected that wouldn't be a problem with Kraven.

Kraven had to take deep breathes and put distance between him and Bat.

He was attracted to her, and it pissed him off. She was mouthy, rude, disrespectful, and everything he usually didn't find appealing in a woman. The worst thing of all though—she was Decker Filmore's granddaughter.

He reached down and adjusted his stiff dick. It seemed to have a mind of its own and became hard every time he got too close to her.

She *did* smell good. It might have something to do with the fact that he'd had to carry her over his shoulder for miles. Their scents had mingled and he'd been breathing her in all day. It had also been a while since he'd touched a woman. Her name had been Violet...and that error in judgment had almost gotten him killed.

The memory of what happened with Violet helped manage his libido. He'd learned his lesson. Women with any association to Decker Filmore couldn't be trusted. The long-legged beauty from Decker's clan had come on to him strongly when they'd met the summer before. He'd fallen for it hook, line, and sinker. He'd even broken his rule of never taking a woman to his own bed, but he sure wasn't going to go to *her* home, considering where she lived.

Images flashed of Violet tearing at his clothes, eager to get him naked and flat on his back. He wasn't normally into women being the sexual aggressors but she'd been incredibly sexy. He wasn't a fool, though he hadn't been willing to slow things down, either. She'd wanted him and he was going to let her have her way. His physical mating urge had been coming on and she'd seemed like a great choice to spend a few weeks with, sharing a bed. It was hell going into heat alone.

It had all been good—until he'd seen the knife flash in Violet's hand.

The bitch had set him up and lowered his defenses to kill him. Instinct had saved him when he'd tensed and jerked to avoid the blade coming toward his heart. The agony of being stabbed hadn't incapacitated him, luckily, and he'd managed to land a fist to the side of her head, throwing her off him. He'd pulled out the knife quickly, rolled in the opposite direction, and stumbled to his feet before she recovered enough to come after him a second time.

He'd made it into the bathroom and locked the door, leaning heavily against it as she'd battered the wood. Her claws had scratched at it but he'd built his house strong. She'd eventually picked up something heavy to bash against the wood, splitting it in places. But by that time, he'd healed to the point he wasn't losing blood anymore and yanked the door open, shocking her with his sudden attack. He'd landed a few punches that had knocked her out cold.

It had been tempting to kill her but instead Kraven had restrained her, wrapped her in his bloodied bed sheet, and tossed her over his shoulder to carry outside.

That day had changed a lot of things for him. He'd fought a woman, something he never thought he'd have to do. He'd been embarrassed to have to tote her through his village in front of the gawking eyes of everyone, and humiliated to have to tell his people how Violet had tried to assassinate him.

His father and brother had returned her alive to Decker's clan. Of course, Decker had denied sending her there to do his bidding. All his father could do was give Decker a warning that the next assassin would die.

Kraven had returned to his house, dragged his bed outside, and burned the damn thing. He didn't want a constant reminder of how close he'd come to death. The bathroom door had also needed to be replaced. His injury completely healed on the outside, but being fooled by a woman had left a lasting scar on the inside.

Decker had sent for his granddaughter to start a civil war. Bat seemed as innocent as she claimed, but it could all still be a lie. He hesitated to trust her, not willing to give her a chance to kill him in the heat of passion when his guard was down. *Been there and almost died doing that.*

He might want Bat, but that didn't mean he would give in to the lust. *Fool me once, shame on you. Fool me twice and I'm a goddamn moron.*

Kraven glanced at Bat and regretted it in an instant. She had a fearful yet confused look on her face. He turned all the way around and sniffed the air. It was slight, but he still picked up her fear. It would make her one hell of an actress if she was deceiving him, to be able to pull off that smell.

Drantos still believed the sisters were ignorant of their heritage. What if his brother was right? What if Antina Decker had never shared the truth of her bloodlines with her daughters?

Goddamn. He needed to know for certain, one way or the other.

He approached Bat and watched as her body stiffened. "We need to talk."

"Just tell me where my sister is."

He studied her eyes. The fear looked real, the worry and the uncertainty. "She's with my brother. He'll keep her safe. What do you know about your family?"

"What's that supposed to mean?"

"What did your mother tell you about her father?"

"Not much. Her mom died, she ran away because I assume her father was overbearing or something, and she started her life fresh in California. She met my dad, they fell in love, and they had us."

"Did you ever see her do anything...odd?"

Her emotions changed and anger narrowed her eyes. "Odd? She was my *mom*. She wasn't some weirdo. Just because we lived in California doesn't mean she was some hippy or something. Not everyone who lives there is *odd*."

"That's not what I meant. She wasn't like other people, was she?"

She just stared at him.

"Do you know the truth? Just admit if you do. I hate playing games. Your mother was different. So are you. *I* know that. *You* know that. No one is around, so you don't have to keep secrets anymore. I'm more than aware of what you are."

Bat blinked a few times and frowned. She said nothing.

"Stop playing with me, Bat. We need to be completely honest with each other. You don't want to tick me off." He closed the distance and gripped her arms so she couldn't get away from him.

Chapter Four

"Okay." Bat wasn't sure what Kraven was talking about. He wasn't making much sense. "I'm an attorney. That's not a lie. I already mentioned that so what's your problem?"

His mouth pressed into a tight grimace.

"Just spit out whatever point you're trying to make!" She glanced around. "I want you to take me to my sister." She met his gaze. "Talk, Kraven." She'd listen to whatever he wanted to say as long as he did it quickly, so she could go after Dusti to make certain Biker Bear wasn't a rapist.

"Fine. I'll start. I'm not completely human."

She blinked, trying to take his words in, and wanted to cringe. A conversation she'd shared with Dusti the evening before flashed. She'd forgotten about it until that moment. Her sister had accused Drantos of being exactly like her friend Greg—a mental case who believed in aliens.

Kraven must be mentally unstable like his brother. It surprised her how depressed that made her feel.

"What are you then? I'm waiting with bated breath to hear this."

"We're VampLycans. We're the descendants of Vampires who overfed on human blood, to the point that they were able to impregnate their female Lycan day guards."

Bat blinked again. *Oh hell. Seriously? So much for believing in aliens. This guy sees paranormal shit that goes bump in the night?* She backed

64

her face away from his as much as she could with his hands still clinging to her arms.

"You're *also* a descendant. You're not as human as you believe."

Why is it that the really good-looking ones are never for me? They're always either gay or insane. Damn. There goes the idea of maybe having a one-night stand. No way am I touching a mental case.

"Are you listening to me?" He arched one of his dark eyebrows.

"Oh yes. I'm hearing you."

"Your mother ran away from your grandfather's clan and bred with a human. Decker is a monster, Bat, who plans to use you to start a civil war with the other clans. He wants to give you to a GarLycan. That's a Gargoyle and Lycan mix. They live in close proximity to our clans, and we're at peace with them, but your grandfather plans to use *you* to force them to fight against us."

She glanced away to peer at the woods. She didn't see an escape route but she sure didn't want to stay with the nutjob either. She needed to find her sister and get them back to the crash site. She'd be happy to send guys with nets after the brothers. They'd get a nice long vacation in some facility until they learned to face reality or the medication they desperately needed kicked in.

"Look at me," he demanded in a gruff voice.

She met his gaze again.

"A GarLycan by the name of Aveoth had agreed to accept your grandmother's sister as his lover. It would have formed a tighter alliance between the GarLycan and VampLycan clans. Her name was Margola.

65

They fed him her blood in hopes he'd learn to care about her, but Margola died before reaching adulthood. Your grandfather wanted to give your *mother* to Aveoth when she matured, but she fled to avoid it. She knew Decker would use her to force Aveoth to do his bidding in exchange.

"Aveoth leads the GarLycans now, and he's still addicted to the blood that runs in your veins. Decker wants to hand you over to him. Aveoth isn't mated yet, so you'd become his lover until he is."

"Uh-huh." She bit her lip, chewed on it, and finally sighed. "I hope he's hot at least. I guess he's really old though, if he was set to hook up with my great aunt. Is he at least rich?" She hoped he'd pick up on the sarcasm.

"This isn't a joke." His fingers dug into her arms but not enough to hurt. "I'm being sincere. Decker told you he's dying just to lure you here. He didn't want your sister because she's defective, in his opinion. That's why he showed no interest in her. He can't use her."

"To give to some Gargoyle half-breed Werewolf."

"Yes. And we don't use the term Werewolf. That's human bullshit. They're Lycans."

She'd dealt with crazy people before but was in *no* mood to humor him. "Her loss, right? I mean, according to you, he's all mine. It must be my lucky day."

A soft growl emanated from deep within the man's chest, the sound alarming. Bat's heart began to pound.

"I'm totally serious and it's the truth. Decker is *evil*. Your mother knew it, and she knew he murdered your grandmother. Anyone vicious

66

enough to kill his own mate isn't fit for living. My brother and I are protecting you and your sister."

"Oh good." She tried to pull out of his hold again but he refused to release her arms. "I'd hate to meet a GarLycan. They sound awful, if they drink blood from women and force them to be their lovers."

"Damn it, woman! You don't believe me." His blue eyes narrowed and his lips pressed into a grim line. "What would it take to convince you?"

"You could let me go. I'd feel less threatened that way."

He released her and backed away. "I'll spank your ass if you run."

She believed that part. "Your fascination with my ass isn't healthy, you know. I'm apparently already taken. My lover-to-be might beat you with his walking stick or toss his dentures at you if you put your gorilla-sized hands on that region of my body."

Anger darkened his features. "You're a menace!"

"At least I'm sane!"

"I'm telling you the truth."

Her gaze slowly examined him, from the top of his head down to his large feet. "So you're half Vampire and half Werewolf?"

"We prefer the term Lycan."

"I'm sorry. I'd hate to insult you." She took a few deep breaths and her body tensed—right before she lunged.

She barely made it a few yards before he spun her, grabbed her waist, and hauled her off her feet, and then she slammed against his body when he adjusted his hold so both arms secured her tight to his tall frame.

Her feet dangled off the ground and she glared at his face inches from her own.

"Put me down, you big ape!"

"I'm a VampLycan."

"You're a nutjob!"

He snarled and the sound terrified her. He had to be one of those insane people who honestly believed his fantasy world, to learn how to make such frightening noises. She wondered if he practiced making them in front of a mirror but wasn't about to ask.

"Please put me down." She didn't struggle, afraid he'd hurt her. He was strong enough to do it.

"Don't run."

"I won't," she lied, staring into his eyes.

He eased his hold enough that she slid down his front, feeling every powerful inch of him. It figured he had to be as big as he was, stronger than most men. It scared her. What if he decided his Vampire side wanted to suck her blood? She shivered and stepped away as soon as he allowed it. She sat on a nearby rock.

"I'm sure you have questions." He crouched close enough to grab her if she tried to flee a second time.

"Not really." She hated the feel of dirt between her toes. She couldn't exactly run around barefoot. "I take that back. Where are my shoes and purse?"

He glared. "You still don't believe me."

"Sure, I do," she lied. "Truth is in the mind of the listener. You have yours and I have mine. I heard what you said. I'm the future snuggle-bunny of some old rock pile who howls at the full moon. Now, what about my things?"

"Forget the goddamn shoes and your stupid purse. I left them at the camp, woman," he rasped. "You're pushing my limit on patience."

He'd already pushed hers way past that point. Though she guessed him calling her woman, rather than a bitch, was an improvement.

They studied each other, saying nothing. He straightened. She watched him pace the clearing. She glanced around the woods, looking for any sign of her sister, every time he turned his back to her. She'd wait until his lunatic brother showed up with Dusti before they escaped. They'd somehow have to find the crash site on their own, while ditching the crazy brother duo.

He began building a fire pit with rocks. She had to admire his survival skills, if not his mental stability. He seemed to know what he was doing. Kraven walked a short distance into the woods but quickly returned carrying broken branches. He whipped out a lighter from his pocket and started a fire.

Meanwhile, Bat's gaze kept searching the woods. Worry ate at her over Dusti's safety.

"You're half human, but you're also half VampLycan." He'd paused near her but she hadn't noticed until he spoke.

Her gaze met his. "Okay."

"I'm serious."

"I heard you. I'm half VampLycan. I'm also an attorney who's good at retaining information and I'm even decent with equations. That means I'm one-fourth Vampire and one-fourth Lycan."

"Yes."

"Odd. I've never wanted to suck someone's blood or sprouted hair during a full moon. Sometimes I get bitchy." She forced a smile. "Now I have an excuse."

"I'm really going to turn you over my knee."

"My future lover will beat you with his walker, or maybe flap his rock wings to knock you out if you do. Don't Gargoyles have those?"

"Damn it, you little hellcat."

"Actually, according to you, I'm not feline. Was my grandfather a panther or a lion?" She crossed her arms over her chest. "That's really going to get complicated if he was. Let me do the genetic arithmetic on that one."

He growled and his hands fisted. "I'm going to catch us something for dinner. You might be more willing to listen if you aren't hungry. I can hear your stomach rumbling."

Bat was relieved when he left her alone. She stood, hating being barefoot, and tentatively looked around the clearing. There were no signs of his brother or her sister. Dense trees surrounded them and the only sounds she could detect were from nature. She hated the great outdoors.

The urge to flee was strong but she had no idea which way to go or how to get back to the crash site. The fire he'd built was the only source of comfort, so she stood close to it, though her temper flared again, resenting that she felt helpless. She would have killed for a satellite phone and a burly security guard who had been a Boy Scout to help in her rescue.

"Kraven is certifiable," she muttered. "Now I have an excuse for why I don't tan easily. It's those pesky Vampire genes." Bat snorted.

She closed her eyes, taking deep breaths. *It could be a lot worse.* She had to keep reminding herself of that. She wasn't dead. It wasn't wintertime. No snow on the ground was a plus. The plane would have been reported as lost sometime the previous night, when it didn't arrive at the airport. She lifted her head and opened her eyes to look for any sign of helicopters or other planes. Nothing.

"Shit."

That Biker Bear guy had seemed saner than Kraven, and wherever her sister was, she could only hope he was taking care of her. Hell, maybe Drantos realized his brother had kidnapped her and was currently looking for them both. She'd just have to endure and be brave.

Growling and grabbiness aside, Kraven didn't really seem dangerous. He had used his big ape body to take most of the lumps when the plane had crashed. She admitted she would have probably gotten more injured if he hadn't. He might be insane, but he hadn't hurt her. He clearly loved to make threats but hadn't carried out any of them.

Her stomach growled loudly, the pains from hunger getting bad. His were probably worse since he had lugged her through the woods.

A light sound of movement drew her attention. Kraven walked out of the woods with something grotesque. She averted her gaze. "What is that?"

71

"A rabbit. I skinned it already so you didn't have to watch."

That was considerate at least. Images of cute little bunnies flashed through her mind but as long as the meat was cooked, she'd eat it. Some of the upscale restaurants she'd been to served far worse. He wasn't offering her bugs or snails.

"Can I do anything?" *Besides making sure you see a shrink when we're saved?*

"Just relax. It won't take long to cook. We have a lot of ground to cover but not much sunlight left."

"We're returning to the crash site?" It was the best news he could give her. Maybe he'd had time to rethink his irrational behavior and would return her to Dusti.

"No. My clan will have heard about what happened and should be searching for us by now. We'll head in the direction they'll be coming from, to hopefully meet up with them before your grandfather sends some of *his* clan this way."

She groaned, not hiding it. "This again? Listen to me, Kraven."

She paused, waiting for him to meet her gaze. He did and she saw how his eyes narrowed, his expression angry.

"There's not some supernatural plot at play here. We were on a plane and it crashed. Maybe you hit your head a little harder than I did so you're not thinking straight. Maybe some of the shit you saw in your line of work, if you're really a cop, made you escape from reality into this fantasy world. I know you sometimes have to actually do drugs if you're working narcotics. Some guys get addicted or it screws with their minds. I get it. I'm a defense attorney. I know just how inhuman some assholes

72

can be, capable of doing things most of mainstream society are better off not knowing about. They'd never have another night's peaceful sleep.

"Now, I'm sure my grandfather is a rotten bastard who probably earned his money by being a heartless prick. The rich often step on people to get to the top. Whatever your reasons for not liking him, I don't blame you. He isn't my favorite person either. But you *need* to return me to the crash site and to my sister. I won't press charges. You saved me from being killed. I'm giving you credit for that."

He blinked. It was better than lunging at her to lift her off her feet again. The rock he used as a makeshift table had the knife sitting there. He wrapped his hand around the handle and her heart skipped a beat.

He cut into the rabbit instead of trying to stab *her*.

"Your mother was a VampLycan. You're half one. It's not your fault that you don't know your heritage, if you weren't told. I'll give *you* credit for *that*. There are four clans of us, and one clan of GarLycans. We live in peace since Aveoth helps us keep it. Your grandfather wants to rule every clan; that's why he'll hand you over to Aveoth. You're his one weakness because of the blood addiction."

She swallowed hard, biting back a sarcastic comment. He wasn't going to be rational.

"I'm almost tempted to hand you over to Aveoth myself at this point, to make my own little deal. He'd kill Decker if I asked him to, with you as leverage, but I'm just not that cruel. You wouldn't survive a month with the GarLycan. You'd open your mouth one time too many and he'd kill you in a fit of rage. I doubt he'd be able to form any kind of attachment to you that would stir his protective instincts enough to overrule his temper.

73

"Marvilella, your grandmother, was part of my clan once. She mated with Decker trying to keep peace between his clan and the others. Decker was unstable even back then. He killed her in the end. Your grandfather has no honor, Bat. He also has no love or compassion in his heart. He doesn't have one. He'd force you into a hellish existence, as long as he got the support of the GarLycans to take out any opposition from the other three clans."

She sighed.

"You don't want to find out how honest I *really* am if Decker's enforcers find us first. There would be a battle to the death."

"Right."

"You're going to do as I say." He shoved meat on a stick he'd sharpened with the knife, holding it over the flames to roast. "Sit down and allow me to feed you."

She sat. The rabbit smelled delicious and she was starving. He passed her the stick.

"Careful. Blow. It's hot."

"I just watched you cook it. I'm not an idiot."

He frowned, putting another piece into the flames. "I didn't say you were. You don't seem the type to eat outdoors much."

"Try never." She blew on the meat and used her fingernails to protect the tips of her fingers while she tested a tiny bite. Her eyes closed as she savored the food. She finished it and opened her eyes, almost jumping when he offered her another piece by waving it right in her face.

"Thank you." She passed him the first stick back, accepting the next one.

She blew on it and ate. They were big chunks. He cooked a few more, letting them cool a little on another rock. He looked at ease in nature, as if he hunted and cooked his meals on a daily basis over an open flame. It would be kind of sexy, if she didn't know how unstable his sanity was.

His muscular thighs and legs were displayed nicely from his crouched position. His pretty gaze flicked her way, and she again found it unfair that he had to have a major flaw.

"More?"

"No." She passed back the stick. "I'm full for now. Thank you. Aren't you going to have some? You haven't eaten."

"VampLycan men take care of women first. You won't find that trait much in the human world. I wouldn't touch the food until I made sure you'd had enough to eat."

Interest sparked inside Bat and part of her softened. "You've romanticized your fantasy world. It's kind of sweet, and a nice change. Most guys would make up more barbaric stuff that degraded women." She smiled. "You aren't so bad, are you? You just need meds."

His head snapped in her direction as he bit down on a piece of meat. He chewed, swallowed, and rose to his feet. "I've lost my appetite. I'm tired of your insults. Stay by the fire, Bat. I need some space."

As he stormed away, regret hit her when she glanced at the rest of the strips he'd left behind. She should have just kept her mouth shut.

A low growl sounded close by and she knew it had come from Kraven. He hadn't gone far. Her belly was full, but he *had* to still be hungry.

"Damn it."

She rose to her feet, ready to apologize. The guy had fed her. Guilt had her walking carefully over dirt to find him.

He may be delusional but he thinks it's real. Believing he's some creature with a hero complex is better than some of the nutjobs I've dealt with. He needs to eat. I'll go play nice to bring him back.

Kraven hands fisted at his sides and he fought the urge to howl out his rage. Bat's insults weren't far off the mark when she'd accused him of being nuts. She was driving him crazy. It was her fault.

How in the hell could she have survived to her age without knowing she wasn't fully human?

Her traits must be almost nonexistent for her not to have learned what she truly was. It meant she was vulnerable and without defenses. The sight of claws growing from her fingertips every time she lost her temper would have clued her in. She obviously didn't have the ability to shift. He'd pissed her off plenty and her eyes hadn't even responded by changing color. Her body was human.

He softly groaned. *Not completely though.* She smelled good to him, enough to tempt his lust. It was bad timing, considering he was giving women a good long rest after Violet had tried to kill him.

Bat had no clue what kind of danger she was in. Her mother had been wrong to keep secrets. She'd probably figured she had more time to warn her daughters, and instead had died suddenly. At least he *hoped* Antina had planned to warn them.

He pondered if Decker had been behind that so-called accident that killed her parents, but he'd never mention that to either sister. The pain in Bat's eyes when she'd spoken of the loss had been too fresh. It didn't sit well with him, the thought of emotionally hurting her that way.

His hands itched to touch Bat. There was something about her that got to him, beyond her scent. It wasn't just her way of pissing him off. She was strong-willed and ornery. It was oddly arousing.

He sat on a wide rock and removed his jacket, tossing it over another. The cooler air felt good against his heated body. Lust rolled off him just *thinking* about Bat. Maybe he was losing his mind, or he'd gone far too long without a woman.

He was also pissed at Drantos. The bastard was being too soft on the sisters. They'd already be at their village if his brother wasn't worried that Dusti might be terrified by their shifted forms. They both could move a hell of a lot faster on four legs, rather than two. Walking through the woods, lugging someone over his shoulder, slowed them down a lot. Drantos had even insisted on stopping at nightfall so the women were well rested. None of that would matter if Decker's enforcers found them and they had a fight on their hands.

He was tempted to knock out Bat, tie her to his back, and shift. He could dump her off as soon as he reached home and someone else could babysit her. Then she'd be someone else's headache and irritation. The downside was, that would leave Drantos alone out here.

Kraven rejected the plan. His brother was bound and determined to ease Dusti into their world. It meant wasting a hell of a lot of time, in his opinion.

Movement drew his attention and the hellion stepped into view. He bit back a low growl, the sway of her hips noticeable as she carefully walked on the ground as if the earth would bite her. It was kind of cute. Though he hated the way his body responded by wanting to rush to her side and pick her up.

"I said I need space."

She kept coming, not taking the hint.

"Go back to the fire. We have to leave soon."

She ignored his order. It wasn't a surprise.

Chapter Five

Bat stopped right in front of him. "You should eat. I'll keep quiet."

His light blue eyes narrowed with irritation when they fixed on her. She clenched her jaw. He wasn't the only one annoyed. He drove her nuts, but at least a little time to cool off would make *her* sane. Not Kraven. He needed a team of doctors with a pharmacy at their disposal to help him find his right mind.

"What are you doing?" His voice came out deep.

She hated the way her body responded instantly when his voice changed to that gruff, sexy tone. Her nipples hardened, making her intensely aware of them. *He's insane, not hot*, she reminded her libido. It was probably just the stress.

His gaze lowered to her feet. "You shouldn't be walking out here barefoot."

"I wouldn't be if you hadn't ditched my shoes when you decided to kidnap me."

Anger flashed in his expression, his mouth tensing. "You'd still have them on your feet if you had decent ones that wouldn't break your ankles."

His pleasing scent was noticeable, being so close to him, and a wave of warmth flooded her body for some reason. He looked tall even sitting down, face level with hers. She'd never liked really large men, they usually intimidated her, but she found his bigger size yet another turn-on. She took a deep breath to quell the anger that attraction also made her feel.

"I'm sorry I hurt your feelings. I'm just a little upset that I've been kidnapped after being the victim of a plane crash. It hasn't exactly been the best twenty-four hours of my life. Please come back with me to eat some food. You've got to be as hungry as I was."

"No. I'll find something else to eat. Return to the fire." He slowly turned his head to look away from her.

Bat grabbed his arm before she even realized her hand had lifted. It really bothered her, thinking about him going hungry. He annoyed the hell out of her but she honestly didn't feel threatened by him. The fact that he fantasized about being something kind of romantic softened her toward him. He seemed to believe he was protecting her, that he was some mythical half-breed creature out to keep her safe from an evil villain.

He froze when her fingers gripped his upper arm. His tan skin felt really warm and definitely firm. He turned his head to watch her with a frown. His gaze shifted to her hand before meeting her gaze again.

"Let go of me."

"*You're* always grabby. I'm picking it up from you. Let's talk as though we're two reasonable adults." A smirk twisted her lips. "How hard can that be?"

He growled. Her heart raced and damned if her nipples didn't harden even more. She wondered if he'd make those animalistic noises during sex. Would he take the Werewolf/Vampire delusion into bed with a woman? She hated that she really wanted to find out. It had to be the hit to her head making her have crazy thoughts. *Yeah, go with that.*

"You're determined to make me spank you, aren't you?" His voice rasped the words and his blue eyes narrowed.

80

I'm a sick bitch, she decided. *Dealing with the scum I normally do has twisted me if I want to jump this crazy bastard. But God, he's totally hot.* "Please eat something? I promise I won't insult you and I'll be nice."

Oh, if only you knew how nice I want to be to you, she thought, glad he couldn't read her mind. He smelled incredible and his eyes made her feel drawn to him for some strange reason. She could get lost inside that intense look he gave her.

He spread his thighs and leaned back, his hands braced on the stone behind him. It moved him out of her reach so she had to let go of his arm, but the picture he created forced Bat to repress a groan. The guy was sex on legs. She gawked a little, taking notice of every inch of him.

Tight, faded jean encased thighs that were big enough to make her fantasize about how strong they must be. She had a real thing about men's legs. With his spread, and his hips tilted just a little, she could imagine him sitting that way to accommodate a raging hard-on. Her gaze lowered but didn't see a telling bulge. She wasn't sure what she'd have done if he were in that condition.

Her gaze zeroed in on his tank top. She would pay good money to see him lift it to flash his abs. His arms were sculpted with impressive muscles and he probably had a washboard tummy to match.

Is he hairy? She hoped not. She hated to lick a matted chest.

Damn it, knock it off, she ordered herself. Her body was really getting worked up and she knew if she didn't stop fantasizing about the big sexy loon, she'd need a new pair of panties to wear until hers dried. *A concussion would totally account for this.*

"Talk," the gruff, deep voice rasped.

She didn't want to. She finally met his gaze and those light blue eyes framed in thick black eyelashes may as well have punched her in the gut. *Damn, I want him,* she admitted. *Right or wrong, crazy or not, I've never been so turned-on in my life.*

"Obviously we're stuck together for as long as you feel the need to keep me. I just hope your brother really is taking care of my sister. We'd both get lost, die of exposure, or fall victim to the dangerous wildlife your state is known for. You and I need to get along until this is over."

"Fine. Don't talk to me and we'll get along just great." He straightened, giving her a look that left no doubt his temper hadn't cooled. "I won't be insulted by some clueless bitch. I've told you the truth."

Anger instantly flashed inside Bat. "I told you not to call me that again."

Kraven's eyes seemed to glow. "I remember. You threatened to castrate me." He gave her a cold smile. "You keep your hands off my dick. You damn near injured me when we crashed. You hurt me one more time and you'll kiss it better."

He was so forceful she believed every word. He'd put her on her knees to get her lips on him. That turned her on more, just imagining the scene. The submissive side she tried to hide shivered just a little at the image of him unzipping those jeans to reveal where she'd "hurt" him.

Bat closed her eyes, the image stuck. She tried to push it back. She heard Kraven sniff deeply a few times and her eyes opened. The first thing she saw was his shocked expression.

"That turns you on?" He whispered the accusation.

"I have no idea what you're talking about," she lied.

He sniffed again and leaned forward. His gaze jerked from her skirt back up to her eyes. "You're so turned-on I can damn near taste you. The scent is that strong."

"That's right. You're part doggy." She moved before she could think or talk sense to her brain, which had obviously decided to take a vacation. She stepped between his spread thighs to stand right before him. With him sitting, she didn't have to look up anymore to gaze into his incredible eyes. "So what do male dogs do when a female one is wet?"

He gaped at her, unmoving.

"I see. For a guy with dog instincts, it's kind of surprising you're not all over me yet…unless you're one of those guys who prefer other ones." She glanced down at his full lips, bit back a groan. She wanted to kiss him so badly she trembled. She couldn't look away from them. "Is that it, Kraven? Am I the wrong sex?" Her gaze lifted.

"I'm not attracted to men."

Her fingers slid down her skirt and curled against the material. She tugged it slowly up her thighs. His gaze lowered to stare at her exposed skin when she inched the skirt high enough to reveal her panties. She stopped there.

A soft growl came from him.

"You don't want to do this." He snarled the words, not looking away from her thighs. "Trust me. You're playing a dangerous game, woman. I know you're just screwing with me but if you don't stop, *I'm* going to be the one doing the fucking."

Desire made her heartbeat accelerate. She ached just at the thought of him doing exactly that to her. She raised her leg and planted the ball of her foot on top of his thigh. She knew it fully exposed her blue silk thong and spread her open to his view.

She released her skirt, cupped his face with both hands, and his gaze lifted from staring at her panties. She closed the distance to his parted mouth...

He turned his head at the last second, avoiding the kiss.

Frustration rose, making Bat want to curse. She wasn't willing to give up though. He'd put her out by taking her into the woods, so he deserved a little payback.

Her lips brushed over his warm throat instead. She hesitated before licking the area just under his earlobe, then closing her mouth on that soft, fleshy part of him. Her tongue and teeth raked it.

His big, strong hands curved around her hips to grab her ass. She made a soft sound in the back of her throat to encourage him.

"I'm going to lose it if you don't stop," he groaned.

She released his ear. "Go ahead. How many more green lights do you need to let you know that I want you?" She dove for the line of his neck where it met shoulder, her mouth open, and clamped down on the skin there, nipping him, not hard enough to hurt but enough to let him feel her bite.

"Fuck me," he moaned, his voice turning so deep it made Bat hotter.

One of her hands slid from his face, brushed down a firm chest and stomach covered by thin cotton, and found his belt. One of his hands helped her unbuckle and get it out the way. She clawed at the snap of his jeans to open his pants. She ached to feel what was hidden inside them. He'd given her an order to fuck him and she fully intended to comply. He grabbed her ass again to squeeze.

The snap gave way after a few tugs and she found the tab of his zipper. The side of her fingers brushed a rigid shape that made her heart beat faster. *Please*, she silently begged. *Don't be tiny like the last guy I had a one-night stand with.*

She pushed that disastrous four minutes of her life out of her mind. That's about as long as the guy had lasted, probably as many inches as he'd had. All she'd gotten for her time was frustration.

Hot, hard skin brushed the back of her hand when she got his pants open. She twisted her wrist, her fingers seeking, and found more than a handful. She tucked her chin down to verify the fact that Kraven probably had the thickest cock she'd ever encountered. Her mouth parted when she got a good look at his sex.

"Jackpot," she whispered.

"What?" His raspy tone lifted her gaze to stare into his.

Pure passion nearly swamped her while she studied his crystal-blue eyes, the paleness of them so breathtaking her lungs froze until she forced air inside them again when she remembered to breathe.

Her hand caressed his velvety shaft up to the tip. Pre-cum beaded the rounded crown of his cock, the slickness spread across the top by her thumb. Kraven softly growled deep in his throat. The purely animalistic sound had Bat's vaginal walls clenching in anticipation of what would come. *Hopefully both of us together*, she prayed.

85

His hands on her ass flexed, dug into her skin for an instant, and then released. She nearly protested but he suddenly grabbed her again and twisted her around, to her surprise, nearly making her stumble when her foot slid off him. His hands roamed down her hips, thumbs hooking the sides of her underwear, and he yanked them down to her knees. They fell on their own at that point to circle her ankles. She lifted one bare foot, freed it of them, and would have done the same with the other, but Kraven grabbed her hips again and jerked her back.

Bat landed on top of his thighs, his free hand fisting her skirt, pulling it higher up her stomach before he shifted again. She gasped, her hands wrapped around his forearms, when Kraven shoved his booted feet between her ankles and spread his legs, forcing hers wide apart. Her knees bent slightly, her legs resting outside of his.

She turned her head to stare over her shoulder. Their gazes met.

"No going back now. You're going to get me," he growled. A look of anger seemed to darken his tan, handsome features. "I'll try to be gentle but don't count on it."

Her mouth parted but the arm at her waist pulled her higher up his legs and his hand fisted the hair at her nape, forced her to face the woods. He bent her nearly in half on top of his lap. All she could grab was his arm over her stomach for something to cling to. His strength amazed her. He totally controlled her body.

"Don't move," he ordered in that deep voice of his that did funny, wonderful things to her.

His fingers untangled from her hair, the tips running softly down her spine to the crack of her ass, and then over one cheek. His soft touch made her nipples ache. She knew he'd discover just how wet she'd become when he tested her by sliding his hand where she was spread wide.

Another snarl tore from his lips, a good indication he took that whole part-animal fantasy in his crazy head to the extreme. His touch left her. She wanted to protest but he moved them both when he shifted a little closer to the edge of the rock, the feel of soft denim under her ass and thighs a bit sexy.

The blunt, thick tip of his shaft nudged her pussy, slid in the wetness of her desire. Kraven growled softly before he pressed his cock against the opening of her sex. She tried to relax but it didn't seem to help much when the broad crown tried to gain entry. The sensation of being stretched, parted, had Bat crying out in pleasure.

He paused just inside her, gave her seconds to adjust, before he released his cock to grab her hair again. He pulled her up into a sitting position by her hair but not roughly enough to hurt. Kraven's hot breath teased her ear when he leaned forward, but he kept his chest from touching her back. He left their bodies separated enough not to allow her to feel his hard body anywhere but under her legs, the arm securing her in place, and where they were connected by his cock.

"You're so fucking tight," he rasped. "I hope I don't break you but I'm too out of control to give you much more than this."

She didn't know what he meant but before she could ask, his arm tightened to draw her closer, until her back came up against his chest. His cock filled her deeper with the sudden move, forcing her to gasp from the excess of sensations that assailed her.

87

His cock felt as hard as steel inside her, her vaginal walls clamped around his thick shaft. She knew the meaning of impalement for the first time in her life. He breathed in short, ragged breaths, another snarl coming from his parted lips, and then he started to rock his hips. Her nails dug into his skin.

She couldn't move, her legs were parted, spread, and her feet didn't touch the ground. He didn't have that problem. He moved in short, hard thrusts, with Bat pinned on his lap. He delved his hand between her thighs until his fingers found her clit. He began to strum it furiously with a fingertip.

Bat moaned loudly, could only get lost in the pleasure of his pounding cock and the ecstasy his finger drew from each rub against the sensitive nerve bundle of her swollen clit. She turned her head into his throat, his scent filling her nose as she panted, and every growl he uttered seemed to draw her closer to climax.

Her walls tightened to the point that Bat wondered if she'd really break. She knew he fought to move inside her, regardless of how slick her need had become, drenching them where they were connected.

"Oh God," she panted. "Kraven!"

He snarled in response and bucked furiously under her, his arm squeezing her hips so tight she knew she'd have bruises, but she didn't care when the first explosion rocked through her brain as she started to come. Her mouth parted, she pressed her lips to his skin and cried out against him.

White-hot rapture gripped her, her back arched against his chest, and she knew her teeth sank into him just a little when she tried to muffle her screams of ecstasy. Kraven tucked his head against hers rather than jerk away, until he threw it back, his body quaking violently, and he started to come inside her.

Bat cried out over and over again, the sounds softer with every hot blast of his semen filling her as he slowed his pumping hips, dragging out his release. She'd never felt anything similar to what she'd just experienced when any other guy had come. His cock seemed to throb, pulse, and flex inside her. More heat flooded her and she shivered from the pressure when he shot again. It didn't stop until they were both left completely out of breath.

Her eyes were closed...she realized she tasted something irony on her tongue. Her vaginal walls trembled with an after-jolt of her climax and Kraven eased his hold around her body. His fingertip, still pressed against her clit, finally pulled away. She instantly missed his touch.

"Are you all right?" His gruff voice came out soft.

Bat opened her eyes. Kraven's face nearly touched hers. Even when she sat on his lap, the guy was taller. She wanted to tilt her head a little and kiss him. His blue gaze studied her until a frown pulled his lips just slightly downward.

"Did I hurt you?" Concern laced his voice.

She had to lick her lips. "You're big but I survived." *Blew my damn mind, just gave me my first screaming orgasm, and I probably won't walk right for at least two days because you're a stallion*, she added silently. Her gaze flicked to something red on his neck that caused her to gasp. "I bit you!"

He turned his head more toward her to hide the side of his neck. "Don't worry about it. You barely broke skin. I appreciate you biting into me rather than scaring off all the wildlife for a good mile."

Bat's heart rate slowed to a more normal rhythm while her body relaxed on top of his lap. She could feel him soften slightly inside her but not by much. Embarrassment came next. She'd bitten the guy, had drawn blood, and when she looked down where her hands still clasped the arm around her waist, she spotted *more* blood. Her nails had literally dug into his skin. The ragged crescent shapes on his arm welled red from the fresh injuries.

"*Damn*. I'm sorry."

"Good thing you weren't facing me." He cleared his throat. "You'd probably have torn my back up."

Bat always hated the part right after sex. She hadn't had much time for boyfriends, had sworn them off after an especially disastrous attempt. Her only sexual encounters since, though far and few between, had been one-night stands. This situation wasn't exactly a typical one, inside a hotel bed where they could roll away from each other to pretend to sleep until she could sneak out, or just part ways as soon as they dressed, never to see each other again.

Then another thought struck.

"Oh hell."

"What?" His voice deepened. "Did I hurt you? Are you in pain? I took you too rough, didn't I? You're so damn tight."

"We didn't use a condom." She wanted to kick her own ass. "I'm on the shot and have a clean bill of health." Hope flared. "You're not by any

90

chance under the regular care of a doctor who's tested you for sexually transmitted diseases, are you? I can't believe I took such a stupid risk! I know better."

He growled low, irritation flashed in his blue eyes, and his arm tightened around her waist as his legs slammed together. He lifted her off him, separated their bodies in a way that made Bat flinch at the briskness of it, and put her bare ass on the rock next to him. She clenched her teeth when cold but smooth stone chilled her butt.

"I don't have any diseases. Is that what you think? I'm some asshole who would have one, yet knowingly take you bareback to expose you to it?"

Her lips parted. "I didn't mean it that way. But you would be surprised at the depraved shit people are capable of doing. I had one client who purposely had sex with women when he knew he had HIV. He figured they deserved it if they didn't make him wear a condom." She hesitated. "I urged him to take a plea bargain and he did. He was scum who deserved to serve time."

He shot to his feet. He kept his back to her while he tucked himself and his shirt back into his jeans and buckled his skull belt.

Bat trembled a little but got to her own feet. She had to shove her skirt down her legs, the material wedged above her hips where Kraven had shoved it, and her knees wobbled slightly. She ached between her thighs enough to know she'd been right. She would be a little sore for days. Their shared passion dampened her thighs and she winced; her gaze studied the ground until she spotted her discarded underwear, and bent to retrieve them. She hesitated, not seeing a choice, and used them to

91

clean up as best she could. They afforded little help in that department but it wasn't as if she had napkins, tissues, or anything else to use.

"Give them to me. I'll wash them in the river and they should dry fast if I squeeze out the water. They're thin enough, it shouldn't take long." He held out a hand.

She hated the blush that heated her cheeks when she dropped the waded material into his outstretched palm. He fisted her panties and shoved them inside the back pocket of his jeans.

"We should get back to camp." He met her gaze, a grim look on his face. "I'll eat before we need to start moving again."

Kraven yanked his leather jacket off a smaller rock and put it back on. He pulled up the collar to his throat. She figured it was his attempt to hide the mark she'd left on him. It irritated her. That was a player move, only there were no other potential women around to hide it from.

She'd just nailed a lunatic playboy sort. *Yeah, I can sure pick them.* She sighed.

"What's wrong?" He stared at her a little too intensely for her comfort.

The color of his eyes seemed to darken. She knew it had to be just a trick from the light. The sun had sunk low enough in the sky to explain it away; it wasn't possible otherwise. "Nothing."

"Do you want me to carry you or can you walk?" He glanced down at her bare feet. "I don't want you getting hurt."

The offer made her opinion of him soften just a tiny bit. He might be a player but he seemed concerned about her, even after getting what he wanted. That was new. "I can walk. I don't enjoy being thrown over your shoulder and now I have to be careful not to flash my goods."

He grinned. "I don't wear underwear. You'll survive."

"You're not wearing a skirt." She tore her gaze from his to carefully watch the ground, to avoid stepping on anything sharp.

He suddenly invaded her personal space and she halted, her chin rising. He cupped her face with his hands. They stared at each other for what seemed a long time. His thumbs slid down her throat, gently caressing her.

"Why?"

"Why what?"

His gaze narrowed.

She licked her lips. She understood that he was asking why she'd hit on him, and even sympathized with the confusion he had to be feeling. She was experiencing it herself. No one had ever made her madder, yet hotter, than Kraven. She breathed in his masculine scent, her body responding again, and she fought the urge to climb the guy to get closer.

"Concussion? Maybe I've lost my mind."

One hand released her to trail down her throat, over her shoulder, and lowered to her waist. His big hand curved there, holding her. "Maybe not. Your Lycan blood is dominant. You've probably never been near a male Lycan and your body must really yearn for mine."

She closed her eyes and jerked her face out of his hold. "Right. God, what was I thinking?" She opened her eyes to stare at him sadly. "I so wish you weren't a nutjob."

He yanked her tight against his tense body; the hand on her hip dove lower and he grabbed her ass. His other hand cupped the other side, both palms gripping her through her skirt, and his face buried in her neck.

"You want proof?" He growled low and his mouth opened against her throat. "Explain this, Hellion."

He nipped her throat, growled again, and Bat clutched at him. He kneaded her ass, grinding his body against hers. His hot, wet tongue teased her skin. Desire shot through her at an alarming rate. Sweat broke out all over her body and she moaned. Her fingers gripped his short hair. She ignored the feel of the gel he had to use to make those spikes that weren't really styled anymore, more of a wild mess on his head, yet still made him appear sexy.

He bit her skin, the sharp nip of pain making her cry out. She could feel damp desire on her thighs. Her nipples tightened, ached, and her belly had funny butterfly feelings fluttering there. He lifted her to her tiptoes, bent his knees, and his hard cock rubbed against the cradle of her thighs through their clothes.

"Kraven," she begged, lifting her leg. She hooked it around the back of his thigh and tightened her arms, trying to pull him even closer.

His mouth left her skin and he lifted his head. She stared deeply into his sexy eyes. Passion flushed his handsome face and his lips pressed together tightly into a near frown.

His Adam's apple bobbed when he swallowed hard, turned his head away, tucking it to hide his features, and took a deep breath. His voice came out so deep it didn't sound human as he spoke.

"Damn. I shouldn't have done that. I could throw you on the ground to fuck you and you'd let me. You'd want it as much as I do." He cleared his throat, took a few deep breaths, and then glared at her. "I bet that pisses you off. You're a hotshot attorney and I'm just some crazy bastard. Explain to me how I can do this to you. Take a deep breath, Hellion. It will only make you want me more. Your scent drives me insane. I'd drop to my knees and fuck you for days in every way imaginable if I had the time. We'd go at it like two animals. My Lycan side attracts yours. No *human* would turn you on this much."

She released his hair but couldn't pull away from him. She'd love to tell him he was full of shit but she couldn't deny the truth. She'd let him do anything he wanted at that moment. She hurt for him again, wanted him more than her next breath. She didn't understand why. No guy had ever affected her the way Kraven did.

"Let go," he ordered.

She didn't want to but finally dropped her leg. It took real effort to force her arms to lower from around his neck. He pulled back as he eased her onto her feet, releasing her ass. She fought the urge to throw her body back against his.

Something was seriously wrong with her. She should slap him, yell, tell him he was full of shit...but he hadn't lied. She not only would agree to him taking her on the ground, she wanted to find out what his imagination could come up with and how many ways he could think of to fuck her.

Kraven backed away more, staring at her with a hungry look. She didn't miss the way his chest rose rapidly as he seemed to be having a hard time catching his breath. One glance down to the front of his jeans assured her he was as turned-on as she was. The hard bulge of his cock couldn't be denied.

"It's the Lycan inside you. It wants the strong male in me...craves me."

That statement made her mind snap back into functioning mode again. "You're full of shit. I don't have any dog in me."

His lips curved into a chilly smile as some of the desire cooled in his gaze. "You were just full of *me*. Want it again?" He growled. "For that dog insult, you can beg me to fuck you. I'll take you like a bitch, from behind on your knees, and show you just how much of a dog I am."

It was an emotional slap. "Asshole."

He turned away. "I'm hungry now." He sniffed the air. "Let's go."

Bat hated the way tears filled her eyes but she blinked them back. It stung that he'd talk to her that way after what they'd shared, as crazy as that seemed. She had hurt his feelings, but he'd hurt hers too.

She trailed him back to the nearby fire. He did walk slow enough that he was easy to follow. He could have just left her to find her own way.

It took every ounce of Kraven's control to keep his back to Bat. His dick throbbed and he wanted to fuck her again. The taste of her blood on his tongue was torment. He'd bitten her throat when he'd grabbed her that last time, too curious to know just how much other she really had inside her. Her blood seemed mostly human with a tiny bit of Lycan. But it was enough.

He'd tasted her—and it had changed everything.

Now it made sense why he was attracted to her...and he didn't know how to deal with the reality of the grim situation.

I just had to taste. He cursed himself for doing it. Her reaction to him wasn't a mystery anymore. He'd resisted biting her while he'd been balls deep inside her pussy but the urge had been there, strongly. He'd fought it until he had to know if it was just Lycan attraction or more. Now he knew.

Nature could be a cruel bitch at times.

He crouched, eating the cooled meat quickly to sate at least one hunger. He needed to be strong in case they ran into any of Decker's clan. The bastard wasn't about to allow his granddaughter to slip through his fingers when he had plans to give her to the GarLycan leader.

No fucking way is Aveoth getting Bat.

Kraven dared to glance at her. She resumed her seat on the rock but avoided looking his way. That was fine with him. He needed a clear head to evaluate the situation. He studied her neck where he'd bitten her, happy to see it nearly healed. His saliva could do that. She seemed unaware of the mark.

Protective instincts gripped him until his body felt made of stone. He needed to get her to the village. Safety was in numbers. Decker wouldn't dare send his men to go against those kinds of odds. His father would offer Bat and her sister protection, since their grandmother had once been part of their clan, but now there was a second reason.

She's my mate. Fuck!

He could deny it but it was pointless. They hadn't sealed the bond, but he certainly planned to. It seemed daunting, though. She wasn't even aware of his world, and she lived in the human one. She'd have to give up everything she knew to be with him. Nothing with her would be easy.

He glanced up at the sky, guessing they needed to get going. He'd keep moving all night but she'd need his warmth to survive. It was too cold for her, and her Lycan bloodline was too weak. He'd have no choice but to stop once the temperatures dropped. His brother would have the same problem with her sister.

"I'm sorry about the dog remark."

He arched an eyebrow when he looked at her. It was odd that she'd apologize, but nice. He still felt leery.

"I was angry."

He blew out a breath. "I see."

"I feel kind of guilty about having sex with you too."

That *really* confused him. He hadn't smelled another man on her and she didn't wear a ring to indicate she was attached in a serious relationship. Humans did that. "Why?"

"Are you even capable of saying yes or no? I mean, there's a valid issue of consent with your mental state in question."

He snarled, enraged. His anger flamed high once more. "Shut up, Bat. I know where this is heading, and don't go there."

"I'm an attorney. I know better. I mean—"

She gasped when he suddenly lunged to his feet, stormed around the fire, and jerked her to her feet. In the next instant, he sat on a log away from the flames—with Bat facedown over his lap.

He molded his hand over her skirt. "I'm going to redden your ass if you imply I'm not competent enough to say yes or no to sex."

She struggled on his lap but he held her down. One hand flattened on her back to push her stomach and chest tighter to his spread thighs, and the hand on her ass slid down her skirt, fingers fisted the edge and jerking it up.

"Let me go! I'm not wearing underwear. Kraven!"

He was more than aware. He never should have grabbed her, but damn, the urge to show Bat that he was her male was too strong to resist. He took deep breaths, trying to calm.

Then his gaze landed on her very tempting ass...and he was lost.

He had to touch it, consequences be damned.

Chapter Six

His palm landed on her ass.

Bat jumped. Kraven didn't hurt her but the feel of his firm touch was enough of a threat. She froze, afraid to even breathe. Fear gripped her. Would he really spank her? She wasn't into pain.

"Please don't."

The hand on her ass held still for seconds before he traced it down the curve of her butt. She sucked in air when his fingers rubbed her inner thigh. It rose higher, until he fingered the seam of her pussy, breaching it enough to make her aware he could fuck her with his finger if he wanted to.

"I *hate* the smell of fear coming from you." His husky voice did things to her. "You're not into too much roughness but you enjoy being controlled. I'm learning more about you each time I touch you. I won't spank you, since I realize you won't enjoy the bite of pain." His finger slid into the slick entrance of her pussy, then out, and he ran the tip of his digit down until he located her clit. "There are other ways to teach you not to insult me."

He tapped the bundle of nerves and she tensed on his lap. Her fingers gripped the leg of his jeans. With her bent over his lap, it was all she could reach. He rubbed her clit and she moaned, the pleasure instant.

"What does it for you, Hellion? The thought of how much stronger I am than you? I could restrain you and do anything I want to your body. I

100

could tie open your thighs and fuck you with my fingers or my tongue. I could play with your pretty little pussy for hours."

Desire shot through her and Kraven softly growled. His hand pressed against her thigh and she spread them to give him more access. A whimper passed her lips when his thumb pushed against her pussy, rubbing the fresh proof of what his words did to her.

"You're getting *so* hot for me." His thick thumb slowly breached her, just barely going inside, and paused. "Apologize as if you really mean it."

She was tempted to tell him to go to hell but he could still smack her butt. "I'm sorry."

"No more insults about my sanity. I don't find it amusing."

She clenched her teeth, her anger stirring. She didn't enjoy being manipulated the way he was trying to do. It was dirty and unfair.

He sniffed at her and chuckled. "My hellion has such a temper." His thumb slid deeper and slowly moved in and out of her as his finger pressed against her clit.

"Fuck you," she rasped.

"*I'm* doing the fucking, aren't I?"

"Asshole." She moaned when he rubbed a little faster, letting his thumb drive into her deeper.

Then he pulled his hand away, withdrawing from her.

Bat wanted to groan. Shame hit her as he released her back and his thighs drew together until her knees touched the ground. She grabbed at him to push up and got to her unsteady feet, backing away from him. She glared as she shoved her skirt down and hated the way her body ached for him to finish.

"Such a dirty mouth." He rose to his feet and reached for the front of his jeans. "Who taught you how to speak? Did you hang out on docks? You must have been around a lot of sailors."

"Go to hell."

"I'm there. Trust me." He unbuckled his belt and unfastened the snap of his jeans. His finger and thumb pinched his zipper, slowly drawing it down.

"What are you doing?" She stared at Kraven.

He lowered his zipper enough for his cock to spring free. It stood straight out, thick, and he kept hold of his pants as he slowly backed to a grassy shaded area under a tree. "Follow me."

"No."

"You ache for me the way I do you. I'm going to use my mouth on you."

Her knees weakened at just the thought and her gaze locked with his. "You want to go down on me?"

"We're going to put our mouths to good use. I want to taste you, and I want that mouth of yours wrapped around me." A soft growl came from his parted lips. "I could eat you alive."

"That's unsanitary."

He had the nerve to grin. "Did you really just say that?"

"We had sex," she reminded him. "We need to clean up first or something." She wasn't really opposed to the idea of oral sex. She was curious—and turned-on.

"Who the hell have you been fucking, my little hellion? It sounds boring. Unsanitary isn't in my vocabulary. Sex is supposed to be dirty and hot. Come here." He backed up a little more.

"We need a shower first, and condoms." She bit her lip. "I don't go down on men without one."

His mouth parted and he looked shocked.

"What? It's less messy that way." She floundered because he was looking at her as if she'd lost her mind. "It is," she insisted.

He recovered and scowled. "Now you're making me feel sorry for you. Are you afraid of tasting yourself? Me? What we did together? I didn't peg you for a coward or a prude."

"God, I don't like you." She took a step to follow him though, and then another. "I'm just letting you know. This is temporary insanity. That's my defense."

He chuckled. "Always the attorney, aren't you? It's kind of hot."

"I'll tell that to my shrink once I'm rescued. She'll love that part."

He snorted. "You see one?"

"The firm demands we do. We deal with a lot of shit."

He lowered to the grass until he was stretched out on his back. He lifted his hips enough to shove his jeans down to mid-thigh, exposing more of his body, and he pulled his shirt up to show off firm abs. The sight of them made her want to touch him. He was beautiful; so in shape, he had to have the best body she'd ever seen. He lifted a hand to urge her on.

"Come on. Live a little."

She stepped next to him.

He gripped her ankle. "Sixty-nine."

Bat only hesitated for a second. "You get bottom. You're too heavy and big." Her gaze locked on his impressive cock. "You'd choke me."

"I know."

The smirk on his face irritated her. She suddenly pulled out of his gentle grip and instead of taking the position he'd demanded, she straddled his thighs, trapped together by his lowered jeans.

His head lifted and he frowned. "You're supposed to face the other way."

"Payback, sweetheart." Her hand wrapped around his shaft as she licked her lips. "I may have a submissive streak but I'm nobody's bitch."

His eyebrows shot up as she lowered her head and took his cock inside her mouth. She didn't go slow; no hesitant licks, no teasing. She took as much of his length as she could without hitting her gag reflect, tightened her lips around his shaft, and sucked hard, moving rapidly up and down on him.

A moan tore from Kraven and his body tensed under her. She looked up at him, her gaze fixing on his face. She watched him throw back his head. His mouth parted and movement from the corner of her vision made her glance that way. His fingers dug into the grass next to his hips. She smiled around him as she worked his cock with her tongue and lips.

His thighs under hers lifted a little as his back arched, muscles tightened to reveal his six-pack abs clearly.

She took him deeper, adjusting to his size.

His cock stiffened even more and he made animalistic noises that turned her on. She wanted to climb up his body to impale herself on his shaft, but she kept going until she knew he was about to come...

Her mouth released him. She sat up and studied him.

Kraven's head rose and his eyes seemed to be glowing as he stared at her, panting.

"Apologize like you mean it for calling me a hellion and a bitch." She slowly licked her lips. "And I might finish you off." She smiled. "If you beg."

His eyes narrowed and he snarled, anger tightening his features. Bat cried out as he swiftly lifted his thighs, tossing her forward, but she didn't dive head first into the grass. Strong arms caught her before she could and he rolled them over. Her back hit the grass with enough force to knock the air from her lungs.

His body came down over hers. His hips shoved between her parted thighs and his cock drove deep into her pussy with one strong thrust. Her mouth opened to cry out from the sheer pleasure of him filling her, but his lips captured the sound, sealing over her parted mouth. He growled and began to fuck her hard and deep. She wrapped her legs around his hips, feeling his hot skin against hers.

Kraven kissed her roughly, aggressively, and she met his passion. She burned to come as his body pinned her tight to the ground. She could only take him. She couldn't even buck her hips to meet his rapid thrusts. The pleasure built until she was the one to twist her head away to break the intense kiss.

She lifted her head, buried her face against his neck, and cried out as she started to climax hard. Sheer ecstasy nearly tore her apart from the magnitude of her orgasm. It only heightened when he found his release. The feel of his semen jetting inside her, the way his stiff cock jerked and seemed to thicken in girth, if that was possible, sent a second climax through her.

Kraven's hips stilled but he remained buried deep inside her pussy, their bodies connected, while they both panted. Bat realized she was wrapped around him, clinging to him with her legs and arms. She tried to relax her tense limbs. Her mind started to clear from the haze of sexual bliss and began to function again.

So much for that apology. The sex was so hot that she was sweating even though she hadn't really moved. Her fingers brushed his back where she had wrapped her arms under his, hugging his broad chest. She wished she were touching skin instead of the thin material of his shirt. She actually felt the need to seek out his warm flesh, some insane obsession making her want nothing between them, but she resisted tearing at his tank top. Instead her palms slid lower, to the bottom of his shirt, where it had hiked up a bit. She found exposed skin.

He was so warm, felt so good as her fingertips caressed his spine. She kept her face buried against his warm throat. She breathed him in, couldn't get enough of the cologne he wore, and figured she may have lost her mind from the stress of the plane crash and being kidnapped. Whatever the reason, she didn't want to release Kraven. She wished they

106

could just remain locked together, and it didn't even matter that she was pinned under his massive body on grass in the middle of Nowhere Woods, Alaska. There wasn't anywhere else she wanted to be.

"Hellion," he rasped. "Are you okay? I was rough again." He nuzzled her a little with the side of his head. "Am I too heavy?"

"I'm great and you're not crushing me," she got out. "I like you here."

"That's why I'm not moving." His arms adjusted until he pinned hers between his biceps and ribs. "I don't want to separate us. It was too damn difficult last time...but we can't stay here for long."

Shit! Dusti! "Right. I need to find my sister."

He nuzzled her again before lifting his head. Bat peered up at him. His ruggedly handsome face looked even more attractive with the small smile that curved his lips. The flush of his features after sex and the way his gaze soaked her in was sexy. She'd even consider that gaze loving.

Whoa! Don't go there. It's just sex.

"We need to have a long talk when we reach my village."

She had to force her gaze from his. Something inside her resisted, but she managed to turn her head to study the tree next to them. "No need."

He softly growled and drew her attention back to his eyes. Anger sparked there now. "There *is* a need. We can't deny what's between us."

"We're attracted to each other. We argue and end up doing this. It's stress."

"You really think that's all it is?" His voice deepened and his features turned harsh.

107

She wanted to say yes. It would be easy to fit what they shared into that neat little box of reason. But Bat just couldn't do it when they were still physically joined, with his lips inches from her own. She wanted to kiss him and she couldn't deny that. It was clearly more than just some crazy one-time thing because she kept wanting Kraven.

"No. We're fire and gasoline, Kraven. The two of us are bad for each other, but we burn so good together when the sparks fly."

All his anger faded. "It's more than just sex."

"It can't be." She hated to say the words. "I'm a defense attorney in Los Angeles. I am about to make partner, nearly killed myself to get there, and you...live in Alaska." *Don't mention he's nuts and that it would ruin my career if word got out that I hooked up with a loon.* "Plus, you kidnapped me. I think it would be bad form to start dating after meeting under those circumstances." She smiled to soften her words.

His lips parted but he said nothing. He lifted his head, broke eye contact, and glanced around the clearing. He took a few deep breaths before he lowered his chin to meet her gaze once more.

"We need to keep moving. Drantos will have left whatever camp he'd made by now. We're trying to keep about a mile apart to cover more ground, but close enough to reach each other if the need arises for backup."

She stopped tracing his spine with her fingers, suddenly aware she'd never stopped, the urge to touch him so strong. "He took my sister? I'd hoped they were still back at the crash site." New worries hit her. "Is she okay?"

"He'll protect her with his life," he rasped, looking sincere. "Release me and I'll get up."

She regretted it deeply but unlocked her legs from around the back of his thighs and lifted her hands from his back. He almost reluctantly withdrew from her body and eased his weight off until they no longer touched. He rolled away, looked elsewhere, as Bat sat up to adjust her clothing.

Her skirt was not only wrinkled but now had grass stains. She rose to her feet. Her hands dusted the thing frantically to push it down her thighs and remove the bits of grass that stuck to it. Kraven stood and fixed his pants, closed the belt, and they faced each other.

"We *are* going to talk, Bat. Prepare for that." His solemn gaze held hers. "But not right now. Let's go." He opened his arms. "I'll carry you."

"Forget it. I'll walk." She took the lead, watched the ground for anything sharp to avoid stepping on it. She paused when they reached the fire.

She'd just turned to Kraven when a horrible, scary sound fractured the woods.

Birds overhead took flight, their wings flapped frantically. Kraven's features paled.

"Was that a bear?" Terror gripped Bat.

"No." Kraven snarled the word, his voice startling her badly at how vicious he sounded. "Stay here. Don't move."

He sprinted off rapidly before she could respond, running faster than she'd ever seen a person move. She stood there in stunned silence until another gut-wrenching roar filled her ears.

Panic struck. Kraven had just abandoned her in the woods.

She debated on rushing after him but didn't want to get lost. A feeling of helplessness brought tears to her eyes before she bent to grab a rock. It was small enough to fit in the palm of her hand, but it was a weapon. She took a few steps in the direction where Kraven had lunged away, her gaze frantically searching for him.

"Come back," she prayed aloud.

Another horrifying animalistic noise rent the air and she inched closer to the fire, grabbing one of the sharpened sticks Kraven had used to cook the meat. Whatever it was, it sounded big and deadly. The crazy idiot had run right in the direction the sound came from.

"I knew he was nuts."

She strained her ears, listening for any other sounds. Time seemed to drag by as seconds turned into minutes. Every bad scenario ran through her head. He could get killed. She'd die without him. She really needed Kraven to come back.

Kraven hated leaving Bat alone but he had to get to his brother. He jumped up on a fallen tree and scanned the woods. He spotted an enforcer within seconds. The wind blew and he inhaled. The scent wasn't familiar.

Enemy. His instincts screamed it.

He quickly removed his clothes and leapt off his higher spot. He was partially shifted as he hit the ground running.

The enforcer was tracking something, his nose to the ground. He didn't see or hear Kraven coming at him until it was too late.

Kraven slammed into his body hard enough that the impact hurt even him. It sent the enforcer rolling into a tree. Kraven was on him before he could recover. He let his claws dig into the man's back, using his weight to pin him down. He grabbed him by the side of his neck as the stunned enforcer tried to draw breath. He bit hard enough to draw blood but not rip out his throat. It was a warning.

Kraven opened his jaws. "She's *mine*," he grumbled. "You aren't taking her."

The guy under him snarled and tried to buck him off.

Fury filled Kraven. "Go home or die. Last warning. Decker is wrong."

The enforcer tried to buck him again and twisted his head, attempting to bite into Kraven's face. He reacted fast by flinching away. He dug his claws in deeper and when the enforcer's body seized from the pain, he lunged. His teeth latched onto the enforcer's throat and tore into flesh.

The enforcer under him shuddered and finally grew still.

Kraven paused, listening to the enforcer take his last breath. He opened his mouth and shoved off the other man. He stood, his body coated in blood where it had splashed on him. He'd killed to protect Bat.

He returned to skin, not wanting Bat to see him in shift. She'd run for her life, surely believing he would attack.

Motion to his left drew his attention as he saw another enforcer in the distance. He wasn't close enough to be a threat to Bat unless he changed direction. Kraven was downwind so the beast probably wasn't aware of him yet. He moved fast to hide behind a tree, tracking the enforcer with his gaze.

The other male paused, looked around, then shoved his nose down on the ground. Decker's man was searching for the women, or perhaps trying to locate the other enforcer, since he had to have heard the fighting. Those first roars hadn't come from the one Kraven fought. Those he'd identified as Drantos. It meant his brother had been found.

Kraven crouched and kept low.

He felt torn between loyalties. Drantos was in trouble but Bat was alone. She'd be defenseless without him sticking close. He dropped to his hands and knees, staying low to keep from being seen until he reached a thick line of trees. Then he straightened, running fast to reach the woman he'd left behind. She was his priority.

He'd almost made it back to Bat when he caught an unfamiliar whiff of yet another enemy. He moved toward the scent with stealth until he spotted motion.

The shifted enforcer leapt over a fallen tree, moving fast toward where he'd left Bat.

The bastard must have caught her scent, or that of the fire he'd started to cook her meal. Kraven's claws shot out from his fingertips and his fangs elongated as he moved to intercept the threat.

Decker's enforcers were well known since they liked to show up at the clan from time to time to make threats, but this wasn't one Kraven had ever met or smelled before.

The male snarled low, probably telling him to move out of his way.

Kraven curled his lip to flash his fangs and held his ground. He decided to try reasoning with the enforcer. "Don't even think about it. Do you know who I am? I'm Velder's son." He hoped the threat of his father would be enough.

The male's eyes narrowed as he softly growled.

Obviously not. "You don't want to fight me. It would be a mistake. That woman is mine. Do you understand me? She's my mate. You *will* die if you try to take her."

"Decker wants," the enforcer hissed.

"Decker can shrivel up and go fuck off. He's gone too far this time and you know it. He isn't going to stop until he starts a war. Is that what you want? Clan fighting clan? To see the bodies of friends and family pile up? To watch women mourn the loss of mates and children?"

The enforcer just stared at him but Kraven saw emotion flicker in his eyes. His tense body also slightly relaxed. It encouraged him to keep talking.

"How many would you kill to protect *your* mate? Is Decker worth dying for? You aren't touching what's mine."

The shifted beast backed up a few steps, indecision in his narrowed stare.

"I'm giving you a chance to live." Kraven flashed his fangs again as he allowed some of his humanity to slip away, the bones in his face shifting. "I've already killed one of you. Big one with black spots on his coat."

A pained whine came from the enforcer.

"You were close to him?"

"Yessss."

"Take him home to his loved ones." He jerked his head toward where he'd battled the other VampLycan. "Don't die on a fool's errand. Decker can't win. Aveoth will never be leashed and controlled as your leader's pet. He'd more likely attack him to make an example of what he does to his enemies. Decker is making your entire clan an enemy of the GarLycans."

Kraven didn't really believe Aveoth would slaughter innocents, but it could happen that way.

The male's stance relaxed and Kraven did the same, but staying on the alert in case it was a deception. "Get your friend and take him home."

The male turned directions, sniffed the air, and tracked Kraven's footsteps to the clearing. Kraven followed him, not willing to trust that he wouldn't go after Bat. The bloodied body lay where he'd left it. A whimper came from his enemy. Remorse for the loss of a life softened some of Kraven's rage.

"I had no choice."

The VampLycan shifted into a boy barely out of his teens. Disgust toward Decker rose once again. It seemed the clan leader not only sent

114

women to do his bidding, but barely full-grown youths as well. Kraven seethed.

"Why do you follow that son of a bitch?"

The boy turned to face him, his shoulders stiff. "It's a matter of honor."

"He *has* none."

"I know." His gaze lowered to the ground. "My father's pledged to him. I must make my family proud by doing his bidding, to keep our honor, whether or not I agree with Decker's orders. My father is a strong supporter. I am not. This was my best friend."

"I'm sorry for your loss."

The teen looked up and held Kraven's stare until he turned to gently lift the body of his comrade. "He's got to be stopped. Decker leads us with terror and kills anyone in our clan who voices dissatisfaction. He ordered us to retrieve his granddaughter. We either do what he says, or he'd have us killed on the spot. I'll die if I go back without her."

It was a plea for help. "Go to one of the other clans and wait it out. Repeat what you've told me. Decker has gone way too far. We're heading home and will tell the other clans of his plot. Aveoth won't be happy to learn your leader planned to blackmail him. No one will allow this to pass without punishment."

"Most of us will be relieved if Decker's no longer in power. We don't want a war with you."

The kid was flat-out telling him the clan wanted Decker removed from position. "How many feel that way?" He wanted to know how their clan was split.

"Just the first generations will have a problem with Decker being gone. We're forced to abide by their decisions."

Kraven understood. Sons and daughters were bound to do as their elders ordered, and they were following Decker. It wasn't honorable to go against one's elders. Few would challenge and kill a parent to take charge of their family. But the dynamics of the clan would change if Decker were gone. The elders would have to follow the new leader. "Is there one amongst you who would be able to lead, and who doesn't share Decker's power lust? A name would help."

The kid hesitated, glancing around first before he whispered, "Lorn. He refused to be an enforcer but Decker didn't kill him. Lorn's father is Decker's chief advisor, but some think that's not why his son was allowed to live. The enforcers tread lightly around Lorn."

They feared him. That's what the kid wasn't saying. "Lorn doesn't like Decker?"

"No."

"Is he sane?"

The kid nodded. "He says he has no tolerance for bullshit and keeps to himself most of the time."

Kraven liked him already. "Do you think your clan would be better off with Lorn leading it?"

"He's only got one flaw."

"What's that?"

The kid glanced around again and lowered his voice. "One of the enforcers was sent into the human world, and he had a child with a human. He brought the baby home with him after the mother died. Lorn protects her."

"You see that as a flaw?" It disgusted Kraven. The kid in question was probably weak like Bat and her sister, unable to defend herself properly.

The kid hesitated and shrugged. "Decker thinks it is. She's still alive because Lorn goes after anyone who threatens her. He practically castrated a few guys who thought she might be fun to fuck with once. He took them on by himself and left them bleeding in the dirt. I saw him fight. He could hold the clan if he wanted to. Most fear and avoid him."

The teen rushed away in the next instant, taking his fallen clansman.

Kraven felt the weight of the world on his shoulders. The new information would help them take out Decker. He just needed to get Bat safely to his village and call the three other clans together to hold a meeting. They also needed to learn more about Lorn. It would be hell to help him gain control of that clan, only to later find out he would be a bigger problem than his predecessor.

He checked on Bat, keeping his distance so she wouldn't spot him. He hadn't retrieved his clothes yet or cleaned up. It amused him seeing her by the fire. She held a rock and a stick. He scanned the area, sniffed, and then decided to quickly check on Drantos. It would only take a few minutes. Bat was safe for the time being. He trusted that the teen wouldn't return.

He'd almost reached where he'd picked up Drantos's scent when the wind blew in his face. He froze as the scent of enforcers filled his nose. There were at least two of them.

He spotted them in the distance, moving fast and heading right toward Bat and the fire. He regretted building the damn thing. He should have caught fish and made her eat it raw.

He spun, rushing back to Bat. He needed to get her the hell out of there. Those weren't enforcers from his clan.

The sight of something caught the corner of Bat's eye and she turned her head, gaping at the person coming at her. It was Kraven, minus his clothes. That didn't faze her as much the fact that he was covered in blood.

She dropped the rock and stick, rushing forward.

"Are you all right? Oh my God."

He had a wild look in his eyes as he threw up his bloodied hands to avoid her making contact. "Don't touch me."

"You're hurt!"

"It's not mine."

She didn't know what to say.

He pointed to his right. "Run, Bat. The river is that way. Cross it and keep going. I'll find you." He turned, giving her with his back. "I'll hold them off."

"Hold off who? Where are your clothes? Where did that blood come from?" It was splashed across his chest, hips, and thighs. He even had some down his back.

"Damn it!" He turned his head, glaring. *"Run!"*

Another loud, scary sound came from nearby and Kraven crouched, seeming to focus on something to his left. "RUN! They're coming."

It wasn't so much not knowing what kind of animal could make such frightening growls as the way he'd snarled the order at her, sounding vicious, that got her moving. She spun, darting in the direction he'd pointed.

The sound of moving water helped her find the river. She paused at the edge, watching it rush by. The hundred or so feet between her and the other side alarmed her. Swimming had never been something she enjoyed.

A roar came from behind her. It was a nightmarish sound, followed by a sharp snap of wood. It was all the motivation she needed to wade in, frantic to put space between whatever Alaskan wildlife could be that thunderous. It sounded huge. The icy water had her gasping but she kept going until the current knocked her over and she paddled for all she was worth.

It's a bear, Bat decided, fighting to keep her head above water. *Maybe a few of them*. Those thoughts motivated her to swim as unseen things bumped into her in the water. Something snagged on her shirt but she was able to get away from it. Her feet touched ground after what seemed forever and she saw the embankment. It was rough finding the strength to crawl out of the water. Her limbs felt heavy and her teeth chattered from the cold.

Chills racked her as she used a tree to help get to her feet. Her head began to hurt more, a migraine of major proportions coming on. It had to be the freezing river that had caused the headache to worsen.

Why was Kraven naked? She had no clue as she turned to peer over her shoulder. The river had swept her away, and it curved out of sight of where she'd gone in. There was no sign of him or the bear that had made that terrible roaring. She'd never heard them make those noises in any movie she'd seen but she was hardly a nature buff.

Her clothes clung to her as she caught her breath, debating on what to do. Pure terror at their situation struck. She was soaked to the skin, night would fall soon, and she didn't see any sign of civilization. Being alone in the woods, at the mercy of nature and hypothermia, would be a deadly combination. She turned, forcing her legs to move, and walked deeper into the woods to find some shelter. It would be nice to stumble upon a random cabin.

She hugged her body and made it about half a mile before her aching bare feet made her stop. Her headache grew worse, until it caused her to drop to her knees. She curled into a ball, absolutely miserable.

Oh God. Am I dying? My head feels as though it's going to explode. Tears filled her eyes at the hopelessness of her situation. *Find me, Kraven. Please.* She reached out a shaky hand, grabbing leaves and trying to cover her freezing body.

Chapter Seven

Kraven used a log to float his clothing and boots across the river to keep them dry. His jacket slid off during the swim over and he hadn't been able to rescue it before the current had swallowed it up. He tossed his remaining things up on the embankment and turned, going back underwater and scrubbing his skin. He surfaced and climbed out, dressing quickly and entering the woods. He needed to find Bat before darkness fell.

It worried him that she might not have made it across. He shoved that thought back, refusing to contemplate that he wouldn't find her. She was alive and out there. He just needed to find her before one of Decker's enforcers did.

He finally found a sign of where she'd come out of the river. He bent, examining the faint tracks she'd left where she'd crawled, then stood. He grinned.

"That's my hellion. I'm coming for you."

It was slow going to track her. She didn't weigh much and was barefoot, barely leaving a trace. The sun went down and frustration rose. *Where is she?* He wanted to call out her name but it could attract unwanted attention. He sniffed the air every time the wind blew, hoping to pick up a hint of her scent. There was nothing.

He started to worry that she'd been caught when he picked up a low moan. It was to his left. He crept forward, alert. Another one followed and he inched closer, prepared to attack—until Bat's faint scent reached him.

He lunged forward, tracking another good ten yards before spotting her shape curled up on the ground. He would have missed her if it wasn't for the faint pained noises she made.

He dropped to his knees near her head. Part of her was covered with leaves. He brushed them away. "Bat? I had a hell of a time finding you. You're lying on a bed of leaves and they masked your scent. It was smart but I damn near passed right by you."

She moved as he touched her shirt. It was still wet and plastered to her skin, the material ice cold. "Kraven?"

He didn't like the way she said his name. It was too soft and pain laced her voice. "Fuck, Hellion. You should have taken your clothes off and wrung them out. You're still so wet. You don't know anything about survival out here, do you?"

"Sorry, not a lumberjack."

He grinned, happy to hear her smartass remark. "Are you hurt?"

He helped her stand up and began to remove her wet clothing. She didn't protest as he stripped her all the way down to her bare skin. He just scooped her into his arms when he was done. "Hold on. I've got you. There's a place real close that will afford us shelter."

He backtracked to a spot he'd found earlier.

"Talk to me, Hellion."

"I feel like I'm dying," she whispered.

He tensed. "You're just cold, but I'm going to warm you up."

She whimpered. "My head. It hurts so bad." He took a seat in the sheltered area under a tree and between two large rocks. It would afford them protection against the wind and help hide their scents from trackers. He placed Bat on his lap and reached up, blindly feeling her skull, sniffing too for any hint of bleeding. "Did something in the river hit you? Did you fall and strike your head? Answer me."

"Thank you."

"For what?" Her words made his anxiety higher. She seemed confused. He couldn't feel any damage. His hands lowered, examining every inch of bare flesh. There were no obvious cuts or bumps.

"Finding me. I was scared."

"I'm here. Where are you hurt? I can't help you unless you tell me."

She shivered in his arms, turning her face against his throat. "My head," she got out. "It feels like it's splitting in two halves. It's never been this bad before. It's agony."

"Did it start in the water? Did you hit it while we were apart? Did something in the river slam into you? Did you fall?" He tried again to get her to answer.

"Plane. Now it's much worse."

She suddenly went lax in his arms and the shivering ceased.

Fear gripped Kraven when he realized Bat had fallen unconscious. He sniffed at her. She smelled of the river strongly, her body chilled beyond safety, but it was her head he worried more about. There was no scent of blood and he didn't find any wounds as he ran his fingers over her once again, everywhere he could touch.

"Fuck," he snarled, realizing how faint her heartbeat pulsed when he ignored the surrounding wood noises to give her his full attention.

123

He allowed his inner animal to ease forward a bit to take control of his instincts. His teeth elongated as he decided he'd do whatever it took to save her, regardless of the consequences.

She'd tasted a few drops of his blood before, when she'd bitten him during sex, and hadn't had any adverse effects. If anything, it had seemed to have a positive effect on her libido. He might be able to heal her. It would start the mating process if he gave her a lot of his blood, but she was his anyway. He bit down on his tongue. Pain lanced through him briefly when he pierced it with his fangs.

The taste of blood filled his mouth and he sealed his lips together and lowered his face. Bat's lips were soft as he forced them open with his own, his tongue exploring hers. He bled into her slowly. She jolted under him, kissed him back as she became somewhat responsive, but the sluggishness alarmed him.

Kiss me, damn it, he mentally urged, despite knowing she couldn't hear him. She did it though, even if it wasn't close to passionate. He curved his hand around the back of her head and used his thumb to gently stroke her throat, urging her to swallow. He could only pray it wasn't too late and his blood would work fast.

His dick responded but he ignored it. This wasn't about sex, but about sharing his strength with her. She was ill and needed him. She kissed him back with a little more eagerness and her hands actually lifted to barely grip his shoulders. She didn't seem to be with it enough to realize she touched a little fur, another thing that alarmed him. His Bat would have freaked-out, but she seemed unaware.

124

His tongue traced over her upper teeth, felt how smooth they remained, and he wanted to howl in rage. She didn't seem to have Vampire traits or she would have started to grow fangs. They would have elongated to cut his tongue more, maybe even bitten into him if her instincts kicked in to feed to save her life. It didn't happen.

He bit himself again, groaned from the pain, and more blood filled their connected mouths. He just hoped it helped.

Bat finally tried to turn her head away and he allowed it, figured that she might have taken enough. She promptly passed out again.

Kraven growled and repositioned her on her back. He sprawled over her and wrapped her with his body, pinning her under him. She needed his warmth.

He zeroed in on her heart rate, listened to each beat, and after some minutes relaxed when it grew stronger. Her body warmed slowly until it wasn't so dangerously chilled.

The thought of losing her left him feeling helpless. He hated that emotion, wasn't thrilled that he felt it, but couldn't deny the truth. He'd never been so emotionally attached to a woman. Ever.

Her breathing grew stronger until her heartbeat told him she just slept and the danger had passed. The huge sense of relief hit. The mouthy attorney mattered way too much. His head lifted and he stared at the pale column of her throat, tempted to take some more of her blood to help cement their bond.

He clenched his teeth together, his fangs gone, and resisted. She didn't need blood loss on top of it all. Bat obviously didn't heal as fast as VampLycans without some help. He hated how human she was at that moment. It made her vulnerable and frail, two things he hadn't wanted in a mate.

He turned his head and peered out at the woods, looking for danger. The wind picked up and he relaxed when he caught Drantos's scent. He cleared his throat and made a soft noise his brother would hear to let him know where he was.

In seconds he got a response. They needed to talk but he didn't want to leave Bat alone. Drantos made another soft call, his way of saying it was urgent. Kraven softly cursed.

"What?" Bat stirred.

"Go back to sleep. I'm going to cover you with my clothes. Rest, my little hellion. I'll be right back."

"Kay."

She didn't argue and drifted right back out. It worried him. He was torn between caring for her and finding out what his brother had to say. He rose and watched her curl onto her side, instantly cold once his body heat was gone. He stripped out of his shirt and covered her with it, then rushed in the direction of Drantos.

His brother waited a few yards away near a tree. "I ran into one of Decker's men. He's toast."

"I ran into a few of them. One made me kill him but I talked another out of going after Bat. He was barely full grown." It still pissed him off. "He shared some info though. Decker is forcing them to do his bidding and most of them aren't happy about it. It's only a matter of honor that they do. He gave me the name of someone in their clan who might be a better leader. Ever heard of Lorn?"

126

Drantos shook his head. "No."

"Me either, but he refused to become one of Decker's personal enforcers. That's got to mean something, *and* he survived saying no. We'll have to have him checked out of it's possible to finally be rid of Decker." He paused. "How is your woman doing?"

"Dusti and I got separated. I'm searching for her. She saw me fight one of them and I had to send her across the river alone. I found where she made it out and tracked her this way. I smelled you and Bat first. Have you seen Dusti? Smelled her?"

"I would have gone after her if I had. Do you need help looking for her?"

He hesitated. "No. You stay here, Kraven. Guard Bat. I know she's annoying but you can get rid of her once we reach the village. Dad will assign someone else to guard her."

"She's my mate." He spoke the only words needed to clarify everything to his brother.

Drantos snorted. "Oh man."

"Yeah. She loves to fight me at every turn."

"How did she take the news?"

"I haven't told her yet. She thinks I need medication to tame my wild imagination."

His brother had the nerve to laugh.

"Fuck you."

"Sorry. I just wanted to check on you. I have to find Dusti. Can I have your jacket? I lost mine. She gets really cold."

"The river snagged it. Sorry. Go. Bat and I are bedded down for the night."

"I'll bring Dusti back this way but we'll give you a little space. I doubt we'll run into any more of Decker's clan soon. I hope not, anyway."

"Me too."

Kraven turned and rushed back to Bat's side. She no longer slept and had sat up, donning his shirt.

A chilly wind blew, reminding Bat of how cold Alaskan nights could be even near summer. The thin material of Kraven's shirt she'd put on barely made a difference in shielding her.

A twig snapped close by. She tried to make out anything in the darkness but she remained blind.

"It's just me," Kraven rasped. He touched her arm, startling her, before he softly cursed. "You're chilled to the bone, damn it."

"I assumed you were making sure nothing was close enough to try to eat us. I would hate *that* a lot more than being cold. I have your shirt. Unless you want to give me your jeans, there's nothing more you can do." Her voice quivered. "It's going to get colder, isn't it?"

"Yes. But I'll keep you warm. How's your head?"

"Much better." The pain was almost gone. "I guess it was from me being so cold and all the stress I've been under. I don't suppose you could build another fire? I'd really like one about now."

"I could but it would only draw attention we can't afford."

The thought of warm flames made her bite back a groan. "Are you sure it's too risky? I thought bears feared fire."

"I can't light one, Bat. Trust me on that, okay? You're on moss. I want you to lay back flat for me. I'm going to use my body to warm yours."

She didn't really want to do that. Waking in the big guy's arms had been bad enough. She'd been turned-on instantly. With her arms wrapped around her legs, tucking them to her chest, it could afford her some warmth. She grimaced but reluctantly stretched out, shivering harder from the cold ground under her. She'd rather be warm than uncomfortable, even if Kraven's body on top of hers gave Bat ideas.

Metal jingled.

"What are you doing?"

"Removing my belt. I doubt you'd enjoy my buckle digging into your skin."

It hit the ground before his hand touched her thigh. He tapped her. "Spread them to make room for me."

"I'm not in the mood for sex, Kraven. I feel like a popsicle." *That is a total lie but say it like you mean it*, she lectured herself.

"I'm not going to fuck you." His anger came across with his snarled tone.

"Though, at least that would distract me from knowing we're under a tree on the ground. I can make out the shape of it above us. There aren't bugs, are there? Tree beetles? Ants? Oh God, please tell me there aren't any flesh-eating insects common to this area."

"No bugs. It's too damn cold for them. Spread your thighs for me now."

She did and when he came down on top of her, the feel of his warm skin sliding against hers made her gasp. "Where are your pants?"

"Body heat works best skin to skin." His upper body remained off hers. "Take off the tank for me."

She hesitated before wiggling around under him to get it over her head, then flattened back down as he spread totally on top of her. She knew her nipples were hard from the cold, that he had to feel them when they dug into his unbelievably warm chest, and she stifled a moan when he adjusted to get more comfortable on top of her.

"Just relax." He whispered the words near her ear.

"You're *so* warm."

"I know. Cold doesn't bother me as much as it would you. Is this better? Are you warming?"

She nodded and turned her face a little to press it against his neck. She breathed in his masculine scent, hating the way her body responded but knowing she'd be on board if he *did* try to take advantage of their intimate position. When he adjusted his big body on top of her one more time, something thick and stiff pressed against the softer flesh of her thighs. It became obvious what part of him touched her.

"You're hard? Really?"

A soft growl came from him. "Ignore it. I am."

"I'm just amazed. In this cold weather I'd think you'd be shriveled. Everything on *me* is."

"So I feel." He relaxed more on top of her.

"Sorry. That happens when I'm freezing."

"Go to sleep, Bat." He drew in a deep breath, nearly crushing her under him, and exhaled. "Morning is a long time away. I know you're exhausted. Crossing that river had to be difficult with your weaker body."

"I'm not weak. I'm just not as strong as you. What do you do in your spare time? Lift weights?"

"Sleep."

"What I wouldn't give for a nice bed right now."

"I know. I promise I'll get you to my cabin before tomorrow night. You'll like it. Picture a big fireplace with real wood burning and a soft bed."

She definitely liked that image.

Her headache had finally faded completely—and its absence brought clarity. "Why were you naked and covered in blood earlier?"

He hesitated.

"Kraven?" No way could he have fallen asleep that fast.

"I ran into a few of your grandfather's people."

She considered his answer. "Oh hell. You *know* you're confusing me. I heard bears, not people."

"You definitely didn't hear bears. They're trying to take you to your grandfather. I won't allow it to happen. I did what I had to, Bat. You're safe."

Did he kill someone? There had been a lot of blood on him. More unanswered questions filled her mind. She should be afraid of him but she wasn't. "Why were you naked?"

"I didn't want to rip my clothing when I shifted."

"Shifted?" She couldn't resist asking.

"Into my VampLycan form." His tone deepened. "I'm too tired to spank you so watch the insults. I know you don't believe me, but it's true. Be damn happy I took out the one who came after you before he got close enough for you to see too much. You wouldn't have liked the sight of a shifted VampLycan."

"It was a bear."

"Right."

"Or maybe a cougar or some type of lion."

"Uh-huh."

He's so damn irritating. "I'm not going to get any answers from you that make sense, am I?"

"No. You don't want to hear the truth."

At least he wasn't denying it. "Fine. I'll let it drop because I'm so glad you found me and you're warm."

He had the nerve to chuckle. "Rest."

The wind whispered through the trees above them and leaves rustled on the ground. The silence stretched and the weight on top of her became heavier. She didn't mind though. Kraven had to weigh over two hundred and forty pounds but his warmth more than made up for the way she had to draw shorter breaths just to fill her lungs.

A loud, short burst of sound filled the night.

Kraven's body instantly tensed over hers and his head lifted.

Bat's heart raced. "What was that?" Fear had her clutching his skin. "Are we going to be attacked by another animal?"

"Shit," Kraven groaned. "It's nothing." He relaxed on top of her, his face lowering again, and he pinned her flat. "Ignore it."

"What the hell *was* that?"

"Your sister and my brother. He found her."

"Dusti?" She struggled to push him up, wanting to know if he was telling her the truth. She needed to see her sister. "What do you mean *he found her*? Was she lost?"

Kraven pinned her tighter. "They're camping nearby."

"Are they hurt? Do they—"

"They had sex," he stated harshly. "That's what you heard. No wonder my brother was determined to stop. And it's not as if we have much else to do while we wait for daylight."

Shock replaced fear. "Are you sure? Dusti and Drantos? *Seriously?*"

"Think I'd joke about that? Trust me. I just hadn't noticed their scents with my face buried in moss. And the two rocks on the sides of us help hide *our* scent, but they also block others from reaching us as fast."

"Scent?" She frowned but her grip on him eased. "Right. Your animal side. How could I have forgotten that?" She hoped he picked up on the sarcasm. "We should check on them."

"You mean *I* should, since you can't see a damn thing in the dark. I'm not getting up. I'm comfortable and your skin is finally warm. They are

133

more than fine. I'd say they're both pretty happy at the moment." He grunted. "At least someone is."

Worry distracted Bat from Kraven. *Is he right? Did Dusti just have sex with Biker Bear?* She had to admit Drantos was good-looking too, in a rough way, and she was sure attracted to his brother. They had near twin body sizes. It wasn't normal for her baby sister to just sleep with some guy though.

But then again, life lately had taken a drastic turn.

She stiffened. "He wouldn't force her, would he?"

Kraven groaned. "No. He wouldn't. Will you sleep?"

"It's just not like Dusti to have sex with a guy she barely knows."

"She's not like you then."

Anger gripped her hard and fast. "No, she's not, and don't take that tone with me. I don't sleep with a lot of men."

"I didn't say you did." He hesitated but then chuckled. "You wouldn't be so damn tight if you fucked a lot of them...unless you just have the bad luck of picking ones with small dicks."

She slapped his chest with both palms. "Asshole."

"Bitch." His body adjusted more over hers. "Want to rip my nuts off still? I think you're a little fond of them now."

Anger burned. "You're lucky I'm cold and you're crushing me to keep me down. Just remember this, because you can bet your ass *I* will."

He chuckled again. "You have that attorney mind for retaining facts."

"Yes."

The silence stretched between them and Bat closed her eyes and tried to ignore the *fact* that Kraven was on top of her. They were in the middle of the woods, lost somewhere in Alaska. She'd survived a lot. Her sister was at least close. It gave her hope of seeing her soon.

"Will you and your brother let us go once you think we're not in danger?" She was trying hard to talk to him in a way that would ensure no harm would come to her or Dusti. "You implied you killed someone. You have to admit that's disturbing."

"You and your sister are in no danger from us, Bat." He sounded mad. "You still doubt that?"

She'd pushed him too far. "Well, on that note, I guess we should get some sleep." Her fingers against his chest rubbed a little. "Good night."

"You don't believe me." His breath teased her.

"You implied you killed someone, Kraven." She kept her tone soft. "Do you see how that could worry me?"

"I've told you the truth. You know what I am and who you need to be protected from. Your grandfather is the enemy, not us."

"You're a ferocious VampLycan and I'm half one. I get the urge to kill people all the time. Especially those assholes who steal parking spaces when you're waiting for one with your blinker on, or the morons who talk on their cell phones while they drive."

He took a deep breath, nearly flattening her under him. He turned his head a bit and rubbed his nose against the sensitive spot of her throat just under her earlobe. A chill jolted through her body, the good kind, and her nipples grew taut again. It irritated her that her body could respond to his tiniest movement.

135

"Bat, Bat, Bat," he whispered. "You're playing with fire."

"I wish I were. I'd be warm and wouldn't need you to blanket me."

"Do you want proof of what we both are? I could give it to you but you probably wouldn't react well. I don't want your sister or my brother rushing over here when you make a lot of noises."

She would never forget what happened in the woods on the other side of the river, and how her body had responded to him when he'd intentionally turned her on. He'd probably just tease her and then leave her hot and bothered without finishing what he started. "I'll pass. I don't want to play the crazy game right now. I'm tired."

He was quiet for a moment. "I know you are. That's why we're resting instead of staying on the move. I still don't agree with Drantos on taking it easy on you both. I'll be happy once we reach home. Sleep."

She tried but it took a long time to drift off, too aware of the sexy nutjob pinning her to the ground with his warm, firm body. She promised to set appointments with her therapist and Dr. Brent when she returned to Los Angeles. Maybe she really *had* sustained a concussion when the plane had crashed.

That could account for why she was risking so much by wanting a man who was a few screws shy of being totally put together.

Kraven wanted to make Bat eat her sarcasm but her earlier physical discomfort weighed heavier on his needs. She'd been ill and needed time to heal from whatever had been wrong.

But he was aware of every breath she took; his dick was so hard it hurt. It took every bit of self-control not to growl at her, nip her with his teeth, and fuck her into oblivion.

Drantos had finally claimed Dusti. It meant his brother had already started the mating process too. The timing couldn't be worse. It was all kinds of stupid to be having sex when they were on the run. In his own defense, they'd had time to kill, since his brother had told him to give the sisters plenty of rest and not to push them too hard.

It was ridiculous. They should just rip off the blinders and show the sisters what they really were. It would also save a hell of a lot of time if he could carry Bat on his back and move faster. He pictured how she'd react if he told her to ride him like a horse.

He could just shift on top of her. The idea of her reaction, after some of the insults she'd tossed at him, was mildly satisfying. She thought he was full of shit and crazy. She'd believe him if she found herself pinned under a hairy, four-legged, so-called figment of his imagination.

Actually, she'd probably freak out and scream. That killed his anger more. The last thing he wanted was for her to be terrified of him, and they were still in danger. Her screams would draw their enemies right to them.

She was in danger. *That* thought sobered him completely. Decker needed Bat to make a deal with Aveoth, and it would destroy the clans. Many would die. The only other option would be to flee to avoid a fight. His family and friends would have to leave their homes and they'd become the hunted once more. It would be stupid to move in a large number together; it would draw a lot of attention. They'd have to split into small groups. They wouldn't have as much strength without numbers and their future would only exist as long as they stayed one step ahead of their enemies.

His temper mounted, thinking about that kind of future. Lycan packs and Vampire nests would probably attack if the clan broke into smaller groups, seeing them as enough of a threat to risk it. Humans could get caught in the crossfire. Innocent lives would be lost.

Fucking Decker. He needs to die.

He bit back a snarl, hating the man responsible for threatening the peace.

Chapter Eight

Bat woke alone. The sun was up and Kraven wasn't nearby as she raised her head, looking around. The view wasn't good though, with a tree at her back and two boulder-sized rocks to the sides of the small area she was in. She shoved at loose leaves, grossed out a bit that he'd probably been the one to cover her legs with them. They kept her warm but she imagined bugs hidden in the mass, regardless of what Kraven had said. His shirt covered her upper body. She put it on.

Her head was fine, the headache totally gone for the first time since the plane crash. She crawled forward beyond the rocks and peered out, looking for him. He still wasn't within sight. It scared her but she calmed after a few panicked seconds. He wouldn't just abandon her. She'd bet on it. He'd found her after she'd swam across the river. He had that crazy hero complex fantasy thing going on.

"Kraven?" She didn't want to yell so she kept her voice low. The last thing she wanted was for a bear or another dangerous animal to find her.

Movement out of the corner of her eye had her turning. Kraven strutted out of the trees. She had to admire him in just a pair of jeans without his shirt. He was tan and muscular, all flat belly and impressive biceps. His hair even looked better without the spikes. It was wavy and thick, a much sexier look. The only flaw was his belt buckle. She wasn't a fan.

He didn't smile when she glanced up at his face. He actually seemed a little angry, judging from the frown marring his lips.

"How are you feeling?" He stopped in front of her and reached out, helped her to stand.

She winced when he plucked a few dry leaves out of her hair, ones she'd missed. "Cold but good."

He leaned down a little, staring deeply into her eyes. "How is your head?"

"It's great now. Where did you go?"

"Boys' room. I didn't think you'd like me to piss right next to you."

"Thanks." She bit her lip. "I have to go too."

That got a smile from him. "I want to watch this."

She stepped back. "Not a chance. I'd give anything for a real bathroom and toilet paper."

"Use leaves."

She grimaced. "I think I'll just try the squat-and-air-dry method. I'm not rubbing dirty debris against myself."

He hooked a thumb in the direction he'd just come. "Right there. Stay close though." He suddenly jerked his head to the right, his nose flaring. "Real close. We have company."

Bat felt instant fear. "Is it a bear?"

"*You* might think so. He's kind of big. It's my cousin Red. Go pee fast. I'll find him and then we'll leave. This is good news. It means the clan has found us."

She let that slide and carefully picked her way across the ground on her bare feet. She'd kill for more clothes and a pair of shoes. Fear of wild animals kept her from going far. She crept behind the first thick tree for privacy. She hated camping and remembered why she never did it. There was no dignity in how she spent her next minute.

She straightened and thought of Kraven's words. *Who would name their kid Red? If he's even a real person. Shit. What if he's a make-believe person?*

Kraven couldn't be *that* nuts. It would break her heart.

She froze, letting it sink in that it really would cause her pain if whatever was wrong with him couldn't be fixed with medication. Some people couldn't be cured of mental illness by taking pills to offset whatever imbalances they had. She had a few clients who were like that. The idea of Kraven spending the rest of his life needing to have fulltime supervision and care just seemed too cruel.

Something caught her eye and she looked up, gasping.

A tall man stood just feet away. He had hair down to his waist—and he was butt naked. She glanced down, then up. And it wasn't his ass she got a glimpse of.

She backed up and her arm bumped a tree. She blinked, too shocked to speak. He had to have seen her squat. He tilted his head, a pair of very dark eyes staring back at her. He was tan and had black, silky hair. He wasn't a bad-looking guy. Just big and muscular.

He reached out as if to touch her.

Bat squealed in fright and spun, running. She didn't care about stepping on bugs or worms anymore. A naked guy was wandering around in the woods. He had to be crazy to do that. Or maybe Alaska had a nudist colony. Or he could be some rapist.

141

She freaked when Kraven wasn't where she'd left him.

"Kraven!" She halted, not seeing him anywhere. She glanced over her shoulder, saw the long-haired man stalking toward her unhurriedly. She spun again, not sure where to run. "KRAVEN!"

He came rushing from her right. "What?" He halted and saw the man. "Hi, Carver."

Bat grabbed Kraven, scrambling to get behind him. She clutched at the back of his jeans and his arm. The name sounded like one a serial killer would have. She didn't miss that. "He's naked!"

Kraven turned his head, peering down at her. He had the nerve to grin. "I see."

"You know him?"

His grin widened. "He's a friend."

She refused to glance at the guy again. She did lower her voice. "Where are his clothes?"

"He probably left them behind to shift, and then figured you'd be less afraid of him in skin than fur, so he shifted back."

Bat's mouth opened but she had no response. She tried to make sense of his words.

"He's a VampLycan too. Remember how I told you we can shift into a different form? It's faster to run and hunt for something when we're not in skin." Kraven turned his entire body to face her, forcing her to let go of the back of his pants. "It would just be weird to see us running around with hairy bodies on four legs, sporting a pair of jeans." He chuckled. "Plus, it would be uncomfortable unless they had enough room to

142

accommodate the other shape. We can pull it off in sweats but again...kind of weird looking."

She realized her mouth hung open. She closed it and swallowed. "There's more like you? What did you guys do, form some kind of club? Like those role-playing games? You have a group?"

All his humor disappeared and he looked angry again. "Goddamn it, Bat. Stop now."

"What?" She wasn't doing anything except trying to figure out if he had friends who were also into his pretend world.

"I know exactly what you meant. I'm not nuts." He was really mad.

"Okay."

He grabbed her and she gasped when he twisted, pulling her forward so they were both looking directly at the naked guy, Carver. He stood there listening with his arms crossed over his chest. He smiled, as if nothing was wrong with being naked. Kraven wrapped his arm around Bat's waist, holding her in front of him, tight to his body.

"Do me a favor, Carver. Shift in front of her."

The guy arched his eyebrows and glanced at Bat, then Kraven. "You want her to see?"

"She thinks I'm a basket case making shit up. Her mother was one of us but her father was human. She smells totally human for a reason. She didn't inherit any traits from her mom. She didn't even know about us. I'm tired of listening to her insult me. Please do it."

"Are you sure about that?"

The new voice startled Bat and she turned her head, gazing up at another stranger. He was big but at least he had clothes on. Bat stared at him but he seemed to ignore her, his focus purely on Kraven.

"This is Red, my cousin," Kraven informed her. "And hell yes, I'm sure. I didn't want to shift myself because she already wanted to get away from me. Now I have backup, so I don't have to worry about hunting her down." His arm around her tightened even more. "She can't run." He looked at the naked guy. "Please, Carver. I've been waiting for this moment since she opened her mouth for the first time and pissed me off."

Carver reached up and pushed his hair over his shoulders so it no longer hung down his front. "You owe me. She looks like a screamer, and I hate that shit. It hurts my ears."

Kraven reached up and planted a palm firmly over Bat's mouth. "No problem."

Bat tried to pull his hand off her lower face but the second she touched him, his naked friend suddenly moved. He just dropped down on his hands and knees. Bat was stunned when he turned his face and winked at her.

He lowered his head then, and his body tensed. He arched his back and soft popping noises sounded, followed by something sickening like bones breaking.

Hair began to grow along his back, over his ass, and down his arms. It spread over his entire body. He threw his head back, his hair tossed out of the way of his face. Thin hairs covered his cheeks, where before it had

144

been clean-shaven. His nose and lower jaw seemed to be expanding outward.

Bat's legs would have given out under her if Kraven hadn't been holding her up. She didn't scream, but she *did* whimper loudly.

The guy wasn't a guy by the time he took a step. He had four legs and kind of looked like some messed-up huge dog. The fur covering his body wasn't overly thick, because she could see some patches of skin. The four limbs were wrong too. They were too muscular, and weren't straight but instead all slightly bent, more similar to a man crouching on all fours instead of an animal.

He turned his head and peered up at her. His eyes were pure black, the irises and pupils seeming to have merged together into one color. He had a snout, his jaw was elongated. His mouth opened and she saw sharp teeth and fangs.

He growled and Bat was glad she'd already taken a trip behind a tree or she was sure she'd have pissed herself. She clutched at Kraven's hand, no longer wanting to remove it from her face. She just wanted to cling to him.

The thing's ears lifted, again like a dog's, since they were slightly pointed. He turned his head and made a soft whine and rushed off into the woods. He didn't move like a horse or a dog but instead...unlike anything she'd ever seen. She watched him until he disappeared behind trees and bushes.

Kraven eased his hand off her mouth and bent down until his lips were near her ear. "What do you have to say now, my little hellion?"

Nothing. She couldn't speak. Her mind frantically tried to come up with a reasonable explanation. She blanked. It was tough to think at all. The image of that thing she'd just seen couldn't have been real but she'd watched the naked man change herself.

The other man, Red, stepped in front of them. She looked up at him. He cocked his head, an expression of pity stamped on his features. He glanced at Kraven. "I think she's in deep shock. Was that really necessary?"

"Oh yeah. It was." Kraven slid his hand under Bat's chin and gently turned her face until she stared at him. He looked amused. "VampLycans are real. Who needs the damn meds now?"

"I hit my head," she got out. "That—"

"Was real," he rasped. "Don't wimp out on me." He leaned a little closer. "And you're awake." He let go of her chin and reached down.

She jumped when he lightly pinched her ass. "Ouch!"

Kraven eased his hold around her middle. "Lock your knees."

She did.

He eased back, totally letting her go. He grinned. "You can't talk, can you? You're speechless. Finally!"

"Kraven!" Red scowled.

"You have no idea." Kraven suddenly bent and one of his arms hit behind her thighs while he wrapped the other one midway down her back. He just scooped her up and then tossed her a little in his arms to adjust her better. "I'm going to enjoy this. Let's go. Wrap your arms around me, Bat."

She did. Kraven smiled.

He was right. She was speechless over Carver turning into some kind of big dog-like monster. A Werewolf/Vampire combination. It wasn't pretty. It had been terrifying.

Everything Kraven had told her started to replay through her mind.

Her mother had been one? It wasn't possible. There was no way her mom turned into one of those things. Her mother hadn't even liked dogs. They'd never been allowed pets, her mom claiming to be allergic to everything with fur.

She muttered that aloud.

Kraven heard her and responded, "She probably avoided them because city animals would fear her and cause a scene when she approached."

Bat let that sink in, thinking about it.

Kraven interrupted her thoughts. "We're coming up on some of my clan, Bat. Are you listening to me?" He stopped walking, holding her stare.

"What?"

"Behave. That means keep your mouth shut. Can you do that? Everyone you're about to meet is a VampLycan. You don't want them to shift and eat you, do you?"

"Fuck," Red hissed. "What is *wrong* with you?"

Kraven ignored him. "That means don't piss them off, Bat. Am I clear? Keep your sharp little tongue firmly inside your mouth and your lips sealed. I smell my father. He's the leader of our clan. Be respectful, or my spanking your ass will seem like a fun time compared to what he'll do."

147

"You struck her?" Red sounded horrified.

Kraven finally broke eye contact to look at his cousin. "No. Of course I didn't hit her. Bat is...difficult. Wait until you get to know her. Just trust me. Enjoy the silence while it lasts." He started walking again, carrying her out of the woods and into a clearing.

Bat stared at the group of people milling around a dirt road in the distance. Two trucks were parked there. A few men approached them but they at least wore pants. Most of them didn't have shirts on. She noticed everyone seemed to be really fit and muscular.

Kraven stopped when they reached the group and eased her down on her feet, mindful of the shirt she wore so he didn't flash the fact she wasn't wearing underwear. He took her hand, keeping a firm grip on it. She squeezed back, not willing to let him go either.

"Good to see you, Kraven." The speaker was a short-haired man maybe in his early twenties. "We were worried when we heard the plane went down."

"Did a rescue crew reach the survivors?" Kraven looked at the men.

"Yes. A human rescue crew found them yesterday afternoon. We ran into a couple of searchers in the woods, who said two couples had disappeared. We told them we'd found you and got you to safety, so they'd stop the search," another guy explained. "We didn't want anyone to get in our way."

"We had a few problems. Decker sent some men after the women," Kraven announced.

The twenty-something man glared at Bat. "Who the hell are they?" He sniffed and frowned, gawking a little at Kraven. "Why is your scent all over her?"

"She's *mine*." He kept his voice low. "I need to talk to my dad. We'll discuss this later, after we reach home." He jerked his head toward Bat. "Enough for now. Got it?"

The men grew quiet. They threw glances at her but it was clear Kraven didn't want them to speak in front of her anymore. She was coming out of her shock enough to function, but it was still tough. Bat wondered if she needed a drink or a doctor more. Both seemed in order.

A good-looking man in his mid-thirties approached. His hair was down to his shoulders and he was fully dressed. Kraven let go of Bat's hand and pulled her closer to his body, putting an arm around her. She let him, still trying to fumble through her thoughts and everything she'd seen.

The new guy stopped a few feet away—and didn't look happy as he gave her the once-over with a sweep of his gaze. Then he fixed his dark blue eyes on Kraven.

"Drantos informed me of the situation."

That perked her up, and she swiveled her head, searching for any sign of Dusti. She spotted her near one of the trucks. She looked okay. She silently urged her sister to look her way.

"This is Batina." Kraven bumped against her. "This is my father, and our clan leader, Velder." He paused. "Remember what I said."

She stared up at Velder and blurted the first thing that came to her mind. "Bullshit."

"Fuck," Kraven sighed.

She recovered. "Sorry." She cleared her throat. "You can't be his father."

Kraven ducked his head and shook it. Then he glared at her. "Why not? I'm dying to hear this."

"You look about the same age."

"VampLycans age differently than humans do. He *is* my father."

Well, she *could* see a resemblance. "Okay."

Kraven grumbled. "I know that tone." He released her and grabbed her arms, twisting her until they were almost nose to nose when he leaned close. "He's my father. My biological, fucked-my-mother-and-knocked-her-up-with-me *father*. Got it?"

"You don't have to get so testy about it."

"Is that really necessary? You're being crude." Velder stepped closer.

Kraven released her and ran his fingers through his hair. "Let's get out of here. Decker has men in the area. I'll explain everything later. Just don't let her piss you off. You've been warned. She's an attorney from L.A. Add in the fact that she was raised in a human world and didn't know about us. She has a mouth on her that would make a saint turn into a raging homicidal maniac."

Velder's eyes seemed to darken. "Don't talk to me that way."

Kraven dropped his hand to his side. "Sorry. It's been a trying few days."

Velder reached out and gripped his shoulder. "I understand. We're all on edge. It's time to head out. She's your responsibility until we reach the village. Then I'll have her assigned to someone else."

"*No.*" He paused. "I'll be the one she stays with. I haven't explained it to her yet but the blood tells. Do you understand?"

Velder growled. He studied Bat again, taking her in from head to toe. "That's what your brother implied about the *other* one. Nature can't be that cruel. I won't allow it."

Kraven suddenly moved, putting himself between her and the other man. "Dad," he whispered. "Don't do this. Don't put me in this situation. You know me too well."

"You just said she's disrespectful and she angers you."

"All true but it doesn't change anything. I'll leave *with* her if you won't allow her to stay."

"We'll deal with this mess later. I already had this fight with Drantos. Right now we need to get back to the village. I'm worried about what Decker is planning, and if he got the GarLycans involved... They could attack."

"Of course." Kraven nodded. "Come on, Bat." He grabbed her hand.

She tried to jerk away. "Not so fast."

He spun on her. "Don't. For one damn time, just nod and do what you're told. Is that really too difficult for you? You thought I was bat-shit crazy this morning but now you know the truth. You're way out of your league, Hellion. Shut up and come with me. We'll have this out later, when everyone isn't watching us."

She nodded, conceding that he had a point. "Fine." She glanced around, spotting Dusti again. "Can I talk to my sister?"

"After we're home. Let's go." He hauled her toward one of the trucks.

A woman handed him a piece of material as they passed the truck's open passenger door, and Kraven accepted it. "Thanks."

He led Bat to the open tailgate and surprised her when he suddenly dropped to his knees and released her hand. He opened the sarong and wrapped it around her waist, tying it at her hip. He looked up.

"Thank you." She felt better with most of her legs covered.

"You're welcome." He stood and hoisted her up into the bed of the truck. "Take a seat."

There were benches on each side of the bed. She sat near the front and Kraven took a seat next to her. He kept close. Bat looked over the top of the cab and watched her sister get into the other truck. Drantos wasn't with her but she recognized Red.

"Where's your brother, and why isn't he with my sister?"

Kraven followed her gaze and frowned. "I don't know. Maybe he's doing something for our father."

"Can't we go to that truck?"

"You'll get to talk to Dusti soon. The priority right now is getting back home where we're safer in numbers. It's unknown how many of your grandfather's enforcers are out here looking for you."

She frowned, remembering what he'd told her. "He really wants to hand me over to some rock guy?"

152

"GarLycan. Yes."

"Does this GarLycan shift into something with hair too?"

"He can grow wings from his back and turn into stone."

She bit her lip, trying to imagine that. It wasn't pretty. "For real?"

"Yes."

"I'd just tell this GarLycan that I'm not interested in being his lover."

"Aveoth wouldn't care what you wanted. It's your blood he craves. You'd be held prisoner at the cliffs."

"What's that?"

"It's just like it sounds. Tall, sheer cliffs where they live in caves. I've only seen the place once from a distance, when I was an adolescent. You'd be trapped thousands of feet above ground with no way to get down."

"How do they— Oh. They can fly. I was wondering how these things get up there."

"GarLycans, not things."

"Whatever." Bat reached down and played with the soft material of the sarong.

Kraven leaned in closer. "How are you holding up?"

She held his gaze. "I don't know."

He surprised her by wrapping his arm around her waist and pulling her closer. "It's going to be fine, Bat. I'll never allow anything to happen to you. That is one thing you can depend on."

He was being sweet and she didn't understand why. "You don't even like me. I've been such a bitch."

He shrugged. "Maybe I like bitches." He smiled to soften his words. "I *do* like you, despite the shit you give me." He lifted his other hand and caressed her cheek. "Trust me for once."

"Your father hates me."

"Don't worry about him."

"You look the same age."

"It's how it is. Didn't your mother look young?"

"It's good genes."

"For those with VampLycan blood. She wouldn't have aged if she'd lived. Not the way a human does. I'm sorry you lost her so young."

It hurt. She was starting to believe everything Kraven had told her...and with it came the pain of betrayal.

"She never said a word, Kraven. Not one. She talked about growing up in Alaska. She loved the woods but she said she never got along with her father. He was controlling and wanted to run her life. That's all she shared about him. Nothing about how they weren't human, or that he was dangerous to us. I should have known though. We always moved when he found us. And Dusti saw it. She's always hated him. Why didn't I see it?"

The truck engine started and the driver pulled forward on the dirt road. Kraven braced his legs, keeping a tight hold on her. "Perhaps Antina realized you couldn't shift, so she thought she was protecting you by letting you believe you were fully human. I'm certain she didn't do it to be cruel. You gave me the impression that she loved you."

154

The truck turned around on the side of the road and Bat clutched Kraven and the edge of the bench seat as they drove over a few large rocks. They were heading away from the clearing. She had a lot of questions for her mother but she'd never get the chance to know the answers. It wasn't fair.

They'd just hit a dense area of trees when something slammed hard into the side of the truck. It happened so fast that there was only a big bang and then Bat was being thrown.

Kraven had latched on to her and they hit the ground with her on top of him. He cursed, rolled, and tried to rise up.

Bat opened her eyes, stunned to find herself flat on her back on the grass.

A huge hairy monster slammed into Kraven, shoving him back down on top of her. Pain radiated throughout her body and the last thing she heard before everything turned black was Kraven's cry of pain.

Kraven twisted his body, fighting the enforcer who had attacked him from behind. The son of a bitch had his claws and fangs dug into his back, tearing into him in an attempt to rip out his spine. He managed to get ahold of its throat and shred major veins with his own claws. The beast fell away, gasping for breath. He watched it almost collapse but it struggled into the thick woods.

He looked down at Bat. Her eyes were closed but she breathed. The steady rise and fall of her chest assured him. He tried to rise to his feet but his injuries prevented that. A quick glance around told him that his clan fought against some of Decker's. He needed to get Bat to safety but the pain in his back was too great and his legs refused to respond. The enforcer had succeeded in crippling him.

He saw two more enforcers from Decker's clan rush out of the woods and he folded himself over Bat, adjusting his body as best he could to hide her from them. His injures were severe enough that his bleeding might mask her scent. He bent his arms to hold up some of his body weight so she wouldn't suffocate under him if he lost consciousness.

He closed his eyes and played dead. The enemy would go after the ones still posing a threat. He really needed to get Bat out of there. His mouth was close to her throat. A decision needed to be made...

He gripped the tank top she wore and tugged it to the side to reveal her shoulder.

Forgive me, he thought.

Then he opened his mouth and sank his fangs into her skin.

The taste of her blood exploded in his mouth. It only reinforced that Bat was his mate. He drank until he could feel his body beginning to heal. He didn't want to take too much so he removed his fangs, bit his own tongue, and licked at the puncture marks to seal them.

It hurt like a motherfucker as the damage to his back continued to heal. It took time for the infusion of fresh blood to work on him, since he was more Lycan than Vampire. He was on the mend though. He just needed the damage to his spine to heal enough so he'd be able to grab Bat and run.

A loud growl behind him—too close—had him holding his breath. Someone sniffed at his back, the hot breath fanning his skin. The bastard backed away and snarled, going after someone else.

Kraven took a shallow breath, and then another.

Come on, he urged his body. *Heal, damn it. I need to get my mate to safety.*

He turned his head just slightly, peeking through thick lashes. He spotted the other truck and Dusti. She was crouched near the front of it. She surprised him when she ran toward their truck. She kept low but sprinted with more speed than he'd give a human credit for. It was probably fear motivating her.

She made it across the opening and disappeared behind the vehicle, which was on its side. She peered around the edge, looking right at him, but her focus seemed to be on his legs instead of his face, or she might have noticed him watching her.

One of Decker's enforcers came into view and Kraven closed his eyes when the thing looked at him.

"Batnna?"

It growled a few times, calling out the name. Kraven tried to move his legs. They still weren't working. The blood he'd taken wasn't healing him fast enough to save them. The bastard would drag Bat out from under him and steal her away.

"I'm Batina," Dusti nearly whispered, her voice breaking.

He was stunned at the courage Bat's sister showed, his admiration for her immeasurable. She was trying to draw the enforcer away, but Kraven still knew he had to act or she'd be taken. He might be able to fight the enforcer off long enough for others to protect the sisters.

157

He sucked in a sharp breath and tried to lung to his feet to attack his enemy—

A surge of white-hot pain shot up his spine, straight to his head. He passed out.

Chapter Nine

Alarm shot through Kraven when someone flipped him over. He tensed, prepared to attack, but it wasn't the enemy crouched over him and Bat, ready to take her away from him. His father and brother were there.

His first concern was for her.

"Bat? Is she breathing? I don't hear her."

"She lives but she's unconscious." His father crouched down next to his side and cupped his cheek. "You acted quickly enough when they leapt out of the trees. You took the brunt of the attack with your back and seemed to have cradled her when you were thrown clear of the truck. Don't try to talk."

"We must protect her." He looked at Drantos then, feeling immense regret. "I heard Dusti claim she was Bat. I couldn't move but I was conscious. She allowed them to take her to save her sister. She should be safe until Decker realizes she lied to his men to dupe them into taking the wrong woman."

Drantos roared out in rage. Fur sprouted along his skin and his fangs elongated as he paced, his fury showing. "I'm going after my mate!"

Their father stood and stepped in Drantos's path. "No, you're not. The clan comes first."

"She needs me."

"She renounced you. It is forbidden for you to go near her."

159

"She doesn't understand our ways!" Drantos snarled.

Kraven opened his mouth to protest their arguing. It wasn't the time. But they were at it again before he could speak. His father took on a haughty tone.

"It is still the law. It's up to our trackers to find her and bring her back."

"No." Drantos refused to back down. "She's *mine*."

"We've been attacked and some of our people are injured. Your own brother is hurt. You need to calm and allow our men to find Decker's granddaughter. They will bring her to safety. *Our* people are your priority right now."

"Let him go, Dad." Kraven's chest felt tight when he spoke and he coughed, blood spilling out. He rolled to his side to make it easier to breathe. He rubbed Bat's leg, the desire to touch her too strong to resist. "They took what they want. They won't be back. He needs to go after his mate."

"She's not his mate." Their father seemed intent on denying the facts.

"I exchanged blood with her during sex but I didn't tell her we had begun the mating process. I planned to explain everything once I had her safely inside my home. She's wearing Red's jacket. It masks her scent." Drantos's temper seemed to fade a little. "Do the trackers know that?"

Their father hesitated before he spoke. "Take a walk with me."

Both men moved away from Kraven. He focused on Bat instead of his arguing family, dragging his body closer, curling around her. She felt

160

chilled but his father had been right. She still breathed. He didn't see any injuries but he worried about what *wasn't* apparent. Her head had been giving her problems. A severe blow could have caused internal injuries. She likely needed more blood but he was too weakened to do it.

He twisted his head to get Drantos's attention. His brother could bleed for her—but he watched as his brother shifted and took off into the woods. His father once more tried to prevent him from leaving but couldn't stop him.

Kraven cursed, biting into his wrist and pressing it against Bat's partly open mouth.

"Goddamn it," his father roared, grabbing his shoulder and gently trying to pull him away from Bat. "Stop it. You're injured enough."

"She's hurt." Kraven didn't bother to turn his head to see his father's disapproval. "I'm just giving her a little."

His father crouched next to him and yanked his arm away from Bat, licking at his wound. "Could one of my sons show some intelligence? Heal yourself first. Then you can heal her."

"She's got some kind of head injury. I gave her blood before but being thrown from the truck probably caused more damage. She's too human. She could die."

His father bit into his own wrist, pressing it against Bat's lips. "I'll bleed for her then. Your mother is going to have a fit, but she'd want me to do it after I tell her why. Have you taken this woman's blood or just given her yours?"

"Her name is Bat. Use it. We've exchanged blood. I bit her before I passed out. The mating process has begun."

161

"These females are weak."

Bat came around a little, tried to turn her head and she choked. Kraven gripped her chin gently. "Drink, my little hellion. Swallow for me."

She did but her eyes remained closed. It made Kraven worry more. He moved his leg, his spine finally repaired enough. He sat up carefully.

His father stopped bleeding for her and licked his wounds. "That's enough. We need to get the hell out of here." He stood, addressing the people around him. "Shove that truck back on its wheels. Get the injured loaded. We move out in one minute."

Carver appeared next to Velder. "This is bad. Decker's enforcers severely injured a few of ours. Two of theirs are dead. They had surprise on their side but we had rage."

Kraven tried to stand but he was too weak. His father jerked his head at Carver. "Put him in one of the trucks."

His friend wrapped his arm around his waist and dragged him to the truck that had just been righted, lifting him up to sit on one of the benches. His father carried Bat to Kraven, placing her in his arms. His dad looked grim as he backed away.

"We'll speak of this later."

"There's nothing to say. You either accept Bat as mine or I leave with her."

"Stubborn bastard."

"I get it from you."

"Don't remind me."

162

"I'm also going to tell Mother you called me a bastard. She might have something to say about that."

Velder actually snorted, some of his anger fading. "Don't you dare."

"Blackmail works."

"Shut up, Kraven. Your blood loss is making you say silly things." His father strode away, issuing orders to their clan.

The trucks were loaded with the injured and Kraven seethed inside over the attack as he cradled Bat to his chest. The bumping around hurt his back when they started the engines and got underway, but he'd live. He stared down at his mate.

Halfway home, Bat finally opened her eyes. "What happened?"

"We were attacked."

"Dusti?"

"Drantos is with her," he lied. He didn't want her to worry. He knew his brother well. Drantos would track the enforcer who had taken her sister away and kill the son of a bitch to bring his mate home.

She relaxed until her gaze drifted to his shoulder. Her eyes widened and she paled. "You're covered in blood."

"I'll be fine. I heal fast." He could control both of his legs now, even had strength in them. "How are you? You blacked out. Is your head hurting again?"

"I feel like I survived a tumble cycle in a washing machine but nothing really hurts." She attempted to sit up to get off his lap.

He tightened his hold. "Be still. The truck is packed and there's nowhere for you to sit."

She tried to twist her head to take a look but he straightened more to prevent her from seeing the injured. It made his back bump against the side of the truck but he managed to hide his grimace of pain.

"Just relax, Bat. We'll be home soon."

"I have to make sure Dusti's okay. She's got to be so freaked-out by all this. She's not as tough as I am."

She didn't give her baby sister enough credit. Dusti had balls of steel, in Kraven's opinion, to willingly allow an enforcer to take her away to protect her big sister. Most would have hidden. She'd shown her love for Bat in a way few would.

"I have a feeling she's much stronger than you give her credit for."

"Are you sure you're okay?" She reached up and touched the blood on his shoulder. "What can I do?"

"Just lay still. Tell me if you're in any pain or if your headache returns." He glanced around. "We're almost to the village."

"Great."

He smiled at her sarcasm. "We'll be safer with more numbers."

"Is your mother young looking too?"

"Yes. Don't insult her, Bat. She's the leader of our women and kind of scary."

"I believe that."

"I won't allow anyone to hurt you. Trust in me, if nothing else."

"As if I have a choice." She wiggled her ass over his lap and gripped his shoulders to sit more upright. "How bad are you hurt? Don't bullshit me."

"I'm healing." He was tempted to tell her that he'd bitten her but decided it could wait. "In just a little bit, I'll be all good."

"Are you serious?"

"Yeah. I'm running on adrenaline." *And fresh blood.* "It helps us heal at a faster rate." *It happens when a mate is in danger. It's nature's way of helping me protect what I love.* He left that out too.

Kraven glanced around, spotting some of his clan in the woods. They'd left the village to meet them, adding extra protection. "Almost there. Just be quiet and let me do the talking."

"Of course. You're terrified I'm going to offend someone."

"What if we were in a courtroom and it was your job to defend me? What would your advice be?"

"To shut up and look pretty. I'd do all the talking. They'd think you were a basket case otherwise."

He chuckled. "This is my courtroom, Bat. Shut up and look pretty."

"That's kind of hard to do since I haven't brushed my hair in days and I'm wearing this getup. It doesn't even match."

She amused him, even under such dire circumstances.

Guilt surfaced next. He'd have to tell her about Dusti soon, but he wanted to be more healed in case she put up a fight to go after her sister. And she would. Bat was the type to set aside reason and charge into any danger for someone she loved.

The truck slowed and he looked away from her. They stopped in front of Macy's home. The healer rushed out with a few of their people, ready to tend to the injured. One of her helpers reached for Bat but Kraven shook his head.

"I've got her."

He rose to his feet, glad his legs felt strong enough to support him. He waited for the truck gate to be lowered and walked to the edge. Two men gripped him by his biceps to help lift him down with Bat still in his arms. "Thanks."

He strode away from his people and headed directly to his own cabin. Bat twisted her head, staring at the village. "It's like a movie set."

"I'm afraid to ask which one. Be nice."

"It's all woods and cabins."

"That's our village."

"Where are you taking me?"

"Up the hill a little ways. That's where I live."

"Where's Dusti?"

"I told you." He really hated to lie but he'd tell her the truth once they had privacy. She could rant at him then, without witnesses. He made it to his home and adjusted her in his arms, twisting the handle and pushing the door open.

"That wasn't locked. What's wrong with you?"

"No one is going to steal from me."

"That's nuts."

"This isn't Los Angeles, Bat. It's Howl. Everyone looks out for their neighbors and VampLycans don't steal from each other. It would be

166

stupid to do so. We'd pick up their scents inside our home." He paused and sniffed. "No one has been here since I left."

"Howl?"

"The name of my village."

"Wow. That's…just wow. Pun intended, right? Since you guys probably howl at the moon?"

He resumed walking, carrying her down the hallway and into his bedroom. He shouldered open the partially closed bathroom door and gently deposited her on the counter between his double sinks. "I'm going to shower, and then you can. I'll fix us food. I know you're starving. I can hear your stomach rumbling."

He backed away and turned to lean into the shower, twisting on the water. Her gasp made him spin back around. Her look of horror had him closing the distance fast, gripping her when she swayed a bit. She looked ready to faint.

"Easy, Bat."

"Your back! It's all fucked up."

"It's okay."

"You're crazy!" She grabbed his shoulders. "You need a doctor. You should be flat on your ass. Sit down. Where's your phone? I'll dial 9-1-1."

"I'm not human, remember? I'm healing. Water will help that happen."

"You need a trauma surgeon, Kraven!"

He liked that she worried about him. He smiled. "Your hospitals are of no use to me, Bat. I just need a shower and food. Then we'll talk."

"Or you'll keel over dead on me and then I'll probably get blamed for it. I don't know the laws in Alaska but I could be held legally responsible if I don't make a reasonable attempt to do something to save your life."

"You already did your part." He'd rather see her angry instead of nearly panicked by the sight of his back. "I drank some of your blood. I'm sorry but I needed it to help me heal."

She gawked at him. "*What?*"

He released her and gripped the tank top she wore, tugging it off her shoulder. He touched the spot, seeing a faint bruise there but the puncture wounds were gone. "Right there. I bit you when I was hurt and you were out cold. Look in the mirror. I sealed the wound but I bit too hard. I was frantic and worried at the time. I wouldn't have done it unless I had to. Your blood helped me heal this fast."

She twisted on the counter, staring into the mirror. She paled but then color infused her cheeks. "Am I going to turn into a hairy beast now too? Don't Werewolf bites change people?"

"No. I needed some blood since I was severely injured. I couldn't move my legs."

She faced him. "What do you mean you couldn't move your legs?"

"The bastard who attacked me from behind left me partially paralyzed."

"You're telling me you healed from a *spinal injury?*"

"I'm VampLycan." He touched his chest. "We can recover from damn near anything, especially if we take fresh blood right afterward. It's the Vampire trait in us. The other injured are probably getting blood from their loved ones as we speak, since we're under threat from your grandfather's clan. They won't want to stay down and heal slower."

"You're such a freak."

He didn't take offense. She seemed to be in shock and struggling with what he'd told her. There was no bristle in her tone. "I'm a freak you like," he reminded her. He leaned in closer. "Don't make me spank your ass, Bat. Behave while I shower. Just sit there until I'm done. Don't try to leave this bathroom."

She seemed to pull herself together. "So…I'm in Howl. Are all the people who live here VampLycans?"

"Mostly, but we do have a few full Lycans. Not all of the original pack abandoned their children when they realized how strong we were."

"Should I even ask?"

He chuckled and backed away from her, removing his bloodied pants. He stepped under the spray of water, turning to watch her. She didn't jump off the counter and make a run for it. He decided to keep her occupied to make sure she stayed.

"Here's the history of VampLycans. Ready?"

She said nothing.

"I'll give you the condensed version. Over two hundred years ago, a group of Lycans and Vampires lived in peace, side by side. It was the first and last time they attempted it, that I know of. Word kind of spread about how it went with that first alliance, so nobody wants a repeat to happen.

"Both sides were being killed by humans in large numbers and were desperate to survive. Vampires could erase the memories of humans who saw too much, but they also burn up in the sun, so they slept during the day and were vulnerable to attack; they lived in constant fear of humans stumbling upon their resting places while they couldn't defend themselves.

"Lycans used to have to move around a lot; it was really the only way to avoid anyone discovering what they were. They only breed in safe environments, so their numbers were rapidly dwindling because of their nomadic lifestyle.

"The two races made an alliance to protect each other that was mutually beneficial. The Lycans could keep Vamps safe during the day, and Vamps could wipe the minds of anyone who found Lycans suspicious. They lived in one place together."

"Seriously?"

"Yep." He leaned his head back, washing his hair. "Relationships were bound to happen between the two races, with them living in such close proximity. Vamps can't breed with each other or humans, but it turned out that Vampires who fed a lot from humans could impregnate female *Lycans*. It was a first, and it changed everything.

"The Vamps turned on the Lycans, killing a lot of their men and raping the women to get them pregnant. They'd tear into their minds, take over, and convince the women they were screwing their mates to get past their natural birth control defenses. The Lycans fought back and escaped, fleeing to Alaska, where they felt the Vampires wouldn't find them. It was remote, not a lot of humans lived here, and Vamps don't like to feed off animals.

170

"The pregnant women gave birth to VampLycans. But when the first generation of half-breed children began to hit puberty, they frightened most of the Lycans. The children were stronger, faster, tougher than regular Lycans, since they'd inherited Vampire traits too. A lot of the full-bloods fled to find Lycan packs to join."

"They abandoned their kids?"

He rinsed out his hair and nodded. "Most did. The children were adolescents by that time. It was fucked up but Lycans mistrusted anything Vampire. I can't blame them after what they'd endured. The children were big enough to fend for themselves. My father is a first-generation VampLycan. His mother left him when he was fourteen. Most of her family went with her, but she'd had a few sisters who stayed. One of them mated with a Gargoyle."

"The rock guy with wings? So he's like a cousin?"

"Aveoth is no relation of mine. Gargoyles were in this area before the Lycans arrived. They weren't happy with a pack of Lycans showing up, especially when they found out some of them were carrying the offspring of Vampires. That's their number one enemy. Some of the single Lycan women offered to mate with them in order to form an alliance. Gargoyles usually breed boys. Girl births are rare among their kind, and long term, that causes a problem... So that's how GarLycans came to be."

"This sounds crazy."

"I'm sure it does but it's the truth. We have four VampLycan clans. They split apart into groups when they first arrived here in case the Vampires tracked and attacked them to retrieve the babies. That way the rest would have time to flee and escape the area. Over the years, the

171

children grew up and the clans remained divided since hierarchies had been established.

"GarLycans have just the one clan, since their home is impenetrable. They don't fear attacks by Lycans or Vampires. No one can hurt them, really...unless maybe they have military-grade weapons and helicopters. And they'd have to know where to look first, and *we're* not even exactly sure where they're living in those cliffs. We have an alliance but it's not as strong as it used to be."

"Why?"

"Full-blooded Gargoyles and their half-breed children still hate anyone with Vampire blood. We don't have any single full-Lycan women to offer to mate with them anymore. The few full Lycans who remain with us are older. All the younger generations are mixed breeds."

"Why would this rock guy want me? My mother was a VampLycan, right? That means I've got some Vampire blood, supposedly."

"His name is Aveoth. You can use it. And they still want lovers. Some of our women have chosen to go live with them but they know it's nothing permanent or lasting. GarLycans have sexual needs like anyone." It pissed him off, thinking about Aveoth getting his hands on Bat. "That's why Aveoth would want you. To warm his bed and to drink your blood. You're like sex and his favorite drug, all rolled into one."

"I still don't get why. Can't he get laid on his own? Find some other moron to drink blood from?"

He sighed. "I'm certain he could, but it's easier to take a lover from a VampLycan clan. She'll know what he is and he won't have to keep her locked up. Humans taken by Gargoyles in the past usually went insane or died while trying to escape. Anyone trying to climb down has fallen to their deaths. Aveoth was set to take Margola as his lover and they fed him her blood, hoping he'd at least come to care for her. He couldn't mate her but the Lycan in him craves some kind of bond. He got addicted, from what we've heard."

"So her blood became like heroin to him?"

He shrugged. "It must be a Gargoyle thing, since blood addiction to a certain family line sure isn't a Lycan trait."

"You also said my great aunt died before she grew up. When did they start feeding him her blood? Was she a baby or something?"

"She was in her early teens. Age of consent is eighteen but she died before then. Her parents made the deal with the GarLycans, trying to strengthen our alliance again by offering her to the son of the GarLycan leader. His father was still in charge at that time but Aveoth challenged him soon after. He now rules his clan."

"He beat up his own father?"

"He killed him." Kraven left the water running and simply wrapped a towel around his waist, not willing to open his healing wounds by trying to dry his back. "Strip and get in, Bat. I'll go cook something for you."

She slid off the counter. "You lay down. I'll shower and hit your kitchen. I'm not totally useless and you should see how bad you look."

He turned and peered over his shoulder at his back in the mirror. It no longer bled and the skin had mostly closed where enemy claws had torn him open. "I'm good."

"You are anything *but* that."

173

"I'm touched you care but food will help me heal too. I'll cook. You get your ass in the shower. We'll talk more afterward."

He faced the mirror and reached for his hair gel. Bat suddenly grabbed it out of his hand. She grimaced after reading the label, then peered up at his hair. "No."

"What?"

"No more spikes. It looks ridiculous. You're not some punk-rocker teenager." She spun away and walked to his small trashcan near the door, dropping the bottle into it. She turned, facing him. "Just let it dry. You're a handsome man without that crap in your hair."

Her expression appeared serious. It was nice to hear her compliment him, even if it was wrapped in an insult. He grinned, deciding to grant her wish. "Fine."

"Thank you."

He strode out of the bathroom, hoping it wouldn't take long to thaw meat from his freezer. He'd just reached the living room when the door opened. He smiled, changing direction when the tall, beautiful woman stepped inside.

"Mom."

"I wanted to check on you. I can't stay, I'm needed by our people." She hugged him and held out a bag. "Here. Fresh meat. I went hunting this morning. Your father said you were injured." She released him and walked around to see his back. "Not bad. I doubt you'll have many scars." She sniffed. "The human?"

174

"She's VampLycan too. Only her father was human. Please don't give me any shit, Mom. I got enough of it from Dad."

"I know. He's worried about the future if both of his sons mate weaklings. He'd hate to have to pass the clan to Redson or someone else. And *I'd* resent having to birth more sons just to make sure our line remains in control. I'm enjoying not having young ones following me around."

Kraven scowled.

"I had you and your brother when I was still in my youth. I had much more patience then."

"You still *are* young, Mom."

"I feel old, especially today. The possibility of war with Decker and the GarLycans is our worst fear." She stepped closer. "I'm being brave for your father but we're both terrified they'll attack and slaughter our entire clan. We could handle VampLycans but the ones with wings? They'd stone-out and our claws wouldn't pierce their shells."

"I have a plan."

"What is it?"

He hesitated. "You won't like it."

"Tell me anyway."

"I need your old Nova. It's flashy, fast, and everyone knows you let me drive it sometimes. I'm going to feed Bat when she gets out of the shower and afterward I'm going to leave with her. I'll skirt Decker's territory so they get a look at us. It'll lead them away from here. They'll chase *us* instead of attacking our people."

"Kraven." She shook her head.

"I'll make it to the airport. I'll take her to Washington. We'll lead them there and vanish."

"You'll be too vulnerable if you leave the clan. You might not make it out of the area."

He chuckled. "No VampLycan runs fast enough to catch your car, and the GarLycans won't take to the air while it's daylight, if they get involved. I have enough time to reach the airport by then. It will give me at least a ten-hour head start before they can begin flying to Washington."

"You're right. I don't like this idea."

"Bat being here puts the clan at risk. Decker needs her to make the trade and Aveoth will come if he knows about her. I'm not letting them attack our people *or* take her. I'll lead them away and make them search for us elsewhere."

"What kind of name is Bat?"

"Batina. Don't start. Please? I've had a rough day."

"Fine. I wish you'd take a few of our men with you."

"We already have injured. I want the clan protected, not short a few enforcers. I won't get caught."

"They won't be needed here if your plan works. You'll be hunted."

"I'd rather be safe than sorry with the clan at risk. I'll do this alone."

"I'll have my car brought here and send one of the women with you to return it."

"No. Leave it at the airport for a few days. Decker's enforcers could attack anyone driving it once they see me with Bat. They'll think the driver will know where we went."

"Of course."

"Thanks for the meat."

"Contact us often to let us know you're safe, and don't make me worry."

"I'll call friends and have them give you messages in case Decker gets access to your phones and puts a trace on them."

"Good plan. I love you."

"Go help our people, Mom. I'd rather Bat not see you and I just heard the water shut off."

"What is wrong with her? You obviously don't want to introduce us."

"Not now, Mom. Please?"

She didn't look happy. "Fine. Only because your father needs me right now to help deal with the stress everyone is under."

She left his home, closing the door. Kraven let out a sigh of relief. His mother and Bat wouldn't get along. He carried the bag into the kitchen and set it inside the sink, opening it. He sniffed and smiled. Elk meat was one of his favorites.

Bat raided Kraven's closet and dresser drawers. She didn't feel an ounce of guilt for hacking off the bottoms of his black sweatpants so they fit her better. He'd kidnapped her and could just deal with her needing to do whatever it took to be clothed again. She only wished his feet weren't

177

huge. There was no way wearing a few pairs of socks were going to make his shoes fit.

The smell of cooking meat had her stomach in knots. She was starving and followed the smell to a nice kitchen. She liked his home. It was rustic but modern at the same time. Almost charming. He still wore just a towel wrapped low around his hips as he stood in front of the cooktop frying meat in a few pans.

His back looked almost healed. She clenched her teeth, studying it. Faint red lines remained of what had been jagged tears in his skin. It was tough to wrap her head around the existence of VampLycans but she wasn't a fool. She'd seen one of them shifted, and that hadn't been elaborate makeup on Kraven's back. He really was healing at a phenomenal rate. No human could do that.

"The food's almost done."

His husky voice shouldn't have startled her. He didn't have to turn around to know she was there. "What is it? Steak?"

"Elk."

"Fantastic."

He glanced at her then and smiled. "It's good. You enjoyed the rabbit."

He had to bring that up. The memory of following him to that rock he'd been sitting on flashed through her mind, as well as what they'd done together. She decided to change the subject. "How are you feeling?"

"Good. Almost a hundred percent. I see you found something to wear."

"Are you going to get mad that I used the scissors in your bathroom to shorten the legs of your sweats?"

"No. I'm glad you didn't pick my favorite pair to mutilate. I just bought those ones a few weeks ago."

"That explains why they didn't seem faded or have any holes in them. Your wardrobe is scary. I've never known a man who owns so many pairs of leather pants and dusters before."

"You've never experienced an Alaskan winter. I like the leather, not that we go out much once the snow starts."

"Do you hibernate or something?"

"Or something." He turned off the flames under the pan. "We stay indoors when the weather is really bad but we do visit each other when it's possible."

"It sounds boring."

"I catch up on movies I put off seeing, read a lot, and do house projects."

"How fun."

He opened cabinets and plated their meal. "I'm ignoring your sarcasm. What do *you* do during the winter?"

"The same thing I do every other time of the year. I work. It's Southern California. We don't get snow. It does get scary when it rains. People freak out and a lot of them don't know how to drive in it. It's fender-benders all the way to and from work."

He frowned as he set them up at the bar counter to eat and retrieved sodas from the fridge. "You really love your job?"

She shrugged. "It's what I do and I'm good at it."

"Eat. We'll talk afterward. You need food."

She was more than happy to do that. It smelled wonderful and he'd made mashed potatoes to go with it. They were instant from a box but she wasn't about to complain. She hadn't had to cook. He got them silverware and took a seat next to her.

Chapter Ten

Bat glared at Kraven. "Say that one more time."

"Decker's enforcers took your sister."

"You waited until now to tell me?" She slid off the barstool and rushed toward the front door. "I have to find her."

Kraven grabbed her before she could reach it and hauled her to a stop. "Drantos went after her. He'll find her. Decker doesn't want *her*, Bat. She told the enforcer who took her that she was you."

"And you let her?" She wanted to slap him.

"I couldn't exactly stop it from happening. I was injured. I tried to get up to attack him but I blacked out. I woke up and she was already gone. My brother will find her."

"How in the hell do you know that?" She jerked out of his hold. "Where's a phone? I'll call my grandfather and straighten his ass out. I'll have him arrested and brought up on charges if he so much as touches a hair on Dusti's head. Hell, I'll kill him with my bare hands. No jury will convict me. I can sell temporary insanity in a snap between the plane crash, my harrowing experience in the woods, near drowning in the river, and being attacked by what I'll claim are dangerous animals."

"Dangerous animals?"

"I could rant about VampLycans and GarLycans to *really* sell an insanity plea but I want to keep you out of it. I think big-ass bears are enough to get the jury's sympathy. We've all seen grizzlies-gone-bad horror flicks. They would relate to that way better than a mythical-creatures scenario."

"Decker doesn't give a shit about your laws. Do you know what happens if you send someone after him? He'll wipe their memory and make them forget it all. Or kill them outright. He's insane, and human law doesn't apply to him."

"Fine. Give me keys to your car and a GPS with his address. I'll go there myself and take care of this mess. *I'm getting my sister back.*"

Kraven scowled. "You're forgetting he's not human. What are you going to do to him, Bat? Beat him up? He's got claws." He suddenly grabbed her around her waist, hauling her off her feet, lifting her so they were face level. "You couldn't even get away from me, and *I'd* never hurt you. *He* would. He doesn't give a shit about you. You're fodder for this war he wants to start. He'd chain you up and send you to Aveoth."

"Better me than my baby sister. I'll deal with this Aveoth. I'm sure he can be reasoned with."

Kraven shook his head. "No."

"Fuck you." She braced her hands on his shoulders. "Put me down!"

He lowered her to the floor and let her go. "Calm down. Drantos will bring your sister back. In the meantime, there's something we need to do. Do you want Dusti to be safe?"

"Of course."

"Then let's lead Decker on a merry chase away from here. Drantos will bring your sister to our village. Decker doesn't care about Dusti, right?

182

You admitted they don't get along. He'd think nothing of killing her *and* the people who live here. We want him to come after *you* instead."

She tried to calm down. "What are you saying?"

"You want the enforcers to stay away from your sister? That means not being anywhere near her. I have a plan, if you'll listen."

It was tough to do when she was worried sick about Dusti. "You have my attention."

"I'm going to pack a bag and borrow a car that's well known to other clans. I want to drive close enough to Decker's territory that his scouts will see us. They'll report it to him and he'll order his enforcers to go after us. Let's lead them away from Dusti and my clan. We'll go to the airport and fly out of Alaska. He'll be able to find out where we went but we'll drop from sight once we hit the lower fifty. They'll start looking for us there instead of here."

"I'm bait to lure them away."

He nodded. "I won't let them capture you. We need to move fast though."

"How do we know Drantos will get my sister back? I need to do something to save her, Kraven. She's my entire world. She's all I have."

"I'll keep my cell phone on until we hear word that Dusti is safe, Bat. You don't know my brother, but he'll do whatever it takes to get her back. She's his mate."

"Excuse me?"

"That's a discussion for another time."

"No, what do you mean, she's his mate?"

He paused, taking a deep breath. "I don't know how else to say it. But he'll kill to get her back, tear apart heaven and hell to find her, whatever it takes. Drantos will protect her at all costs. I have absolute faith in that. He loves her and she belongs to him."

"She can't be his *mate*. We're not animals."

"Do you want to debate that or do something useful, like make Decker come after you instead of your sister, who his enforcers think is *you* right now? We need to get them off Drantos and Dusti's trail."

"If he even found her."

"You don't know my brother."

"You're right, I don't."

"You didn't see him when he found out she'd been taken. He was enraged, and there's nothing more dangerous than a VampLycan whose mate is in danger. He *will* find her and he'll bring her home. The best thing we can do is give Decker a big target to go after instead. You're the one he wants."

"Fine."

He grabbed her hand. "Help me pack."

"No."

"I'm not letting you out of my sight. You're upset. Besides, it will go faster if we do this together."

"You should have told me the truth right off."

"I'm sorry. I wanted you to shower and eat first. There was nothing you could do but worry, Bat. You're going to need your strength since we'll be the ones running. I did what I thought was necessary."

"Don't lie to me about my sister ever again. Got it?"

"Yes." He tugged on her. "Come on. The longer we waste time, the longer Decker's enforcers are focused on the wrong sister."

"This better work."

"Decker is going to come after you. He needs you to make a deal with Aveoth. He knows his plan is out in the open now. He's got to be desperate."

"What the hell does that mean?"

"It means he pissed off three clans. He'd lose if we all attacked his. He needs the GarLycans on his side or he's screwed. Understand?" He led her into the bedroom. "Grab a duffle bag out from under my bed." He crossed to the closet, throwing open the door. He began tossing things on the bed.

Bat dropped to her knees and dragged out the large black bag. She started rolling his clothes and shoving them inside. It made her feel better knowing she was at least doing *something*, anything.

"I don't have clothes."

"We'll buy you some once we hit Washington State. Right now it's about making a show of leaving the area and giving them something to follow."

"I need my damn purse. It costs money to travel and I have no ID. They ask for that at the airport. Did you think about that?"

"Of course. We're avoiding large airports with heavy security and cameras. We'll only use the smaller airports."

"They'll still ask for money and identification."

"Stop worrying. I know what I'm doing, Bat. I have a plan."

"Right."

He growled and stopped grabbing clothes. "I do. I'm not an idiot. I'm also not poor. I'm old enough to have made some good financial decisions."

"Right."

"I'm older than you think."

"Really? How old are you? Thirty-something? A *young* thirty-something?"

"I'm eighty-one."

She stopped rolling his duster, glowering at him. "Right. And I'm the Pope."

"Don't you dare call me nuts again. I'm eighty-one years old."

She stared at his face, looking for any indication that he could be that age. "You're old enough to be someone's grandfather? That's disturbing."

"Goddamn, woman," he snarled. "Stop picking fights. I'm sorry I told you. The point is, I have money and I know how to get us to Washington." He stormed over to the wall and grabbed a painting of a forest scene, taking it down. It exposed a wall safe. He'd opened it less than a minute later and began pulling out stacks of cash. He had to move a few weapons to do it.

"Are you a drug dealer?"

186

He spun, glaring. "What?"

"No one keeps that much cash on hand unless they got it illegally. Hidden safe, weapons, and tons of cash?"

"I don't trust your banks. And no, I don't sell frickin' drugs."

"What do you do for a living?"

"Lots of shit but nothing illegal. Now let's go." He slammed the safe shut and dumped the money into the bag.

"Do you want to get dressed first?"

He looked down and cursed. "You drive me nuts." He stomped across the room and entered his walk-in closet.

Bat turned around to give him privacy. She glanced at the still open bag, guessing he had at least thirty grand in there. Maybe more. It made her wonder once more how he'd gotten it. In the end, she supposed it didn't matter. Dusti was her priority, and doing whatever it took to keep her safe. Kraven could bribe airport officials with enough cash. The best thing she could do was get away from her sister.

Kraven came out a few minutes later sporting black jeans, another black tank top, and he had one of his leather dusters over his arm. The kickass black boots were nice. He zipped the bag closed and hoisted the strap over his shoulder. "Let's go."

"What about your cell?"

"I'll grab my spare on the way out."

"Drug dealer," she muttered, following him.

"I heard that."

"You have lots of cash, weapons, and spare burner phones? Give me a break. Who do you think I defend?"

"I lost my personal phone while we were being pursued. This is my work one for clan business." He had a cell phone plugged in on his counter. He removed it and the charger, shoving both into a side pocket of the bag. "Move your ass, Bat."

He walked outside and she was stunned to see a bright red classic Nova parked in front of his house. It hadn't been there when they'd entered. He yanked open the passenger door and tossed the bag over the seat into the back. "Get in."

"Nice wheels."

"Thanks. It belongs to my mother."

That had Bat arching her eyebrows. "Okay." She took a seat.

Kraven slammed the door and rounded the car, climbing into the driver's seat. The keys were in the ignition. She opened her mouth to tell him how easy it would be for someone to steal it but changed her mind. He'd just tell her again how VampLycans didn't steal from each other. He twisted the key and the engine roared to life.

"Seat belt," he demanded.

She had to put on two. One was a lap belt and she guessed the shoulder strap had been later added to the car. Kraven didn't put on his before he threw it in drive and punched the gas. She cursed, grabbing hold of the seat.

"Maniac. We're in town. You're going to kill someone."

He laughed. "They know to get out of the way."

She was glad when he turned away from most of the houses and drove on a dirt road. The ass end of the vehicle slid a bit when he took turns and she clenched her teeth until she couldn't hold back anymore. "Are you trying to get me killed?"

"It's been a while since I drove this baby. I want to get a feel for it before we hit Decker's territory line."

"Unless you wrap the car around a tree and get me killed first."

"Can't you just enjoy this?"

"No. I don't find it fun to drive at excessive speeds on dirt roads and have my life flash before my eyes."

He snorted. "Your life sucks, my little hellion. You're all work and no play. That's about to change as we spend time together."

She closed her eyes, gripping tightly to anything she could hold on to. It made it worse when she could feel the car skidding around, her brain imagining them slamming into a tree or going airborne. She opened her eyes and muttered curses.

"Your language is offensive."

"So is your driving."

He laughed. "It won't be long before the scouts spot us. Roll down your window."

She stared at the crank handle. "Why? So you can choke me on dust? It's tough to bitch when I'm unable to breathe."

"Tempting but not the reason." Kraven accelerated. "I want them to pick up our conversation. I can take a hand off the wheel to roll this one down if you want?"

189

"Don't!" She released her death grip on the seat and reached forward, opening the window halfway. "Don't you guys have real roads out here?"

"Not between our borders. Decker's is coming up. I'm going to start talking loudly when I spot his scouts."

"Why?"

"So they can hear your name and report it to their leader. Don't take it personal."

"Take what personal?"

"Hang on."

She stared ahead and her mouth opened, a scream trapped inside her throat. There was a gap in the road where it dropped off to a lower section. It looked as if part of it had washed away at some point.

The car left the ground and flew across the small gap, landing hard on the other side. The belts dug into Bat.

Kraven swerved the wheel and they skidded a good twenty or so feet before he recovered, straightening it out to avoid striking a tree. "That's what I'm talking about, Bat!" he yelled. "Come on. Don't be squeamish. I swear you've got no sense of humor, Batina. What kind of lawyer are you if you can't handle life in the fast lane?" He paused. "Stop moaning, Batina. It's fucking annoying."

He lowered his voice. "It worked. They're on our ass. They heard."

She peered into the rearview mirror and spotted two of those ugly beasts running after them. They looked like demented mutant dogs.

190

She said something she was sure she never would since getting in the car.

"Drive faster!"

He laughed. "Hang on, Batina. I'll get you out of here."

She couldn't take her eyes off the beasts following them. It was tempting to lean over to glance at the dash, check their actual speed, but those things were almost on their bumper. She could even see their open mouths and sharp fangs as they panted in the side mirror, hauling ass to keep up with the car.

"Oh shit. They can *run*."

"Yes, we can." Kraven almost sounded proud. "We're about to hit a paved road. Close your eyes, I don't want you to scream. I'm just hoping there isn't any cross traffic. We'll lose them then. Pavement is going to hurt their feet after a good mile."

She should have listened. The trees thinned and she saw a paved two-lane road ahead. She could also see a big truck barreling down it, toward the dirt road they were on—and Kraven accelerated more. Pure terror filled Bat when she realized the truck would probably slam into them if he didn't hit the brakes.

He twisted the wheel when the tires hit pavement, sending them skidding again. The truck blared its horn and tires screeched in protest as the driver hit his brakes.

The truck barely avoided hitting them as they slid into the other lane and Kraven got control of the car, taking off in the opposite direction.

Bat panted, tears blinding her. It took her a good minute to recover enough to remember to look in the side-view mirrors. Only one of the beasts followed, and Kraven was putting distance between it and them.

"It's okay." Kraven reached over and patted her leg. "I'm a great driver. One of them was almost hit by the truck but they didn't collide."

"It's *not* okay."

"I'm sorry that frightened you. I was hoping there wouldn't be any traffic at all. Only truckers and the random tourist use this road as a shortcut from the main highway."

"Don't *ever* do that again."

"Look. He's giving up."

She glanced in the side mirror and the beast slowed even more, seeming to stop pursuing them. "You don't get it. That's how my parents died, Kraven. A big semi T-boned their car."

"Ah shit. I'm sorry."

She reached up and wiped at her tears. "I think I know how they must have felt now. I always hoped they never saw it coming but I can't see how they didn't. That truck looked huge."

He rubbed her leg. "I'm really sorry. The good news is they heard me saying your name, they followed, and they'll report back to your grandfather that we took off toward the airport. Dusti will be safer now."

"If your brother manages to get her back."

"Have faith."

She stared out the window, deciding she really hated vacations and Alaska, and she regretted ever boarding that airplane. The prospect of inheriting a lot of money hadn't been worth it.

Kraven hated the way Bat had grown silent. He glanced at her every few seconds. She seemed lost in thought. He felt guilty for scaring her, and for making her think she might die the same way her parents had. He promised to make it up to her somehow.

He kept alert as he drove. It was possible Decker might have thought about assigning a few of his people to the airport in case the sisters made a run for it. He should have put the cell phone in his pocket but he knew it would take hours for Drantos to reach the village, even if he'd found Dusti right away. He'd have to walk her there.

He hadn't lied to Bat. Drantos was driven to get her sister back safely. His big brother would stop at nothing to protect Dusti. He had no doubt he'd succeed. Drantos wouldn't settle for anything less.

He watched his speed. State troopers usually didn't patrol this far out but he couldn't risk being pulled over. Even a few minutes to deal with wiping the human's memory of ever seeing them and ordering him to go away were minutes he couldn't afford to waste. He needed to get Bat to the airport and in the air before Decker could launch an attack.

"Why don't we just drive and not fly? I really don't look forward to getting on another plane after the last one we shared."

He was grateful to hear her voice, and that she seemed to have recovered enough to complain. "GarLycans can fly. They'll be in the air by nightfall if they're working with Decker. This car is fast but traffic will slow us down. We'd hit plenty near the cities we'd eventually pass through."

"We could switch out cars so they don't know what to look for."

"Or we could just play it safe and go by plane. You're going to need to trust me, Bat. I know what we're dealing with. You don't."

"Aren't they afraid to be seen? You know. Like someone stargazing and then there's a big freaking guy with wings flying overhead?"

"They can change their flesh tones to dark gray and their wings are black. You'd be surprised how well they can blend into a night sky."

"How fast can they fly?"

"Fast. I've never exactly clocked one but I'd guess about seventy miles an hour if they're motivated. Maybe faster."

"How is that even possible? Are they super skinny or something so their wings can support their weight?"

"They're about my size, for the most part, and they have large wingspans. They don't stone-out completely while they're flying but they can control their coloring if they need to. It's how they've never been detected. They just have to watch out for radar devices in bigger cities."

"I *liked* Gargoyles, damn it."

He glanced at her. She looked perplexed, staring at her hands in her lap. "What does that mean?"

"They were cute, you know? Part of old buildings that gave it character and charm. Now I know they're real and dangerous. Is that clear enough?"

He tried to put himself in her place. She'd learned a lot within the past few hours and hadn't broken down yet. It showed her strength. "We're not usually under threat from them. I've liked some of the ones I've met. You're doing great, Bat. I'm proud of you."

"Great."

He smiled. "Look on the bright side."

She turned her head, staring at him. "Is this going to make me want to smack you?"

"Probably but I'm driving." He jerked his head to the road they traveled. "You don't want me to wreck."

"I'll keep that in mind. What smartass thing did you want to say?"

"You know I'm not crazy now."

"I wish you were. Then I'd be sane. Now *I'm* the nutcase."

He felt empathy. "You're not. It's just that life has gotten more complicated since you discovered the truth."

"No shit. My grandfather is a conniving lunatic monster and apparently I need to buy a diamond collar to put around my throat since I'm part dog."

"Lycan. There's a difference."

"I'm dying to hear this."

He grinned. "I've never licked my balls or chased my tail."

She dropped her head and sighed.

"Don't forget the Vampire bloodline. I bet some of your clients have called you a bloodsucker when they received the bill for your services.

195

Now you can smile over that because it's not an insult anymore. You ancestors on your great-grandfather's side did that to survive."

She lifted her chin, stared at him, and actually smiled. "Stop. I'm trying to dislike you."

"You like me, my little hellion." He met her gaze. "You're going to like me even more tonight after we find a safe place to rest."

Her features sobered. "That's not happening. We can't do that again."

"Right."

"No, I mean it."

He wasn't about to argue with her. She was his mate, even if she didn't know it yet. The attraction between them couldn't be denied. She was his weakness but it meant he was hers as well.

"Did you hear me, Kraven? I'm serious. We're not going to have sex again."

"I heard you."

"You have this smug look on your face that I don't like."

"I'm just relieved we got out of there without any trouble."

"You think having two monster mutant dogs chasing us wasn't troublesome?"

"They didn't catch us, did they?"

"No."

"See? We're golden."

She stayed silent for a bit. "What are you worried about right now?"

"Who says I am?"

"You keep chewing on your bottom lip. It's a tell, Kraven. What's on your mind?"

"I'm just plotting our next move. They usually have planes fueled and ready to fly someone somewhere during the day. We're going to have to hijack one."

"You're joking, right? I don't want to go to prison for the rest of my life."

"We won't be arrested. You're forgetting that I can take control of human minds. I'll make any passengers for that flight decide to take a later one. The pilot will be paid to fly us. The airport only has a few employees. They'll be easy to handle. I'm just hoping your grandfather doesn't have anyone posted there already. I'll drive the car directly to the hangar where they store the planes."

"Aren't these small airports only for short flights?"

"There are a few jets that fly in and out of this one. Big-game hunting is lucrative. A few pilots cater to the rich assholes who want to experience Alaska up close and personal. I'll get us on one of them."

"You make it sound easy."

"It is for me. I tell them what I want them to believe."

"Really?"

"Yep."

"So you can just walk up to any human and say you're the president of the United States and they'd buy it?"

"I haven't done that, but it's possible. I could convince them of almost anything."

"That's so wrong."

"Why? Because *you* can't do it? It's nature's way of helping us stay alive in your world, Bat. Every predator has a set of skills. That's just one of ours."

"You had to say that, right?"

He chuckled. "I won't lie. I'm not exactly harmless if the circumstances are right." He didn't want her to be afraid of him. "I'm no danger to *you*."

She grew silent and he regretted mentioning that he wasn't as normal as she probably wished. "Your mother was like me. Remember that."

"I keep racking my brain trying to remember anything out of the ordinary about her. I should have seen something."

"Can I be honest?"

"Sure."

"She would have made you forget anything that gave her away. You have a susceptible mind to our kind, Bat. You could have seen her shift and all she had to do was tell you it was a dream you should forget."

"What do you mean I have a susceptible mind? Did you make me want to sleep with you?"

"No! I've *never* influenced a woman to have sex with me by mind control. That's fucked up and pathetic." He felt insulted that she'd even accuse him of that, but then remembered this was all new to her. He reluctantly admitted it was reasonable to be suspicious. "I told you to sleep when I carried you from the crash site. You went right out like a baby and stayed that way for hours. That's what I meant."

"What else have you done to mess with my head?"

"Nothing. I give you my word."

She remained quiet for long seconds. "Okay. I believe you. Your ego is huge."

"What the hell does that mean?"

"You wouldn't have a problem getting women into bed. That's all. You know it."

He let it go, deciding to take that as a compliment.

"My mom should have told me the truth. I can see why she'd keep it from Dusti. My sister is horrible at keeping secrets."

"I agree that Antina should have told at least one of you. She must have had her reasons though, and I'm sure she figured you'd be safer in the human world not knowing."

"I brought my sister here. I wouldn't have done that if I'd known why our grandfather really wanted to see me. Mom and Dad always made me promise to look out for Dusti if anything ever happened to them. How was I supposed to keep her safe if I didn't know the danger? It makes me furious." She paused. "Looking back—it's almost as if they *thought* something might happen to them, like they feared dying and leaving us alone. It makes me wonder if my dad knew the truth about my mom."

"Were they close?"

"Very. It used to embarrass me when I was a kid. They were always kissing and hugging in public. They held hands all the time. I'd catch them making out on the couch if I got out of bed to get something from the kitchen after my bedtime. When I got older, I wanted that kind of relationship. I guess I always assumed any couple in love would be like them. But I learned later on that what they had was one in a billion."

It made him wonder about her past with men. Had someone hurt her deeply? He fisted the steering wheel and resisted asking. It wasn't the time.

"I was almost glad they died together. It was the only good thing that came out of their accident. I don't think one of them could have survived without the other for very long. They were that in love. It sucked for us, but I think it's how they would have wanted to go. Together."

"Did your father age?"

She shrugged. "I didn't really notice. Girls tend to focus more on their mothers' looks since it's a way to kind of guess how we'll age as we get older."

He checked the mirrors, his gaze drifting to their surroundings. He didn't see anything to alarm him but he maintained a fast speed, just not too far over the limit. They would reach the airport soon.

"Was there anyone in your life who was close to your mother?"

"Not really. We moved a few times. My dad's parents were alcoholics. He lost his dad in high school and his mom two years later, so they were both gone by the time I was born. He said they'd burned their bridges with any family so he wasn't close to anyone on either side growing up. He always said we were the only family we needed."

200

"Think, Bat. Was there anyone who was around your mother for years?"

She seemed to consider it. "Dr. Morton Brent. He's been our doctor for as long as I can remember. He and my mom were on friendly terms. She was paranoid about doctors... Damn it!"

"What?" He glanced away from the road. She looked angry.

"She was always riding our butts about never trusting anyone but Dr. Brent. He *must* know the truth. It all makes sense now! She made us promise to never go to emergency rooms or see other doctors. She called them all hacks who would get us killed via malpractice. She even made a point of endlessly pointing out news stories about doctors misdiagnosing their patients and doing them harm, or worse." She paused. "Could a regular doctor or hospital tell that our blood is wonky if they ran tests on us?"

Bat was smart. He nodded. "Definitely."

"He treated Dusti for free after our parents died and we didn't have medical insurance. I thought he was just a sweetheart who felt sorry for us. Instead, he was helping to hide the truth. God! What I wouldn't give to talk to him right now. Too bad you broke my phone or I'd be calling him to get some answers."

"He's in California?"

"Yes."

"You need clothes. We could make a trip there to speak to him and pack you a bag. I'd like to have a conversation with this guy too. We'll fly to Washington first but we can catch another flight straight there. I told

201

you we'll have about ten hours' head start. We'll have to get in and out of California fast, but it's doable."

"Good."

He saw the sign for the airport ahead. "You need to do everything I say, Bat. Don't argue with me until we're in the air."

She sighed. "Fine."

He was pleasantly surprised. "Thank you."

"It's better for Dusti if I get far away from here. I'm the bait. That's not something one forgets."

Chapter Eleven

Bat watched Kraven literally control someone's mind. At the moment, the pilot stared at him silently, a blank look on his face while Kraven told him what he wanted.

"I can get us out of here in thirty minutes."

"Make it ten."

The pilot hesitated. "We have to wait on other planes taking off and landing."

"I'll deal with traffic control. We're wheels-up in ten. You're going to let the lady on the plane now. We're very important clients. Go. Make it happen."

The pilot spun away, rushing inside the hangar. Kraven's eyes were still glowing bright blue when he turned his head and met her stare. They faded to a lighter color as she watched.

"That's freaky."

He shrugged. "Grab my bag and get on whatever plane he's at. He's supposed to have the nicest aircraft here right now. I'm going to have to go inside for a few minutes. Stay out of sight."

"You can *really* control people and mess with their minds!"

"Not now, Bat."

An airport worker came around the side of the building and Kraven's eyes began to glow again. "You. Come here."

The man paused, but once he looked at Kraven, he walked right to him.

"See the car? I want you to park it somewhere safe and out of sight. You protect it like it belongs to the person you love most. A friend of mine will come get it at some point. Give them the keys and show them where it's at so they can take it. He or she will say 'Kraven sent them'. You don't talk about that car to anyone. Do you understand?"

The man nodded mutely.

"What's your full name?"

"Mike Marlin."

Kraven glanced at Bat. "Get the bag out."

She moved, unsure if she was doing it because his eyes were still glowing or if she had her own free will. She pulled the bag out, gripping it tight. Kraven looked back at the worker. "Move the car now and forgot you saw us. Just remember my instructions."

The stranger walked away from Kraven, opened the driver's door, and climbed inside. He started the engine and drove behind a few hangars.

Kraven's eyes dulled to light blue again as he pointed at her. "Go after the pilot and get in the plane, Bat. We don't have time to waste. I'll be right back."

"You're going to pull that mumbo-jumbo on the people inside?"

He nodded. "Yes. Move! Decker's enforcers aren't far behind us. Ask questions later." He strode off.

She sighed and walked inside the hangar. The pilot was talking to another guy. Bat approached them, half expecting trouble, but it didn't happen. The pilot rushed to her side to take the bag and carried it onto his plane. She followed him up the steps inside.

"Make yourself comfortable," the pilot encouraged. "There's a fridge near the front with cold drinks and various sealed sandwiches if you get hungry. There's also a container next to it with chips and snacks. Have whatever you want." He flashed a smile.

"Thank you."

It was a decent-size plane for being a private one. She counted eight seats to accommodate passengers and some empty space near the front for possible storage. It was far bigger than what she and Kraven needed but she wasn't going to complain.

Bat slipped into a seat and watched the pilot leave the plane. She sighed, trying to relax. Her mind kept fixating on what Kraven could do. A little jealousy surfaced. It would be amazing to be able to control people. She could order clients she hated into confessing that they were pure scum. Then there were the occasional ones who were actually innocent. She could have a little glowing chat with the prosecutor and convince them they had the wrong person.

A list started to form of people she'd love to mess with. Her bosses were at the top. She'd order the three partners to be nicer to their employees and not stare at her ass. She'd become partner in a snap, too. That caused her to grin. She'd make Jacob leave the firm and go anywhere else. He was a conceited asshole who was one of the partners, and he'd stood in her way too many times to count. He didn't view anyone with a set of tits as bright enough to be his equal.

Maybe Kraven can do me a few favors while we're in Los Angeles. She chuckled over that.

The pilot entered the plane and stopped in the aisle, smiling at her.

"So is this business or pleasure?"

She hesitated. "Business."

He glanced at her and his expression clouded with confusion. "You don't have shoes on."

Shit. "I took them off. It's been a long day. I hope you don't mind. High heels are a bitch." She silently hoped Kraven would return soon.

Kraven seemed to almost read her mind, as he boarded the plane seconds later. He had to crouch a bit not to hit his head on the top of the cabin. "We're ready to go. The tower is waiting for you to contact them, Norman. Are we fueled?"

"Yes, sir."

"Let's get on with it." Kraven took the seat opposite her.

Bat waited for the pilot to go into the back to close up the door and then enter the cockpit before she spoke. "I'm glad you're here. He was starting to ask questions."

"Like what?"

"Business or pleasure trip? Where are your shoes? I was afraid he was going to demand my driver's license or something next."

"Not a problem. I would have handled it."

206

She bit her lip as the pilot started the engines. Fear of flying was new but the crash was still foremost in her thoughts. "Are you sure we can't just drive?"

Kraven surprised her by shifting his ass a little, stretching his long legs out as much as possible. He opened his arms. "Come here. I'll hold you."

She hesitated.

"I won't let anything happen to you, Bat. I already protected you once when we crashed. I'd do it again. What are the chances of that happening twice in one week? Not very likely. Let me hold you."

She was grateful there were no witnesses or she would have flat-out refused. It was a matter of pride for her to never show fear, but Kraven had already seen her at her worst. There was no denying she had her moments. The crash was one of them. It helped her make the decision as she fumbled for her seat belt and released it.

The plane started to move as the pilot drove it out of the hangar and toward the runway. She stood and crossed the space that separated them. Kraven helped her settle across his lap sideways. He wrapped his arms around her and she tucked her head against his shoulder.

"Thank you."

He surprised her again by brushing a kiss over her forehead. "Just breathe. In and out. You're safe with me."

She closed her eyes and shifted her head a little, picking up his steady heartbeat. It helped her relax and feel less afraid.

"I'm not a big fan of flying either. I always say I would have been born a GarLycan if I were meant to soar in the sky."

His chatter helped distract Bat when the plane paused, probably preparing for takeoff. She could hear the pilot talking to someone, most likely the control tower. The words were muffled by the engines. She cuddled firmly into Kraven and he held her a little tighter.

"Tell me about Gargoyles. Do they really turn into stone statues and hang out on tops of buildings?"

He laughed. "I hope not." He stroked her back. "Although it would be funny if Aveoth did that. Did I tell you that we used to be friends when we were kids?"

"No."

"We were. We'd meet him in the woods between his territory and ours. He could stone-out but I wouldn't want him hanging out on my roof. It's kind of cool though. His skin turns gray and we call it 'shelling'. He can harden his body. He took me flying once."

"Really?" The conversation was helping her remain calm as the plane started to move again and picked up rapid speed. They were taking off. She kept her eyes closed. "Tell me about it."

"We had to do it at night so no one would see us together. Lord Abotorus, Aveoth's father, was a total asshole." Kraven shifted his body a little, bracing his legs better. "He was a snob who would have hated his son hanging out with a couple of VampLycans. There's no other way to put it. Anyway, Drantos loved to have Aveoth take him flying but I've never been a fan of leaving the ground. They kind of teased me until it was a matter of pride to accept. I have to say it was beautiful. I know how a bird feels to soar."

Bat tried to picture that. "Weren't you afraid he'd drop you?"

"No. We're pretty damn strong. And I hadn't pissed him off." He chuckled. "That's about the only way it would have happened. On purpose."

The plane lifted off the ground, sharply gaining altitude. Bat clutched at Kraven, clinging to him. He stopped rubbing her back and rested his chin on the top of her head. "I've got you, Bat. It's okay. Anyway, Gargoyles don't express many feelings. It was kind of cool to see Aveoth laugh and kid around with us. He taught us sword fighting since they're big on that in his clan, and we taught him a lot of Lycan tracking skills. I hated it when those times ended."

"What happened?"

He hesitated.

"You said he's a threat, so I take it you aren't friends anymore?"

"Winter came one year and traveling is difficult that time of year. He can fly, but it's not exactly smart or safe to do it during storms. And we're snowbound on the ground during the worst of it too. He wasn't about to visit our village to say hi, even if he wanted to fly during the coldest months. Anyway, word spread that he'd challenged and killed his father. Some bad shit had to have gone down for Aveoth to do that. I knew they weren't close but he never talked about wanting to take his father out. Drantos and I never saw or spoke to him again after that. We went where we used to meet him, in hopes he'd show up, but he never did. Drantos tried to contact him a few times but his requests were ignored."

"You said his dad was an asshole."

"Yes, he was. It still came as a shock, though. I mean, to kill your own father? Think about that."

209

"I bet my mom thought about doing that before she had to run away from home to avoid forced sexual slavery."

"Very true. Antina was just a girl though. There's no way she would have been able to challenge her father and win. Our laws require a fair, equal fight to take leadership. She wasn't as strong as him and weapons aren't allowed."

"So she couldn't just shoot his worthless ass and call it a day?"

He shook his head. "VampLycans aren't permitted to use weapons against each other, only when we're battling another race. We have to be in the same form, and fight each other in a fair challenge. There's no honor in a shifted person attacking someone in skin." He paused. "Decker absolutely has no honor. He violated our laws today when his enforcers attacked us in the trucks."

"Then *why* couldn't she have just shot him? He's an asshole. Everyone seems to know that."

"The other clans would have had a problem with it. They would have punished her. All VampLycans are accountable for their own actions. Decker will pay for attacking us. He can't deny what happened this time."

"It sounds like they should have awarded my mother a medal if she'd shot his ass."

"We're better than Decker. Your mother's only hope would have been if either of her two brothers challenged him. They were older and equal in size to their father. But they didn't."

That had Bat tensing, her eyes snapped open, and she pulled back to stare at him. "I have uncles?"

210

"Your mother never told you about them?"

Anger stirred. "No. Big shocker, right? It was a theme of hers, apparently."

"They're like Decker, Bat. I've met both of them over the years and didn't like either."

"Fantastic. Is there anyone else I should know about? Any aunts? Cousins?"

"No aunts by blood. Your mother was Decker's only daughter. One of your uncles is mated and has three sons. They travel a lot for Decker. The other hasn't found a mate yet, last I heard."

"So what about my cousins? Are they pricks too?"

"I've never met them. To be blunt, Decker doesn't want anyone to be able to use his family against him. He's probably afraid we'd kill them or something. That's what *he'd* do. We usually only hear they were in the area after the fact. Decker sent them away after he murdered Marvilella and Antina made a run for it. Maybe they were angry with him for taking their mother and they chose to roam for him."

"Roam?"

"Attend to business outside of the clan. Enforcers sometimes go on short missions in your world but it's possible Decker set them up somewhere far from here on a more permanent basis."

She let that information sink in. "I wonder why my uncles didn't take that bastard out if he really killed their mother. I mean, homicide seems like how you guys handle things since there's no real law."

211

"We *do* have laws. They're just different from the ones you know. It could be the simple fact that they thought they couldn't take Decker in a fight. It's also less accepted in VampLycan clans to kill a parent for leadership. Of course, this is all somewhat new to us, considering how short of a time we've been in existence. First generations still run all four clans. Aveoth is the only second generation to take over a clan, but he's a GarLycan."

"Got it. You live in a weird world, Kraven." She rested her head on his chest again. "I'm going to be glad to return to mine."

Kraven rested his chin back on top of Bat's head and hid his scowl. He wasn't happy they were venturing into the human world. His height and stature always drew attention. There were humans his size but not many. Six feet five tended to make him stand above a normal crowd.

He'd have to be leery of women too. He'd be putting off hormones with Bat around. Humans were naturally drawn to Lycan men when they were horny. He was pretty certain that was going to be a problem, unless Bat stopped resisting their attraction. He didn't want her to become pissed off if women came on to him.

For his part, he'd want to kill anyone who approached Bat for sex.

He'd just have to make certain they bonded stronger before they had to deal with that issue. Bat was stubborn and wasn't about to easily give up her life. She'd resist admitting they were a mated pair.

It might be a mistake to take her back to Los Angeles. It would only show her what she had to lose once the danger passed and they could return to Alaska, where they both belonged. But it was important to

212

speak to the doctor who had helped Antina Filmore. He'd hold answers that Bat needed. And Kraven was a little curious himself.

He stroked her back, staring out the window. It might give her peace if the doctor turned out to have all the answers to her questions. Kraven just hoped he didn't have to spill much blood to force the Lycan or Vampire to talk; he was certain the doctor had to be other.

He chewed on his bottom lip, contemplating how to go about that without making Bat fear him. He'd usually just unleash his claws and start cutting until his prey was willing to tell him any damn thing he wanted to know. She might not enjoy that kind of violence.

"Is this going to be a long flight?"

Her question jolted him from his thoughts. "I'm not sure. I know commercial flights are about three and a half hours. It doesn't matter. The GarLycans can't come after us until nightfall. We have a huge head start. The control tower is going to tell anyone who asks that we're flying into Seattle."

"Aren't we?" She jerked her head off his chest and peered up at him.

"No. There's another airport we're heading to. I don't want Decker or Aveoth calling Lycan packs so they're waiting for us when we land."

"What if we crash again? You fucked with our flight plan. How will they find us?"

He hated that he'd scared her. "We're good. You saw me stop and ask that first guy we met who had the best plane and flying record. That's Norman, our pilot. Just relax and try to get some rest."

"As if," she sighed, but she did rest her cheek against his chest again. "I'm a little jealous of you."

That surprised him. "Why?"

"That mind-control thing. It's kind of cool."

He found that admission amusing. "I see."

"I wonder if I could do it but just didn't know to try."

"You can't."

She looked up at him again and frowned. "You don't know that for sure."

"It's a Vampire thing. I've tasted your blood. You didn't inherit enough to get that trait. Sorry."

"That sucks."

"You have me," he reminded her. "I got us on this aircraft without any problems."

"Yes, you did. I'd love to have you in court with me."

He snorted. "So I could look pretty?"

She smiled. "I'd never lose a case again. You could order them to believe everything I say, like my client is innocent."

"We only mess with minds in emergency situations." She had a lot to learn. "It can cause damage to some humans, so we avoid it whenever possible."

"What kind of damage? You mean like telling them they're a cow and then they'd spend the rest of their lives mooing and trying to eat grass?"

He laughed. She did have a great sense of humor. "No. The mentally unstable can become more so. Some humans have a slight resistance to

214

our kind and we have to push them harder than normal. It causes them pain; sometimes a brain bleed can occur. It's rare but it's a risk. It's why Drantos and I didn't mess with any of the survivors from the plane crash. They already had injures and we didn't want to accidentally kill them. Then there's the totally immune…" Though Kraven wasn't sure if he should tell her about those.

"What about them?"

He should have known she'd ask. "A very small percentage of humans are immune to Vampire suggestions. But it's law that humans can't know about other races. It puts all of us at risk."

"And that means what for the humans?"

He didn't know if he should answer.

"I'm waiting. Spit it out." She peered at him.

"It's a death sentence," he stated. "There's always that risk when we use our power of persuasion, that it'll fail and we'll reveal too much to a human and can't fix it. They might try to convince other humans of our existence. Ever hear of Vampire hunters? Some of those stories are based on history. Immune humans have tracked and killed Vamps during the day while they slept. It got even more dangerous to allow those humans to live as technology evolved. They could stalk us easier, film us to provide proof to others, and there are more effective weapons to kill anything not human. Past hunters started with Vampires and eventually learned about other races. They wanted to slaughter us all. So…" He paused. "It became law."

Bat studied him, her expression grim. "Good thing I'm not totally human then. Would you have to kill me too?"

"I voluntarily told you what we are. I'd never hurt you."

"So you're just going to let me go after all this is over and done with?"

No. Never. He couldn't say that to her though. "Do you plan on becoming a Vampire hunter?"

"I like to sleep at night. I'll pass."

"Most Vampire hunters kill when the sun is up. That's when Vamps are most vulnerable."

"I'd be in court."

"You're good then. You're also smart. Most humans don't believe in our existence. They think the ones who do are mentally unstable. That's fortunate for us."

"How so?"

"It gives us time to clean up messes when they happen."

She seemed to ponder that. "I'd make a horrible Vampire slayer. It sounds dirty and disgusting. I'd much rather spend my free time getting a manicure or a pedicure."

It was a reminder of how different she was than any of the women he'd ever known. Most of them were tough females who loved to go hunting.

He didn't mind, though. His mate was more human than not. It would be an adjustment but he'd make it work. They'd both have to compromise.

He suddenly couldn't resist touching her more intimately. He lifted his hand and gently caressed her cheek. Then he dropped all his restraint and lunged for her surprised mouth, kissing her. Bat tensed in his arms but she caved quickly, meeting his tongue with her own.

He slid his other hand lower to cup her ass. She moaned in response and he leaned forward a little so she had room to wrap her arms around his neck. She couldn't deny that they belonged together when they touched. He wouldn't allow her to put emotional barriers between them.

My mate. The instinct to bond with her became almost unbearable. He wanted to slash open a vein to make her drink his blood, and take more from her. It would help their bond strengthen until they could feel each other's emotions and even share thoughts. He resisted though. He wanted her to accept what they were on her own terms, not because his pain over her rejection would be something she felt. He never wanted his Bat to hurt.

She jerked back, breathing hard. Passion showed in the way she looked at him. "We can't do this."

"We can."

"The pilot—"

"Won't come back here. He's busy flying."

He kissed her again, capturing her lips with his. She didn't protest. He realized soon enough when she began to grind her hips on his lap that the seat wasn't going to work. He pulled his face away from hers, both of them panting, and frantically looked around for an option. The narrow aisle between the seats looked to be the best place.

"Hold on tight," he ordered.

She wrapped her arms around his neck. He braced one arm around her waist and grabbed the seat in front of him to pull them both up. He nearly slammed his head on the low roof. He twisted sideways and took them both to the floor, ending up on top of her. The space felt pretty tight for someone his size, but all he cared about was making sure he didn't crush Bat. Then he discovered another problem. She no longer wore a skirt. The sweatpants hugging her lower body meant he'd have to get her at least partially naked.

Sexual frustration rolled through him but he refused to stop. He was going to have his mate. They were safe for the time being. No GarLycan would dare attack the plane in flight, even if they were insane enough to do it during the day. It would put Bat's life in danger, not something they'd be willing to do, since Aveoth would order them to bring her to him alive and well.

He lifted off Bat, assessing her. Her cheeks were flushed a bit, her mouth a little swollen from his kisses, and her nipples were taut, showing through the shirt she wore. He inhaled, picking up the scent of her, as turned-on as he was. She wanted him too.

He reached down and shoved her legs together, lifting them so she had no choice but to bend her knees to her chest. He snagged the waistband of the sweats at her spine and tore them down her legs to her knees. He spread her thighs, ducked his head, and scooted forward so her bunched-up pants ended up behind his neck. It put her exposed pussy right under his mouth.

"I'm not a pretzel." Bat lifted her head, holding his gaze.

He grinned. "Relax and enjoy, my little hellion."

218

It was the only warning he gave before he dropped his chin and began to feast on her. She moaned when he lapped at her clit with his tongue. She stabbed her fingers into his hair. He almost expected her to pull at it, try to stop him. She surprised him by doing the opposite. She just curved her hand along the back of his head, almost as if she were afraid he'd stop and wanted to force him to stay exactly where he was. Her moans were soft and throaty. He loved the sounds she made.

He adjusted his hold when her hips began to rock against his mouth. He pinned her tighter by her thighs to keep her still. He sucked on her stiffening clit, knowing she was really close to her climax. He'd normally want to draw it out and torment her a bit but his dick demanded release from his constraining jeans.

Bat came loudly. She cried out his name, her fingers fisting his hair. Kraven eased off her clit and ran his tongue down her slit. The sweet taste of her, aroused and needy, was the best thing ever. She could become his addiction. He let go of her thighs and maneuvered one hand down to unfasten his jeans. He had to twist his hips a bit to shove them down enough to free his stiff shaft. He wished he could strip them both entirely but he'd make do with what was possible.

He reached up and behind him next, blindly finding one of Bat's feet. He yanked on the sweats until he freed one of her legs, then crawled up her body. Bat's eyes opened and their gazes locked. He had to have her.

He braced his elbows above her shoulders since there was no room next to them. "Wrap around me," he demanded.

Bat didn't hesitate. She hugged his ribs and wrapped her legs around his waist. He shifted his hips until his rock-hard dick was in position, entering Bat in one long, slow thrust. A groan passed his lips.

Bat felt like heaven. She was wet, hot, ready for him.

"Yes," she moaned.

That was all he needed to hear. Bat was his for the taking.

He was never going to let her go.

Chapter Twelve

"What's the problem?" Bat kept her voice down. There were a lot of people in the airport, despite its smaller size.

Kraven glanced down at her feet. "Nice shoes. Are those flowers printed all over them?"

"Shut up. It's all the gift shop had and they aren't even my size. That store was a joke. I've seen larger bathrooms. Can you say limited merchandise choices? They should. Did you get us another plane?"

He shook his head.

"Why not?"

He gazed at her with those intense eyes of his. "There are cameras everywhere."

"So?"

He gripped her arm, pulled her into an alcove with a large fake plant and invaded her space. One of his hands lifted, as if he were rubbing his temple. The color of his eyes sharpened, brightened, and the blue began to glow neon. They were gorgeous.

"I have to look this way to control minds. Do you see the problem?" The brightness faded to a pale shade. "I figured since it was a small airport it would be more like the one near home. There are cameras all over in here. It's a nightmare."

"You can't use your power."

"Nope." He dropped his hand and stepped back, pulling her away from the wall. "I can't."

"So we just hire someone. Simple."

"The two pilots I talked to just came off flights. They refused. I looked up and saw cameras on us so I couldn't change their minds."

"What about Norman?"

"I let him go after I paid him. He was tired. I could see it. We don't want to crash again and having a pilot who can't keep his eyes open isn't the brightest move we could make."

"That's true."

"I also couldn't take over his mind once we left the plane. They have surveillance *every* damn where." He looked pissed.

"Welcome to the human world."

He scowled.

"So we have to fly commercial?"

"We can't be tracked and you don't have identification."

"Got it. No eyes. We're screwed."

"We need to get out of here. There isn't a lot of time to waste if we're being hunted by Lycans." His gaze lifted and he turned his head, watching the people around them. His nostrils flared. "I haven't seen any so far or picked up their scent. We're going to have to rent a car."

"That's a long drive to Southern California." She cringed.

"We don't have a choice."

"Damn."

"I agree." He shifted the strap of his bag on his shoulder and offered his hand. "Come on."

"Won't that leave a trail?"

"It won't matter if they find out I rented a car in Washington. They already know we flew here by now. Let's go."

She clasped his hand and he led her to the car rental area of the airport. There was a short line. Kraven passed her his bag and pointed to a chair. "Go take a seat. This won't take long."

"I'm hungry."

"We'll grab something in the car."

"Fast food. Awesome." She rolled her eyes.

"I'm sorry, Bat."

"I'm being a pain. I know. Go. I'll sit right here and guard your bag."

He flashed a smile before getting in the line and Bat took a seat on a plastic chair. A woman a few seats over shot her a dirty look and curled her upper lip. Probably because of how she was dressed and the generic tennis shoes she wore without socks. *Judgmental bitch.* Bat reached up and rubbed the bridge of her nose with her middle finger. The woman gasped and jerked her head in the other direction.

Bat relaxed and watched Kraven. He was the most interesting thing in the airport. And it quickly became apparent she wasn't the only one paying attention to him. Women walked by, their gazes lingering on him as they slowed.

"Yeah, he's hot. Move on," she muttered.

Kraven turned his head, regarding her over his shoulder. One of his eyebrows arched. She shook her head and he faced forward. Damn, he had really good hearing. She'd have to remember that.

Another woman walked by, nearly tripping in the process of admiring Kraven. It irritated Bat, and her irritation just got worse when he reached the counter. The cute brunette he rented a vehicle from grinned widely and appraised him like a side of prime beef. Bat wished she could hear what was being said.

Long minutes passed and Bat had finally had enough when she watched the brunette laugh and have the gall to reach out and purposely touch Kraven's hand. She stood, grabbed the strap of his bag, and lifted. It was heavier than it looked and she had to battle to carry it to his side. She dumped it on the floor.

"What's taking so long, sweetheart?"

That killed the brunette's cheery smile as she took notice of Bat.

Kraven signed his name on the digital screen and dropped the stylus pen. "Nothing, honeybun. I got us a car."

"Fantastic." Bat held the brunette's gaze. "We're going on a romantic getaway."

"How nice." The brunette walked over to a printer, her movements jerky. "I'll get you a copy of the rental agreement. They'll bring the car around and hand you the keys then."

"Thanks." Kraven turned his gaze on Bat, looking far too amused. His lips twitched as if he wanted to laugh.

"Don't even," she mumbled. "I said I'm hungry. I didn't want to wait while you continued to flirt."

All humor vanished and he leaned toward her, putting his face closer. "You're the only woman I want. Should I fuck you on the floor again to prove it?"

He spoke loud enough that everyone around them, including the clerk, had to have heard. Bat swallowed hard. It was a good thing she didn't embarrass easily or was the type to back away from any kind of a challenge. "Does this car have a backseat? We haven't tried that yet. Confined spaces sound exciting."

The brunette slapped the papers on the counter. "There you go. Follow the sign and someone will bring your rental around in a few minutes. Next!"

Kraven folded the papers and pocketed them in his duster. He bent, gripping his bag. "Come on, honeybun. Let's go find out how roomy this car is." He offered his elbow.

Bat slid her arm through his and allowed him to lead her outside. She avoided looking at him.

"I like it that you felt the need to stake your claim on me."

She refused to look at his face. "Give me a break. I was just annoyed."

"Too bad. I also liked you calling me sweetheart. It had a nice ring to it."

"Bite me."

He chuckled. "Invitation accepted. I'm part Vamp, Hellion. I have fangs and I'm happy to use them."

"You know what I meant. Keep your fangs sucked up."

"They're actually retracted."

"Shut it."

A silver sedan pulled up to the curb and a kid slipped out of the passenger seat. He wore a shirt with the rental company logo over his chest. Kraven unhooked his arm from Bat and removed the paperwork, passing it over to show the employee.

"Here you go, sir. It's fully gassed. I strongly suggest you return it with a full tank." He handed over the keys. "Have a great day."

Kraven nodded, pocketed his paperwork again, and walked over to the car. He opened the back door, threw the bag in, and stripped off his duster to toss in too. He opened the passenger door next, flashing Bat a killer smile.

"Come on, honeybun. It's got a roomy backseat. It's our lucky day."

Seems he wasn't about to let that go. She sighed and climbed into the car. Kraven closed the door and rounded the vehicle. She put on her belt as he adjusted the mirrors and seat on the driver's side, before driving away from the curb.

"Can you do me a favor?" Kraven glanced at her.

"It depends on what you want."

"There's supposed to be a map in the glove box. Get it out and find us the nearest highway."

She leaned forward and found the map, unfolding it. "Map reading isn't my best skill. Fair warning."

"I just want to put some miles between us and that airport."

"Got it." She studied the map and found where they were on it, giving him directions. "I really am hungry. That sandwich I ate on the plane was mostly frozen."

"I know. You barely touched it. You only took three bites."

She wasn't sure how to feel about him being that aware of her actions. "And I'm not a fan of fast food."

"I picked up on that. Let's put some miles behind us and I'll find a restaurant. I doubt it will be very nice but there won't be a drive-thru window. Can you hang in there for at least half an hour or so?"

"Yes."

"Good."

He was being sweet and she appreciated it. She suddenly had a thought and laughed.

"What?" Kraven glanced over at her.

"I just realized we're going on a long road trip together but at least you're willing to ask for directions. That puts you above a lot of men."

"I don't get it."

"Men never ask for directions, especially from women."

"Humans might not but this isn't familiar territory to me. Maps are needed and you're the one who can read it without having to steer at the same time."

She smiled, telling him which turns to make. "This map only covers Washington."

They reached a freeway and Kraven drove them onto it. "We'll pick up more maps when we need to fill the tank."

They drove for a good ten minutes before Bat saw a sign listing the distance to major cities. Dread struck as she read the miles posted for Los Angeles. She quickly did the math. "Shit. We're looking at about fifteen hours of drive time to reach L.A."

"I don't require as much sleep...and we'll be able to cut down that time."

"How do you figure that?"

He glanced at her. "I'll have any law enforcement forget they saw us if I'm pulled over for speeding."

"Forget it. One, you said it could be dangerous to the person if they're immune, and two, most cops wear body cameras now."

"Why?"

"Because people are assholes. It's for their protection against false claims being filed against them."

He sighed, staring forward.

"Do the speed limit. I'll take turns driving with you. Just tell me when you get tired and we'll switch."

"I'm not human, Bat. I don't require as much sleep as you do. I can stay up for a few days without it becoming a problem."

"Lucky you. You still might get sick of driving. Don't you trust me behind the wheel?"

"I trust you. You can drive if you have an overwhelming desire to. Let's find somewhere to eat. I can hear your stomach rumbling."

She put the map away and closed the glove box. Kraven had to be the most agreeable person she'd ever taken a road trip with. It might not be so bad after all. He didn't even turn on the radio. Her sister loved to blast loud music that gave Bat a headache.

* * * * *

Kraven reached over and gently adjusted Bat's head to a more comfortable position. She'd fallen asleep an hour before. Traffic had slowed to a crawl and red lights flashed ahead in the darkness. He hoped it was just an accident and not a trap. Decker's enforcers could have forced the human police to narrow the lanes to one in hopes of finding them if they were aware the two traveled by car.

He got closer and saw two tangled vehicles in the distance. Paramedics were attending one of the victims from the back of an ambulance. Another human, presumably the other driver, spoke to a law enforcer who was taking notes. Kraven let out a relieved sigh and relaxed.

It was taking longer than he'd hoped to travel via vehicle with his mate. She demanded they stop at restaurants instead of just grabbing quick premade food, and had a tendency to waste a lot of time when they refilled the gas tank. The mini mart had seemed to fascinate her as she'd strolled around picking out a few snacks. He glanced down at the bag resting on the passenger floor. She hadn't touched anything she'd bought but had seemed comforted by having the food nearby anyway.

Must be a human thing. He sighed.

229

A slight noise drew his attention and he twisted, reaching into the backseat. He blindly felt around for his bag and finally located the pocket. Kraven withdrew his cell phone and glanced back and forth from the screen to the slow-moving traffic ahead of him. The text from Carver wasn't long but the message made him feel a hell of a lot better. He debated about waking Bat to let her know her sister and Drantos had safely returned to their village, but she looked exhausted. The news could wait.

He used his thumb to type back.

Decker?

The response came quickly. Being hunted.

That put a smile on Kraven's face. It didn't last long. He typed again. Aveoth?

Uncertain.

Is Dusti or Drantos injured?

Wasn't able to see or talk to them. He took her right home but no healer was called. I assume they're both fine.

That was good news. Kraven dropped the phone onto his lap when he saw one of the human law enforcers directing traffic. He smiled at the man and drove past. The lanes opened and he pressed his foot down on the gas, accelerating. He waited until it was safe to lift his phone and glance at it again. A message waited.

Drantos is being punished for defying your father.

Shit! Kraven felt his gums ache, his fangs wanting to extend. He typed with his thumb, glancing frequently from the screen to the road. How bad?

Lycan whipping. He got off easy.

Some of his anger faded. He agreed. The punishment could have been a hell of a lot worse. His father would have had to punish Drantos in some way to keep the peace. That fate was tame in comparison to some. Tell him we're safe.

Will do.

Thanks. Out.

Kraven reached back, returning the phone to the bag, then he glanced over at Bat. She slept peacefully but he considered pulling over and finding somewhere with a bed. He decided against it quickly though. It was best if they remained on the move and inconspicuous. He'd also asked for the most popular car available at the rental company. He'd seen hundreds of the same ones on the road since they'd left the airport.

Bat stirred, waking. She stretched and turned to look at him. "Was I out long?"

"No."

"Sorry I nodded off."

"It's okay." It was a good time to share the news he'd received. "Drantos brought your sister back to the village. Your grandfather doesn't have her."

He expected her to be happy. He flinched when she reached across and slapped him hard on his arm.

"What the hell was that for?"

"You purposely waited for me to drift off to make a call? I wanted to speak to her myself!"

"I got a text from Carver and heard the phone vibrate."

"Oh."

"Decker's being hunted. I guess Drantos got to your sister before she reached your grandfather, or he'd be dead."

"Is she hurt?"

"Our healer wasn't called to Drantos's house. I'll assume not."

She unhooked her belt.

"What the hell are you doing? Put that back on."

"Where's the phone? I'm calling her." She turned and knelt on her seat, and tried to reach into his bag.

Kraven softly growled and reached out, grabbing her ass as he looked in the mirrors, steering to the side of the highway and slowly bringing the car to a halt on the shoulder. "Are you crazy? Don't do that again."

"I'm calling Dusti. Where the hell is the phone? It's dark back here."

He let her go, unhooked his own belt, and grabbed her hips, yanking her down onto the center console. She glared at him when their gazes met in the dim glow of the dash lights.

"Don't ever do that again. You could have caused me to wreck. You keep your ass in the seat and the belt on. You're too fragile to survive if we crash otherwise."

"I'm *calling* my sister." She glanced down at his chest. "Do you have the phone?" She opened her hand. "Give it up."

"You're not calling her. Didn't you hear me? Decker is still on the loose. They're hunting for him. That means *he* could be hunting for *you*. I'm not going to let you help him find us. No direct calls to my brother or parents in case he's put a trace on their lines."

"How in the hell could he? Do you know how difficult it is to get a warrant for that? I do."

"He just has to send one of his enforcers into the nearest phone center. We use human technology too, Bat. He can manipulate anyone into turning it against us."

"Bullshit. You just don't want me to talk to my sister for some reason. Are you lying to me? Is she really okay?"

She could really piss him off with her lack of trust and wild accusations. He dropped his control and allowed his eyes to glow. Hers widened in surprise but he didn't stop. He focused on her. "Look down, Bat. I'm holding a frog in my hand. See it." He released her hip and opened his palm inches from her.

She gasped, trying to jerk away. He reigned in his power and hooked her around the waist, keeping her close. He guessed she was afraid of frogs from the expression on her face, and already regretted losing his temper.

"Easy. You saw the frog, didn't you? It's not real. I was making a point. We can control human minds. Decker could easily convince a human to track our phones."

"That was a shitty trick."

"But effective. You thought I had a frog in my palm."

She licked her lips. "He could be tracking your phone anyway then."

"It's my work phone. Without knowing the number, he'd have to trace over fifty of them. At least that many were assigned to our clan members. I would have removed the battery once I got word but I was driving."

"Kraven, I need to talk to Dusti." Her voice softened. "She's probably scared."

"You underestimate her, Bat. I saw her after the attack on the trucks. She was very brave to step out and claim to be you. A coward wouldn't do that, neither would someone weak. She wanted to protect you, and was willing to be taken in order to save your life. Don't blow her sacrifice by asking me to call Drantos's home and possibly get traced. She's really safe. I wouldn't lie to you."

She looked uncertain. He gently released her. "Sit and put on your belt. I'll show you the texts." It stung that he even had to make the offer.

She scooted over off the center divider and buckled back in. He twisted in the seat and retrieved the phone but kept hold of it, leaning over to show her the screen. He scrolled to the top of the conversation to allow her to read it all. When she was done, he removed the phone's battery.

"Believe me now?"

"What was that about a Lycan whipping?"

"It's complicated."

"Uncomplicate it for me."

"Fine. Drantos and my father argued in front of some clan members. That's a no-no. So he has to be punished. We're not a democracy. My father leads our people and Drantos openly questioned his authority. The punishment is to discourage others from doing the same. Drantos will take some lashings. It's no big deal."

Bat frowned.

"You know we heal fast," he gently reminded her. "My father would have attacked and killed anyone else for arguing with him. He would have seen it as a challenge. Others can't see him as weak, even for his own sons. Drantos needs to be punished in some form for what happened."

"Sounds kind of messed up to me."

"My people come with claws and sharp teeth, Hellion. It's about the alpha mentality. Weaknesses aren't abided in a leader."

"Got it."

Kraven put on his belt. "We need to go. I figure at the rate we're traveling, we should reach Los Angeles sometime tomorrow afternoon."

"I have to pee."

He clenched his teeth. "Or perhaps tomorrow evening."

"Just find me a bathroom."

"Fine, but it slows us down every time we have to stop."

"My bladder doesn't work on a schedule. Don't take me to one of those horrible rest areas either. They have the most disgusting bathrooms."

Kraven checked traffic and accelerated on the shoulder, merging over into the slow lane. "You're really demanding."

"It's called having standards. I can't just whip it out and aim. Women need to get up close and personal in a stall. Men have it easy. I don't think it's asking too much to find decent facilities." She pointed. "There. See that sign? A restaurant has health inspectors."

Kraven sighed.

"And I'm hungry again."

"You bought some snacks at the gas station, remember? They're in the bag at your feet."

"I'm in the mood for something hot."

"Maybe we'll arrive in Los Angeles the day after next."

"Don't be a drama queen."

He grimaced. "I don't even know how to take that."

Chapter Thirteen

Bat was glad the road trip had ended. Kraven had refused to stop at restaurants after the second one, determined to arrive in L.A. before nightfall the following day. His mood had turned outright snarky when that hadn't happened.

The taxi finally stopped in front of her building forty minutes after they'd dropped off the rental car. Traffic had been a nightmare. She tried to get out of the vehicle the moment it stopped but Kraven grabbed her arm.

He shoved money through the slot to pay the driver. "Stick close to me."

She jerked out of his hold and shoved open the door, stepping out onto the sidewalk. He slid out after her, dragging his bag.

"Wait." He closed the door and latched on to her hand, slinging his bag over his shoulder.

Bat tapped her foot until the taxi pulled from the curb. "I just want to take a shower and eat real food. That stuff you tried to shove at me earlier tasted like cardboard. Hustle it."

He had the nerve to growl.

"Don't even. I'm never taking another long road trip with you again."

"It was no picnic for me either. I've got kinks in my legs from sitting and drive all night and day."

"I bet you love picnics, living in Dog Bark."

"Howl."

"Whatever. I'm cranky." She could easily admit the obvious. "So are you."

He inclined his head. "Agreed. It's been a trying day."

"Nobody likes shit traffic jams. Your snarling and blowing the horn didn't help either."

"Humans are stupid."

"Not all of us are," she snapped. "But yeah, there seemed to be a lot of morons out on the road today."

"I thought you wanted to pack some of your things. Well? We're at your building."

She turned her head, staring at the large glass doors of the elegant building across the street. Some of her anger faded. "I wondered if I'd ever see it again."

"We're not staying long. In and out. That's it, Bat. Twenty minutes, tops. You pack one bag and we're gone."

"We'll be safe here. You'll see." She spun, striding toward the crosswalk.

Kraven hurried his pace and caught up to her, clutching her hand. She allowed it since they'd joined a group of people clustered together waiting for the lights to change. It was bumper to bumper traffic. The walk sign lit up and Bat stepped off the curb. He stayed at her side.

"What in the hell does that mean?" Kraven finally asked.

"I'm going to sleep in my own bed tonight."

"No, you aren't."

She decided to stop arguing with him. Her stomach rumbled from the distant memory of the inedible lunch she'd tried to choke down. She'd kill for a shower too.

Bat led him to the front doors that automatically slid open. The reception area was a glassed-in space with couches and a few artificial plants. She spotted Doug at the front desk and grinned. He stood up behind the glass security walls that separated him from the rest of the room. He clicked on the intercom.

"May I help you?" His gaze gave Bat a once-over and his upper lip curled.

She'd forgotten what she was wearing. Kraven's cut-up sweats and oversized shirt, plus she probably looked horrible. Her clothes were wrinkled from being in a car for so long. "Yes. You can let me in. I don't have my keys."

Doug actually rested his hand on his holstered gun. "Excuse me?"

It sank in that he didn't recognize her. Bat felt irritated but quickly let it go. She wasn't wearing makeup and he'd never seen her less than impeccably dressed. "It's me, Doug. Batina Dawson."

Doug's eyes widened and his mouth dropped open. His gaze lowered down her body again, then he seemed to study her face closely.

"Seriously?" Her irritation grew. "I give you a two hundred dollar Christmas bonus every year. You just had a little boy with your wife over the summer. You named him Mike. He's got your wife's green eyes but looks just like you. You show me pictures of him often. He's just learning how to crawl. I sent catered food to your house once when the security team said you and your wife both had the flu and I figured neither of you

239

probably felt like cooking; I had soups and specialty breads delivered. Ring any bells?"

"Ms. Dawson." Doug released his gun, still appearing stunned. He gave her one more inspection from head to foot. "You look so different."

"I was in a plane crash and just survived the road trip from hell."

He paled. "Shit."

"That's putting it mildly. I lost everything. My luggage. My purse. I'll need my spare key from the safe."

Doug nodded but his gaze slid to Kraven. "Who's your guest?"

She had never asked him his last name. "This is Mr. Kraven. He was nice enough to bring me home. He's a fellow survivor. We met in Alaska."

Doug nodded. "You know procedure."

"Of course." She'd forgotten. She turned her head to peer at Kraven. "You need to step outside for a minute."

"What?" Kraven frowned.

She pointed at the glass barriers in the room. "See those? We need to be buzzed through. No one can get past them without a resident's permission. You need to step out so he knows you're not forcing me to let you in."

Kraven just gawked at her.

"It's for the safety of every resident in the building. I told you the security here is excellent. Go outside and take your bag with you. I'll wave you back in when he knows you're not some criminal intent on robbing me or worse. You could be threatening to shoot me, or have a bomb in your bag ready to go off if I don't do whatever you want. See where I'm

240

going with this? Just step out and he'll know you're here because I want you to be and not because I'm under duress."

"Unbelievable." Kraven released her hand and stormed toward the sliding doors.

Doug released his gun and stepped over to the controls. The doors locked with a buzz after Kraven exited the building. Bat waited for Doug to look at her again.

"He's really a friend."

"Okay. Are you alright, Ms. Dawson? Do you want me to see if one of the doctors are home and can take a look at you?"

"That's so sweet but I'm fine. I just need real clothes again, and food. I'll be ordering something so expect a delivery." She grimaced, glancing down. "I really did lose everything."

Doug released the exterior locks with another buzz. Bat waved at Kraven and he strode back inside. He didn't appear too happy. Doug opened the interior doors for them both, and Bat led Kraven through before Doug locked the doors again and came around his desk.

"I'm glad you're okay, Ms. Dawson. I'll need your code for the safe."

"Of course. Three, three, six, nine, zero."

"I'll be right back."

Doug walked over to the door behind his desk and pressed his thumb on the lock, then punched in a code. As soon as he disappeared, Bat turned to Kraven. "It won't take long. He's just grabbing the spare keys to my place."

"Code?"

241

"Every resident has a small safe inside the security office where we store spare keys."

"Why?"

"In case we lose ours."

"I meant, why a safe?"

"In case of a breach. That way thieves can't just grab the keys to everyone's units. They'd have to get past reception to here, which is tough, since that glass is bulletproof and rated to withstand small bombs. Next, they'd have to break through that security door to the next office." She paused. "After that, they'd have to deal with individual safes to obtain keys. The police would arrive and arrest them around that time, so the residents are pretty safe."

"Unbelievable."

"That's the second time you've said that. It's a high-security building. I also need a key card for the elevator. Every key is coded to a floor. My card takes us directly to the fourteenth floor, and the general floors like the lobby and parking garage. That's it."

"Who the hell lives here to warrant that kind of paranoia?"

Bat crossed her arms over her chest. "This is Los Angeles. Not Howl. Crime is high. This is how we avoid home invasions, some residents have stalkers...then there are the paparazzi. They can't be allowed into the building."

"You didn't answer my question. Who needs protection from all that?"

"Other attorneys. Doctors. Trust-fund kids." She shrugged. "There're a few movie studios who keep apartments here, so we get plenty of movie industry people. Musicians. You name it. If they have money and want to live in a safe place, this is it."

He glanced around. "I bet it costs a fortune."

"Hence why I said 'if they have money'. The association fees alone are nearly three grand a month."

"That's insane."

"It's worth every penny."

Doug returned, holding an envelope. "I'll send Brian up with the food as soon as it arrives, Ms. Dawson. Welcome home and I'm glad you're okay."

"Thank you." She smiled. Doug was one of her favorites.

"Call down if you change your mind about wanting a doctor to look you over. I'm pretty sure Dr. Mitchells and Dr. Young are going to be home for the rest of the evening."

"I appreciate that but I'm fine." She reached out and patted his arm, accepting the envelope. "Thank you."

Bat used her fingernail to unseal it and led Kraven to the elevators. She pulled out the keycard and pushed the button. When doors opened, she entered and he followed her inside. She slid the card in a slot, the doors closed, and the elevator began to lift.

"You didn't push any buttons."

"I don't have to. We're at the lobby." She reached inside the envelope again and withdrew the single key to her home. "I'd have to

243

press a button when I leave my floor. I could go to the lobby, or parking garage one or two."

Kraven shifted his weight. He didn't look very comfortable. "Who's Brian? What food?"

"He's one of the runners. They run errands for the tenants. Food deliveries are accepted at reception, since we can't have delivery people inside the building. It's a security risk. One of the runners brings food to the tenants. All employees here have had extensive background checks done on them, as well." She licked her lips. "I'm starving. I plan to order us something."

"Why can't you just go down and get it yourself?"

Bat grinned. "Because I don't have to, and it's part of the perks of living here. I mentioned those steep association fees."

"Unbelievable."

"Is that your new word for the day?"

He glared.

The elevator stopped and Bat stepped out first. "You're so grumpy. Come on."

She stopped at her apartment and grabbed the mail off the table next to it before unlocking the door.

"They just leave your mail there?"

"Yes."

"Aren't you worried someone will steal it?"

"There are only six residents who have access to this floor and there's a camera." She jerked her head toward the far corner to indicate where it was located. "It would be stupid of them; they'd be caught." She shoved open the door and flipped on the lights, stepping aside for Kraven to enter.

She watched his face, curious about his reaction.

He took a few steps inside and looked around. His mouth pressed together in a tight line. She guessed he didn't like her decor. She glanced around too as she closed and locked the door. The walls were dark, the floors white, and it complimented her black furniture.

"You don't like black and white?"

"It's fine."

"I like it, and it's my home." She bent, tearing off the shoes. "Let's order food. I'm starving. Don't bother arguing with me. I know what you're going to say but I want cooked food from a real kitchen, by people who take pride in their work. Does Chinese sound okay? They're the closest and can deliver quickly."

"Sure."

She walked into the kitchen and opened a drawer. "Here's the menu."

"Just order whatever you usually do. I guess we can eat." He dropped his bag on the floor and entered her living room, seeming interested in some of the photos she kept of her and Dusti over the mantel of the gas fireplace.

She removed the right menu and dialed, recognizing the voice of the woman who answered. "Hi, Vera. It's Batina Dawson." She sized up

245

Kraven. He was a big man. "Send me the variety dinner spread I usually order. Make it for six people. Charge it to my card with the normal tip."

"Of course, Ms. Dawson. You said dinner? Not just appetizers?"

Bat realized it must be later than she thought. "Yes."

"What time does your company arrive?"

"Immediately."

Vera chuckled. "You forgot you have guests coming again?"

She sighed. "It was a spur-of-the-moment kind of thing. I invited some of the interns over to my place. We've had to put in a lot of overtime and they've been busting their ass so they deserve a reward," she lied. "Thank you."

"Not a problem. We always appreciate your business. We'll have it there in about twenty-five minutes."

Bat hung up and frowned. Kraven had moved to her shelves, reading the titles of books displayed. "I'm going to go take a shower."

"We're not staying long. I told you that. Go pack. We'll eat and then we're out the door."

"You saw the security my building has. We're safe here, Kraven. No one is going to get past reception."

He abandoned her shelves and entered the dining area near her. Bat narrowed her gaze, leery as she watched Kraven take notice of the framed headlines she'd carefully cut from newspapers to hang on the wall. They were some of her toughest cases that she'd won. Most hadn't earned her public likability but she was proud of beating the seemingly impossible odds. His mouth twisted into a grimace but he didn't speak.

"You don't approve?" It was a good guess.

He turned and held her stare. "You helped killers remain free."

"Everyone deserves the best defense possible. Even pond scum. I'm supposed to win because that's my job. Some people are actually innocent of the crimes they're accused of, you know. I do a lot of good in some cases."

He glanced over at the wall, then back at her. "Why do you hang these?"

She gave up on the idea of an immediate shower. "Do you want something to drink?"

"You didn't answer me."

She yanked open the fridge, removing two bottled waters. The island was between them when she spun, slamming both of them down. She used her toes to close the door. The silence in the room grew uncomfortable as they watched each other.

Kraven advanced until he paused on the other side of the granite slab. "Why keep trophies if you hate the people you represent?"

"I'm good at what I do."

"Why are they there, Bat?"

He reached over and rested his bigger hand over hers. She jerked away and he lifted one of the bottles of water, twisting the cap open. He took a long sip of the drink and she watched him swallow. He didn't fit into her apartment with his rugged good looks and biker clothing.

"Answer me. I refuse to let this drop."

She believed that. "Fine. I *do* hate my job. But I beat the odds on some of the toughest cases. It's a challenge. I like to look at them in the morning when I'm having my coffee. It helps motivate me to go to work."

He blinked a few times but didn't say a word.

"Go ahead. Judge me. Everyone else does."

He put more space between them and she stiffened. His reaction hurt. He didn't walk away though, instead rounding the island. She held his narrowed gaze until he paused close enough that they nearly touched.

"I respect the difficulty of your job, Bat. I might not like it, but I've been an enforcer since I became an adult. Not all my duties have been agreeable, yet they were mine to fulfill. You fill a need in society. Someone has to defend them." He lifted his hand and gently trailed his thumb along the side of her face. "I understand."

Tears filled her eyes and she dropped her gaze before he could see them. It was the first time someone outside her firm had said anything that even remotely implied they didn't detest her for doing her job. "Thank you."

"We can't stay here."

"We can."

"Decker's enforcers could order Doug to let them inside and have him bring them right to your door. That glass he stays behind won't protect him from our eyes."

She lifted up the key she still had in her hand. "They can't get in without this. There are no more copies."

"They can break a door down, Bat."

248

"It's reinforced. It might look like mahogany but it's steel-lined. That's why I bought a condo here. I wanted to sleep at night without fearing some lunatic would be able to get to me."

"You really have enemies?"

"You saw the wall."

He glanced over his shoulder at the framed reminders of her cases before looking back at her.

She backed away to prevent him from continuing to touch her. "Imagine I'm the lawyer who defended the guy you think murdered your brother. I don't make it easy for them to get to me. Some of my clients are morons too. They need me to save them from going to prison but they might feel I'm a liability after the fact. A dead attorney tells no tales. You think I'm paranoid for living here? You've never met real lowlifes. Who knows, maybe they've all taken too many drugs to be rational. As if I'd be stupid enough to try to blackmail them or write some tell-all book one day." She snorted. "But you can't convince them of that. I can think of four off the top of my head who would love to see me dead and might pay some bucks to make it happen."

"You know where the bodies are buried."

"Not literally, but I know more than they're comfortable with."

Kraven scowled, staring at her. "They can't be tried for the same crime twice, right? What's the big deal if you know they're guilty?"

She took a sip of water. "Let's say for the sake of argument that you've been accused of murdering someone and you actually didn't do it. Instead you were screwing around on your wife. You have to tell your attorney where you really were and what you were doing, so she can help

249

figure out how to prove your alibi without the mistress being involved in any way." Bat tapped her chest. "That would be me. So I do my job and prove you innocent...but I still know about the mistress. You might sleep better at night if I died so you don't end up losing a chunk of money in a messy divorce. See how that goes, Kraven?"

"That's all kinds of fucked up."

"Welcome to my world. I take precautions."

"What's to keep them from bribing someone who works in this building to turn on you? You want me to think like one of your criminals? That's what I'd do. I'm assuming your clients are rich."

"I make sure they know I have a safety deposit box with all my notes. I might imply that upon my death, the box will be turned over to someone with access to major newspaper outlets. Most of them probably believe it. It's the few who don't that worry me."

"Is that true?"

She shook her head. "I'd never chance a bank being robbed and those kinds of notes getting out while I'm still alive. I'd be disbarred at best, sued for certain, and have so many hits out on me that I wouldn't survive a week. I also have Dusti to think about. They'd kill her out of spite. It's just a bluff I tell my clients."

"Has anyone ever come after you before?"

"Four years ago, my firm hired security for me because I was almost killed. I used to drive myself to and from work. Now I'm escorted."

"What happened?"

She swallowed hard, remembering. It was tough to talk about. "I had court. I was running late because it was raining. Traffic was shit, like normal, but it was worse that morning. One second I'm sitting at a red light and the next thing I know, a guy on a motorcycle pulls up between my car on the passenger side and the truck next to me. He pulled out a gun."

Kraven moved closer.

"I guess when he'd weaved through traffic, he'd tagged the truck's side mirror, so the driver started screaming at him, oblivious to the gun because it was pointed at me. He distracted the shooter for just a second. I slammed on the gas as he opened fire. Lucky for me, he was a bad shot and I wasn't creamed by traffic. He chased me for two blocks, firing at me. There was a cop who saw it go down and pursued. The motorcycle broke away and took off."

"Shit." Kraven reached out and gripped her arm, turning her toward him.

"Yeah. They dug out six bullets from my car. At first we thought it was road rage. That happens here. Then four hours later, they found the suspect next to his motorcycle in an alley. He'd been shot in the head execution style. My picture was found inside his pocket. The police realized it wasn't random after all. Whoever hired him to kill me was pissed enough to take him out when he failed, or maybe wanted to make sure he couldn't blab to the police. My firm immediately took action. Now I'm picked up every day and dropped off at night."

"That was nice of them."

Bat debated on telling Kraven the truth or not. She decided to be honest. "The police were all over me, trying to figure out which of my clients would send a hit man. They were certain that was the cause. My firm just wanted me to keep my mouth shut. We have a reputation to uphold. Clients come first and foremost. They offered me armed security and, in exchange, I refused to give up possible suspects to the police that would help them arrest anyone we'd defended."

"Was it one of your clients?"

She shrugged. "I have no clue. Probably. The police were never able to solve that one. It's still an open case."

"Your firm wanted to protect one of the killers you defended, rather than see justice for *you*. That's what you're saying."

"Alleged killers. We're not certain it was one of our clients. My firm did right by me, regardless of the reason. And that's only one reason for the security detail. The firm helped me upgrade to this place too. You have to have recommendations to get approved to buy in this building. I'm safe."

He growled low, a furious sound. *"Unbelievable."*

"There's that word again." Bat tried to break the tension with a little humor. "This coming from a guy who can make people think they're a Saint Bernard if he wants." She leaned in closer, peering into his eyes. "Woof!"

He didn't crack a smile the way she'd hoped. He looked furious.

"Lighten up, Kraven. I work for them. They aren't family or my friends. It's business."

"I don't like your world."

"Yours wasn't so hot either. Mine has delicious takeout food and they deliver. Speaking of, it should be coming soon."

He released her and spun away. "You need to pack."

She grit her teeth. He was stubborn as hell. It was exasperating.

Kraven left Bat in her kitchen and walked down the hallway to explore the rest of her home. The guestroom was to the immediate right. It was a small, impersonal space with a closet and bathroom. He exited and entered her bedroom. Her scent lingered strongly there, even after her absence.

The four-poster canopy bed with white scarves hanging from it surprised him. It looked exotic, instead of cold like the rest of her furnishings. A teddy bear lay on the plush overstuffed pillows on the bed. He crossed the room and lifted the brown animal, curious about the tattered old toy.

"My parents gave him to me."

He turned.

She stood in the doorway. "That's Puffin."

He arched his eyebrows. It was an odd thing to name a stuffed animal.

She seemed to understand. "I couldn't say muffin when I started to talk. Apparently, that's what I was going for. Puffin stuck."

He gently replaced it on the bed. A framed picture caught his attention next and he strode to her dresser to lift the eight-by-ten photograph. "Antina."

"I thought you never met my mom?" She came closer.

"I wasn't close to her but I saw her from afar a few times. Decker didn't want anyone to get too close to his only daughter, especially men. He had plans for her. She looks very much like her mother did. That's your father?" He studied the smiling blond man with his arms around Batina's mother. He could see a family resemblance. Bat and Dusti took more after their father in coloring.

Bat came up and took the frame from him, replacing it on the dresser. "Yes. That's one of the last pictures I have of them together. It was taken a week before they died. I got a new camera for my birthday." Emotion laced her voice. "I took it."

He wanted to pull her into his arms and hold her but she spun away, marching to an open doorway.

"I'm going to take a shower. Get the door when the food comes. It's already paid for."

"Do I tip the runner, Brian?"

"No. We're not supposed to do that with building employees. We give them holiday bonuses every year in lieu of tips. I think it's a stupid policy but I don't make the association rules." She closed the door behind her.

He strode across the room and tested the knob. It opened. He entered her master bathroom, which was bigger than the one attached to the other bedroom. Bat glared at him as he leaned against the doorway.

"Do you mind? I shut that for a reason."

"I came in here to make certain it was safe."

"You saw security downstairs. No one broke into my place, no one's hiding in here. We're fourteen floors up. It's not as if they can come in through a window."

"It's night, and that means GarLycans will feel safer taking to the skies."

"I highly doubt they would fly all this way to come after me."

"Aveoth could have a pact with Lycans in the area and may have assigned them a guardian. Decker *has* to know where you live. This is where they'd start if they're looking for us in L.A." He pushed away from the jamb and moved around her to the window. "Why don't you have curtains?" He stared out at the city lights below.

"Do you see any other buildings this high within clear view? They'd have to have a high-powered telescope to see in. Most of those other buildings are businesses, not personal homes. There's no reason for covering them."

"Go use the other bathroom. There are no windows."

"Are you serious?"

He inclined his head. "Yes."

"So you think a winged guy is going to bust in through a window and grab me while I'm in the shower?"

"I'd rather not take the chance. I'd hear glass breaking if they attacked but I want you where it will be harder for someone to take you until I have a chance to fight them."

255

She frowned. "You *are* serious."

"Yes."

"That's a real threat?"

"It is if Aveoth sends anyone from his clan to retrieve you."

She bit her lip but nodded. "Fine. Let me grab some of my things and I'll go use that shower."

He had expected her to argue more. "Thank you."

"I can be reasonable."

"Good."

"About some things. We both want to talk to Dr. Brent. We'll do that in the morning. He only keeps office hours during the day and I don't know where he lives. That means we should spend the night here."

"No way in hell."

"I want to sleep in my bed, not in some cheap motel."

"Who said we had to?"

"This is my city, Kraven. Nice hotels ask for identification and credit cards. We're supposed to stay under the radar if we're being hunted. That means leaving few traces. They're too afraid you'll throw a party and destroy the room if you pay in cash. That means staying in a seedy part of town where they take cash and don't give a damn what you do, as long as you don't leave a dead body in one of the rooms. Those places are *already* trashed. No thanks. I refuse to sleep on a bed where some hooker just earned fifty bucks."

"I'm certain I'll find somewhere suitable."

"You won't be able to pull the eye trick on them. Nice places have surveillance cameras. It'll be the airport all over again."

"Not all of them will."

"Bullshit. I'm not leaving. We can stay here tonight. I'm done moving around. We were in a car for almost twenty-four hours. Stick a fork in me. I'm done. Forget it, Kraven. I'm going to take a shower, eat, and sleep in my own bed." She approached him and fisted his shirt. "That's not up for debate. Play your cards right and I'll let you sleep with me. You can take the side next to the windows, since you think some rock dude is likely to come smashing through one."

He ignored her flippant tone. "You thought I was crazy about VampLycans being real. GarLycans *will* come after us if Aveoth tells them to. Fourteen floors up will make it easier to attack. Less witnesses to possibly see them."

"It's safety glass. Some stockbrokers live here."

He gave her a blank look.

Bat grinned. "Bad joke. Really bad. You could pick up a chair and smash it against those windows. They were made to withstand earthquakes. The only thing that will shatter them is a lot of bullets."

His eyebrows arched.

"Do your rock guys carry guns?"

"No."

"Then we should be good. Relax, Kraven."

"I need to keep you safe, Bat." She frustrated him with her inability to understand the depth of the danger she was in.

"I disagree that they'll come here. This is the last place they'll look for us. Hiding in plain sight and all that. My grandfather knows we're together and he'll figure you'll take me somewhere woodsy. It seems to be your thing. Either way, I'm sleeping in my bed tonight. It's a highly secured building. We're good."

"Damn it, Hellion."

She winked. "I'm going to take that shower in the other room. See? Compromise. We can sleep here tonight and argue about where to go tomorrow after we talk to Dr. Brent. His office hours start at eight a.m."

"Go." He needed time to think.

Bat released his shirt and collected her toiletries, striding out of the bathroom. He followed her down the hallway until she entered the other bathroom, waited for the door to close, then went out into the living room to retrieve his bag. He placed a call home to one of his friends.

"Yeah."

"Hey, Red. It's me. Is everything good there?"

"We haven't been attacked. You shouldn't call family."

"It's your enforcer line."

"True. Just keep it short."

Kraven already knew that. "I need you to relay a message. Tell my brother that I'm going to talk to the doctor. He'll know what that means. That'll take place in the morning. I'll call back tomorrow night with an update."

"You doing good?"

"We're keeping on the move." He glanced around Bat's condo. He hated to lie to Red, but he wasn't about to admit the little attorney might have talked him into making a stupid mistake like staying where they were until morning. "Thanks."

"Keep in contact."

"Will do."

Kraven hung up and removed the battery from the phone before replacing it in his bag. The doorbell rang. He approached it with caution, avoiding the peephole. "Who is it?"

"Brian."

The male had a very human pitch to his voice. Kraven unlocked the door, yanking it open, prepared to attack if necessary.

The guy who stood there looked young, perhaps just out of high school. He held a large open box packed with food containers. The smell of it filled the hallway.

Kraven glanced behind the kid, spotting no one else. "Thank you." He took the box.

"You're welcome, sir. Have a wonderful evening." Brian hurried away.

Kraven kicked the door closed and locked it with his free hand, sniffing at the food. He carried it to the long island and set it down. His stomach immediately rumbled. Bat had been right. The fast food they'd eaten for lunch hadn't done the trick of keeping his belly full. Her Chinese food did smell good.

He moved around her kitchen, opening cupboards. He located a few plates and silverware, placing them on her dining room table. He heard when the water turned off in her shower. Minutes passed before Bat came out of the guestroom. She only wore a towel wrapped around her middle.

"Great. The food came."

Kraven stared at all of her flushed, warm skin exposed and lost interest in food. He wanted *her*.

Bat ignored him as she entered the kitchen. "I'm starved."

"Me too."

She twisted her head, eyebrows arching. "Why'd your voice turn so deep?" She peered into his eyes. "Oh, I know that look—and forget it. I'm eating."

She wasn't going to drive him insane. He was already there. "Fine."

Chapter Fourteen

Bat was amused that Kraven had ordered her to put on a set of pajamas before they sat down to eat. She wasn't about to complain that he found her distracting when mostly naked. It had been a long time since a man had made her feel sexy. Kraven did.

That killed her good mood.

She was falling for him, and it spelled disaster. They were from two different worlds. *Hell, two different species.* She believed her mother had been a VampLycan but she really had nothing in common with Kraven. Her body was totally human. She hadn't inherited any traits, despite wishing she could control minds. It wasn't a bad thing that she couldn't shift. The idea of turning into a beast with hair didn't appeal to her in the least.

"What's wrong?"

She looked up from her food, the fork paused in midair. "Nothing."

He arched an eyebrow, staring at her. It was clear he didn't buy it.

"Nothing I'd like to share," she corrected.

"Bat."

"Kraven." She stabbed her fork into a chunk of sesame chicken. "I was just thinking about something. That's all. My thoughts are private."

"What are you plotting now?"

"Who says I am?"

"It's what you do. Tell me what put that expression on your face."

"I was worried about Dusti, of course."

"Don't lie to me. Something else is wrong. I told you she was fine."

He seemed to be getting to know her a little too well. She refused to admit it depressed her, thinking about when he finally went home. They could never make a relationship work between them. He didn't seem comfortable in her world and she never wanted to step foot in Alaska again.

She studied him across the table. Kraven was a very attractive man. There was no denying that. His eyes were unusual with their light blue intensity, and fascinating. She could stare into them all day. He had handsome features but no one would ever compare him to a pretty boy. The hair looked a thousand times better without the spikes. His broad shoulders and muscles couldn't be ignored either. He dwarfed her dining room table and looked out of place in her condo.

It was best if they just ended it for good.

A memory flashed of the day before on the plane, when she'd told him they wouldn't have sex again. That had lasted about five minutes or less. He'd kissed her on his lap and she'd ended up joining the mile-high club. It was impossible to think when he touched her. The sexual attraction was too strong.

She was screwed. *Literally and figuratively*, she admitted.

She'd invited him to share her bed. That had been a mistake, but one she didn't regret. The time they had would be over once her grandfather gave up whatever the hell he'd hoped to do. She wasn't going to agree to live with some guy who did a statue impression in his spare time.

"Bat," he urged. "I'm waiting."

"Fine." She looked up, holding his gaze. "It's been a rough few days. My life has changed and I'm evaluating what that means." That was close to the truth.

"I won't let anyone hurt you."

Who's going to protect me from a broken heart? She shoved a bite of chicken into her mouth. It tasted sweet for such a bitter moment. She's sworn she'd never fall in love with another man. The first time had been too painful. But she feared Kraven would make the past look tame in comparison.

"I'd do anything to protect you."

She swallowed. "Stop."

"What?"

"Don't say things like that."

"It's the truth."

"Well, it shouldn't be." She stabbed another piece of chicken with her fork. "Just like you urging me to trust you. Enough already."

"What's wrong?"

She lost her appetite. "I'm tired. That's all. I'm going to bed."

"You barely touched your food."

She set the fork down and pushed away from the table, standing. "I'm getting a headache. It's probably because we're finally out of that damn car. Like reverse motion sickness." She just needed to put some space between them to think. He was too damn appealing. "Make yourself at home and climb into my bed if you really think some rock guy is going to burst through the windows at some point."

263

Kraven frowned.

"Good night."

He rose fast and came around the table to block her from escaping. It wasn't a surprise. He wasn't the type to just let a woman walk away. She stared up at him.

"Hellion," he rasped. "What's wrong? Talk to me."

"Stop calling me that."

"You like giving me hell. It fits."

She'd give him that. "I just need some space, okay?"

"Why?" He reached out, seeming intent on stroking her arm.

"We just spent a really long time sharing a front seat. Isn't that enough?"

He tried to touch her again.

She backed away and bumped her ass on the edge of the table. "Don't."

"This again?"

"What?"

"Are you going to keep fighting what's between us?"

She held his gaze. "No. I learned that lesson yesterday. You can seduce me easily. I have the carpet burn on my ass to prove it."

That earned her a scowl. "You're hurt? Let me see."

"Forget it. It's not bad. I'm just a bit tender in that region. The skin isn't broken or anything, just a little red. I wasn't even aware of it until I used body soap. It burned a bit. Sitting in a car through three states probably didn't help either."

"I can heal it."

"No thanks."

"I want to take care of you."

She decided to just be honest. "That's the problem. I don't want to trust you. And I don't want you to make offers like that."

"Your life has changed, Bat, and there's no going back to the way it was."

"Bullshit." Her temper flared. "My grandfather will get a damn life or drop dead, whatever works, and you'll go back to Alaska. I belong *here*. You don't. This can't go anywhere. I don't want to depend on you for anything, Kraven." She glanced down his body, then back up. "So keep your hands to yourself and let's make it easier on both of us when the time comes to say goodbye."

"That's not going to happen."

"Yes, it will. You're Alaska and I'm Southern California. See the problem?"

His frown deepened.

"I'm a lawyer. You're an enforcer. I don't really even know exactly what your job entails but I have a good idea. You kick ass with your body for a living and terrify people. I use my mouth to defend the type of people you probably beat up. You can control minds and literally go all beast. I can't do that. Sex isn't everything—and that's really the only thing we have in common. It's not enough. It's all good at first but we have to get out of bed at some point. You know what I mean. Then what do we have? Nada. Nothing."

He inhaled and blew it out. "You're my mate, Bat."

"No." She shook her head. "Hell no."

He actually smiled. "I thought that myself when I realized what you were to me. I understand we're vastly different." His expression sobered. "It doesn't change the truth. We *are* mates. You're mine and I'm yours."

"I'm not an animal. I can't have a *mate*." She slid along the table to avoid touching him. "I refuse."

He sidestepped and pinned her with his big body. "It doesn't work that way."

"This is your problem, not mine. *No*."

"We've already begun the bonding."

She sagged against the table, happy it was behind her as she used it to support her weight. "What in the hell does that mean?"

"I've taken your blood, and you've had mine." His tone softened. "Remember when you had that headache after crossing the river? I fed you my blood to heal you. And I took a lot of yours when my back was torn up. I'm certain we're mates. You might not have the instincts I do, but trust me, it's a fact. We're going to be together."

She just gawked at him, speechless. It couldn't be. She wasn't an animal. Animals mated. People dated, made commitments, and married. Then divorced, more often than not.

"Easy, baby." He reached out and gently grasped her upper arms. "Breathe. You're hyperventilating."

266

She was. She forced her eyes closed and focused on her body. Her heart pounded and she was having a hard time catching her breath. She also felt faint. It made her panic. Passing out was for wimps, something she wasn't.

"Fuck." Kraven just scooped her into his arms.

She opened her eyes as he carried her through the living room, down the hallway, and into her bedroom. He took a seat on her bed, keeping her on his lap. He rested his chin on the top of her head, holding her close.

"It's going to be okay."

"No!" She shook her head and tried to wiggle off his lap.

He let her go. She got up and paced the carpet between the bed and dresser, shooting him a dirty look. "I'm not living in Alaska. My life is *here*. I busted my ass to make partner and guess what? I'm finally there. They're going to give it to me. I went through hell to earn it." She knew she was ranting but she couldn't stop. "Do you know how many times I had to kiss ass and overlook shit, when I really wanted to deck a few of those assholes I work for? One of them pats my ass when we share an elevator. All I want to do is break his damn fingers—but I don't. I smile like that prick is being cute. Then avoid being alone with him. I earn my way on my feet, not on my back!"

"Calm down, Bat."

She stopped. "Fuck you!"

He stood. "I understand."

"Do you?"

267

"Yeah." He crossed his arms over his chest. "I wanted a mate who would actually be *happy* when we found each other. You weren't my ideal person either."

That hurt but it seemed justified. She bit her lip and turned away, staring at the wall.

"We'll make this work." He came up behind her and wrapped his arms around her waist, pulling her close. "I *want* it to work."

She closed her eyes. He smelled so good, and it felt right having him hold her.

"I know you're scared." He leaned down so his soft words fanned his breath against the shell of her ear. "I am too. We're vastly different but life will never be boring, will it?"

She gripped his arms but just held on to him. "What are we going to do?"

"Fighting it won't work. I could return to Alaska and you could stay here once you're safe from Decker, but we'll both be miserable. You'll be thinking about me and I'll be thinking about you." His arms tightened and his voice took on a raspy tone. "I'll hunt down and kill *any* man who touches you, including that prick who palms your ass. I'm hoping you have enough Lycan blood to detest any man's touch that isn't mine, now that you know you have a mate. It should make you want to rip off his face and watch him choke to death on his own blood, instead of just breaking a few bones. That happens with mates. We only want each other, and there's never any cheating.

"I'll be the horniest, loneliest VampLycan in Alaska without you." He rested his head against hers. "I'll eventually snap and come after you. Not

268

to hurt you," he quickly amended. "I could never do that, but I can't promise rug burn won't occur again. Mates are meant to be together. You could send me away afterward but I'll always come back. I can't live without you for long."

She wanted to cry. Tears filled her eyes and she rapidly blinked to prevent them from spilling. He painted a sad picture for both of their futures.

"We could stay here, if it means so much to you."

That gave her hope. "Really?"

"I'd do anything for you."

She pulled her head away from his and peered up at him. "You won't miss your woods? Your family?"

"I will, but you come first."

It made her feel selfish.

"We can try it. It beats the alternative. You're mine, my little hellion."

"That's not the most endearing thing to call me."

He smiled. "It fits."

"You said that."

"I mean it. You like to give me hell. I don't mind."

"I don't want to get hurt," she confessed. "I've been there and done that."

"Hurting you would mean hurting myself. I'm not a masochist."

"Good to know."

"I don't know how strong our bond will become, with you being so human, but I'm hoping we can share emotions. What you feel, I'll feel. And vice versa. It tends to make mates really pay close attention to each other's needs and desires."

"That's weird."

"It's just the way it is." He shrugged. "How do you fear being hurt? I'd never hit you. You should know that by now, since you've pissed me off more times than I can count."

"No. You just have an abnormal obsession with my ass."

"I'll take any opportunity I find to touch it."

She laughed, some of the stress fading. She slowly turned in his arms. "I don't know how to handle this."

"We take it one day at a time and talk things out. Don't hide things from me."

"You seem pretty good at reading my emotions. That scares me. I worked hard to build walls to keep people distanced."

He eased one arm from around her and reached up, brushing her hair back from her face and stroking her cheek with his thumb. "You like to feel in control of everything. I can respect that, and understand it was something you needed to do to survive. Things have changed. I'm here now. I'm the one person you can always count on. There's no pain here, Bat. I'm safe."

"I want to believe you."

"Time will prove it. I'm not going anywhere."

She slid her arms around him and buried her face against his chest. "I'm going to freak out sometimes. I'm just being honest. I want to run."

"I'm a damn good tracker. I'll find you if you do. Just try to avoid it until I'm the only one who might come after you." He kissed the top of her head. "Let me protect you first from the real danger."

"Okay."

"Promise me."

"I do."

He pulled her against him tighter. "Will you eat now? I can hear your stomach rumbling still."

"Yeah. I could eat. I just..."

"What?"

She sighed.

"Open your mouth and spit it out. It's not so hard, Bat. You're great at expressing your thoughts when you're angry. We just need to work on you doing that when you're not."

"I know. I was thinking earlier about how difficult it's going to be when you return to Alaska, and how much it mattered to me. I just wanted to get away from you at that moment, put some space between us. You kind of messed that up when you got in my way."

"Give me the name of the man who hurt you and I'll kill him."

She jerked her head up, startled.

"You don't trust easy and you bolt when you start to feel too much for me. It doesn't take a genius to add it up." His lips tightened into a grimace. "Did he strike you? I've got no qualms about burying his ass. Just

271

give me a name and I'll take care of it as soon as I can leave your side for a day or two. He won't ever get near you again."

"It wasn't like that."

"How was it?"

It hurt her pride to even think about it but she found herself talking. "He was a conman. A good one, too. I never saw it coming. I should have. He was too charming, too smooth. You know? The perfect boyfriend. I actually felt lucky. Most of my friends bitched about the men they were with but I was with someone who always gave me thoughtful gifts and paid attention to me. All the while he was stealing my identity."

Kraven frowned. "I don't understand."

"He opened credit cards in my name and had the statements sent to another address. He paid them at first, got them to up the limits, and opened more credit lines in my name. I wasn't aware of any of it. One day he called me to say his sister had been in a bad car accident and he was on his way to Italy. That's where he claimed his family was from. He had a lovely accent. I never heard from him again. I tried to track him down, worried that something had happened. We were in love." She knew the bitterness sounded in her voice. "At least he had me *convinced* we were. I couldn't find anyone who'd ever heard of him, his family, or his sister. Everything he'd told me was bogus. He probably learned Italian taking night classes or something."

Kraven growled.

"Yeah. Everything about him was a lie. I was so involved in my busy life that I didn't exactly check into his too much. He'd supposedly moved here from Italy less than a year before we started dating, had told me his entire family and all his friends were over there. All I got to meet were the work friends he'd made since he'd started his job. They were as shocked as I was that he wasn't who he'd claimed. The police got involved because of the fraud. He'd racked up about forty grand in my name. I pressed charges. My credit was ruined for a while but I battled that until it was cleared.

"It turned out he'd done this to other women. It was his scheme. Wine and dine a woman, spend half a year building credit lines, all the while working on his next target. I got to see some of the charges on those credit cards. He'd bought jewelry and flowers that weren't for me. There were hotel charges. We didn't live together and I worked a lot. It was easy for him to date other women without me being aware. He was already working on his next marks."

"Is he in prison?"

"He was sentenced to sixty days in jail. His rich new wife paid restitution to some of his victims and hired him some great lawyers." It still made Bat angry. "He was good-looking and a damn good conman. I can attest to that. He latched on to some sixty-two-year-old woman with a lot of money. I felt bad for her. He dumped her as soon as her usefulness was up and took her for a shitload of money in the divorce settlement. She got screwed over way worse than I did."

"No wonder you have trust issues."

"He talked about our future all the time. I bought into it, Kraven. He said everything I wanted to hear."

"I'm nothing like him."

She nodded. "I know that." A grin broke. "You're not charming or smooth. You're more like a sledgehammer."

He chuckled. "Come eat. We'll stay here tonight." He glanced at the windows. "I just wish you had curtains."

"I can buy some but no one can see in." She swallowed. "Unless they can fly. Do you really think we'll be attacked by Gargoyles?"

"I hope not. GarLycans would try like hell to avoid flying in a city this size. We've survived all these years because we take great care to protect our existence."

Kraven led Bat back into her dining room and helped her sit. He retook his seat across from her. It was a bad idea to stay in her condo but she needed a little stability tonight. One night hopefully wouldn't hurt. Tomorrow he'd talk her into moving locations after they spoke to Dr. Brent.

He needed to gain her trust. The idea of her running away from him made Kraven break out in a sweat. She knew the human world far better than he did. It was a miracle no Lycan pack or Vampire nest had ever attacked her or Dusti. The talk with the doctor might shed some light on it. She smelled human but her blood carried a slight scent of other. At some point she had to have suffered cuts. Everyone did.

He watched her eat and went through the motions of filling his own stomach. His thoughts were elsewhere. The things she'd shared about her past helped him understand some of her resistance to let him get close. Betrayal was tough to recover from. He'd barely known the woman who'd tried to stab him in the heart. Bat implied she'd spent at least six months with the man who'd used her. She'd fight Kraven at every turn.

Something his mother always said floated through his thoughts. *Nothing worthwhile in life is ever easy.* Those words finally made sense. Bat came with a complicated past but he had motivation and desire to stick it out.

They finished eating and Bat offered to clean up. He shook his head.

"I'll do it."

"Let's make a deal, okay?"

He waited.

"I'll put away the leftovers while you shower. I'm sure you want to take one after all that driving you did. We'll meet up in the bedroom in about ten minutes."

He turned his head, studying the door.

She easily read his concerns. "No one is going to break in."

"VampLycans can get past your security downstairs, Bat."

"I promise to haul ass shouting for you if someone so much as knocks. Okay?" She lifted her hand and crossed her finger over her chest. "I swear. I also won't run around with scissors or do anything dangerous."

She was cute as hell. "Fine."

"I left my shampoo and conditioner in the guest bathroom. There are fresh towels under the sink."

"I'll hurry."

"Okay."

He strode over to the door and lifted his bag, double checking that her locks were secure. Bat began clearing the table as he went to the guestroom. The desire to keep her close was strong but she was right. He wanted a shower. It would just be a fast one.

He left the bathroom door open and dumped his bag on the counter. He stripped quickly and turned on the hot water. The stall wasn't as large as his one at home. Humans were so much smaller. He sighed, stepping inside the confined space.

Chapter Fifteen

Bat closed the fridge and glanced around to make certain she'd thrown away all the empty containers. The counters were clear. She was heading toward the hallway when the phone rang. She switched directions, walking over to the machine. The readout flashed the number and name of her caller.

She snatched up the receiver. "Hello, Jacob."

"You're back? I thought you'd be gone for a few more days."

She opened her mouth to explain but he cut her off before she could say a word.

"I'm glad I reached you. I was just going to leave a message and hope that you checked your machine daily. Are you familiar with Travis Bales?"

"The name sounds familiar."

"He lives in your building and he's a new client. He's out on bail."

That news didn't shock her. It wasn't the first time one of the building's tenants had had trouble with the law. "What was he charged with?"

"We'll discuss that in the morning. We're holding a seven o'clock meeting at the office. Don't miss it."

She winced. No way would Kraven agree to that. He didn't even want to stay in her condo for one night. "I was in a plane crash."

"What?" Jacob gasped.

"It's a long story. I'm not going to be able to make that meeting. I have no idea when I'll be returning to work. I have to go see my doctor first thing in the morning." It wasn't exactly a lie. She planned to talk to Dr. Brent.

"Mr. Bales is a close friend of Warren's. You know what that means."

She clenched her teeth. Warren Otis was a one of their special clients. He brought in a lot of referrals and she was pretty sure he was a major player in organized crime. It could kill her future with the firm if she let their big fish down.

"Warren personally called me and insisted you take care of Mr. Bales, Batina. I've been trying to reach you all day to tell you to get your ass back home immediately but you didn't answer your damn cell. I was desperate enough to call your home phone, hoping you at least checked *those* messages. Get patched up first thing tomorrow. Mr. Bales is having a little cocktail party tomorrow to meet with the team that will represent him. Wheel yourself there or go on crutches. I don't really give a damn. It's at six sharp inside your building. It's being held in some lounge. I assume you know where that is? Be there. It's not a request. Warren will be there too. Am I clear?"

It irritated her that her boss didn't seem to give a shit that she could have possible injuries. He didn't even ask. That wasn't a surprise. "Crystal." She grit her teeth. "I'll take pain pills if I have to."

"That's the spirit. Just don't take too many of them. Six sharp. And Batina? Don't fuck this up." He ended the call.

She slammed the phone down and spun, bumping right into Kraven's damp chest.

278

He gripped her as she stumbled back. He looked furious when she looked up at his face. "Why did you answer the phone? Now someone knows you're here."

"It was one of the partners at my law firm. I looked at the caller ID first." She lowered her gaze, appreciating the sight of him with just a towel wrapped low on his hips. He had an amazing body. She wanted to reach out and touch him. And there was really no reason not to. He said they were mates. She might as well take advantage of the perks of having one. Sex sounded like more fun than stewing over what a jerk Jacob could be.

He shook his head, still glowering.

"I wish I *hadn't* answered it. Does that help?"

She reached out and used her fingertip to catch a drop of water that had threatened to fall off his taut nipple. She brought it to her lips and sucked on it, peering at him. His eyes narrowed. She put her other hand on his biceps and rubbed. Her finger left her mouth so she could flatten that palm on his chest.

"Don't do that. What was so damn important that you had to get that call?"

"It was work."

His eyes narrowed. "I'm pissed at you."

"How is that working out for you?"

"Stop touching me and avoiding my questions. What was that about?"

"Work. I'm not lying." She released him and backed up, skirting him and strolling down the hallway. "You look really good though. Sexy."

"I hate avoidance, Bat. And we need to leave now that you've answered that phone." He followed her.

She stopped and turned to confront him when she got inside her bedroom. "It wasn't anything related to my grandfather, so it doesn't concern you. Let's just go to bed."

"Did it ever cross your mind that it would be a smart move for Decker to grab one of your bosses and make them call you to find out where you are?"

"No. Because I'm not paranoid."

"Damn it, Bat. You're in *danger* and every human you know can be mind-controlled!"

"Give me a break."

"It's possible."

"I don't want to fight with you. Are we having sex or not?"

A muscle in his jaw twitched. "Not."

"Fine."

"I won't be manipulated. That's what you're doing. You know you screwed up and you're trying to seduce me to get your way. We need to leave."

His accusation stung, as if she only wanted him for that reason. "I can't believe you just said that to me."

"Isn't it true?"

"No. You said we were mates and you gave me the long spiel about what would happen if we denied it. You have an amazing body. Excuse the hell out of me for wanting you. My mistake. Let me give you some advice for the future—you'll get laid a lot more if don't open your mouth." She took a few steps, paused, and shot him a dirty look. "I wasn't trying to use you. I was trying to get lost in you. Think about that."

She stormed over to the bed and yanked back the covers, climbing under them in her pajamas. She punched the pillow, rolling on her side until her back was to him.

"Bat."

"Tell it to the hand." She threw up her arm and flipped him off. "I'm going to sleep. You can take the floor or the guestroom but you're not welcome in my bed anymore. Invitation revoked."

"We need to get the hell out of here."

"*You* leave." She dropped her hand and curled her arms against her chest. "I think I'd rather take my chances with some rock guys crashing through my windows. Though I highly doubt that will happen. I'm going to sleep. I'm tired of all the bullshit I've been through."

He loudly sighed.

She closed her eyes and snuggled against her soft mattress. "Turn off the light. Maybe that will fool the flock of Gargoyles you believe are flying around outside into thinking we're not home."

"Sarcasm is not an attractive trait."

"Neither is being an asshole, so I guess we're even."

"You drive me crazy!"

"We have something in common."

"It's safer if we leave."

"It's safer for you if you shut up and let me go to sleep."

"I'm getting dressed. I'll be right back."

"Go for it."

He did flip off the light on his way out of her bedroom. She relaxed, trying to slow her breathing. They were fire and water. The two just didn't go well together, one always putting the other out. She couldn't win with him. It was just one argument after another. She liked a good fight inside the courtroom but not in her bedroom.

"Damn," she whispered.

She was falling in love with Kraven and it wasn't going to end well. Their relationship was doomed. It didn't come as a surprise but it still hurt. The urge to cry surfaced but she was afraid he'd hear her, or worse, see it. She'd be damned if she gave him the satisfaction of knowing how he affected her. She had her pride.

Kraven put on a pair of black sweatpants and ran his finger through his wet hair, shoving it back. Bat had been clear she wasn't about to allow him to take her from her home. He brushed his teeth in the guest bathroom and glared at his reflection in the mirror. Razors hadn't been packed so he'd need to buy some. His facial hair grew fast if he didn't remove it daily.

His thoughts drifted inward as he stepped back from the counter. Her words echoed in his head.

"I wasn't trying to use you. I was trying to get lost in you. Think about that."

He was. She'd looked upset when she'd gotten off the phone, and he'd picked up anger and stress in her voice. He hadn't heard both sides of the conversation but his mate was clearly upset. She'd looked to him for comfort. It was possible she linked sex to that need.

He'd fucked up by getting angry with Bat. She was just so damn naïve about the danger she faced. Anyone with a lick of sense wouldn't have answered that phone. Her carelessness made him see red. He'd said things he regretted.

He flipped off the bathroom light and crept down the hallway, checking out her apartment to give her a little time to cool off. They'd just fight again otherwise. He didn't blame her for being angry.

He walked to the large windows in the living room, staring out at the city. He leaned against the wall next to the glass and admired the view. He could see why Bat might enjoy it. All those lights were spectacular.

He and Bat may as well come from two different planets. The parts of the world they lived in were vastly dissimilar. She liked the city. He craved the woods. She'd been raised human. She made phone calls to get things done. He just did everything himself. It was going to be tough to find some kind of middle ground they could both be happy with. *If it's even possible. I'm starting to doubt it.*

Movement over the top of a distant building made him tense but he identified it as a helicopter. It wasn't a threat. He scanned the sky but didn't see anything else that shouldn't be there. Aveoth might hesitate to send any guardians into Los Angeles to search for Bat. Humans had cameras and surveillance videos all over the place. It would be impossible to avoid being spotted on all of them. He just didn't want to discount the possible threat.

His skin prickled and tingled. Kraven clenched his teeth. The stress made him want to shift and run for miles to burn off his excess energy. There was nowhere to do it inside her small condo. Bat would probably have a fit if he shed any fur on her expensive floors, or worse, he'd terrify her if she got out of bed and saw him on four legs. She hadn't exactly taken it well when Carver had shown her the truth of what they could do with their bodies.

His possible future flashed in his head and it appalled him. Bat would want him to stay in the city. He *had* offered, so that was his own damn fault. He'd wanted her to calm down after breaking the news of them being mates. Part of him had hoped she'd understand what it would cost him, but he kept failing to take into account how little she knew about VampLycans. There would be nowhere for him to run. He'd be trapped inside her home when he shifted, the only safe place away from prying eyes or discovery. No running free in the woods. No hunting to keep his skills sharp.

He'd also have to visit every damn Lycan pack and Vampire nest in the area to let them know not to fuck with his mate. They might target Bat otherwise, when they discovered him living in their city, viewing him as a threat. He stared out into the night, pondering how many asses he'd have to kick or kill. He'd have no idea how many there were until he'd learned the territory he was about to become a part of.

He'd have to do it alone, without backup. It would be worse if he asked his cousin Red to fly out and help him. The less intelligent packs and nests might think they were trying to claim the area and declare outright war if they had to deal with more than one VampLycan. It would start a shit storm. Bat wouldn't be allowed out of his sight, day or night. That would probably piss her off, not that it would dissuade him. Her safety came first.

The impulse to shift became stronger so he turned his head away from the glass and forced his body to relax. He slowed his breathing and tried to focus on something else. Bat was his mate. She was worth anything he might have to do or give up. They'd argue all the time but that sounded better than returning to Alaska alone. Misery would drive him to return to her within two weeks or less.

He pushed away from the wall and quietly strode down the hallway. He paused inside the bedroom door, his gaze fixing on Bat. Her slow, steady breathing assured him she slept peacefully. Kraven crept forward and just watched his mate sleep. Exhaustion had wiped her out. *So damn fragile. I was too hard on her. I need to stop doing that by remembering this is all new to her.*

He backed away and moved to the bedroom window, staring out at another sparkling view of Bat's beloved city. Vehicles filled the streets, their head and brake lights helping him determine which directions they traveled. He lowered his chin, watching humans walk on the sidewalks far below. There were too many of them, even later in the evening. Vampires were out hunting but the humans were oblivious to the danger of becoming a quick meal.

He didn't belong in a city, and he sympathized with his mate about how she'd feel living in Howl. The only difference between them was he didn't fear anyone or anything in her home. Carver's shifting had frightened Bat. She'd be surrounded by people who transformed. In time she'd adjust, but it wouldn't be easy for her. The only saving grace would be Dusti.

That perked him up. Bat would want to remain close to her sister. No way would Drantos leave home to move to the city. He couldn't. Their parents would throw a shit-fit. His older brother would one day lead their clan. Kraven glanced back at Bat, wondering if the love for her sister would make her agree to move to Alaska.

The hope quickly died. It would be a shitty thing to do, using Dusti to persuade her to make that choice.

"Fuck."

Bat stirred. He clamped his lips together. She rolled onto her stomach and her breathing assured him she slept on. He stared back out at the city lights.

Kraven suddenly felt trapped, caged by glass and all those tall buildings. A shudder racked his body. The prickling sensation along his arms returned and he allowed his fangs to slide down to help relieve some of the pressure his desire to shift forms caused. Some hair growth happened on his face, arms, and chest. He closed his eyes and concentrated on his breathing.

Breathe In. Out. In. Out. Calm. I can do this for my mate. I'm not trapped.

Kraven snapped his eyes open and scanned the sky again, searching for danger. He almost wished Aveoth would send a guardian. A good fight would work better than going for a run, something he couldn't do. But he didn't spot any danger. And unlike Bat, he wasn't tired. He had too much on his mind to sleep.

The doctor's office would open at eight. He guessed Dr. Brent would be a Lycan who Antina had turned to for medical help when her youngest daughter had been born flawed. A Vamp would keep night hours. He glanced at the clock on the nightstand.

He'd wake Bat up around six a.m. to give them plenty of time to get ready, eat, and leave her time to pack a bag. They wouldn't be returning to her condo. She might put up a fight but he'd win. Her safety came first and foremost.

It's going to be a long night.

He left the bedroom every ten minutes, making a security check throughout Bat's home, before returning to keep close to his mate while she slept. Eventually the sun began to peek over the horizon of buildings. Kraven rolled his shoulders and stretched. It was time to wake her up.

Chapter Sixteen

Bat watched Kraven take the lead as they exited the elevator. He waved his hand behind his back, indicating she should stick close and stay behind him. He acted like one of her bodyguards on high alert. He even paused to run a sweeping gaze down both sides of the corridor. It was kind of cute, if a little annoying. She decided to go with being amused. So far they'd avoided an argument, even when he'd informed her to pack. She had done it just to shut him up.

He hadn't been happy about her suggestion to take her car. No way would she trust some stranger with their bags while they talked to Dr. Brent, and toting them around a large medical building sounded like a pain in the ass.

Kraven had examined her car and sniffed at it.

"I'll assume you're worried about a bomb. That would imply blowing someone up. I thought you said my grandfather wants me very much alive."

He'd shot her a dirty look. "You have other enemies. We're around too many humans."

"They'd have a really tough time gaining access to the parking area. I'll say it again. I live in a high-security building for a reason, Kraven. It's so I know I can park my car without anyone fucking with it. Do you want to talk to Dr. Brent or not? I'd like to get there before he starts seeing patients. The idea of waiting in the reception area for an hour or so doesn't appeal to me."

"Which way?"

His voice brought her back from her thoughts of earlier that morning to the present. She walked around him and strode left down the hallway. Kraven growled low and lengthened his stride to get ahead of her again. He spun and gripped her hips firmly.

"Stay behind me."

"I've been here hundreds of times. It's not dangerous. Most of his patients are kids and pregnant women. You're being paranoid. Do you want to talk to Dr. Brent or not?"

"That's why we're here."

"Let's go."

He released her and took a step back. "At least stay at my side." His nose flared. "I smell Vampire."

"Okay." She took a deep breath and continued down the hall to room B2. She opened the door and entered the waiting room. There wasn't a receptionist at the desk but instead, a sign to push a bell for assistance. No patients had arrived yet. She reached out to put her finger on the bell but Kraven grabbed her wrist.

"No."

"This is how we're seen. Push and wait. Just like the sign says. Dr. Brent will come out as soon as he's able."

He kept hold of her as he moved to the inner door and tried to open it. It was locked.

Bat sighed. "That's also why you push the button."

Kraven gripped the handle tighter and the metal creaked, then made a popping noise. He shoved open the door and dragged her into another hallway. He sniffed the air and pulled her forward. He paused at one of the doors and suddenly released her.

He threw open the door, storming inside.

Bat peered into Dr. Brent's personal office. He sat behind his desk doing something on his computer.

His head snapped up and he stared at Kraven—then his mouth opened and sharp fangs flashed as he loudly hissed.

A second later his chair clattered to the floor as the older man seemed to leap backward in some crazy acrobatic way that shouldn't have been possible. He landed feet first on his five-foot-tall file cabinets in the corner.

Dr. Brent had fangs.

Bat gawked at them. Their family doctor hissed again, reminding her of a pissed-off cat. He didn't spare her a glance. His full attention was on Kraven. Some of the shock wore off as long seconds passed and it sank in that Dr. Brent might actually be a Vampire. Her gaze lowered down his body. He was sure tan though for someone who should burn up from the sun.

"I have questions, and you *will* answer them," Kraven snarled.

His harsh tone caused Dr. Brent to spin on his feet and claw at the wall, as if he wanted to tear through it to get away. Sheer terror showed on his expression as he twisted his head to stare wide-eyed at Kraven, and he *did* do some damage to the drywall. Small chunks of it rained down onto the file cabinets.

290

"Stop it!" Bat had known Dr. Brent most of her life. Whatever he was, she felt bad for him in that second.

Morton Brent was usually an easygoing man with a good sense of humor. She'd always liked him. It bothered her to see him terror-stricken, almost as much as it bothered her to learn he had sharp fangs.

"It's okay, Dr. Brent."

His gaze turned to her and he stopped trying to dig through the wall. He stilled completely. She wasn't even sure if he were breathing as she stared back. The fangs were still present and really disturbing.

Kraven growled.

She reached his side and threw her arm out, smacking his stomach. "Enough!"

Dr. Brent turned to face them but kept pressed tight to the wall from his perch on the cabinets. His arms raised in a defensive motion, as if he feared being strangled when he covered his throat with both hands. It looked ridiculous.

Bat glanced at Kraven. He glared at the doctor, his expression intimidating. She looked back at Dr. Brent.

"Get him away from me," Dr. Brent pleaded.

Bat stepped in front of Kraven, putting her body between him and the doctor. "It's okay. Nobody is going to hurt you."

"He's a Vampire. Get behind me, Bat!" Kraven gripped her arm.

She spun on him and tore out of his grasp. "Stop grabbing me! I know Dr. Brent. He's never hurt me."

Kraven refused to stop glaring at the doctor. "Did you see the way he moved? The fangs?"

"I did, and I'm duly freaked-out by that. Now stop being a bully. He's scared. Can't you see that? Back off. Let me handle this." She turned, took a step closer to the desk, and tried to remain calm. "Hi, Dr. Brent. I'm sorry for showing up without an appointment. This is Kraven. He wants to ask you some questions about my mom. He isn't going to hurt you. Can you come down from there?"

Dr. Brent closed his mouth and licked his lips. He didn't remove his hands from around his throat or climb down though. "He's going to kill me."

"No, he's not." Bat motioned with her hand for Kraven to back off. She wasn't sure if he did it or not, her focus remaining on Dr. Brent. "Please come down."

"No."

Kraven was a big man. She understood how he could frighten someone much smaller in stature. "You were friends with my mom," she reminded Dr. Brent. "Dusti and I went to go visit our grandfather in Alaska but then—"

"What?" Dr. Brent lowered his hands. "You did *what*? Why didn't anyone mention that to me?"

"There was no reason to, unless Dusti was going to be gone for an extended amount of time and would have run out of her shots."

Dr. Brent jumped off the file cabinet and landed gracefully on his feet behind his desk. "I feel faint. I need to sit." He bent, lifted his chair—and surprised Bat when he straightened, holding a gun. It must have been attached to the back of it somehow. He trained it on Kraven. "This will blow a nice hole in your heart and it will take you time to recover, VampLycan. Bat, get away from him right now! Your grandfather's people are a danger to you."

Bat didn't budge.

Kraven tensed but he held still. "Don't shoot. You could hurt Bat by accident."

"I'm aiming at you, and I wouldn't miss, VampLycan."

"Kraven is with another clan. He's not one of my grandfather's." Bat managed to keep her voice calm. "Lower the gun. Please? He's been protecting me."

Dr. Brent scowled. "You can't trust them. They'll just want to use you. Your mother lived in terror that one day her father would send men after you."

"Please put down the gun." She moved over a foot so it was pointed at her instead of Kraven. "Why didn't my mom tell us the truth?"

Dr. Brent lowered the weapon slightly but he still appeared scared. "She tried a few times, Bat, but you never took it well."

She gaped at him. "She did?"

The doctor sighed. "Yes. She tried to tell you for the first time when you were twelve, right after your grandfather found you the second time. You thought she'd lost her mind. Your mother had to wipe your memory of the discussion she'd had with you. You're mostly human, and only inherited a little of her Vampiric bloodlines. You had no natural immunity to mind control. She hated to do it but you left her with no choice."

293

Dr. Brent leaned forward and placed the gun on the desk. He collapsed into the chair. "Your sister is the opposite. Antina couldn't wipe her memories. She learned that when Dustina was a small child. Antina could stop her from throwing tantrums and make her go to sleep, but your sister remembered us testing different blood substitutes on her. She eventually resisted coming to my office so your mom would put her to sleep and bring her in. Eventually she forgot, as most very young children do. We were mindful of every word and action in front of Dustina. I couldn't wipe her memories either. I tried but she has a very strong mind. I could make her hold still but she remembered everything."

"My mom really told me, Dr. Brent?" Bat felt confused and hurt.

"Yes. Antina had no choice but to make you forget, Bat. She tried to tell you again when you were sixteen and more mature. She shifted in front of you to prove her words." He paused. "You were hysterical at first. Then you were angry and wanted to confront your grandfather, to end your mother's fear of what he might one day do. You thought that telling your grandfather you refused to be gifted to a GarLycan would just end the problem. You were raised human, and were already set on becoming a lawyer. You mentioned all the laws he'd be breaking if he attempted to force that kind of life on you, swearing you'd see him in prison... You're very stubborn, Batina. You always have been. There was no reasoning with you. Antina had to wipe your memory again."

Bat remembered her teenage years. She'd definitely been difficult, at best.

"Antina always believed you'd be ready at some point but she also wanted her daughters to have normal, happy lives for as long as possible.

294

Once she died, I watched out for you both. She would have wanted me too."

"You did a shit job." Kraven stepped close enough to press against Bat. One of his arms wrapped around her middle. "Decker almost got his hands on both of them."

Dr. Brent glared at Kraven. "They always tell me when they take trips." His expression softened when he looked at Bat. "I would have prevented you from going to Alaska if you'd mentioned it."

"You wouldn't have been able to," she stated simply. "I was set to go. I thought our grandfather might leave us money in his will and I wanted it for Dusti."

Dr. Brent tapped his fingers on the desk. "Remember when child services came for Dustina right after your parents' deaths? Who do you think *suggested* you sell the house and move where you did until your sister turned eighteen? I arranged it so you'd be safe. You wanted to fight them and stay here, Bat. But that damn case worker had a natural immunity to mind control. It's rare but it happens with some humans. I realized I couldn't make her back off the case, and it might land suspicion on *you* if I just had her killed. So I took you both out of the equation. I sent you into a territory that was out of her jurisdiction but where I had alliances, so you'd both still be safe."

Bat let that information sink in. "You fucked with my head?"

"I did what was best for you and Dustina."

She fisted her hands, the urge to slap him strong. "What else did you fuck with my head over?"

"Nothing, Batina." Dr. Brent sighed. "I only did it that once, and I would have called that an emergency."

She couldn't deny that. The state had wanted to take her sister away from her. It had worked out well enough in the end. They would have had to sell the house anyway. She calmed down a bit. "So my mom really was a VampLycan."

Dr. Brent leaned forward and placed his hands flat on the desk. "Antina came to me four days after Dusti was born. I didn't even know a VampLycan was in the area. Your sister was very ill and Antina was terrified to take her to a hospital. She'd birthed her at home with the aid of a midwife and controlled the woman's mind to help her avoid blood tests or anything else that would have revealed the truth. Dusti was lethargic and your mother suspected she'd gained more Vampire traits than Werewolf ones."

Bat let that sink in. She opened her mouth but Dr. Brent continued before she could ask questions.

"I ran my own tests on Dustina and concluded that your mother was right. Your sister was the first baby with Vampire traits I'd ever treated. The last, too. It was hell trying to determine what to do for her. Dusti didn't develop fangs so she had no way to feed herself. At first your mother would mix blood in with Dusti's formula, then her drinks, but we later switched to the shots as your sister grew older."

"Why would you help a VampLycan?" Kraven eased his tight hold on Bat but kept his arm around her.

"I felt sorry for her." Dr. Brent seemed to relax a little. "Antina was on her own with two small children and only a human to help her protect them. She was terrified other VampLycans sent by her father would come after her family."

"Who helped her?" Bat asked.

"Your father."

"Dad knew what she was?"

He nodded. "Yes. Antina took blood from him but she wouldn't give him hers. It helped her smell human. She'd wear a lot of his shirts to mask her scent as well. He came in with her the first few years you were my patients, until he learned to trust that I wouldn't harm his family. He amused me. He carried holy water and a stake, as if they could ward me off if I attacked." He smiled slightly. "Your mother asked me to pretend to fear them. She was very protective of his feelings, and particularly his desire to believe he could protect her. Your father was a brave human."

Tears filled Bat's eyes, memories of her parents surfacing. Her father had known, yet he'd loved his family, despite them being different. He'd been a wonderful dad. Now she tried to picture him facing off against a Vampire because he loved his wife and kids. It didn't surprise her.

Dr. Brent's expression softened even more. "I know this sounds wrong but I'm glad they died together. I doubt either would have survived long without the other. They couldn't complete a formal blooded mating bond because your mother feared it would put a target on his back if he carried her scent, but you wouldn't know it from the way they loved each other. Antina planned to seal the blood bond with him once both you girls were out of the house. She feared losing him to old age if she didn't. He was my patient too. Vampire blood can heal. She'd rush him to me anytime he was ill."

"Dad was sick?"

"Nothing serious. She'd panic every time he caught a cold. Both you and Dustina inherited her immunity traits but he had none. He'd run a fever and she'd bring him to me. Humans can receive small amounts of blood from my kind without it doing them any lasting harm or staying in their system beyond a few hours. It heals them though. He'd be cured within minutes."

"So those shots you give Dusti are blood?"

"It's a special plasma mix I created just for her. I had to adjust it over the years as she grew. It's also laced with a light sedative. It was pure hell inventing something she wouldn't have to keep refrigerated that could last weeks without spoiling. That's why I insist on seeing her at least once a month. It's a powder substance, and the liquid I use is the sedative and a preservative." He paused. "Where *is* Dustina?"

"She's safe." Kraven's tone softened, as if his anger had edged back. "My brother is her mate."

"I see. He'll be sharing his blood with her then. That's good. It will keep her stabilized." Dr. Brent pulled his chair closer to the desk. "Would you mind taking a seat? You're making me nervous, VampLycan."

Kraven actually released Bat and pulled two chairs closer to the desk. He sat, and Bat took the other seat. "You may call me Kraven."

"I'd rather not." Dr. Brent studied Bat. "You never physically needed my help to survive. I mean, I'd give you checkups. You're remarkably human unless your blood is spilled. You faintly carry the Werewolf scent."

"Lycan," Kraven interjected. "We hate that term. Why didn't any of the packs or your kind attack Bat?"

298

"Antina made bargains with the local pack masters, and she held the gratitude of my nest. We're the dominant nest in this city. The smaller ones knew they'd face retribution from us if the girls were harmed in any way."

Bat leaned back in her chair, confused.

Kraven didn't seem to be. "Grateful for what?"

"At first Antina kept herself and her babies hidden but she couldn't keep them housebound forever. They needed to go to school and that put them out in the open. She knew she could trust me to help her find a solution. I became a doctor because I believe in saving lives, not taking them."

"Why are you a suckhead?" Kraven's tone became rude.

Dr. Brent hesitated. "My nest master was a fourteenth-century Vampire. He turned anyone he found useful, willing or not. I wasn't asked if I wanted to become a Vampire. He needed a doctor, so he grabbed me thirty-six years ago after I ended my shift at the hospital. My old master lost his arm during a sword fight and believed I could find a way to get him a new one. His had turned to ash seconds after it was severed."

"Did you?" Kraven asked.

He nodded. "I was horrified. He killed people and chopped off their arms, forcing me to try to attach them to him. It took me months but one finally took. I mastered attaching the nerves. His blood did the rest. I thought he'd kill me at that point but he loaned me out to the Werewolves. I would set bones so they didn't heal wrong, and remove bullets so they didn't walk around with them inside their bodies. Especially after metal detectors began to be used more frequently by

299

humans. The packs like to keep a low profile, not trigger alarms and be subjected to body searches. I made my old master money and earned him favors from various packs."

"That's why your master allowed you to treat Antina's children? He wanted favors?" Kraven leaned forward a bit.

"I never told him about them. He gave me enough blood so I was awake and mobile during the day but he never came here himself. I feared he'd steal the children from her. He could have used them to force Antina to assassinate other masters around the city." Dr. Brent grimly regarded Bat. "He would have ended up killing you both, and possibly your mother, when he got what he wanted from her. I refused to let that happen. He was a real bastard."

"Was?" Kraven leaned even closer.

"Antina killed him, earning her the gratitude of every Vampire in the city. He terrorized my nest, plus the other ones in the area. He was the oldest and most powerful master in this territory. He forced everyone to pay him tribute."

"What does that mean?" Bat glanced between them.

Dr. Brent grimaced. "He would literally make us kiss his feet, for one. And he took whatever he wanted from all Vampires. Money. Property. Hell, he even stole a few brides from another nest, and wiped it out completely when they complained, just to set an example to others. Antina knew he'd use her daughters against her if he ever learned of your existence. She killed him for all of us, as well as for her own safety. She made a deal with the nests, including a few members of mine, before she let her presence be known to my old master. You VampLycans are devious and brilliant. As was her plan."

"Which was?" Kraven asked.

"I hated my master, and Antina figured some of the others in my nest might feel the same. None were strong enough to take him on, and the Vampire Council would have come after us anyway for killing our sire. They would've wiped out our entire nest as punishment."

"There's a Vampire Council?" Bat was stunned.

"Yes. There's no law against someone else killing a master if they don't belong to the nest he created." Dr. Brent smiled. "Antina was beautiful and a VampLycan—two things he couldn't resist when she offered herself to him as a lover. She played on his vanity to get his guard down and took his head before he knew what happened."

"My mom cheated on my dad?" Bat was horrified.

"No." Dr. Brent chuckled. "She just pretended she wanted to join forces with my old master, to be the most powerful couple and rule the city. His greed was his downfall. He would be in charge of the Vampires and she could gain control of the packs. They went to his bedchamber together but she walked out alone. It was done, and every Vampire in the city owed her their gratitude." He looked pointedly at Kraven. "Her children have always been safe with us."

Kraven didn't seem appeased. "What about the Lycans?"

"They were treated badly by my old master. They owed gratitude to Antina as well after his death. Lycan packs no longer have to pay money to live in peace with us. It was one of the terms she made with the nests. Peace between the two and no more cash demands. She left them alone

301

and they gave a wide berth to her and her children. Her family was deemed off-limits by all."

"Wasn't anyone tempted to go after her daughters once Antina died?" Kraven shifted his weight in the chair, making it creak. "No one likes VampLycans."

"They are weak and harmless. It wasn't worth pissing me off."

Kraven arched an eyebrow.

"I treat a lot of the packs. It's why I keep day hours. They can't go to human hospitals and few of them have the patience to go to medical school. You know how they are."

Kraven nodded.

"*I* don't know. Clue me in," Bat stated.

"Werewolves are moody creatures."

"Lycans," Kraven corrected. "And I wouldn't say they're moody, so much as intolerant of sitting still for long hours. They enjoy working physically demanding jobs, rather than careers that call for years of schooling."

"It bores them," Dr. Brent added. "So I give them ultrasounds to see if their next pup is a girl or a boy. They enjoy finding that out. Sometimes there are breech births. I make sure the mothers don't suffer and the pups live. Parents like to know their pups are healthy and growing strong. I examine their children to alleviate their worries. I dig out bullets from time to time still, so they don't have to heal around them. It can cause nerve damage and enduring pain otherwise. I'm still excellent at setting broken bones. Sometimes I'll stitch one up if he or she is really torn up from some pack disagreement. I'm useful to them, and we're on friendly terms."

He addressed Kraven. "I tell everyone I'm Batina and Dustina's godfather. They respect me enough to never give them trouble. Batina has earned their respect on her own, with some of the legal help she's given them."

"Some of my clients are Werewolves?" That surprised her.

"Lycans," Kraven muttered.

She ignored him. "I had no clue. Which ones? Give me a few names."

"I can't. They know you aren't aware of what they are." Dr. Brent sighed. "Your mother was a highly respected woman who did a lot of good when she was alive. You're safe here in the city, Batina. You never should have left. Is she in danger, VampLycan?"

"Yes. Her grandfather wants to use Bat to start a civil war between the four clans."

"Don't tell anyone else that." Dr. Brent stood and paced behind his desk. "It'll be bad if he sends his enforcers here. Especially if he offers favors in return for help finding her." He stopped, staring at Kraven. "There's always some tension between nests and packs. A VampLycan promising to kill their enemies would be too tempting to resist for some. The newest packs or nests especially, if they're promised power. They're low in the pecking order of our society. Youth is notoriously stupid."

"Agreed." Kraven stood. "Are you the new master of your nest?"

Dr. Brent shook his head. "No, but Michael is a good man. He was grateful to take over leadership and allows me a lot of leeway, especially

303

about the Dawson girls. He knows I'm fond of them and I help keep the peace between us and the packs."

Kraven frowned. "Why didn't *you* tell the sisters the truth? You never answered that to my satisfaction."

"There was no need. They were safe. No one saw them as a threat and they were too weak to be used in any way that mattered. I also feared they'd be frightened of me if I told them the truth. They certainly wouldn't have believed a Vampire existed unless I showed them proof." Dr. Brent held Bat's gaze. "I could make *you* forget if you reacted badly, but not Dustina. I had nightmares that you'd flee to somewhere else. Are you afraid of me now?"

She debated it. He still seemed to be the man she'd known. Even if he could do some weird backward leap onto cabinets and had fangs. "No."

He smiled. "Good."

"I do have a question."

"Ask me anything, Batina." Dr. Brent retook his seat.

"How are you so tan if you're a Vampire?"

He grinned. "I do what every other Californian does when their schedules don't allow them to bathe in the sun. I go to the spa every week. They give me a manicure and spray my skin so I'm a nice golden brown."

She let that sink in. "Ah."

"It helps us fit in easier with humans and avoid suspicion."

"You have golf clubs in the corner."

His grin widened. "I go at night. I'd burn in the sun. I used to love to play before I was turned. My enhanced night vision helps a lot since the lighting isn't the greatest on most golf courses. It's just hell finding another Vampire to play against. Not many do."

"This has been interesting." Kraven stood. "We should leave now."

Dr. Brent rose to his feet too. "There's one more thing I need to tell you." He gazed at Bat. "Your body chemistry changed a little during your teens. Remember when I began to give you birth control shots to help you with painful periods? You stayed on them afterward when you became sexually active."

Bat nodded. "What about them?"

Dr. Brent hesitated. "The pain wasn't exclusively from your menstrual cycle. You displayed mild symptoms of going into heat. Those shots keep you from getting pregnant...but they also keep your mild Lycan traits dormant."

Kraven growled and Bat stared at him. She looked back at Dr. Brent, stunned.

"It was for your protection. Werewolf males would have gone after you if you'd gone into heat and you'd have been vulnerable to their seduction. At best, it may have confused you and left you at the mercy of hormones. Your mother wanted you ruled by your mind instead."

"Have the shots permanently hindered her in any way?" Kraven's voice came out harsh.

"No. Of course not. A lot of pack women take the same shot when they want to avoid going into heat, and have been doing so for years. But I can finally tell you the truth, Batina." He held her gaze. "You just need to

305

stop taking them when you wish to get pregnant or decide you don't mind going into heat, now that you'd be aware of what's happening."

Bat didn't know what to think. She was stunned. Questions began to stream through her head.

Kraven spoke up. "Bat and I will have a discussion about this later. She's heard enough. We're out of here."

"One last thing, VampLycan. Is Dustina really safe?"

"She's with my clan in Alaska. My brother will make damn sure Decker Filmore doesn't get her."

"Tell her mate that she doesn't need to be fed often, but it gets worse when she's under stress. She'll turn lethargic and drift into a Vampiric coma if she's starved for too long. I don't know if it would kill her or not. We never allowed it to go that far. She's very human, so it's possible it could be life threatening."

"I'll pass it along."

"What about the rest of your clan? Is her mate high positioned? Will they help protect her?"

"My father is our clan leader." He suddenly reached over and grabbed a letter opener off the desk and jabbed his skin near his wrist. "Smell."

Dr. Brent backed away and bumped into his file cabinet. His expression turned fearful.

"What?" Bat stood too, confused. She glanced between them. "What the hell are you doing, Kraven?"

306

"He's strong-blooded," Dr. Brent whispered. "That's what he's proving. Whatever Vampire blood he has is very strong and very old. Powerful. He also smells like an alpha Werewolf."

"Lycan," Kraven snarled. "I hate being called that. Say it again and I'll make you regret it."

"Stop it," Bat demanded. "You're scaring Dr. Brent."

"He *should* be afraid."

She turned on Kraven and fisted his shirt with both hands. "Hey!"

He stopped glowering at the doctor to hold her gaze.

"Knock that shit off right now! You heard him. He's kept Dusti and me safe. Don't threaten him. Stop being an asshole."

"He could have harmed you with those shots you were given."

"He said he didn't."

"Don't argue with a furious VampLycan," Dr. Brent hissed. "He could kill you in a rage."

"Kraven's not going to hurt me, Dr. Brent. Everybody please calm down!"

Kraven cupped her ass with both of his big hands. "You should take his advice, Hellion. Show me submission."

"In your dreams. Get your gorilla-sized mitts off my ass."

"Never. It's *my* ass."

Dr. Brent gasped. "You're having an affair with him?"

Kraven snapped his head up. "Affair? Don't insult us. She's *mine*."

"Stop." Bat released Kraven's shirt and smoothed the crumpled material with her fingers. "I get it. You're a mega-badass in your world. No need to beat someone up to prove a point."

"I apologize." Dr. Brent seemed to consider his next words more carefully. "I didn't mean any insult. I didn't know she was your mate."

"We need to go." Kraven still seemed furious. "Now." He glared at the doctor. "Don't tell anyone we were here or what we discussed. I'll come after you otherwise. Understand?"

"*Stop* threatening Dr. Brent." Bat smacked his chest. "You're such a dick!"

He lowered his gaze, eyes narrowing. "You're asking for it, Hellion."

"Yeah, yeah. You're going to spank me." She rolled her eyes. "I'm shaking in my high heels." She looked over her shoulder. "Thank you, Dr. Brent. For everything. I'll be in touch with you soon."

"Or not," Kraven muttered.

Bat shoved away from him and stormed toward the door. "Come on. Let's go. I can't take you anywhere. You're such a bully."

"Wait!"

Bat stared at Dr. Brent. "What is it?"

"Can you please exit out the back? I have a patient who's arrived. She's pregnant." His gaze slid to Kraven. "You'll terrify her."

Bat arched her eyebrows.

"Were— Lycans," Dr. Brent sighed. "The females need to avoid high stress when they're pregnant. The trauma of confronting a VampLycan at this stage of her pregnancy could send her into early labor. She'll try to

308

flee and could possibly get hurt, at the very least. Take a left out the door and after that, a right at the end of the corridor. There's a freight elevator. It's clearly marked. It's how I sneak in severely injured patients if they need surgery."

"Sure." Kraven nodded.

"Thank you."

Kraven led Bat into the hallway and turned left. She had learned a lot and needed to mull it over.

Her father had known her mother was a VampLycan—and her mom *had* tried to tell her the truth.

Kraven worried about his mate but didn't say anything until they reached her car. He gently deposited Bat into the passenger side, then took the driver's seat. "Are you okay? You're too damn quiet."

"I'm just thinking," she murmured.

He put the key in the ignition but rested his hands on the steering wheel, instead of starting the engine. "Do you mind sharing?"

She looked at him. "Dad knew and accepted what my mom was."

"The Vamp said they were in love."

"I know but he stuck it out with her."

"Why does that confuse you?"

"I'm impressed more. I always thought he was a good man but it takes a lot to get over the fact that the person you're with isn't human."

"You're with *me*."

She licked her lips. "I'm not who I thought. My entire life was a lie."

He released the wheel and reached over, taking her hand. She didn't resist. It made him worry more. "You knew the truth about your bloodlines before we came here."

"Yeah but it was more believable coming from Dr. Brent."

He tried not to be insulted. She had known the Vampire for most of her life. "You're the same woman you've always been. Your bloodlines don't change that."

Irritation showed in the way she looked at him.

"You know what I mean, Bat."

"Yeah. I guess I do. It makes it worse knowing my mother tried to tell me and I didn't take it well."

"No one would. It had to come as a shock."

"Don't be nice to me. I don't want to cry. Tears are for pussies."

"Where the hell did you hear that?" The things that popped out of her mouth sometimes left him astonished.

"One of my law professors. He was a dick but he was right. Crying doesn't do a damn thing but show others you have a weakness they can take advantage of."

"You've known some fucked-up humans."

"Yes. I have. And I happen to be one of them right now. Dr. Brent is a real Vampire. He has a spray tan."

"I told you they exist. I'm a *Vamp*Lycan. Remember how I said we came into existence? Vampires and Lycans breeding…?"

"It's kind of hard to forget. Why did he say you smell of a really old Vampire?"

"Are you sure you want to know?"

"Yes. I do. You definitely have my full attention now. You said Vampires and Lycans joined forces but shit hit the fan. Tell me more."

"Here?"

"You don't want to go back to my place and I'm not letting you take me to some shithole. It's early in the morning. Check-in times at a decent hotel wouldn't be until later this afternoon, unless we go somewhere that rents to prostitutes by the hour. Pass."

"You might have a point."

"I do. So tell me again about how VampLycans came to be now that I'm not so distracted."

He opened his mouth.

"Skip the shit you already said. I remember. It's kind of etched into my mind."

"What exactly do you want to know?"

"Why do you smell old? I mean, you said you're eighty-one. Is that what Dr. Brent meant? He looks fifty and he said he was turned into a Vampire thirty-six years ago. That puts him at around eighty-six, at least. You're younger than him."

"Vampires gain strength with age. A newly turned one is weak. They need to sleep during daytime; it's a natural defense against the sun. They get an overpowering urge to go somewhere dark and safe before dawn. They lapse into a coma-like sleep until it's safe to move around again."

"I get it. Go on."

311

"A hundred-year-old Vampire can move when the sun is up. It can still burn and kill him, but it doesn't put him to sleep during the day. He gains strength with his abilities too. He's stronger, faster, doesn't require as much blood as he did before."

She nodded.

"A two-hundred-year-old Vampire is twice as strong as a hundred-year-old one, and so forth."

"The sun?"

"He'll still fry, but he can take tiny amounts of exposure. He'd suffer severe burns if he had a sudden urge to streak outside from one place to another for some reason. He'd survive but it would hurt like hell, even after a short distance. He'd need blood immediately to heal or go a bit crazy from the pain."

"How short?"

Kraven glanced around, spotting the other parking structure across the street. "Let's say his lair was invaded and he needed to flee. He could run at full speed from this building to that one and survive. He probably wouldn't make it much more than a city block. He'd collapse and turn to ash." He watched her response.

She peered out the windshield. "Okay. That's comforting."

"It is?"

"Yeah. It's not far."

She amused him. He couldn't follow her logic but it obviously made sense to her.

"So how is Dr. Brent moving around? He's thirty-six in dead years."

"Vamps aren't really dead."

"Whatever. Why isn't he snoozing? It's a bright, sunny day. His ass is awake."

"He said his master was from the fourteenth century. Feedings from his master would have strengthened him. He'd have kept that strength, even after his master's death."

"Like a blood transfusion? Get enough blood from an old one and their abilities are transferred?"

"To a certain point, yes."

"So Dr. Brent is as strong as his master was?"

Kraven shook his head. "No. A master would never allow that to happen. Their strength over others is part of what makes them a master to begin with. He'd have fed Brent enough blood to make it possible for him to work during daylight hours but nothing beyond that."

"Afraid the ones he made would kill his evil ass if they could take him in a fight?"

"Yeah." He chuckled. "Something like that."

"Okay. So why do *you* smell old?"

"Vampires can't have children...or at least, they couldn't until a nest made an alliance with Lycans."

"Yeah. You told me this. They were both being hunted by humans and thought it would be safer to band together. Get to the point."

"The master who discovered shifters could breed with Vamps invited some of his friends from Europe when the Lycans began to conceive."

"Why?"

"Who the fuck knows? Maybe he thought he could trade the knowledge to get his fangs invited into the vein of someone even older. Vampires can be pretty damn greedy that way, wanting to suck on someone stronger to increase their strength. It's possible he just wanted to rub it in their noses that he'd accomplished something they hadn't. It could have been to make alliances with stronger nests if he planned to go to Europe. I've heard they're pretty territorial over there and will kill Vampires who aren't part of their nests. Could be any reason. I'd ask him myself but nobody knows what happened to that betraying asshole. The fact is, he let some very old masters attack Lycan women. He offered them up to be raped and impregnated against their wills. My grandmother was one of them."

Bat cringed and squeezed his hand. "I'm so sorry."

"He ripped into her mind as easy as if she were human. Lycans aren't normally easy to mind control. And they're aware of the intrusion unless that Vamp is really powerful. A Lycan will fight or flee to protect themselves against becoming a suckhead's puppet. But she didn't stand a chance. He was too strong physically, and with his abilities..." He took a deep breath. "The bastard knocked her out and killed her mate. Then the son of a bitch convinced her that *he* was her mate. That's how they got past the Lycan birth control. Just took over her mind, told her it was safe to get pregnant and urged her to ovulate to breed him a pup. She was kept under his control until her body complied. That's how my father came to be. Her mind was released from his will after she was pregnant. She woke to the horror of what he'd done."

"I hope he's dead."

314

"It's uncertain. I told you the strongest males and the older Lycans fought the nest to give the women and younger ones time to escape. It wasn't like they were willing or able to go back to see who survived and who didn't. The survivors ended up in Alaska. It still belonged to Russia at the time. They figured it would be remote enough to hide from the Vampires if they were hunting them to retrieve the unborn babies. My father was born with very strong Vampire and Lycan traits. The power and strength were inherited."

"So you smell like some old master?"

"I carry the scent of a powerful Vamp and an alpha Lycan. My grandmother was the daughter of an alpha. It's probably why that suckhead chose her to be his breeder. She was one of the strongest Lycan females in her pack."

"It boils down to you getting the best genetics from both races, and that makes you one tough son of a bitch who scares others."

He grinned. She was so damn cute. "Yeah, Hellion. That sums it up."

Chapter Seventeen

Kraven wanted to kick his own ass. Bat had him wrapped around her little finger. Otherwise she couldn't have talked him into returning to her condo.

He slammed the door and locked it. Bat turned and grinned.

"Don't gloat," he warned.

"I told you no decent hotel was going to accept cash for a room. And I didn't say anything until the *fifth* clerk demanded a credit card, did I?"

"You didn't have to. The smirk said it all."

"I'm impressed by how reasonable you're being, and the security here is far better than at a five-star hotel."

"Let's drop it."

"Thank you."

He sighed.

"Really. I know you'd prefer we stay on the move but I have to meet with a client later. It could cost me my job otherwise."

"That's what you said. I don't want to have another argument. You gave me a headache."

"My job is important and I want to keep it. I'm going to call Marla." She turned around, heading toward the phone.

He dropped her bag and shrugged his off his shoulder, stalking after her. "No phone calls."

She swung to face him. "Marla works for me. I need her to go grocery shopping so we have some food in the fridge and I have to replace some of the things I lost. She can do that for me."

"It can wait until Decker is no longer a threat."

"I don't have a license, Kraven. Marla can get me another one. I need her to call my credit card companies to have them send me replacements. She handles all my personal affairs. I trust her."

"It can wait." He wasn't backing down. "Your grandfather could be looking for any activity on your accounts."

She bit her lip and looked guilty.

"What?"

"I ordered food on my card. I didn't physically need it. They have it on record." She glanced at the door. "Nobody has come here. I think we're good. Let me have Marla start getting me replacements."

He had assumed she had some kind of tab at the restaurant. "Damn it! Pay in cash from now on."

"Fine."

"We're leaving after your meeting. That's final. Don't get too comfortable, Bat. It's harder for someone to find us if we stay on the move."

"*Fine!*" She shook her head and spun, walking into the kitchen. "I have an idea."

"What?"

She kicked off her shoes behind the counter and opened the fridge, taking out a soda. "Want one?"

"No."

She closed the fridge, opened the can, and took a sip. "We'll switch condos with someone on another floor. Some are rented out to tenants if they have family come in. I'll just tell them I need one. How about that? I'll get my secure building but we won't be easy to find."

"I thought you didn't want me messing with someone's mind? I'd have to make them forget they know where we are if we do that."

She grimaced. "You're too paranoid."

Kraven arched his eyebrows.

"It just sounds like a big pain in the ass for my grandfather to send men down here and personally mind-bend every person inside the building, if he even bothers to look here. He'll figure this is the last place you'd take me."

"That's because it's incredibly stupid to be here."

She put her soda down and approached him. "I suppose you're going to insist on coming to my meeting with me."

"Yes. I'm not letting you out of my sight."

She walked around him, staring at his clothing. "Your outfit won't do. We're not in Barking Dog anymore."

He knew she did that on purpose. "Howl."

"Whatever." She stopped in front of him and grinned. "I say we go shopping. We have a few hours to kill before six."

"No."

"I'm not talking anything tailored. It's too late for that. I have some connections but you're so tall and broad that they'd have to make you a

318

suit. The jeans are fine but you need a nicer shirt and jacket to pull off the security-guard look here. Those boots need to go, too, for some nice dress shoes."

"No way in hell. Tell them I'm your boyfriend."

"Oh, that will go over great with the partners. I'll bring my date to a client meet-and-greet for an upcoming criminal case." She rolled her eyes. "I'm going to this so they don't can my ass, Kraven. You're my new bodyguard, as far as they're concerned. It's the only way I can take you with me."

"I'm not going shopping. I don't give a damn what anyone thinks of how I dress *or* my boots."

"Fine. I'll just tell them I hired you in Alaska. That might explain it— but absolutely no duster. Nobody wears long coats in L.A unless they're the Hollyweird crowd."

"The *what*?"

"Movie stars and celebrity types. They wear odd shit just to get attention."

"It hides my blade."

"You can't take weapons to a client meet-and-greet. He's probably got his own security and they'll pat you down."

"I'm not going anywhere without my blade, Hellion."

She shoved open his coat, searching and finding his shorter blade strapped to his hip. "Geez. You've been wearing that all day?"

"Yes."

She bit her lower lip and backed off, releasing his coat. "Compromise. Ever heard of that term? I'm agreeing to let you tag along but the coat and blade have to stay here."

"You're one to talk. Do you even know what compromising means? You're not leaving my sight. I don't care what you agree to or not. The blade stays. I can't exactly shift and attack someone coming after you. Claws and fangs won't do a damn bit of good against a GarLycan anyway. Only steel will hurt them."

"I need a stronger drink." She left him to return to her kitchen, opened a cupboard, and removed a bottle of vodka. "Want one?"

He followed her and swiped it off the counter. "You're not drinking. I want your full wits about you since you're determined to put yourself at risk by being here."

"Fine."

He appreciated her caving so quickly. It also made him suspicious. "What are you plotting?"

"Nothing."

"You're lying."

"That's not nice. You don't want me to drink. I get it. It's probably for the best. We have a few hours to kill. I think I'll take a nice, hot bath. And I know—guest bedroom. You don't want me near a window."

"It's daylight. No GarLycan can fly right now."

She smiled. "Good to know. Okay. You guard the door and I'll go relax in my bathroom. That tub has jets."

He watched her leave but still felt like his Bat was up to something. He waited a few minutes and crept down the hallway. He entered her bedroom and opened the bathroom door to follow the sound of water. Bat turned from the counter.

"Can I help you? I'm just waiting for the tub to fill, Kraven. I'm about to tweeze my eyebrows, if you were wondering."

"I was just checking." He glanced around but didn't see anything suspicious.

"There's no boogieman hiding in here. Just me. I'd prefer to do my eyebrows in private but you can have a seat if you're that curious."

"I'll be in the living room."

"Okay. I'll be in here."

He backed up and closed the door. He didn't go far. She remained in there and he listened as she turned off the water. He finally relaxed enough to leave the room when he heard her sink into the tub, sloshing some of the water, followed by the soft motor sound of the jets.

Kraven ended up in the guest bathroom, studying his reflection. There wasn't a damn thing wrong with the black button-down shirt he wore, or the pants. He sighed and went in search of his bag. He hadn't packed expecting to go to anything formal. He settled for a pair of jeans and a fresh black long-sleeved shirt, carrying them and his toiletry bag back into the bathroom.

He shaved with a razor he'd picked up while they were out, and then dressed, taking his time. His boots had seen better days but he really didn't give a damn what anyone thought of him at Bat's work meeting.

Her safety came first. That's all that mattered. He quit the room and strode into her bedroom.

"How are you doing, Bat?"

"I'm fine. And in the bathroom still. Stay out."

He took a seat on her bed. "You've been in there for a while."

"I'm relaxing, and then I have to do my hair and makeup again. Chill out."

He resigned himself to waiting. It would be a lesson in learning patience with a mate. His father swore his mother could take forever to get ready for certain events the clan held.

He finally heard her moving around after she got out of the water. When the bathroom door opened—nearly two hours later—he gaped.

"What in the hell?" Kraven was on his feet in an instant.

Bat grinned. "What do you think?"

"You look like you got into a fight and lost!" Kraven stepped closer, sniffing. "Makeup?"

"Of course. I wasn't really going to hurt myself." She cocked her head. "How did I do? I haven't dressed up for Halloween in forever but I once had quite a talent for it. Does it look like my eye is bruised? My cheek?"

"Yes. Badly."

"Good." She moved past him to her closet, throwing open the door.

"Why would you do that to your face?" He followed her inside and tried to touch her. It disturbed him seeing her marred skin, even if the injuries weren't real. It caused his protective instincts to go a bit crazy.

She jerked away. "Don't mess it up!" She turned her back on him to evaluate her dresses. "I know the partners. They're going to demand I start building a defense for our new client immediately. Then you'll throw a shit-fit and refuse to let me go to work. You'll probably think the interns I'd need to invite here are possible assassins under mind control." She chose a black dress suit and lifted it off the rack, turning to stare at Kraven. "This is called the pity maneuver."

He just gawked at her.

"It'll make Jacob and the other partners look like total dickheads if I show up looking like shit. They'll have to give me a few days to heal up. I represent the firm. Can you say 'really bad public relations'? It'd be pretty bad if they have one of their counsel appear before a judge or reporters looking like something that went through the tumble cycle in a washing machine."

"This wasn't necessary."

"Bullshit. Give me a break, Kraven. I'm trying to make you happy and save my job. Those two things are working against each other right now. You're demanding I avoid people and they'll want me to lead this case. I can't do both. This is my plan. It will give me some time."

"I *meant*, I could just use mind control to convince your boss to use another attorney and put you on vacation leave."

Bat suddenly felt like an idiot. "Shit. I should have thought of that."

"I knew you were up to something. This is why you need to learn to talk to me."

"Excuse me for forgetting I'm dating a guy with super powers. This is new to me."

"We're not dating. I'm your mate."

She couldn't miss his anger. "You have two hot spots."

"What does that mean?"

"Being called a Werewolf or my boyfriend pisses you off."

"Go wash that stuff off your face."

She debated it but shook her head. "No. I'm going with my plan."

"You don't need to."

"What if they have security cameras in the lounge? I never exactly looked around to find out. I've only been there once and that was four years ago. I thought meeting the neighbors at a Christmas party the association held would be fun. It turned out I was wrong. They should have dubbed it the dateless and desperate mixer for losers."

"Men made advances on you?"

"I was the only single woman there. I got out as fast as possible and never went to another association party. They do them a few times a year for the holidays. I make other plans or spend those evenings with Dusti." The thought of her sister made her sad. "I hope she's doing okay. Can you turn on your phone and see if there are any new texts?"

"I said I'd call back tonight with an update."

"Why not now?"

"I keep my word. I said I'd call tonight."

Bat sighed, irritated. "Really? You aren't going to call and check on my sister for me because the sun is still up?"

"Yes."

She closed her eyes. The sound of his chuckle snapped them back open.

He looked really amused. "I know that look. I feel that way all the time. You drive me crazy. Turnabout and all that."

"You were just messing with me?"

"Yeah. Of course I'll make the call."

"I want to talk to Dusti."

"No. I'm calling my cousin Red and keeping it short."

"Come on, Kraven. I just want to hear her voice."

"Not until I know the situation there."

She debated that. "Fair enough."

He strode out of her bedroom and she followed hot on his heels. The outfit he'd changed into looked nicer than the one he'd had on before. She didn't mention that though. He sure couldn't return the compliment with her looking as if she'd been battered, thanks to the blue eye shadow she'd used to contour her eye and cheek to look as if she had bruises.

His bag was in the guest bathroom. He slid out the phone and she watched impatiently as he put in the battery.

"Put it on speaker," she urged.

He nodded. "Fine, but be quiet."

"I'll try."

She impatiently waited for the call to connect. Kraven gripped the phone in his palm, far out of her reach. It clicked and rang twice.

A deep male voice answered. "What did you learn from the doctor?"

Kraven didn't hesitate to answer his cousin. "Here's the short version. Tell Drantos Antina had help from a nest of Vampires to keep the daughters safe. She killed their master and they left her family alone as a thank you."

Bat couldn't resist anymore. "How's Dusti? Is she okay?"

There was a pause. Red spoke. "She's fine. Hello."

Kraven glowered at her. "So much for staying quiet."

"I'm worried." Bat shrugged.

"Interesting news," Red stated before they could argue. "Decker took six bullets but survived."

"Who got to him?" Kraven pointed at Bat, then put his finger to his lips.

She sealed hers shut.

"Dusti shot him." Red chuckled. "With Drantos's gun. He was pissed that she stole it and snuck out of his home to meet Decker, but she's unharmed and safe."

"*What?*" Bat lost it. Pure fear and panic filled her. "What happened? Son of a bitch! Is she okay? Did you say Dusti *shot our grandfather*? Like with a gun? What was she doing with a weapon?" She reached out and slapped Kraven's arm. "You said Biker Bear would keep her safe!"

"Goddamn it, Hellion," Kraven growled. "Shut up."

"Don't tell me to shut up! I want answers, damn it!" Anger flooded Bat.

"Both of you stop," Red demanded. "Here's the highlights. Lord Aveoth isn't going to go after *either* sister. He's been made aware of Decker's plan and it pissed him off. Maybe the blood addiction is bullshit, because Drantos said Aveoth will stay away from both of them. Drantos also made it clear to the GarLycan that Dusti is his mate and their bond is solid. Lord Aveoth's clan is helping our clans track down Decker. You'll be safer here than you are out there now, since Decker's fled. Your father told me to tell you to come home when you called. When should I expect you both?"

Bat's temper faded as quickly as it had flared. She stared into Kraven's eyes.

He'd want to take her back to Alaska.

He held her gaze, his expression unreadable. "I'll have to get back to you on that, Red. Expect a call later tonight." Kraven hung up and removed the battery.

Bat backed away and leaned against the wall. "Are you going to make me go?"

He shook his head. "You've made it clear that you prefer Los Angeles. I'd never force you to live somewhere that would make you unhappy."

She felt torn for the first time in her life about what she wanted to do with her future. Dusti was in Alaska. Bat's life was in L.A. It was a situation she'd never thought she'd have to face. She and her sister had always remained close, just half an hour drive apart at most. They went to dinner at least every few weeks. Now it would be a long plane ride to see her.

"You don't look so good. I'm not talking about the makeup job either."

"It just kind of hit me."

"What?"

"Dusti is never coming back here, is she? You said she mated your brother. Will Biker Bear move to California?"

"No. Drantos will lead our clan one day. It's his duty to stay there."

"What if Dusti wants to come home?"

"He *is* her home now."

She turned away and tried to put some space between them before Kraven caught her. He wrapped his arms around her from behind. Bat didn't struggle, instead gripping his arms. Kraven sighed, lowering his head to put his lips close to her ear.

"You look so sad, Hellion. She'll be happy there. Drantos will make sure of it and we can visit her anytime you want."

"You said the winters are shit."

"I didn't."

"You become a movie-watching couch potato and do home projects. I don't even know what that means but it sounds boring."

"That's because I lived alone. They'll have each other to spend time with. Mated couples love the winters. Drantos will have shorter shifts to work and they'll just make love all the time."

"What if he's bad in bed? My poor sister will be stuck with him."

Kraven laughed.

She twisted her head, staring at him. "I'm not trying to be funny. I mean it. Do you know how annoying it is when a guy hounds you for sex when you're not interested?"

"You're so damn cute. I'm willing to give my brother the benefit of the doubt but worst case, he'll hone his skills as a lover with his mate by the time the snow starts melting."

"Wipe that grin off your face. I'm serious."

"I know." He chuckled but seemed to get control of it. "I could keep you happily amused during an Alaskan winter. And Dusti will be fine. Drantos will make certain he meets her needs. Her happiness will be the most important thing to him. Stop worrying so much."

Bat turned her head and glanced at the clock on the nightstand. "It's almost six."

"Ignore the time. They'll wait until we arrive. You're upset. We'll talk until you feel better."

"I need to work. It's what I do best." She pulled on his arms around her waist. "We need to go. It's better to get there a little early than to be late."

"Bat..."

"Let go."

Kraven opened his arms. She stepped away from him and turned. "We have to go over some things first."

"Like what?"

"You don't talk after we enter the lounge. It's a large room with a bar and some tables. Not a word. You stand about four feet behind me and look mean. That's what bodyguards do. I don't know if Mr. Bales has his own security guard or not, but I know Warren Otis has two with him at all times. They'll pat you down. Don't fight it. Just act stoic and bored. I'm sure you can pull that off." She ran her gaze up and down him. "You can't take the blade, Kraven. They'll find it."

"I told you, the blade goes with me."

"And I heard your cousin on the phone. Rock guy is cool now. You won't be facing off against any of his winged men."

Kraven didn't look happy but he finally nodded. "Fine."

"Okay. Oh, and if you do talk, don't call me 'Hellion'. I'm Ms. Dawson. You're pretending to work for me and that's the title you'd use."

"I still don't like this."

"I'm sure that's true, and thank you."

The way his eyes darkened was a bit disturbing. She stepped closer, peering at them. "What does it mean when your irises and your pupils become the same black color?"

"Let's get this over with." He spun, stomping toward the door.

Bat cringed. She'd somehow pissed him off. Again.

"Damn." She hurried to catch up to him.

Chapter Eighteen

"Don't lose your cool, no matter what. Jacob is one of the partners and he'll be here. He's condescending, a first-rate prick, and he will sputter off shit that will make you want to smash him in the mouth. I know, and I sympathize, but ignore it." Bat smoothed down her dress, glancing at Kraven in the elevator as it lowered them to the ground floor of her building. "Just remember what I said. Don't talk or show any emotion."

"I heard."

"I didn't mean to upset you."

"I have a bad feeling about this."

"Welcome to my work world. We're likely about to meet a criminal, and who I believe is his boss. I always try to make a mental challenge out of these ordeals. You know, like let's see how much shocking shit I can take and still pretend I'm fine with it. I just hope whatever Mr. Bales has been charged with isn't something that's going to make me lose my appetite. They usually hire good caterers for these things so we might as well enjoy the snacks."

"He probably murdered someone."

She only hoped this client was one of the innocent ones. There were a lot of crimes Bales could have committed that were far worse than killing someone. The elevator doors opened and Kraven took the lead. He blocked her from exiting until he'd scoped out the area. Bat sighed, resigned that he'd play his role to the hilt. Protecting her was what he seemed to do best, after all.

"The lobby is safe," she reminded him. "Protective glass and all that."

"Give me a break. I don't want to hear it again."

"Fine. Go left, then make a right. It's those two large double doors. They're always kept closed but Mr. Bales obviously rented the space from the association. We just go inside."

Kraven stayed in front of her and at the lounge doors, he gripped a handle, opening one a few inches. He sniffed. She noticed his body stiffen and he blindly reached back, found her arm, and forced her to the side as he closed the door quietly.

"This isn't inside," she said, pointing out the obvious.

"Lycans," he whispered.

It took Bat a second for his words to sink in. "What do you mean?"

"I smell them." He tightened his hold on her arm. "We're out of here."

"Wait." She dug in her high heels to prevent him from pulling her down the hall. "Dr. Brent said some of my clients are Werewolves. I mean Lycans. This isn't so alarming."

"I don't want you near any packs or nests!"

"You thought Dr. Brent was dangerous. He wasn't. This is just some guy in trouble with the law and he wants the best representation available. I'll consult with him and hand him off to someone else. It won't take long."

"I don't like this."

"Noted." She reached out and tried to pry his fingers off her wrist. "I still have to go inside. I refuse to give my law firm an excuse to kick me to the curb when I'm so close to making partner. I'd face off against the devil himself. I'm a lot of things, but chicken shit isn't one of them. Now let's go inside."

"I think this is a mistake, Bat."

"A Vampire could mind control a victim and witnesses to make them forget something. It makes sense a Lycan would get into a jam sometimes with the police, right?"

"Maybe."

"Okay. This is probably a Lycan in trouble, and he asked for me. I'll excuse myself from the case because I look like shit. Jacob won't want me in front of cameras if this is going to be a case the media follows. We're just going to walk in there and put on a little show that will save my job. Relax. We knew there were Lycans and Vampires in L.A. No big shocker."

He released her. "You stick within three feet of me and we're out of there at the first sign of something I don't like."

"Deal." Bat fixed the sleeve he'd messed up.

"You don't fight with me. I say we're out, and you do what I say."

She nodded. "I said deal."

"You also love to argue."

"You're my bodyguard." She tried to lighten his mood. "I'll trust your instincts but don't be a bully. You'll probably terrify the client just by walking in the door, with the old smell you carry. I'm glad I can't pick it up, by the way. Try to behave, okay?"

"This is a damn bad idea, Bat."

"So is losing my job." She inched around him and gripped the handle of the door. "Just follow my lead and don't talk."

Bat pulled the door open and stepped inside.

Four men waited across the room. One of them she recognized, the other three were new faces. She didn't have to glance back to know Kraven remained close on her ass.

Jacob's mouth dropped open when he saw her. It made her feel a bit pleased with her makeup job.

Her gaze shifted to the client. The two men standing close to him had to be his bodyguards. They weren't wearing suits. She fixed her gaze on the blond in custom Armani.

"Hello, Mr. Bales." She approached him and remembered to limp slightly. "I'm Batina Dawson."

He didn't meet her gaze but instead stared over her head at Kraven. His nostrils flared. She glanced at his bodyguards. They did the same. Jacob just kept gawking at her.

Okay, I know who the Lycans are. That was easier than I thought it would be to figure out who's who. Jacob's obviously human.

Bat paused several feet away from Travis Bales. She was pretty sure if she reached back, she'd touch Kraven. He wasn't exactly keeping that three feet of space she'd asked for. She studied her client. The thing that surprised her most was his short, stocky body. She expected all Lycans to be tall like Kraven. Mr. Bales stood about five feet seven. The suit he wore

334

did seem a little tight in the arms and chest, indicating he was muscled and probably worked out quite a bit. She plastered on a smile.

"You look like shit," Jacob accused.

She turned her attention to him. "I just survived a plane crash. I mentioned that, *and* the fact that I had to see a doctor this morning."

"Are you well, Ms. Dawson?"

Bat stared into Mr. Bales's light brown eyes. "I've had better days."

"Who is your friend?" he asked, studying Kraven.

"I'm the guy who'll break bones if you so much as look at her wrong," Kraven responded. "Three against me aren't good odds. I'd keep that in mind if I were you."

Bat's smile faltered. "Gentlemen, let's not having a pissing contest. A lady *is* present."

"How dare you!" Jacob advanced a step, openly hostile to Kraven. "You're fired."

"He's not working for the firm." Bat tried to defuse the situation before it blew up. "I personally hired Mr. Kraven. Let's just all take a deep breath—and *not* through our noses." She hoped the message was clear to the Lycans and the man behind her.

"What in the hell does that mean?" Jacob seemed confused.

"Shut up, Jacob. Keep out of this," Mr. Bales ordered. He looked at Bat. "I was told you were unaware of certain things. I was misinformed."

"It's a new development." She kept her tone cool. "As you can see, I haven't had the best week. I'm unable to represent you at this time but I

335

can highly recommend Paul Tomis. He's excellent. I'd want him to defend me."

"Warren said I wanted you."

"What were you charged with?"

"Domestic violence. My girlfriend and I got into a fight. I never touched the bitch but she wants money for me dumping her. This is her sad attempt at blackmail."

That cleared up a few things for Bat and why they'd insisted on her. And he probably meant the woman he'd dated was a Lycan too, and wasn't just calling his ex a bad name. "Gracie Barton is also excellent. A woman attorney is smart to have in this case but the last thing you want is for me to represent you in my current condition. Some might jump to conclusions. First impressions count."

"You'll heal by my first court appearance." He cocked his head, seeming to take in the bruising. "It should be gone by tomorrow."

"I'm not quite like you, Mr. Bales. Bruises can stay with me for weeks."

"What in the *hell* are you all talking about?" Jacob stepped closer.

"I said shut up." Mr. Bales shot him a glare. "Now."

Jacob didn't look pleased but he stopped talking. Bat knew he'd take it out on her later when they were alone but he wouldn't want to piss off their new client, especially since he was associated with Warren Otis.

The doors opened and Bat turned. She had to lean a little to see around Kraven.

Warren and two of his guards entered. Kraven inhaled and she could tell by his body language that he was on alert.

"Ah. More, I take it?"

Kraven gave a short nod, affirming her suspicions. It didn't surprise her. Warren had sent Mr. Bales to her firm. It made sense that he'd be a Lycan too. She watched as Warren and his two-man security team came to an abrupt halt, all three focused on Kraven. Their nostrils flared.

"This is unexpected." Warren stayed by the doors and didn't come any closer. He addressed Bat directly. "Would you mind introducing us?"

"Who the fuck cares? It's some security guard she hired." Jacob crossed the room and offered his hand. "I got her here, just like you asked, Warren."

Warren motioned to his security to spread out. They moved off to the sides of the room. He slid is gaze to Kraven. "Your alpha already has a deal with us. I expect him to keep it."

"I don't understand." Jacob glanced between Kraven and Warren. "What's really going on here, Warren? You said your friend wanted Batina to defend him."

"Did Jacob have to be here? He's starting to annoy me." Mr. Bales took a seat on top of one of the tables. "He's *your* pet. Leash him."

Warren growled low. "Are you giving me orders, Travis?"

"No." Travis Bales slid off the table and dropped his head. "Sorry. He's just really annoying."

"I'm aware." Warren advanced a little, his men doing the same. "This changes nothing, VampLycan. Your alpha and I came to an agreement. I delivered."

Kraven backed up and hooked an arm around Bat, pulling her close. "What did Decker offer?"

Bat was glad Kraven loosely held her because her knees suddenly felt weak. Warren had obviously set her up. She'd worked with him since starting at the firm and he'd sold her out. Jacob obviously didn't have a clue what was going down.

"Don't you talk to your alpha?" Warren asked. "Two hundred grand. That's pocket change to me, but the offer of twenty of *your* kind at my disposal for two weeks was too much of a temptation to resist." He smiled at Bat. It was chilling. "Sorry, sweetheart. I enjoyed watching you keep my enforcers out of prison but one bitch is as good as another. You can be replaced. I only asked Jacob to hire you as a favor to me. I didn't believe the Vampires when they said you were weak. It helped me keep a close eye on you."

One of his men snorted. "He thought about fucking you to get close but your *smell* puts most of us off."

Bat glared at Warren. "That wouldn't have worked. You're not my type."

His guard growled and took a threatening step forward. "You'd be lucky to have our alpha fuck you." The man flashed his fangs. "Weak bitch. You're going to apologize or bleed."

Kraven reacted by shoving Bat behind him. He opened his hands and claws grew out of his fingertips.

338

Warren motioned with two fingers. "No, Cary. Be nice. Back off. I promised she'd be handed over unharmed. The VampLycan would take your arm for trying to get near that weak-blooded bitch."

"She's a Werewolf too?" Jacob gawked at Bat. "I had no idea. You never said a word, Warren. You should have told me."

Bat recovered and her temper replaced the shock as she stayed mostly behind Kraven. "Rethinking all those times you palmed my ass, Jacob? How do you even know about Lycans?" She glanced at Kraven. "Is he one?"

"No. He's completely human. I'm curious about that myself."

"They're going to turn me." Jacob grinned smugly. "I've known about Werewolves for a few years now. I'm earning my way into becoming a pack member. I'll be young and strong one day soon."

"Shut up," Warren snapped.

"Sorry." Jacob closed his mouth.

Kraven surprised Bat by suddenly laughing. She moved closer to him, pressing against his body. "What's funny?"

"Is that what they told you, Jacob?" Kraven shook his head. "It doesn't work that way. Being turned is brutal. At your age, and given how out of shape you are, you'd die within minutes of receiving multiple bites. And I have no idea why you think it'll turn back the clock. That's absolute bullshit. The strength is accurate, but I'll state again—you won't survive being turned."

"What's he talking about?" Jacob's tone took on a whining pitch. "You said I'd get a blood transfusion and become young again after I became one of your kind."

"He's full of shit." Warren growled again. "Shut up, VampLycan. Your alpha made a deal! I called him last night to let him know where she is. If you have her, that makes you one of mine for the next few weeks. The other nineteen VampLycans I was promised better be on their way. You're going to help me become top of the food chain in this territory."

"Ah. You want us to take out the Vampires and stronger packs for you." Kraven kept remarkably calm.

"There *is* no stronger pack than mine. I've got that handled. It's those fucking Vampires. They're like damn rats in the sewer. They spread like a disease and think they have the right to tell us what to do. I'm fucking sick of it! No team I've sent after them ever returns. But they won't stand a chance against twenty of your kind. I want Michael's fangs torn from his mouth before you ash that fucker. I plan to wear them as a necklace."

Kraven took a deep breath. "Decker Filmore believes Lycans are beneath him, and won't keep his word. He'll use you to get what he wants. Any promises he made are lies. Twenty VampLycans *will* show up—but they'll slaughter your entire pack before he allows you to tell any of his enforcers what to do."

Warren's face twisted with rage. "That's not true."

Bat took the opportunity to speak. "Did Decker inform you that I'm his granddaughter?"

Warren couldn't hide his surprise.

"Let me handle this, Bat." Kraven sounded pissed.

340

"Shut up and look pretty," Bat snapped, keeping her attention on Warren. She'd dealt with him plenty of times. "Do you know why Decker wants me, Warren? My mom ran away from him because he wanted to sell her into sexual slavery to some GarLycan clan. You have two sisters...I've met them. I've seen the love you feel for them. Would you sell them?"

Warren scowled.

"That's what I thought. Decker Filmore is my grandfather, but I'd shoot the bastard between the eyes if I got the chance. He lied to *me*, and I'm his own flesh and blood. Be reasonable, Warren. Be smart. He's scum with the morals of a longtime drug addict. Remember Bradley Mars?"

Warren growled low. "I killed that bastard."

Bat inwardly winced. Her client had gone missing and she'd suspected he'd met a bad end. Now she knew for certain. "But when he worked for you, you paid me to represent him. He wanted to make a deal with the DA, regardless of how many times I told him he didn't need to. I could have had his charge knocked down to a misdemeanor. At worst, he would have only been looking at sixty days in lockup and I could've had it reduced to half that. I even told him I could probably get him off with monetary fines." She shot a dirty look at Jacob. "I wondered how you'd found out he'd requested to speak to the DA. Mystery solved." She held Warren's stare. "Regardless, I bring it up because he wanted to rat you out in order to avoid any possible jail time. And he was a standup guy compared to my grandfather."

"Brad was human. They're weak and have no loyalty. VampLycans have a reputation for being honorable."

341

"Most." Bat licked her lips. "Do you have any bad Werewolves in your pack? You're an alpha, right? Don't you ever have to punish any of yours because they do bad shit?"

He said nothing.

Bat felt she was on to something, despite only making educated guesses. "There are always bad apples in every group. Decker Filmore is on the top of that rotten barrel. He's greedy, power hungry, and he'd stab you in the back the first opportunity he finds. He'll send enforcers here to pick me up, but they won't take orders from you. He's going to fuck you over—because it's what he does best."

Warren seemed to consider it for long moments. "That's a shame." He glanced at his men. "Plan B."

Bat startled when shots rang out but Kraven had already jerked in front of her, his body nearly knocking her over. His knees buckled, and she tried to hold him up briefly by latching on to his waist, but he was too big and heavy so they both went down. He twisted though so they landed on their sides.

Kraven had been shot.

The horror, the suddenness, and the shock slammed into her all at once. She sat up and yanked on him, pulling him to his back. Blood soaked his clothing. It was dark and wet, spreading as she watched.

It didn't matter that men stood behind her with guns. She shoved at Kraven's duster, getting a better look at where he'd been shot. At least three bloody spots were revealed.

"No, no, no," she whispered, bordering on hysteria. His chest rose and fell but his eyes were closed. She slapped her palms over the worst

342

two and leaned forward, using her weight to apply pressure. "Call an ambulance!"

"That would be defeating the purpose of killing him. Move out of the way so my men don't accidentally shoot you when they put more rounds into him."

Bat whipped her head around and wished she could shoot Warren Otis. "You son of a bitch! Why would you do this?"

"I'm going to force the VampLycans to kill my enemies or you're going to bleed out next to him. You're important to Decker Filmore for a reason, if he wants you so bad. Now he'll do exactly what I say—or I'll send you to him in pieces."

"You didn't say anything about killing anyone," Jacob sputtered. "I can't be here for this. I need to leave."

"Ball-less coward," one of the guards spat. "Pathetic."

"Knock it off," Warren ordered. "You want to become one of mine, Jacob? Blood and death are part of it. Stop being so damn squeamish. Grab the bitch so we can put more bullets into the VampLycan before he begins to heal. I have a phone call to make and new terms to set. *Nobody fucks with me.*"

Bat remembered that Kraven had kept a knife in his boot in Alaska, and hoped it was still there. "Don't touch me!" She released his chest and turned a little on her ass, gripping one of his legs as if to steady herself while tugging at the material. "I'll get up by myself."

She slid her hand into the boot on his right leg and her fingertips brushed against a metal handle. She slowly got up, using her body to hide the motion of withdrawing the knife.

343

"Un-fucking-believable," she loudly protested. "I try to give you advice and this is what you do? Kill my bodyguard?!" She turned, pressing her hand against her side to keep the hunting knife hidden. "He didn't work for Decker. That was totally unnecessary."

"He's not dead yet. I can hear him breathing." Warren looked at one of his men. "Take off his head just to be sure he stays down. Who the hell knows what it takes to kill one of them, but that should do it."

Kraven needed her. He seemed unconscious. No way would she stand there and just allow them to decapitate the man she loved. "You got his heart. He's toast. I'm an expert on VampLycans. I *am* part one, remember? Hit the old ticker and it's just a matter of time before he takes his last breath if he's not given blood right away." She stepped closer to Warren. "Someone probably heard those shots. We should go."

He frowned, looking unconvinced. "You *should* want the cops to come."

"I'm still an attorney and you keep our firm on retainer. I'm advising you to get the hell out of here before they arrive."

"You expect me to believe you're okay with this? I don't buy it." He stalked forward. "You're my insurance that I get those damn Vampires dusted so they aren't my problem anymore."

He reached out to grab her. Bat tightened her fisted hold on the knife handle but allowed him to grip her arm, jerking her closer. He let go and looked at his men.

"Do it. Take the VampLycan's head. I want to keep it as a trophy."

Bat knew time was up. She fisted his belt buckle and shoved the tip of the blade between his slightly spread thighs. "How attached to your dick are you?"

Warren's eyes widened and he looked down.

"I don't know how to kill a Lycan but I'm pretty sure you don't want to spend the rest of your life as a eunuch. Tell your men to back the fuck off and stay away from Kraven."

He wrapped his hand around her upper arm, the one attached to the hand gripping his belt. "I'll crush the bones."

"Too bad that's not the arm holding the knife. You do it and I start slicing. That's going to hurt just as much. Tell your men to do as I said."

"Do it," Warren snarled to the guards, glaring at her. His eyes took on an inhuman look, yellow showing in the irises. Some hair began to grow on his cheeks.

"Wolf form or human, balls are balls, Warren. Want to keep them? Ease your paw off me, and remember, you move, I move with you." She tugged on his belt. "And so does the knife."

"Do you really think you're going to get out of here? That you can escape?" He grew fangs but he let go. "You stupid bitch."

She shook her head. "No. You're stronger, faster, and have extras that I don't. I'm just going to stand here and think about my options. You do the same."

"Just put down the knife," Jacob ordered.

Bat refused to look away from Warren or move her head, since she could see the other Lycans from the corner of her eye. "Screw you, Jacob.

345

You're such a kiss-ass moron. Kraven was right, you know. You've been lied to. They aren't going to change you, and you sure as hell aren't getting any younger." She pressed the knife tighter against Warren. "Have your men toss the guns. What do you care, anyway? You don't plan to shoot me, right? You need me alive to compel Decker to do what you want. I hate guns."

"I'm going to make you pay for this."

She studied Warren's eyes. "It's so rare to see such honesty from a client. Have them toss the guns."

He didn't so she slid the knife just a little.

He snarled. "Throw them."

"We can still shoot her," one of his men said. "In the arm. She'll drop the blade."

"It's not your nuts on the line. Toss the damn guns!" Warren yelled. "Now. She won't get away."

They threw their guns and Bat breathed a sigh of relief. *Come on, Kraven. Get up.* She started to pray he'd recover; she just wasn't certain if he could do it without blood.

The doors from the hallway opened suddenly. Bat assumed it would be more Lycans from Warren's pack. She tightened her grip on the knife and turned her head.

Instead, Doug walked in, wearing his security uniform. He pointed at Batina. "There she is."

At least twenty men filed into the room on his heels, led by a tall brunette man sporting all leather. He wore a trench coat and shoved it apart in the front, his hands resting on a set of guns strapped to his thighs.

Oh shit. All hope for her and Kraven faded with their arrival. A sweep of her gaze revealed they'd all opened their coats, displaying more guns. It was like something out of a gangster movie. It had to be the rest of the pack.

"My ears were burning," the brunette stated. "What are you up to, Warren?"

"Fuck you, Michael."

They weren't Lycans, but Vampires. One glance and Bat figured they must use the same person to get their spray tans as Dr. Brent. There wasn't a pale-faced member in the group.

The tall Vampire leader cocked his head, his gaze lowering to Bat's hand. "Am I interrupting something?"

"Just me, trying to survive and stall for time," Bat answered. "Are you here to use me against Decker too?"

Michael shook his head. "No. A friend tipped me off that Warren was up to no good and that he was heading here. I'm aware of where you live, Batina. We wanted to check on you."

"I have no idea what you're talking about. I'm just consulting my attorney," Warren lied.

"I would have hired Batina myself if I'd known she conducted business in such a kinky way." Michael grinned.

347

"Could you please stop joking around? I'd like to back away without getting my arm broken in the process, or worse." Dr. Brent had implied his nest wouldn't want any harm to come to her. She trusted him.

Michael pulled one of his guns free of its holster and aimed it at Warren's face. "I always like to accommodate a woman. He won't move, or I'll shoot."

Bat backed away but kept hold of the knife. Warren didn't do anything but stand there very still. She relaxed when she reached Kraven's side.

He surprised her by leaping to his feet and grabbing her around her waist. She gasped as he lifted her, putting her behind him.

"No one touches her," Kraven snarled.

"Are you okay?" Bat couldn't see how he *could* be, with bullets in his body.

"Worry about that later," he muttered.

Warren slowly moved his arms and gripped his suit jacket, taking it off. He threw it to the floor. "Put away your toys and let's deal with this like real men, Michael."

Michael cleared his throat. "Doug?"

The building security guard turned to him. "Yes?"

Michael's eyes began to glow. "Return to your station. Everything is normal, regardless of what you hear, and if calls come in, tell them everything is fine. Do you understand? We're not here. We were never here. Delete all the video surveillance for the evening. Can you do that?"

"Yes." Doug walked around the men and left the lounge.

"I told you your security would be shit keeping out Vamps," Kraven murmured.

Bat flashed him a dirty look. "Really? You're going to say I told you so *now*?"

Michael withdrew his second gun and pointed it at Warren. "The Dawson girls are off-limits. You were warned there would be repercussions if you fucked with someone under my protection. I always keep my word." He lowered the barrel of one gun and shot the Lycan in the knee.

Warren screamed out and dropped into a crouch. Blood stained the carpet under him. Kraven hooked Bat around her waist and lifted her, moving swiftly toward the wall and far from everyone else in the room. She couldn't look away though as Warren's white dress shirt started ripping and he began to transform, his skin quickly disappearing under fur.

Motion drew her attention away from him to the Lycan men who'd come with Warren and Travis Bales. They shifted too. The Vampires spread out, blocking the door, sealing them inside.

"Jesus!" Jacob yelled, throwing himself under one of the tables.

Bat could relate. The Vampires held their guns steady while the Lycans changed forms. They weren't anything like what she'd seen in the woods of Alaska when Carver had shifted into a scary beast. Warren and his crew looked more like actual wolves, only larger.

"Stay behind me." Kraven shoved her against the wall and planted his body in front of her, but she still had a great view of the violence about to take place between the two races.

"No problem."

349

"Crazy bastards."

Bat could agree with Kraven's assessment as the Vampires took well-aimed shots at the Lycans, targeting their legs. Warren tried to stagger toward Michael and his men but the lead Vampire fired again.

Warren dropped to his belly, whining.

Dozens of shots rang out but it ceased almost as soon as it began. Michael holstered his guns and crossed his arms over his chest as he glanced between the downed Lycans. A few of them tried to crawl but their injured limbs prevented them from getting far.

"I don't want you dead, Warren. I'd have to deal with a new asshole if I did and at least I have *you* figured out. This was just a friendly reminder that I'm watching everything you do, and I'm *always* aware of your actions. You can't get anything past me." He sighed. "You might view us as rats but I know a certain doctor who will pull those slugs out of you and set the bones. Now muzzle your men and I'll have mine take you to Morton. I called ahead and he's prepared to treat all of you."

Michael jerked his head and some of his men moved cautiously forward, scooping up the furry bodies. They carried them out of the lounge, a few more Vampires leading the way and taking care of opening and closing the doors. Michael and eight of his nest remained.

Kraven stepped forward and dragged Bat with him, keeping her at his back. "Do we have a problem? I won't let you take her. She's my mate."

"Batina is safe. I didn't come here to fight with you, VampLycan. We have spies in the pack." Michael shrugged. "Warren took over when his father stepped down eight years ago. He still has a lot to learn. It's a big territory to share. We'll never see eye to eye but I try to keep the peace. Wars are too damn messy with so many humans around us."

"I'm surprised you'd care."

Michael smiled. "I love humans. They're not only a source of food, but endless entertainment. I'm a huge movie fan. You could say I'm more progressive than most masters." His expression sobered. "I've also been around long enough to see too much blood spilled." He turned his head, glancing at the carpet. "Someone call in a cleanup crew, please. I don't want to have to pay to replace the flooring of a room this size." He looked at Bat next. "We'd like to move you to a safer location. Word has spread you're here and there's a bounty on your head."

Movement caught Bat's attention. Jacob crawled out from under one of the tables and tried to make it toward the back of the room and the fire-escape exit.

Michael didn't turn around but he did lift his hand, making a signal. "Get him before he triggers an alarm by trying to flee that way."

One of the Vampires by the door rushed over to Jacob and grabbed him by the back of his suit, lifting and forcing him to walk over to them.

Michael studied Jacob. "Friend of yours, Batina?"

"Not really; he's a partner at my law firm."

"He set up this meeting so the Lycans could take her. They promised to make him one." Kraven's disgust sounded in his voice.

Michael snorted. "I'm aware of how Warren works. He offers humans what they desire most to get them to do his bidding." He turned to stare down at Jacob. "Hello, sweaty human. Nervous? Scared?"

351

"I didn't see anything," Jacob whispered. "I swear."

"I noticed you didn't say you didn't *do* anything. Betrayal of one of your own is low." Michael clucked his tongue. "I'm considering your punishment."

Jacob blanched. "It wasn't like that! I didn't know."

Michael's eyes began to glow brightly. He reached out and fisted Jacob by his tie, hauling him closer. "Did you know Warren was a Werewolf? Tell me the truth now."

"Yes."

"What was the reason you believed he wanted Batina? Tell the truth. All of it."

"I thought he might kill her," Jacob blurted. "She's been a thorn in my side since day one. I hate her. She talked to my partners about sexual harassment charges if I didn't stop trying to fuck her and they threatened to use the buyout clause to get rid of me if I didn't cease. She's made a name for herself and brings in more clients than I do. I wanted Warren to get rid of her."

Kraven growled.

Michael leaned in closer. "You're a pathetic human being. I don't want you to ever forget what you are. Now stand there and sleep until you're ordered to waken."

Jacob closed his eyes.

The brightness in Michael's eyes faded as he turned to face Bat and Kraven, releasing Jacob's tie. "I'll send one of my men home with him to make sure he doesn't have a stash of evidence of the pack's existence hidden. Humans exposed to us love to do that shit." He reached out and grabbed Jacob's arm, shoving back his jacket to expose his dress shirt. He unbuttoned the wrist, baring skin.

"You're going to feed from him?" Bat tried to hide her distaste.

"No." Michael lifted Jacob's arm. "Your mate is. It's the least this asshole can do for setting you up." He shifted his gaze to Kraven. "How many hits did you take? Three? Four? I did my research on VampLycans once I became acquainted with Antina. Blood will heal you faster than letting those bullet holes heal on their own. Do you need our doctor to dig them out first or will they push out while you heal? I can have Morton come here now. The Lycans can wait if you need assistance. You carry both scents strongly so I'm not sure what traits you get from your parents."

"Grandparents. I'm second generation. My body will reject foreign objects as I heal."

"Blood is right here. Take it. You can kill the bastard if you want but just let us interview him first so we can destroy whatever evidence he has on the pack."

Kraven shook his head. "No thanks."

"Do it," Bat urged. She couldn't stand that he was hurt.

He looked down at her.

"Please? I'm the one who asked you to bring me here. Drink blood if it heals you."

"Your coloring is bad," Michael said. "It's safe to feed in front of us. Batina is considered one of ours and you're her mate. Feed, VampLycan.

353

We're not enemies. I'd rather you take it from this asshole than her. My girlfriend is human and I have to be very careful how much I take from her. There's nothing worse than the guilt of seeing them weakened because of our blood needs. This is how I feed, since my Christa is a jealous little thing. She wouldn't abide it if I took blood from any woman that isn't her."

That interested Bat. "You're dating a human?"

Michael smiled. "Yes. She doesn't know what I am yet. It's getting more serious. We'll have to have the talk soon."

"How do you feed off her then?"

"Very carefully, at passionate moments." He winked. "Now urge your mate to drink. He's being very brave and tough for you but he's hurt. I'd hate for him to accidentally hurt *you* when he takes you to bed later. He'd feel like shit after he drank too much."

"Goddamn it," Kraven rumbled. He held out his hand. "Fine."

Bat averted her gaze while Kraven bit into Jacob. But she didn't feel bad if it hurt the conniving son of a bitch when Kraven's fangs dug into him.

Chapter Nineteen

Kraven lifted his shirt when he stopped feeding off Jacob and grimaced. The bullets hurt as they left his body, dropping onto the carpet. He glanced at Bat, only to find her staring across the room. He released the human after licking his skin so the wounds would heal fast and nodded thanks to the master Vamp.

Michael pushed Jacob toward one of his men. "Deal with this."

"Kill or salvage?"

"Wipe him if possible. Otherwise, he looks like a man on the edge."

"Understood." The Vampire grabbed Jacob and led him out of the room.

Kraven waited until Michael looked back at him before he asked questions. "You're going to have him jump to his death?"

"My life would be easier if I said yes, but I value human life. Sometimes the exposure has lasted too long to erase it all, so we'll mess with his memories a bit until he's unsure of his sanity. He looks like he can afford a nice room in a mental health clinic. I have some experience with this, thanks to those damn Lycans. We just suggest the aliens told them about Werewolves or something, if we can't totally remove the memories, then urge them to verbally share every unkind thought they have to every person they come into contact with for a few months." Michael laughed. "Let's just say it doesn't gain them sympathy or friends. No one will believe anything he says and just peg him as a crazy asshole."

Kraven chuckled. "That's kind of mean."

Michael shrugged. "I feel no guilt. He'll live."

Bat suddenly bent and picked up the bullets from the floor. Kraven watched her pocket them. She looked up at him. "What? They have your blood on them."

"We'll clean the scene." Michael held out his hand to Bat. "You can give those to me."

Bat backed up closer to Kraven. "I'll hold on to them. No offense, but I'm a defense attorney. I have no idea if you'll dispose of them properly. I'd hate for them to be found and given to some forensics lab. It's not that I don't trust you, but let's be honest. I don't know you."

"Fair enough. You should feed your mate, VampLycan. Her injuries are bothering me."

"It's just makeup," Bat explained. "I was trying to get out of representing a client. It washes off."

Michael studied her face but turned when the doors opened. Men entered wearing uniforms with a cleaning service logo over their chests. "Get every drop, every bullet. Don't miss anything."

The men went to work. Bat sighed. "Nice."

"They're mine," Michael admitted. "We expected trouble so I had them on standby outside the building. No one can remove traces of blood better than us. But we should leave. Someone probably heard the gunshots and might come to investigate. I'd like them to just find men working."

"To clean up blood." Bat frowned.

"Wine," Michael corrected. "That's what they'll believe when my men tell them so."

Kraven felt thankful to the nest. Being shot hadn't been expected and he'd been helpless while he'd healed long enough to get up. It could have turned bad. Michael had good timing.

It didn't mean he trusted them completely or wanted to go anywhere with them.

"Thanks but I'm going to take her out of here."

"She's got a bounty on her head." Michael removed his phone and tapped the screen, turning it. It showed a photo of Bat wearing a nice suit with her hair pulled into a bun. "This was sent to the Vampire Council and they spread it to every registered nest. They've ordered us to bring her in alive. The Lycans aren't as organized but they have a system in place to share information. Within days, she'll be the most known human to both races. I know from speaking to Morton that her grandfather is the culprit behind this hunt."

Kraven reached out and gripped Bat, preparing to fight. "I'm not allowing you to turn her over to that bastard."

"I'm not giving her to the council or her grandfather." Michael stepped back and opened his hands. "We're not enemies. I do keep my word, VampLycan. I swore to Antina I'd protect her daughters from all harm—and that includes the council. She made me master of my nest."

Kraven glanced at the other men in the room. Michael seemed to guess his thoughts.

"They are absolutely loyal to me. Drackamus, the one who led our nest before, was a twisted bastard. That probably wasn't even his real

357

name; he idolized the horror accounts of the first Vampire humans ever wrote about. He tortured us, abused everyone he held power over, and used fear to rule. And the council assured we couldn't rise against him, with their threats of slaughtering any nest that killed a master." Anger deepened Michael's voice. "Let's just say we're not so loyal to them, and have worked to ensure they aren't a threat to us much longer."

Kraven arched an eyebrow.

Michael hesitated before he spoke. "I'm not the only master who's tired of being given orders by a bunch of old, outdated moving mummies who rule Vampires across the world. We've worked in unison to assassinate a few of them so far. Some are more elusive, but we *will* find them. The council needs fresh, younger blood in charge. The old ones aren't human friendly. They still dream of enslaving all other races. We've more of a mind to live in peace. It's just stupid to kill your food source."

He glanced at Bat. "Sorry. I like humans. I'm just putting it bluntly. Even Lycans have the right to live. I'm friendly with quite a few and I'd hate to see them slaughtered. There are a lot of masters of the same mindset. We're modern. The council is not. I'm showing you trust, VampLycan. They'd send every nest they could at us if you shared that information. They have no idea we were behind some of the so-called *accidents* that have taken the lives of some of their members."

Kraven considered everything he'd been told. "They aren't suspicious?"

A wide grin spread across Michael's mouth. "Like I said, I love movies. Let's just say I get some really good ideas from watching them. And technology is an amazing thing. Did you know you could steal a fresh body from a morgue—for instance, a pilot who'd recently suffered a heart attack—erase all records of his body being found, and put him in a plane? And having friends who can hack into the autopilot controls of that plane to make certain it crashes right into the home of a council member is priceless. Containers of jet fuel might have been placed onboard to level the house and make certain everything inside burned. Just an accident that happened in broad daylight. We weren't blamed. It's not *my* fault some of the ancients still believe they should sleep in wood coffins in their basements.

"He was one of the worst. I would have loved to have seen his face when he realized he was trapped after his burning house caved in on top of him. He didn't like being near humans so we didn't have to worry about innocents being harmed if the flames spread. Clean kills. He and his guards were the only ones taken out. I felt a little bad about those but he had already killed them on the inside. It was a mercy."

"He hired humans to be his day guards?" Kraven knew some Vamps did.

Michael shook his head. "*Hiring* would imply he trusted a free-thinking human. It was far more barbaric. Old ones like him think nothing of tearing into human minds and ripping out all aspects of the lives they once had, turning them into killing machines with only one objective—to protect their master. We can't fix that kind of damage. It's permanent. I've heard of a few attempts to deprogram them but they took their own lives at the first opportunity. The suggestions are placed too deep to remove. The master dies, they die. Period."

"Fuck." Kraven grimaced. "That's…"

"Fucked up," Michael agreed. "Yes. What do you want to do, VampLycan? You said she's your mate. We're willing to hide you both and keep you safe."

Kraven turned to Bat. "I'd like to take you back to my clan. The GarLycans are on our side. You'll be safest there. We'll have the protection of both."

Bat didn't look pleased with the idea of returning to Alaska.

"He's right," Michael rasped. "Everyone fears VampLycans and GarLycans. I can arrange an immediate flight back to Alaska."

"You can?" Kraven studied the master.

"I have connections. L.A. is my town. I can have a jet fueled and ready to go within fifteen minutes. It will take us that long to reach the airport. All I ask is that you ensure the safety of my pilots during the day until they can fly back tomorrow evening. I wouldn't trust anyone else to take you. They're not only part of my nest, but my friends."

"Done." Kraven would have some of the clan meet them at the airport to guard it and the Vampires while they slept. "That's easy. There are hangars. We could park the jet inside if your pilots don't mind sleeping on the plane. Is four guards enough?"

"VampLycans?"

"Of course."

Michael smiled and withdrew his phone. "I'll have them meet us there and get the jet prepared. We have people at the airport already in place. They can handle all the arrangements to get you past security and right onto the tarmac." He turned his back, making the call a few feet away.

"I didn't agree," Bat whispered.

Kraven reached out and cupped her face, stepping closer. "You're not safe here, Hellion. You heard him. Decker asked the Vampire Council to put a bounty on your head. We'll be safer with my clan, now that we know Aveoth isn't going to try to take you. You heard what Red said."

"What if it's a trap?"

He considered that. "I would rather trust the known than the unknown."

She seemed to debate that, glancing at Michael. "How do you know we can trust him?" She mouthed the words.

"I don't for certain, but he hasn't shot me."

She dropped her gaze to his chest and reached out. Her hands trembled as she lightly touched the wet material. "I'm so sorry."

He forced her head up. "Don't. You're new to all of this. You didn't even realize Warren was a Lycan. I should have said no and not let you come to the meeting. This was on me when I let you talk me into this. I should have put my foot down."

"I insisted."

"I'm not arguing with you about this, Bat. I'll ask Michael to have the Vampire with Jacob implant a suggestion so you have some time off without issues. I'm not saying you can't come back to L.A. but we need time until Decker is apprehended and dealt with, so you're completely safe. This bounty needs to be taken off your head. Think of it like a vacation. You deserve one. I get the impression you work too damn much."

"In Alaska?" She made a cute distasteful face. "I'd rather go to the Bahamas."

"Wouldn't we all." Michael said, approaching. "There's an established nest that's laid claim to those islands. They're loyal to the council. I couldn't ensure your safety there."

"Bat," Kraven drew her attention, "let me keep you safe. It won't be forever. You'll get to see your sister."

"That's a low blow."

"I know," he acknowledged. "We need to return to Alaska. I'm sorry." His mind was made up. He'd do whatever was best for his mate, even if it meant tossing her over his shoulder and carrying her onto that damn jet with her kicking and screaming every step of the way.

"I heard what you said. I'll have Lance take care of Bat's work situation. I'd be happy to even send him to speak to the other partners at her firm, so they're all in agreement on needed vacation time. Her job will be safeguarded until her return. Batina, you should listen to your VampLycan. I could hide you in the city but I'd have to secure you in one of my underground bunkers. We've modernized them a bit but I doubt you'd enjoy the accommodations. We've had a few issues with rats. I think the exterminator took care of most of them but there's always more."

Bat grimaced. "Alaska it is. We need to go up to my condo first. I'm not leaving without some clothes."

"We can do that. Let's go." Michael backed away.

Kraven didn't miss Michael's amused expression. He released Bat and motioned her to go first. After she turned away, he looked at Michael. "No rats?" He mouthed the question.

Michael shook his head.

"Thanks."

"You only want what's best for your mate. I would too," the Vamp whispered, soft enough for only his ears. "Her mother was stubborn. I know the daughters inherited that trait."

"You knew Antina well?" Kraven kept a close eye on Bat, his voice low. The other Vampires opened the door for her and two walked ahead of her, their body language those of men on alert.

"She was smart and determined to protect her young. I admired everything about her. It deeply saddened me when she and her husband died. Antina had a good heart and sympathized with the plight of others being controlled by a domineering asshole. She said her father and Drackamus were cut from the same cloth. She told me that she couldn't stop Decker, but she wanted do something about our problem. Our own demons always seem far worse than those of others."

Kraven summed it up for him. "It wasn't against the law for her to kill your master. Unfortunately, the laws were not in her favor regarding her father."

"Sometimes we live in a fucked-up world."

Kraven agreed. "But there are things that make up for it." His gaze lingered on Bat as she led them to the elevators.

363

"Very true," Michael agreed. "Love is our one weakness, and I'm very grateful for it."

* * * * *

Bat took a seat on the jet. "Wow."

Kraven dropped into the one next to hers. "It's definitely luxurious."

"Did you peek into the bathroom? I think the fixtures are actual gold."

One of the Vampires came out from the cockpit. He was a young-looking blond sporting a tailored blue pilot's uniform. "I just got off the phone with your father, Kraven. He's sending out a team to take control of the humans on the ground. They'll be waiting at your airport when we arrive. Just expect us to brake hard after we touchdown. We'll warn you on approach."

"I told you they'd give you anything you need, Ronnie." Kraven accepted the cell phone the pilot returned to him.

That pilot's words made Bat leery. "Why would we have to brake hard?"

"It's a shorter runway than we're used to, but we've landed in trickier situations. My copilot, Georgio, is prepping us for takeoff. We have clear skies and don't foresee any issues. Just relax, enjoy anything you want from the kitchen area, or let us know if there's something you need. We're estimating we'll be there in just under six hours."

"Will we make it before dawn?" Bat imagined the pilots bursting into flames if they didn't.

364

"Yes, but this is a Vampire aircraft." Ronnie grinned. "We can darken all the windows, including the windshield, and see via cameras that are specially outfitted just for the jet. We prefer not to fly during the day but in an emergency, we could. It's just not recommended."

"In case you crash?" Bat was worried about that. She'd never get on a plane again without having flashbacks of that traumatic event.

"That, and we couldn't leave the jet. We'd be trapped onboard until the sun set."

"You're strong enough to move around during daylight?" Kraven asked the question.

"Michael made sure of it." Ronnie paused. "He's fed us enough of his blood so we'll never pass out at the controls if the sun rises. You're completely safe."

Kraven wasn't done. "Are you aware that your master is helping her escape from the council?"

Bat threw him a warning look. She wasn't certain why he'd blabbed that.

"We're aware." Ronnie took a step closer. "May I be candid?"

"Please do," Kraven encouraged.

"My father was a pilot, and I've been flying since I was a young boy. I was grabbed on my twenty-first birthday by three Vampires outside a bar, and spent seventeen years doing laundry for my first master and his guards. I complained once. That cost me three months being chained to a wall and starved to near insanity. They tortured me. Michael took over and sat down with every person in our nest; he got to know us and he

365

assigned jobs we'd enjoy. He wants us to be happy. He paid for me to get my pilot's license under a new name. He freely shares his blood with us as well, so we're all strong enough to be mobile during sunlight hours. The council would order him destroyed if they found out. It's standard practice for a master to keep his underlings weak and use fear to control them. Michael doesn't. We respect *and* like him. He's our master, but he makes certain we know he sees us as equals. So the council can kiss my ass. I'm happy to do everything I can to go against their directives. It's pretty much a nest motto."

Kraven nodded. "I understand."

Ronnie addressed Bat next. "You seem nervous. There's no reason for it, Batina. Just relax. You're in great hands with Georgio and me. We once landed this beauty on an old road between two cornfields without incident, at night, without proper lighting. The nest there held torches so we could see it." He chuckled. "We're flying to an actual airport this time. This will be a breeze."

"Why cornfields?" Kraven asked.

"We have alliances with other nests, and that one was located in Indiana. There was a territory war between two Lycan packs and they needed help trying to manage all the humans who saw too much. Michael sent his friend Buck fifteen of ours to help wipe minds and negotiate peace. It's never good when there's a war. We're all exposed."

"But why not just use an airport?"

"We'd been ordered by the council not to help. Buck pissed them off when he refused to allow their enforcers to integrate with his nest. They would have taken over, destroyed Buck and anyone loyal to him. It's what

366

they do if they feel a master isn't strong enough. An airport would have left a trail of our presence. So we dropped them off in the field and our men made their way back via cars a few nights later, after Buck had things in hand and the Lycans settled their land dispute. The council never found out."

That made Bat curious. "Do Lycans fight a lot?"

Ronnie grinned. "It's the nature of the beast. Now, it's time to leave." He nodded at them and returned to the cockpit, closing the door.

Kraven turned his head, regarding her with his beautiful eyes. He opened his arms. "Come here."

Bat lifted out of the seat without hesitation. "This is becoming a habit."

"I'm not complaining. I love holding you."

She straddled his lap instead of sitting across his legs. The seats in the jet were plush and roomier than those on the other jet they'd been on. Kraven grinned in response and wrapped his arm around her waist as she settled down on him. She slid her fingers into his hair and leaned forward so she could peer into his eyes.

"I have something very important to say to you."

"You do?" He smiled. "Tell me."

"From now on, wear an armored vest when you're acting as my bodyguard."

He suddenly appeared irritated. "I'm pretty tough, Hellion."

"I don't care." It choked her up, remembering him being shot. She had to swallow hard. "Buy one and wear it when there's danger." Bat

367

released his head and placed her hand over his heart. He'd showered and changed shirts before they'd left her condo but the memory remained of all the blood he'd lost. "You protect this better."

"I'll try."

"Do. Not try."

He snarled, his lips pressed firmly together.

"What's wrong? That makes you mad?"

"I thought you had something else to say."

The jet moved. Bat tried to ignore it, focusing on him instead. "Do you know why I want you to wear a vest?"

"I can't protect you if I'm dead."

She stroked his shirt. "You promised not to hurt me, Kraven. You dying would kill me too."

His expression softened. "Bat."

Tears filled her eyes but for once she didn't blink to conceal them. "Yes, I love you. Big surprise. You're kind of hard to ignore."

He grinned.

"Don't gloat, badass. This is where you tell me you love me too, or I've made an ass out of myself and I'd hate that."

"You're my entire world, Hellion."

"Words, Kraven. I need to hear you say it."

"I love you too. You've known that for a while."

"I hoped but I wasn't certain."

"You're my mate."

"I'm still confused about how that happened. Is it just a blood thing? Like you're stuck with me, even if you don't want to be?"

"It can be that way with Lycans, but I'm more. It's part attraction, part chemistry, but most importantly, I had already begun to fall for you when I tasted your blood. Call it a bit of all that and instinct—you're the woman for me."

"I just think you're really hot and you get under my skin." She smiled, teasing him.

"I'll take it." The arm around her waist tightened and he gripped the armrest with his other hand. He also moved a bit under her to shift his legs.

Bat heard the jet accelerate and the engine noise increase. She shifted her upper body a little and buried her face in Kraven's neck. They were taking off. The sick feeling hit when the wheels left the ground and the aircraft rose.

"Easy, Hellion. I've got you." Kraven pressed his cheek against hers. "Want to have sex? I know I do. There's an actual bed in the back and a lock on the door. I was more interested in that than the bathroom."

She nodded, waiting for the jet to level out. It seemed to take forever as the pilots climbed to whatever elevation they needed. Bat sat up a bit, staring into his eyes. "Distract me."

"It's going to be fine, Bat. You know I'm not a fan of flying either but the chances of being in another crash are slim to none."

"We're going to Alaska. I'm not a big fan of *that*. Your family is going to hate me."

"Why would you say that?"

"Come on. We both know I'm no one's idea of the perfect daughter-in-law. I usually avoided meeting the families of men I've dated, since it never went well the couple times I did. They found me too forward, too pushy, and that's just to list a few complaints I've heard."

"I don't care." He used his arm to stand, keeping a hold on Bat. "Your ass is mine and I'm never letting you go. Mates are forever. I'm not worried about whether or not your sister likes me. She'll have to deal."

"She's with your Biker Bear brother." Bat wrapped her legs around his waist and he walked toward the back of the cabin. "It's not like she has any room to talk."

He chuckled. "Exactly. If it makes you feel any better…" He turned sideways, squeezing them through the door and closing it. The lock clicked. "My mother wasn't anyone's idea of my father's dream mate. Some of the clan thought she wasn't strong enough to mate with their leader. They saw her as too beta for someone so alpha." He eased her down onto her feet. "Strip."

Bat didn't hesitate to kick off her shoes and begin to remove her dress. "And the point is?"

"She loves my father, and he worships the ground she walks on. They mated anyway. He kicked some ass until they didn't dare grumble anymore. He taught her how to fight better, and *she* beat the shit out of women who gave her any lip." Kraven removed his shirt and let it drop. "She was shy once, and hesitant about standing up for herself. No one will ever accuse *you* of that, Hellion. You might not have claws but you're

370

fierce with your mouth." He took a seat on the bed and yanked off his boots. "Do you really give a fuck what anyone thinks?"

Bat considered it as she removed the rest of her clothes. It was almost instinct to deny it but when she looked at Kraven, she didn't want to lie. "I kind of do. These are people who are important to you. I'm afraid it's going to taint what we have."

He stood. "Nothing and no one could come between us." He stepped closer and gripped her hips.

Bat gasped, grabbing his biceps as he lifted her, turned them both, and tossed her on the bed. She landed on her back and watched as he peeled down his pants. He'd forgone wearing underwear. She sat up a little, using her elbows to brace herself.

"It's easy to say that now, but we're going to be staying with these people for a bit until we can return to L.A. Wait until they're pulling you aside to point out what they think of me and how big of a mistake you've made."

Kraven climbed on the bed and lowered next to her on his side. She went flat as he leaned over her, using part of his chest to push hers down. "We're not human. It's a done deal. I'll kick their asses for being morons if they dare say shit about you. They know it. You should too." He reached up and used his fingers to tangle in her hair. "I hate it up."

Bat helped him remove some of the pins from her bun until it was free. "Better?"

His gaze ran down her body. "Perfect." He looked at her then, the light blue of his eyes showing sparks of a brighter shade. "Stop worrying, Hellion. It's a wasted emotion when you could be feeling other things."

She smiled. "Like what?"

He took possession of her mouth and rolled over farther, pinning her under him. Bat wrapped her arms around his neck. Kraven could make her forget her own name when he kissed her. She didn't care about his family or his clan anymore.

Chapter Twenty

Bat clawed at the pillow behind her head and bit her lip. Kraven's hands kept her thighs pinned wide open as he tormented her with his mouth. She refused to beg him to get her off. It was a battle of wills and she was determined to win. He seemed to have had enough, though, when he growled, sucking on her clit. His lower teeth gently rubbed the swollen bud, sending her over the edge finally.

She groaned, reveling in the aftermath.

He released her and climbed up her body, hooked her thigh with one hand, and lifted it. She helped by resting her other calf on his thigh, and opened her eyes, staring into his. He slowly entered her, his cock stiff and thick. Bat reached up and cupped his neck, dragging him down for a kiss.

"You'll taste yourself," he warned.

"I don't care."

He grinned. "Not such a prude after all, huh?"

"Fuck you."

"I'm the one doing the fucking, Hellion." To prove his point, he slid his hand under her ass, getting a firm grip, and thrust deep. He paused there, just watching her.

Bat adjusted her hold on him, digging her nails into his back. "Don't stop."

Kraven twisted his head and bit her throat lightly, growling. He started to move, fucking her slow and steady. "So demanding."

She lifted her legs higher, digging her heels into his muscular ass. "Faster."

He nipped her harder but complied. Bat clung to him, lost to all the sensations of making love to the man she loved. She was no longer worried about the jet going down. Kraven had kept her preoccupied for hours now, and she had no complaints. He brought her to climax with him and groaned her name.

"This is how we could spend winters in Alaska."

She caught her breath, caressing his skin. "No offense but I'm hoping we're back in L.A. by then."

"I understand. Three clans and the GarLycans are hunting for Decker. He'll be found."

"It's a big world," she reminded him. "What if he leaves Alaska and hides with some Lycan pack or Vampires?"

"It will just take longer to find him but he's made too many enemies."

"What about the VampLycans my grandfather rules? The ones in his clan?"

"I'm certain my father and Drantos have reached out to them after the attack to see where they stand as a whole. The GarLycans won't back Decker in a fight. That's pretty damn clear. It would be suicide for the whole clan if they don't challenge him for leadership and have someone new take over."

"Do you think they're hiding him?"

Kraven seemed to consider it. "He'd know better. That's the first place we'd look. He'll want to keep mobile and out of reach of what he believes are the deadliest threats. That's Aveoth right now."

"I have to meet this guy."

Kraven's expression hardened. "Why?"

"He seems to be the boogieman of Alaska. I'm curious what terror on two legs and with a set of wings looks like."

"I don't want you anywhere near him. He'll be attracted to your blood. I won't risk him changing his mind."

"I'm *your* mate. He's shit out of luck."

"I'm still keeping you far from him."

Bat smiled. "Are you afraid I'll think he's hotter than you?"

"No. I'm worried that he'd snatch you away from me and carry you off to the cliffs."

That killed her teasing mood. "Oh."

"Yeah. I don't have wings, Hellion. Neither do you."

"I get it."

"Let's use that nice bathroom before we land. I'll wash your back." Kraven lifted off her, untangling their bodies. "You're going to want to see your sister as soon as we reach Howl, and I need to have a meeting with my father and brother. It's probably better if we don't scent like we just spent hours in bed."

"But we did."

He crawled out of bed and offered her his hand to help her up. "And we'll do it again once we're done with our families."

Bat sat up and clasped his hand, grateful as he pulled her to the edge of the big bed. She stood and followed him into the bathroom attached to the bedroom. Kraven turned on the water as she used her fingers in the mirror, trying to get out some of the tangles.

"You look beautiful, and I'm about to wash your hair."

She turned, holding his gaze. "I was just kidding about thinking anyone could be hotter than you are. That's not possible."

He winked. "You're biased. You know what I can do to you with my tongue and hands."

She lowered her gaze down his body. "You're forgetting to mention your other generous qualities."

His deep, throaty laugh was sexy. "Come on, Bat. We should be landing soon."

"Really? How long were we going at it?"

"Longer than you think. I was making up for all the times we were rushed."

She approached him. "Thank you."

"For what?"

"Just being you." She shrugged and stepped into the shower stall.

It was a tight fit when he came in behind her, closing the door. "I don't seem to annoy you when I take off my clothes."

She closed her eyes and tilted her neck, allowing warm water to pour over her head. Kraven pressed against her body, wrapping one arm around her waist and using his other to help wet all of her hair. She

376

blindly reached out and gripped the curve of his shoulder to help steady her balance.

The jet dipped at that moment. She bumped against him. Her eyes opened, staring at his face.

"It's just more turbulence."

"More?"

"It happened a few times while we were in bed."

"I didn't notice."

"Good. Don't be afraid. I'm right here. Close your eyes and I'll wash your hair. Just focus on me and nothing else."

She allowed him to tend to her. It was nice that he'd do such intimate tasks. He wasn't like other men she'd known. It made her think about the whole mate thing. She still wasn't completely onboard with the concept but it was growing on her. So was he.

Bat relaxed as he used his fingers to massage her scalp with first shampoo, then conditioner. He rinsed it all out, turned her, and pulled her close. She wrapped her arms around his waist, holding on to him.

"It's going to be fine, baby."

"I know."

"You're being too quiet and that means you're overthinking whatever's on your mind. Do you want to talk about it?"

"Mates."

"Still resistant to that?"

"More confused than anything," she admitted.

"You're never going to lose me."

377

It wasn't such a bad notion, spending the rest of her life with Kraven. She'd once feared dying alone, without ever knowing real love or happiness.

"Tell me what's bothering you," he urged.

"It's kind of scary."

"Look at me."

She lifted her chin and opened her eyes, peering into his.

"There's no pain here, Hellion. There never will be. What are your fears?"

A list of them streamed through her mind. Kraven released her waist and turned off the water. He shoved open the door, grabbed a towel, and handed it to her. She took it. He stepped out of the stall and used a second one to dry off. She did the same.

"I'm waiting. You really do need to work on your communication skills."

She nodded. "I don't know. What if you cheat? What if you decide I bug the living hell out of you in six months? What if your family goes nuts when they meet me and realize I'm the last person you should be with? We're fire and water."

"We're fire and gasoline. You were right the first time. We burn together, not put each other out." He wrapped the towel around his waist and removed a third one from the shelf near the stall. "Turn around. Let me get your hair."

She did, holding still as he worked to get a lot of water out of her long strands. "I know you say it's forever but that's a tall order for two people who barely know each other."

"You're not completely human, and I'm not at all. Don't hold us to the standards of the world you came from. You're stuck with me." He jerked her against his body, holding her from behind, and bent his lips close to her ear. "I'm trying to be patient with you because I realize this is new and foreign, but you're all I want. I don't give a fuck what anyone else says or does. You're mine, Hellion. I'm never letting you go."

"Promise?"

"I swear on my life. I always keep my word. I'd die before I'd hurt you in any way."

She hoped he meant it. It would destroy her if he ever walked away or did something that broke her heart.

Kraven counted to ten to cool his temper. He really wanted to track and kill the human bastard who'd done a number on his mate. She reminded him of a skittish animal that had been abused at the hands of others. He finished drying her hair and led her back into the bedroom. The bags were in the other room so he retrieved them in case one of the Vampire pilots came into the main area of the cabin. He didn't want them to see her in just a towel.

Bat thanked him and opened her suitcase. He threw his bag on the bed and removed comfortable clothes. He reminded her to do the same.

"It will be very early morning when we arrive. Most of the clan will be just waking and starting their day."

"So jeans and sweater?"

"Yes."

"No high heels?"

He was grateful to see a two pairs of flat-soled shoes inside her bag. "Definitely not. You shouldn't have brought *any* of those ankle-breakers."

"Don't you people have social events?"

"Not where those would be welcome."

"Fantastic. I guess I shouldn't have packed a few dresses then. I repacked while you washed off the blood and changed clothes, before we left my place."

He finished dressing and put on his boots. He leaned over, peering into her bag. "What did you bring?"

"Jeans and slacks. Some sweaters and short-sleeved blouses. I remembered you said something about picnics."

"I'm surprised you own jeans." He admired her in a pair of tight ones as she zipped them closed. "I like them."

"Thank Dusti. She bought them for me last Christmas. She said I screamed 'mugging victim' when I visited her apartment in anything I bought myself. She'd always meet me at the street and pay some teenager to watch my car so it wasn't stolen."

Kraven hid his distaste. He didn't like much about the human world. "I love how you look."

Bat smiled. "They're tight."

"Your ass looks especially amazing." He eyed it as she bent over to put on her shoes. "It almost makes me regret bringing your clothes."

She straightened and turned to face him. "Flattery will get you everywhere. I'm going to take my makeup bag in the bathroom and spruce up a bit to meet the in-laws, or whatever I'm supposed to call your parents."

"You can call them Mom and Dad, or their names, whichever you're comfortable with. Mating is just like marriage. They're family to you now."

"So we're official?"

"We need to share blood more. I wanted to wait until the danger has passed."

"Why?"

"I'm hoping for a strong bond between us, but that will mean spending days in bed, if not weeks, once the bond snaps into place."

She grinned. "Killer sex, huh?"

He grinned back. "The best."

Bat came closer and held out her wrist. "What's stopping you? Show me the fangs."

He snagged her hand and yanked her onto his lap. "That's not where I'm going to bite you, and I certainly won't do it while we're dressed."

She wrapped her arms around his neck and seemed content on his lap. "Let's not half-ass this. You said we're mates so we should make it official."

"I've been trying to give you more time to adjust."

She licked her lips. "It's better if you don't allow me to stew over things. It just makes it worse."

He understood. "Tonight, we'll share blood."

"Good. Is this going to be gross?"

"There will be lots of sex to keep you distracted."

"You're really good at that."

"I'm motivated."

A knock sounded at the door. Kraven lifted Bat and placed her next to him, going to answer it. Ronnie stood there. The pilot smiled.

"Sorry for interrupting you, but we're about to land. You'll want to strap in tight."

Kraven stepped out and closed the door behind him. He lowered his voice so Bat wouldn't hear. "Do you think there's any chance we'll crash? Give it to me straight."

"I've landed on worse. It's just a shorter runway than is recommended for this aircraft. I don't foresee problems but I'd hate for you or your mate to be flung out of your seats when we touchdown and lay on the brakes hard."

"Got it. Thank you."

Bat tried to open the door. Kraven let the handle go and spun to her.

"What in the hell was that?"

"Nothing. Let's strap in. You heard Ronnie."

She paled. "We're screwed, aren't we?"

"No." He hooked her waist, leading her to the seats. "We aren't."

"Why did you shut the door? What else did he say?"

Kraven hated to lie but he did at that moment. "I just wanted to make certain my people are on the ground waiting for us. They are."

382

"So it's safe? We're not going to blow up in a ball of flames?"

He gently deposited her into a seat and crouched, hooking her belt snuggly over her lap. "What did I say about our chances of being in another crash? Slim to none." He took the seat next to her and put on his own belt.

"I see you're not inviting me to sit on your lap this time."

He twisted in his seat and leaned toward her, firmly gripping the armrest on her other side to pin her in place better. He picked up the panicked tone in her voice. "Look into my eyes. I can take away the fear."

"You're willing to go all glowy for me?"

"Only with your permission. I'll never use this power otherwise."

She gave a sharp nod. "Do it. I can feel we're losing altitude." She gripped his arm with both hands. "Please. Just don't make me think I'm a cow. I'll be pissed if I get the urge to eat grass or moo. Fair warning."

"I would never do that." He focused on her, allowing his Vampire traits to slowly ease out. "There's nothing to be afraid of. I'm right here, Hellion. Just relax and remember the things we did in bed a little while ago."

The tension left her features and she smiled. "You're too good in bed. You blow my mind."

"I feel the same way about you." It was really tempting to implant that she could trust him, but he refused to take advantage of his mate that way. He'd have to give her time to get to know him better and earn her trust. "I think you're beautiful, and I love you." Those were things he'd already told her but he wanted her to hear it until she believed. He just

383

had to choose his words carefully while he had the ability to control her mind. "You're going to see your sister soon. Think about what you want to say to her."

"I'm going to ask if Biker Bear is good to her. I'm worried about that. He's not her type."

"You're a loving sister." Kraven was aware of the engine noises changing and heard something along the belly of the plane. It was probably the landing gear coming down. "Are you going to discuss Dr. Brent with her?"

"I'm going to tell her everything. She'll be relieved that our dad knew what Mom was. I know I am."

"Brace," Ronnie said over a speaker in the cabin.

"I want you to go to sleep until I say wake," Kraven ordered. "Now, Hellion. Sleep."

She closed her eyes and her body went lax. He ignored the belt painfully digging into his hips as he strained his body closer to her and tucked her head against his chest.

The jet hit the runway and bounced slightly. Kraven gripped the armrest tighter, his other arm wrapping around Bat. The wheels touched down firmly and the pilots applied the brakes. The engines grew louder.

Kraven hissed as his body lurched from the jarring pressure, and he cushioned Bat's limp form. The belt held but he might have bruises later. They'd fade fast. The armrest he gripped made a popping noise but didn't come loose.

The momentum eased quickly and the jet came to a halt. He took a deep breath and kissed her cheek.

"Wake up, Bat. It's over. We're on the ground safe."

She stirred and her eyes opened. "Thank you."

He released the armrest and straightened, unbuckling his belt. "Not a problem." He slid out of his seat to his knees and got in front of her, unfastening her belt. "Anything hurt?"

"Did we overshoot the runway?" She looked around.

"No but the belt might have dug into you a little. I think I kept you in place fairly well, but I want to make sure."

"I feel great."

He climbed to his feet and helped her stand. "We're back in Alaska...and we didn't crash this time."

"Oh, goodie. How thrilling."

She amused the hell out of him. "Try to hide that sarcasm around my parents. They love this state."

"Got it. Lie my ass off and pretend I'm in the Bahamas."

He chuckled. "Exactly."

"Does your mom really look as young as your father?"

"Yeah. VampLycans don't age the way humans do."

She grimaced. "Shit. Does that mean you're going to look the same in say a hundred years and people are going to mistake me for some cougar grandma dating a hot young dude?"

"No. You already look younger than you really are, but sharing my blood will show your aging process down even more."

385

"That's a bonus. You should have mentioned that when you told me we were mates."

He cocked his head, confused. "Why would that matter?"

"You're such a man. Never mind."

Ronnie came out of the cockpit. "Do you want to deplane now or do you want a ride to the hangar? Georgio is about to back up and drive us there."

"Where are my people?"

"Outside. They're leading us to where we're supposed to park for the day."

Kraven's phone buzzed. He reached down and answered it. "Yeah."

"Are you coming out?"

He grinned. "Hi, Red. Thanks for coming."

"There are eight of us. Four will protect the Vamps until they can fly out tonight and my team will escort you home."

"We're heading out." He hung up and nodded to Ronnie. "Just open the side door. We're getting off here." He spun, strode into the bedroom, and collected his bag and Bat's suitcase. He carried them back into the main area of the cabin.

Ronnie had already unsealed the door and had it open. "Do you want me to extend the stairs?"

Kraven walked to the opening, looking down. "No need. Red! Head's up." He tossed out the bags one at a time.

"Dickhead," Red yelled, but caught each one.

Kraven chuckled and spun around, scooping Bat up in his arms next. "Time to meet the family."

"Don't you fucking dare," she ordered.

He turned sideways to avoid bumping her against the opening and jumped. Bat screamed and tightened her arms around his neck. He bent his knees a little, landing gracefully on his feet before straightening.

"You rotten son of a bitch," Bat ranted. She fisted his hair with one hand and gave it a tug. "You suck ass. That was a horrible thing to do. What if you'd dropped me? What if you broke your legs and we both ate shit?"

He ignored her and lifted his head, staring up at Ronnie. "Thanks for the ride," he called out.

"Good luck." Ronnie closed the door.

"Are you listening to me? Don't jump out of planes! What's wrong with using the stairs?"

"This is why I'm single."

He turned, grinning at Red. "You don't know what you're missing, cousin." He held Bat's gaze. "I'd never drop you. It saved time to just jump. Do you want down or should I keep carrying you? Our escort home is here. You remember Red, don't you?"

Bat turned her head. "Hi. Is he always this damn crazy?"

"It was only about twelve feet. That's nothing." Red shrugged. "I'd worry if it were fifty feet or so, since he's carrying you. That can fuck up our balance a little."

Bat buried her face against his neck and groaned. "Why did I even bother to ask? You're all nuts."

She always amused him. Kraven winked at Red. "It's good to be home."

"At least you didn't toss *her* out at me." Red had the nerve to laugh.

Bat jerked her head up and glared at him. Kraven grinned. "I'd never do that. She's a keeper."

"Let's go." Red bent and hefted up their bags he'd placed on the tarmac.

Chapter Twenty-One

Bat paced the living room of Kraven's home, her gaze constantly straying to the front door. "Where is she?"

Kraven sat on the couch, watching her. "They were sleeping. Give them a few minutes to get dressed. They'll be here." He sighed. "All of them."

That halted her. "What does that mean?"

"My parents will show up too. Try to remember they lead this clan, and are used to being respected, okay? Pretend they're some high-end client or something."

He actually seemed worried. She admitted some nervousness on her part too. "Kiss a little ass. I got it."

The front door opened and Bat spun, spotting Dusti. Her sister entered first, with the big Biker Bear right on her heels. Their gazes locked and Bat rushed at her, grabbing her around her waist and hugging her tight. Relief that she looked fine, despite her messy hair and baggy clothing, brought tears to Bat's eyes.

"I'm okay," Dusti assured her.

Bat eased her hold enough to get a good look at her sister's face. "You *shot* our grandfather? What were you thinking? You've never touched a gun in your life! You could have been killed!"

"It's a long story." Dusti squeezed her arm. "Come on, are you really surprised? You know how much I've always hated him. I only regret that he didn't die. Who *does* that? I got him six times!"

Bat would never forget Kraven taking three bullets to the chest. "They aren't human. Why would you go after him? That's something *I'd* do."

"I was being you."

"What?" Bat was confused.

"He grabbed a little girl and wanted to exchange her for you. The moron thought you were the one in Howl, instead of me. So I played *you*." Dusti wiggled out of her hold and straightened her shoulders, lifting her chin, and her expression hardened. "It wasn't too hard. I just threw some lawyer terms out there and ranted about my messed-up clothing." Dusti smiled and her body relaxed. "The dumbass bought it right up until I shot him."

"You still could have been killed." Bat tried to remain calm but the thought of Dusti with a gun, facing off against their grandfather, terrified her. She looked at Drantos. "How could you let her do that?"

He shook his head. "I didn't. She snuck out—and my *mother* helped her do it. Don't blame this on me. I'm still furious."

"Hey." Dusti drew her attention. "Ease up, big sis. This was all on me. My plan. That kid was just a baby. You'd have done the same thing. Not to mention, you know how much I've always hated Decker Filmore. I don't regret shooting him but I'm sorry he's still alive. He deserves to die for all he did to Mom and us."

Bat just gawked at her, stunned.

"Are you disappointed in me for saying that?" Tears shone in Dusti's eyes. "I know you think it's important that we have family but I don't agree. He's a piece of shit."

"I had a change of heart," Bat admitted. "I wish the bastard was dead too. He put you in danger. I'll never forgive him for that."

Kraven came up behind Bat. "It's good to see you, Drantos. Do you have any leads?"

"He never showed up at the airport, but someone reported a bush pilot missing forty miles from here. We sent an enforcer with one of Aveoth's men to that location. They picked up VampLycan scents at the man's home, including Decker's. They must have forced him to fly them out of the area in his helicopter."

"Damn." Kraven wrapped his fingers around Bat's hip and tugged her back against him.

She allowed it, glancing between the brothers as they stared at each other. Both of them showed grim expressions. "What exactly does that mean?"

Kraven answered. "He could be anywhere. Alaska. Canada. Hell, Russia. It depends on the range of the helicopter or if he just had it fly him to somewhere with other transportation. Trains, buses, or other airports. For all we know, he could have avoided civilization altogether."

"He'll go for the cities," Drantos predicted. "It's easier to get lost and we don't venture there often."

"I agree. He had the Vampire Council put a bounty on her head so he's buddy/buddy with them right now."

"Fuck." Drantos snarled.

Bat pressed back against Kraven. His brother's fangs had extended and he looked scary. He wrapped both of his arms firmly around her waist and held her close.

"He reached out to the Lycan packs too," Kraven added. "I'm guessing he's on his way to L.A. That's why I wanted to get the hell out of there. One of the packs tried to turn Bat over to him. They admitted being in contact with him. The Vamps stopped them and flew us home."

"Against council orders?" Drantos frowned.

"That's another long story," Kraven admitted. "I need to talk to Dad."

Drantos leaned and placed a kiss on Dusti's cheek. "You stay here with your sister. Kraven and I are going to see our parents. I asked Maku to keep an eye out for you two. He's right outside. Stay put...for once."

Dusti turned and wrapped her arms around the big Biker Bear, grinning up at him. "Promise."

Bat studied the couple. Some of her reservations about their relationship disappeared at observing the loving way they gazed at each other. Drantos hugged her sister close, kissing her again.

Dusti suddenly laughed. "You're so bad. Is that my reward if I'm good?"

Drantos winked at her sister and she laughed again.

"What am I missing?" Bat looked up at Kraven.

He held her gaze. "They've bonded."

"So?"

He lowered his head, putting his lips close to her ear. "They can think words and hear each other without actually speaking them aloud," he

392

whispered. "Watch them. They're having an entire conversation. We just can't hear it."

Bat studied her sister and her Biker Bear again. They were staring into each other's eyes, and sure enough, their expressions changed, almost as if they were talking. Drantos kissed her sister once more and reached up, brushing her cheek with his fingers. Dusti suddenly placed her hand on his stomach and shoved at him, laughing again. He grinned in response.

It kind of freaked Bat out. "Dusti?"

Her sister turned her head, looking at Bat. "Sorry."

Kraven eased his hold. "I'll be back soon."

Bat nodded. She waited until the men left and the door closed. She had questions and she wanted answers. "What was *that*?"

"It's called mate bonding. It's kind of hard to explain." Dusti smiled. "I have a lot to tell you."

"No shit. You have telepathy with Biker Bear?!"

Dusti took her hand. "This is a conversation best had sitting down."

Bat just nodded and turned, taking a seat on the couch. Dusti kept hold of her hand and sat next to her. "Hit me with it."

"Drantos is my mate. I was weirded out by that at first but...he's amazing, Bat. I love him so much. He loves me too." Dusti smiled wider. "We can send thoughts and words at each other if we're close. I can feel what he feels too. The sex is amazing when we're linked."

Bat tried to take all that in.

Dusti squeezed her hand. "I know it sounds crazy. It's real though. I didn't believe it until our bond snapped into place. I can feel my hands on him like it's my own body. You know how we joke about how it sucks sleeping with men who can get off so easily during sex when it's tougher for us? Not anymore. Drantos getting off gets *me* off."

It was tough for Bat to wrap her mind around.

"I take it you and Kraven haven't experienced that yet?" Dusti's tone softened. "He's *your* mate, Bat. Did he tell you that? He is. Drantos shared that information with me."

"Kraven told me."

Dusti leaned closer. "You're fighting it, right? Stop. For once in your damn life, listen to what I'm saying. Having a mate is the best thing that ever happened to me. I don't know Kraven, but I do know Drantos. And they're brothers, so I'll give him the benefit of the doubt that he's an incredible person too. You've always been afraid of being hurt again. These guys aren't like the ones we've known. My marriage was a damn joke. A sad, unfunny one. What I have with Drantos doesn't even compare. It's intense and beautiful. He'd never hurt me. He can't without hurting himself. It will be the same way with Kraven if you stop fighting becoming his mate. He'll feel what you feel. He hurts you, he does it to himself too. He makes you sad, *he's* sad. It's how it is. Really."

"I don't know what to think," Bat admitted.

"I know. I was reluctant to believe until I experienced it firsthand. It seemed too damn weird." Dusti smiled again. "But you trust me, and I wouldn't lie to you. I'm not brainwashed or anything either. I'm just in love and really happy."

"Doesn't it bother you that they're VampLycan?"

"So are we, to an extent. We just didn't know it."

Dusti had a point. "I talked to Dr. Brent." Bat shared what she'd learned and everything that had happened in L.A. "So Dad knew about Mom being a VampLycan, and she did try to tell me the truth. I feel like I let her down. She had to erase my memories every time she let me in on our family secret."

Dusti released her hand and wiped away tears. "Stop beating yourself up. You were just a teenager, Bat. Hell, I'm an *adult* and didn't take it well until the truth was unavoidable. I accused Drantos of being nuts."

"I'm guilty of doing that to Kraven too."

"Drantos understood why I was so resistant to believe. I'm sure Kraven doesn't hold it against you either." Dusti pulled her legs up, kicking off her shoes to get more comfortable on the couch. "I'm sorry that one of your bosses tried to set you up, but you knew he was an asshole. You've told me about Jacob. He's the tool."

"You're trying to change the subject."

Dusti laughed. "Guilty. I hate seeing you sad. I prefer mad."

"I *am* pissed. Warren Otis admitted he told the firm to hire me. He wanted to keep an eye on me and Jacob was his little yes man, willing to do anything to become a Lycan."

"You're an awesome attorney, Bat. They were lucky to get you. Plenty of law firms offered you jobs. You got where you are on your own merit."

Bat blurted out what was on her mind. "Everything is different now. I'm so confused!"

"I know." Dusti gave her a sympathetic look. "It's easier for me. I didn't really care much about my job and I won't miss my apartment. Drantos needs to live here. The winters are going to suck but he's assured me I won't have to go out in the snow unless I want to. I guess a lot of mates just hunker down and spend a lot of time in bed together. I'm kind of looking forward to that. Did I mention the sex between mates is amazing?"

Bat felt torn. "I'm happy for you, but I hate that we're going to be living in two different states. Kraven offered to move to L.A."

Dusti's expression sobered. "He'd be miserable, Bat. You realize that, don't you? He's a VampLycan. They love the freedom of living in the woods. Where is he going to shift forms and run? And they're a pack-mentality kind of species. I've learned a lot about them over the past few days. He'd be alone, without family and friends. You might as well stick a wild animal in a cage. That's what you'd be doing to him by making him live in L.A. Drantos loves to climb out of bed and go for a run while shifted in the mornings. They can do that here. It's a human-free zone, except by the main road. Drantos just steps out the back door, shifts into his other form, and it's safe for him to do it."

"Kraven said he'd live there with me."

"Okay." Dusti nodded. "But when you start feeling really sad and depressed, just know that emotion is actually coming from him. You'll feel what he does. He might try to shield you by closing the bond, to protect you from his pain. That's going to hurt too. Right now, I can't feel Drantos

396

because his parents' house it too far and I feel like a part of me is missing. You love Kraven, don't you?"

"Yes." Bat had never lied to Dusti about the important things.

"Is your job worth hurting him? You could always take the bar or whatever you need to do to practice law here. It's not as if you owe your firm anything after what Jacob tried to do. Do you really want to work with that asshole ever again? And Warren Otis is there. You'll be stuck defending him or his employees if he stays with your firm, and that's if he doesn't try to kill you for what happened. Think about that."

"I'm so close to making partner, Dusti."

Dusti scooted closer, giving her a look. "It didn't make you happy, Bat. You've been dying inside for years. I watched and said nothing because I didn't want to be one of the people you pushed away. You've done that ever since our parents died. It hurts you to care. I get it. Now things are different. *We're* different. You love Kraven and you have something to lose again. What's more important? That's what you need to figure out."

Bat looked away, battling tears.

"Hey."

She met Dusti's gaze. "What?"

"Close your eyes."

Bat hesitated but then did as she asked.

"It's six months in the future. You've made partner and just won a big case that nobody thought you could." Dusti released her hand. "You go home to your empty condo. Kraven is in Alaska. Put yourself at your table,

397

staring at your wall of accomplishments. What do you really want, sis? That damn wall? Or to be with the man who loves you?"

The couch cushion shifted and Bat opened her eyes. Dusti stood. "Really think about that. I'm going to raid Kraven's kitchen and find us something to eat. I'm hungry. This is something only you can decide. Close your eyes and picture your future. I'm going to be fine, whatever you decide. I have Drantos. But I know you can't be selfish enough to ask Kraven to live in a cage, so you need to let him go if you return to L.A., Bat. That's the big point I'm trying to make; I've told you about the mating bond. It's not too late. Love him or set him free. Decide what matters most. It's not fair to expect a relationship to work on just your terms. That's a dick move, and you're not a dick."

Bat watched Dusti enter the kitchen, opening cupboards and the fridge. Her little sister always had a way of putting things into perspective. And Bat had some thinking to do.

* * * * *

Kraven shifted in the seat, wishing he could just go home to Bat. He worried about her. His brother seemed to guess his thoughts.

"Dusti won't let her run away."

He turned his head, holding Drantos's stare. "She can be pretty persuasive. What if she talks your mate into leaving with her?"

Drantos grinned. "Dusti won't leave me."

His brother's confidence in his mate irritated Kraven. "Fuck you."

"Knock it off," their father ordered. "Maku won't let either of them leave. He's protecting them. Get your minds back on the matter at hand."

398

Drantos broke eye contact first. "We need to reach out to Decker's clan and get a feel for what's going on there. He didn't make friends by kidnapping one of the children. That pissed some of them off. They also suffered grief from the deaths his orders caused."

"Have we heard from anyone in that clan?" Kraven shifted in his seat again.

"We've had some people reach out to family." Their father leaned forward, resting his elbows on his desk. "Lake's sister and her mate are furious that their daughter was taken. They asked to join our clan and I accepted. Decker took most of his enforcers with him when he fled. It's a good time for some of them to flee without repercussions. I made it clear we'd welcome any families who wish to join us. I've ordered some of our men to start building temporary cabins to house them."

"What if most of their clan wants to leave Decker's?" It could become a headache to house a bunch of families, and there was the issue of where to put them. Kraven decided he'd help any way he could, even if that meant chopping down a lot of trees for building materials and sharing some of his land with newcomers.

"I've spoken to the other two clans. They'll take in families if we get a lot coming to us." Their father shrugged. "It means fewer numbers we'll have to fight if Decker starts his war. They'll swear their allegiance to their new clans."

"What about Lorn?" Kraven would hate like hell to have to switch clans, if he were in their shoes. "That kid I spoke to said he might be strong enough to challenge and take over the clan. He spoke of Lorn in terms that made me believe he isn't anything like Decker. It might be

399

better to support leadership change in their clan instead of expecting families to start over."

"It's risky." Drantos shrugged. "We don't know him. What if Lorn is worse?"

Kraven snorted. "As if that's possible."

"He could be an option. I'd prefer we not break up clans." Their father glanced at both of them. "We buy up any land that becomes available or lease it from the state, but spacing is going to become an issue if we take in large numbers. It could cause friction between new neighbors. I'd like to avoid that."

"I agree." Drantos stood. "We should reach out to this Lorn, then, and talk to him. I could go there."

"No. I'll call him. They could see it as an act of aggression if we show up unannounced. I'll offer Lorn support." Their father glanced at the phone. "I'll send him some of our enforcers to help him deal with any of the hard-core Decker supporters, but only if he agrees. Who knows how many were poisoned in their minds by that bastard's lack of integrity?"

"Decker encouraged them to break laws." Kraven guessed some were beyond caring about honor. "They won't want someone new stepping up."

Drantos sat back down. "But you're both right, taking a chance on this Lorn is better than having to move a bunch of people and completely uproot their lives. Most of them might be willing to throw their support behind him if it will keep their clan together."

Their father picked up the phone and dialed.

"Are you calling Lorn right now?" Kraven asked.

"No. I'm calling Lake. He knows more about the people in that clan than I do, since he visited his sister often. I want his opinion." He quickly asked the enforcer to come to his home and hung up. "He's on his way."

It didn't take long. Lake entered, giving Drantos a wide berth. It made Kraven curious but he didn't ask what the problem was between the two. He'd find out later. His father spoke first.

"Do you know a Lorn, from Decker's clan?"

Lake nodded. "He's a big bastard, keeps to himself, and not real popular with Decker's enforcers. May I ask why you're asking about him?"

"I spoke to a kid who said Lorn might make a good candidate to take over Decker's clan," Kraven shared. "We're discussing it but we don't know much about him. Relax and take a seat. You look tense. Tell us everything you know about Lorn."

Lake gave a wary glance to Drantos, who nodded and pointed to a chair. Lake sat. It made Kraven even more interested in what had transpired while he'd been gone.

"I like Lorn. He's the first son of Ladius."

"Decker's advisor?" Their father's tone implied he didn't like the VampLycan.

Lake nodded. "It's no secret that Lorn and his brother Lavos are distanced from their father. Both refused to become personal enforcers for Decker but they have the strength for it."

"What else can you tell us?" Drantos crossed his ankles. "Give us your best impression of Lorn."

401

Lake nodded. "He's a bit of a loner but not someone to fuck with. I was also warned by my sister to avoid speaking or even getting too close to a particular woman in the clan. She smells completely human but her father is a VampLycan. Lorn is her protector."

"The kid I met said something about a human," Kraven remembered.

"Kira. That's a mystery I couldn't solve. Nobody seems to know why Decker would allow her to live there, unless it has something to do with her father. Davis runs their community center and hosts events for the clan. Maybe he and Decker are friends or they made a deal." Lake shrugged. "I was surprised to smell a human there but was assured Davis is her biological father."

"Is Lorn her mate?"

"She's an outcast, Velder. I witnessed the way she was treated on occasion while visiting that clan. No one speaks to her and they avoid contact. I think Lorn might feel sorry for her. My sister does."

"That *is* strange. Davis must have something on Decker," Drantos assessed. "I'd love to know what that secret could be. Friends wouldn't allow the daughter of one to be shunned. Are you close to Davis, Lake?"

The enforcer shook his head. "No. He keeps to himself too. Decker's clan isn't as social as ours. It's got a whole different vibe there."

Their father leaned back in his chair. "Do you think Lorn would be interested in taking over his clan?"

Lake took his time before he spoke. "I'm not sure, but he'd make a good leader."

"What makes you think so?" Their father's eyes narrowed.

"I've seen him interact with the clan. Kids like him and he's good with them. One of the enforcers, Nabby, tends to be cruel. He picked on a group of teens, trying to assert his dominance. None of the youths challenged him. He just seemed to want a fight. Lorn went chest to chest with him and forced him to back down. My sister told me that people go to Lorn for help if they have problems with Decker's enforcers. He makes them back off."

"I'm surprised Decker hasn't killed him." Their father scowled. "This Lorn sounds like a natural enforcer, yet he won't work for him?"

"Decker is longtime friends with Ladius. He might not want to infuriate him by killing his only sons. Decker needs every ally he can keep. The brothers are tight. They'd kill or die to defend each other." Lake stood. "May I go? I'm on duty in a few minutes."

"Go. Thank you." Their father gazed at Kraven and Drantos, waited until Lake closed the door. "We'll reach out to Lorn by phone and test the waters. It would be best if the clans remain divided, providing this VampLycan has honor."

"Agreed." Kraven wanted to go home too. "Are we done?"

"Yes." Their father snorted. "I forget you're both newly mated."

Kraven led the way back to his cabin. "How did Mom take meeting Dusti?"

"Bad. I mean, she didn't attack Dusti or anything. Mom advised her to get pregnant right away since she's so human."

Kraven winced. Bat would lose her temper if their mother ever said something like that to her. "Shit. How pissed is your mate at you?"

"She damn near got herself killed confronting Decker to prove her worth to the clan and our parents. Dusti will say otherwise but it boils down to that. We're good, but you'd better point out to our mother that your mate is less tolerant than her sister."

"You're the first son. I'm not under pressure to produce offspring for future generations."

Drantos growled. "Fuck you."

Kraven chuckled. "It's good to be the younger brother."

"I'm just glad you're finally here. It will give Dusti more support to have her sister to talk to and commiserate with."

His good mood fled. "Bat wants to return to L.A."

Drantos stopped and gripped his arm. "You'd hate it there."

He faced him. "I know, but she's my mate. I'm not giving her up, regardless of what it takes to keep her."

His brother studied him with narrowed eyes. "You fear if given the choice between the life she had and the one you could offer her, she won't chose you?"

"We've barely exchanged blood. The bond isn't strong. Hell, I'm not even sure if we can form the kind you have with Dusti. Those Vampire traits help with the telepathy link with a mate. Bat is barely Lycan, and I don't taste any Vamp in her at all."

"You'd feel trapped in the city."

"It would be worse being without her."

Drantos released him and sighed. "I'm so sorry. Why'd we think finding mates would be so damn easy?"

"We were younger and naïve. She's worth it. Whatever the cost, I'm not letting her go. She's mine."

"I understand."

Chapter Twenty-Two

The front door opened and a tall dark-haired woman entered.

Bat frowned, assessing the uninvited intruder into Kraven's home. She stood, ready to confront her. Suspicion that it was one of his ex-lovers immediately came to mind. Dusti rushed to her side.

"Hi, Crayla." Dusti elbowed Bat. "This is Drantos and Kraven's mother."

Bat managed to keep her mouth from falling open. Kraven had warned her that his mother looked young, but she seemed to be the same age as her sons. "Hello."

Crayla closed the door and openly studied her. Her nostrils flared as she sniffed the air. "You smell just as human as your sister. That's a disappointment. I was hoping you'd carry a Lycan scent but I can't pick it up."

"Excuse me?" Bat took offense.

"You're as weak as your sister. It's disappointing. Isn't that clear enough?"

Her temper boiled fast. "Listen up, bitch. Don't you dare walk in here like you own the place and—"

"Okay," Dusti yelled, slapping her hand over Bat's mouth. "Let's not get off to a bad start."

Bat reached up and yanked Dusti's fingers away, glaring at Kraven's mother. "Don't ever do that again, Dusti."

"She can shift," Dusti whispered. "Calm down."

"As if I care." Bat took a step forward and lifted her chin, refusing to look away from Crayla's steady gaze. "I won't be talked to that way. My sister let me in on how you treated her. How *dare* you? We might be more human than you'd like but at least I don't have to spend a fortune on razors." She glanced down at Crayla's body. "I hope you invested in one of those companies, what with those long legs of yours. That's a hell of a lot of space to keep shaved."

Crayla's mouth parted and she appeared a bit stunned.

"What? I'm sure you don't see turning into a big dog as a bad thing but from my point of view, that has to suck. I spent a small fortune on laser hair removal. That's how much I detest body hair. I won't put *you* down if you lay off the insults too. That's the only way we're going to get along. Is that clear?"

Crayla firmly sealed her lips.

"That's right. I don't take any shit, lady. I'm also not getting pregnant anytime soon, so don't even go there. I'm Kraven's mate. You don't have to like it but it seems pretty set in stone, from what your son told me. We can either call a truce to get along or holidays are going to be pure hell. That's entirely up to you."

"I see." Crayla crossed her arms over her chest but then smiled. "I can respect that."

"Great," Dusti muttered.

Bat relaxed. "I don't want to have a bitch war with you, Crayla. I love your son and he loves me. Dusti and I aren't used to having family besides

407

each other, but I want us to all get along. It's not a requirement though if you keep being nasty."

"I like you. You're very outspoken."

"That's who I am," Bat admitted. "So, truce?"

Crayla grinned. "Yes. It's a shame you can't shift. I bet you'd have made a wonderful predator."

"I don't need claws or fangs. I've got a mouth and a mean temperament when riled. I have no qualms about picking up the nearest sharp object and going after someone if I'm pissed."

"You'll do." Crayla chuckled. "I approve."

"That's just great," Dusti mumbled again.

Both Crayla and Bat looked at her.

Dusti shook her head. "I tried to be nice to keep the peace. Did she approve of *me* right away? Hell no. It's not fair."

Bat put her arm around her and smiled. "That's because you're the nice one."

"You *are* very polite," Crayla admitted. "You're living with VampLycans, Dusti. We're a tough race. You need to stand up for yourself more."

"That's what I've always told her." Bat smiled at Kraven's mom. "Maybe we *will* get along."

"I hate you both right now." Dusti pulled away from Bat. "Really. You're both assholes."

"That's better." Crayla laughed.

The front door opened and Kraven and Drantos stepped in. Kraven's horrified expression at seeing his mother amused Bat. "Hi, baby."

He strode to her side quickly. "Is everything okay?"

"We're great." She put her arm around him and leaned in close to press against his side.

Drantos cleared his throat. "Dad could really use your attention right now, Mom."

She glared at him. "Are you trying to get me to leave?"

"He's irritated that both his sons want to spend more time with their mates, rather than sitting with him in his office discussing politics. Could you please talk to him? We'd appreciate it."

She walked toward him. "I'm old, not stupid. Fine. I'll leave." She glanced over her shoulder. "I'll talk to them later."

The tension eased from everyone once she'd left. Drantos held out his hand. "Let's go home, Dusti."

Her sister almost ran to Biker Bear. "I missed you."

"I missed you too." He lifted her and planted a kiss on her lips. "Later. Dinner tonight? My place? Say six o'clock?"

"Sounds good," Kraven answered. "We'll be there."

Kraven eased away from Bat and locked the door after the couple left. "I'm sorry about my mom. I didn't know she'd come over so soon." He approached. "Did she upset you?"

"She's a bit aggressive but she's also part Lycan. That's to be expected, right?"

He smiled. "You're not mad?"

"I was. We had a few words but she backed off."

"My *mother*?"

"I speak bitch," Bat explained. "Any word about my grandfather?"

"He's still missing but everyone is looking for him. It's only a matter of time before he's caught."

"You don't look convinced."

"Like you said, it's a big world and we don't leave ours too often. It will help if someone else takes leadership of Decker's clan. That way, he'll lose all hope of starting his war. He can't wage it with only a handful of enforcers."

Bat let that sink in and felt dread. "Are they asking you to take his place in that clan?"

"No. They'd never accept an outsider."

"That's good." She could breathe easier.

He stepped close and peered down at her. "I gave you my word that I'd take you back to L.A. as soon as the danger has passed. I'd never ask you to give up your life for me. This is just temporary."

I'm just asking you to give up yours. Dusti's words replayed in her head. Kraven would be miserable living in a city.

She made a decision. "Take off your clothes."

He tilted his head a little but amusement showed in his eyes. "You want to have sex?"

"I want to see you shifted."

His expression sobered in an instant. "I don't think you're ready for that."

"I am." She took a seat on the couch. "Show me. I won't run away or scream. I need to see all of you, Kraven."

He bent down, pulling off his boots. "I'd never hurt you. I might look vastly different but it's still me."

"I understand. You're not going to turn into a mindless animal."

"Exactly."

Bat pulled up her legs and tucked them under her. Her heart pounded; she was nervous. In order to make plans for the future, she needed to face the present. That meant knowing all the facts. It was one thing to see Carver change into a big dog beast but she needed to see Kraven that way. He was her mate.

Kraven revealed his beautiful body. He stood straight, letting her see every inch of him bared. "Are you sure about this, Hellion?"

"Absolutely. Rip off the bandage and let's get this over with."

He laughed. "Okay. Here goes." He slowly crouched, his gaze locked with hers. "I'd *never* hurt you."

"I'm counting on that. I won't scream or run out into the woods. I'm not a lumberjack. I like being indoors."

"My eyes turn black. Don't be afraid."

"Thank you for the warning. Just do what you're going to do. I'm ready."

He took a deep breath and blew it out, watching her. Bat tensed when hair began to slowly grow on his cheeks. Her gaze traveled over his body, watching hair spread everywhere. The sounds came next as his bones seemed to pop and adjust to the way his body changed. His form took on a more animal one, and became hairier by the second, but it was his face that stunned her the most.

His nose and mouth pushed out, becoming snout-like. His forehead stretched back a little and his ears became a bit pointy. She stared into his eyes, watching the color of them disappear, changing from light blue to total black. Even the whites of his eyes bled away until they were nearly impossible to see.

It ended when he sat on his haunches, watching her from a few feet away.

Kraven wasn't a man anymore. Bat felt fear but she pushed it back. He wasn't about to hurt her, despite the fact that the hell dog version of him could give most people nightmares for life. She regulated her breathing and forced her legs to move. She slid off the couch to the floor, just studying him.

He held unnaturally still and she appreciated that, realizing he was doing his best to alleviate her fear of him. She inched closer, crawling to him. His size was about the same, a little bigger, but his shape had completely changed. Her hand trembled as she reached out and gently stroked one of his shoulders. The fur was softer than she expected.

He tilted his head just a tiny bit, watching her.

"I'm okay," she got out. "Can I see the teeth?"

His eyes narrowed but he actually opened his mouth just enough to flash some wicked-sharp fangs. A soft whine came from him. It wasn't a scary sound.

"I'm going to stand. Just hold still."

She got to her feet and carefully walked around him, taking in every inch. He had a tail. His paws were massive, with some fierce claws. They were thick, curved, and a few inches long. She brushed her hand down his back and her thoughts returned to what her sister had said about a VampLycan living in the city. There was no way anyone could confuse Kraven for some domesticated dog. It would cause complete panic if he were seen. People would scream, call 9-1-1, and probably whip out their camera phones to get some footage for YouTube. He looked like something right out of a horror movie.

Bat sat down in front of him again, staring up into his eyes. She'd thought Carver looked evil, but not Kraven. The shape and color of his eyes weren't anything close to human but he didn't have that dead look some killers carried. She'd seen that plenty of times over the years in her line of work. Kraven's gaze felt warm, almost loving.

He moved slowly and lowered his muzzle closer.

All her fear evaporated and her hand no longer shook when she reached up to stroke the side of his face. "I can deal with this. I get it."

Boy, do I. It all hit her at once. Dusti was absolutely right. Kraven couldn't shift and run anywhere in L.A. He'd only be able to transform inside her condo. Her condo was big, but Kraven was a huge hulk of a beast. It would be like owning two Great Danes in a tiny apartment. She'd always felt it was cruel to contain dogs in small spaces without a yard, one of the reasons she didn't own a pet.

He started to shift to skin and Bat scooted away until she had the couch at her back. Kraven's light blue eyes were a welcome sight, along

413

with all that smooth skin. He sat down in front of her and drew up his knees, silent.

"How often to you usually change and go for a run here?"

"Daily."

"Dusti said her Biker Bear likes to go running every morning. Do you?"

He nodded. "What are you thinking? You look sad, Hellion."

"It's not going to work."

His mouth pressed into a firm line and he glanced away, then back. "I knew it was too soon. You're my mate, Bat. I'm not letting you just walk away. I'll fight to keep you. We belong together."

"I wasn't talking about us. What happens if you don't shift for days or weeks?"

"I can deal with it."

"What happens? Don't bullshit me. Does it make you sick or something?"

"Not sick but the urge gets stronger. It's a part of me. Over time it can weaken me a bit, trying to contain my other side." He seemed to guess her thoughts. "I'll be fine in L.A."

"Don't lie to me, Kraven. Please."

"You know what I look like now. I can shift inside your condo if the urge becomes too strong to resist."

"It's sixteen hundred square feet of living space. What do you plan to do? Buy a treadmill for the guest bedroom?"

"If I have to."

414

"You'd be happier here, wouldn't you?"

"You'd be *unhappy*. I can withstand anything for you."

"God, I feel like a selfish bitch right now. I didn't get it until this moment."

"We'll make it work. I can't lose you, Bat."

She bent forward and crawled to him. He lowered his legs and she just climbed onto his lap. It helped being close to him. She hugged his waist.

"I don't want to lose you either. I just need to think."

"There's nothing to think about. We're here until Decker is captured and then we'll return to L.A. Don't worry about me. I'll be fine as long as I have you."

She believed he meant the words, but over time, he might begin to resent her. Bitterness would eat into their relationship and poison it. She rested her cheek against his warm chest and closed her eyes.

"We'll make it work." He held her tighter. "I'm determined."

"Me too." That much she was certain of. Kraven was her mate. She loved him and she didn't want to face a future without him.

"We're both tired. Why don't we get some sleep?"

"I *am* exhausted."

He lifted her off his legs and helped her stand, then took her hand once he got to his feet. "Come on, baby. We'll cuddle. I love holding you."

"I love that too."

He led her into his bedroom and pulled back the covers. Bat stripped and got into bed first. Kraven pulled her close, spooning her from behind. "You're safe and I'm right here."

Bat turned her head, staring at him. "I love you."

"I love you too, Hellion."

She smiled and closed her eyes. A lot was on her mind but exhaustion muted her thoughts.

Kraven knew the moment Bat drifted to sleep. He couldn't. It worried him when she'd said she needed to think about things. She had a tendency to be stubborn and irrational when it came to matters of the heart. A human had hurt her and that wound ran deep. He understood, but he no longer felt she could be a threat, not the way Violet had been. That bitch had merely tried to stab him in the heart. Bat could tear it from his chest with words and actions.

I can't lose her. She had taken seeing him shifted extremely well. He needed to strengthen their mate bond. He pulled his head back a little, openly admiring her bared throat and shoulder. His fangs slid down without him meaning them to and his dick reacted by hardening. He wanted to claim his mate but she needed to rest first.

He began to plot out the best ways to have sex with Bat that wouldn't make taking his blood traumatic for her.

A light tapping at the door drew his attention and he eased away from Bat, careful not to wake her as he got out of bed. He walked to the dresser, withdrew a pair of boxers, and quickly strode into the living room. He unlocked the front door to find his brother standing there with an irritated look on his face.

"What? I know it's not dinnertime yet, so we aren't late."

"Dad called. You don't seem to have your phone on so I had to come give you the message." He glanced down Kraven's body and sniffed the air. "At least you weren't interrupted during sex. I can't say the same."

"What does Dad want?"

"He talked to Lorn and asked for a meeting. He agreed but it has to be a secret one. He's coming here later today. Dinner is now being held at our parents' house."

"This Lorn is going to eat with us? Has hell frozen over?"

Drantos smirked. "I know. A Decker clan member breaking bread at the family table." He sobered quickly. "Lorn's going to drive in. He wants anyone watching him from his clan to believe he's going to town. Two representatives from the other clans are coming too. Lorn didn't want to sit at a table with all three clan leaders though, so two enforcers will join us. Dad said Lorn still wasn't comfortable with that, but he agreed to the terms after Dad made it clear all the clans want to be a part of this discussion. It affects us all."

"Why doesn't Lorn want to meet with the other leaders?"

"I'm not certain but we don't want to scare him off. Dad said Lorn seemed a bit paranoid, not that I blame him."

"No shit. Decker has to have some who are loyal to him; they'd probably murder Lorn if they knew he had agreed to a meet with us."

"Exactly."

417

"What time?"

"Five. Be there early."

"Are you bringing Dusti?"

Drantos nodded. "Come with your mate. Dad hopes Lorn will be more comfortable with our females present."

"That's a good idea."

"It's important that we build trust with this guy and get to know him."

Kraven reached up and rubbed his neck. "Do you think he'll take over the clan?"

"It would sure solve a lot of our problems but I don't envy the bastard. He's going to come up against opposition. The first generations are set in their ways and they've been led by Decker since the beginning. Change will go down hard for them. They'll resist and want that bastard back."

Kraven silently agreed. "We're offering support though and Decker is a dead man walking. It's just a matter of time."

"*We* know that, but does everyone in his clan realize he went too far and there's no way for him to dig his way out of the grave?"

"I think the dead bodies of their loved ones probably clued them in."

"No shit." Drantos leaned against the doorjamb. "Are you alright? You look upset."

"Bat is starting to realize what a VampLycan is, and everything that goes along with having me for a mate. She's taking it better than I'd expected, but I'm worried she'll use it as an excuse to keep me distanced."

"You need to strengthen the bond. Why haven't you?"

"We've been kind of busy, bro."

"You're having sex with her. That was apparent to everyone the moment you stepped foot in the village. We know what you were doing on the way home. How damn hard is it to bite and bleed for her?"

"Baby steps. I'm trying to cushion the blows as they come. She just saw me shifted for the first time a little while ago. There was no screaming involved so that was a plus."

Drantos sighed. "You said *I* was being too easy on Dusti."

"It was easy to say when it wasn't *me* in the situation."

"Agreed." Drantos straightened. "She's your mate, Kraven. You're way more aggressive with Bat than I am with Dusti. That's the man she fell for. Why stop doing what's worked for you so far? Bite her and bleed."

"I will."

"Do it now. She's in your bed, I assume. Don't forget Aveoth—he might stop by around dinner too. Dad invited him."

"Fuck." That pissed Kraven off. "I refuse to allow him anywhere near Bat!"

"He's not as bad as we'd feared. I saw and spoke to him. He won't snatch her and take flight. Just make sure he can smell that you're mated. That means she needs to carry more of your scent than just physical contact."

"I don't want him near her, Drantos."

419

"I understand, but he backed off wanting to meet her when I told him she was yours. Maybe thanks to our old friendship, he has a soft spot for us. Who knows with him? Don't give him a reason to reconsider. Strengthen the bond before dinner. Now you don't have an excuse to put it off." Drantos grinned. "Talk about motivation. Get to it."

"We'll be there."

Kraven waved and closed the door, locking it. He stormed into the bedroom and removed his boxers, getting back into bed. The idea of Aveoth meeting Bat made him fear losing her—and that wasn't going to happen.

He gently gripped her shoulder and pulled her onto her back. She woke, confused as she peered at him.

He extended his fangs. "I want you right now."

"Is everything okay?"

She had a sexy voice when she mumbled, still sleepy.

"It will be." He leaned over her, going for her throat. She stiffened for a second at the feel of his fangs but he didn't bite, just lightly nipped and kissed her. Her arms wound around his neck and she pressed her breasts against his chest.

"Yes," she urged.

He pulled away just enough to stare into her eyes. "It's time to link our bond stronger."

"What do we need to do?"

"I'm going to bite you and you're going to drink some of my blood."

She glanced at his mouth. "I don't have those."

"You don't need them." He lowered his head, brushing kisses across her throat. He shifted his weight on her, reaching down and tapping her thighs. She parted them wider. "Relax, Hellion. I'm going to distract you, and when I say so, drink."

"Okay."

He slid his hand between her thighs, found her clit, and rubbed gently. Bat moaned his name and stopped worrying about what would come next. Kraven made her hot and achy, turned-on to the point that she was instantly prepared to beg him to fuck her. He seemed to sense that and lifted up.

Kraven rolled Bat onto her side and spooned her. He gripped her thigh and she lifted it, arching her ass to help him enter her from that angle. The feel of his thick shaft stretching her, sinking deep inside her pussy, caused her to groan his name.

"I'm going to bite my wrist and put it to your mouth. Drink while I fuck you. I'll bite you when I know it won't hurt. Ready, Hellion?"

"Yes."

She didn't watch him actually sink his fangs into his skin but she saw the aftermath when he brought his arm in front of her face. She swallowed once and then opened her mouth. Kraven began to move slowly inside her when she pressed her lips over the wound and warm, wet blood filled her mouth. The coppery taste somehow seemed muted with the feel of his cock driving in and out of her. Pleasure instantly swamped her senses.

He rolled them so she lay on top of him and his other hand delved between her thighs. She spread them a little farther apart. He used two fingers to strum across her clit.

Bat moaned. Kraven was so good at distracting her. The need to come overruled any objections she had to drinking his blood. He fucked her harder, driving up into her, and his mouth clamped down on the top of her shoulder. She felt wetness, his sharp fangs, and then a soft jab of pain that quickly faded.

Fucking and sucking. She got the concept now—and it felt pretty amazing. The climax built quickly with Kraven inside her and manipulating her clit. She had to pull her mouth away from his wrist to avoid choking.

"Yes!" Pleasure tore through her.

Kraven snarled against her shoulder and rolled them onto their sides again, curling around her. He held her tight, their bodies twitching together. He gently stopped biting her and licked at her skin.

"It will heal up fast."

Bat opened her eyes, seeing that blood had spilled on the bed. "I can't say the same about your bedding."

"Fuck it. That was worth it. I own more."

She laughed, finding that funny. "We've got blood on us too."

"I like my sex messy." He growled low at her. "It's more fun if we get dirty. How about a shower? I want to nail you against my tile."

"Give me a minute to catch my breath."

"One. Then your ass is mine." He reached down and cupped her butt. "All mine, Hellion."

Chapter Twenty-Three

Bat took a sip of wine and glanced around at the men seated at the long dining room table. They were all big, muscular guys. Dusti leaned over enough to bump into her right side.

"Is it just me or are the testosterone levels in here off the charts?" Dusti whispered the words.

Bat gave a slight nod. She agreed.

"Aren't those two men supposed to be from friendly clans?"

Bat gave another nod.

"Should we remind them of that? They look as if a fight might break out at any second."

"They can hear you," Kraven stated from her immediate left.

Bat met his gaze. "It's a valid question. We're not used to men snarling at each other over dinner." She turned her focus to the tall dark-headed stranger across the table. "You're Wen, right?"

"Yes."

She glanced at the man to his left. "Brady?"

"Brody."

"I was close." Bat hesitated, glancing between the two. "I understand that your clans are nervous about asking an unknown candidate to take over a neighboring clan, but let's be honest. Anyone would be better leading it than Decker Filmore. Am I right?"

"Enough." Velder growled from the head of the table. "Be silent."

424

Her new father-in-law irritated her. He might be big shit in Dog Bark but after listening to the men around the table argue over trivial things for the past hour, her patience was gone. She pushed away from the table and stood.

"Bat, no," Kraven hissed.

She met his pleading stare, almost able to read his thoughts. He had warned her dozens of times not to cause any trouble or talk. *Shut up and look pretty.* He'd thrown her words in her face in a teasing manner, but he'd meant them.

"I can't. I'm sorry." She fixed her gaze on Velder. "No disrespect to you but I have some experience settling disputes. Not everything needs to go to court. We're getting nowhere, so please let me try."

Velder growled low but threw up his hands. "I'll listen."

She studied the men around the table. "Let me sum it up. No one knows much about Lorn." She openly appraised the beefy blond at the table. He was an attractive guy with a calm demeanor and some seriously unique gray eyes. "My statement stands though. *Anyone* would do a better job at ruling or leading—whatever you call it—the clan he comes from. He's not really talkative but he doesn't know anyone here. I wouldn't want to play twenty questions with a bunch of strangers either. Some of the things you've asked are totally out of line." She pointedly stared at Brody. "Why don't you tell us about *your* sex life?"

He glared at her.

"Exactly. Do you believe he's a sexual deviant? That he'd take advantage of women? In other words, *what is your point*? Spit it out." Bat waited, crossing her arms over her chest.

425

"He's earned a reputation amongst my clan of being cold to women when he visits us every year during his heat."

"Does he abuse them? Hit them? Force them to do weird shit they don't want to do?" Bat wasn't completely certain what "his heat" meant, other than the little Dr. Brent described, but she knew they were part animal. She could make an educated guess. "Are you accusing him of being a rapist or something?"

"No," Brody snarled. "He's just cold. He doesn't cuddle them after sex."

Bat sighed. "So he acts too human?"

That seemed to confuse the big dark-haired Brody.

Bat shifted her gaze to Lorn. "Is that a requirement in the VampLycan world? Is it a rule or something?"

"No. I'm not looking for a mate."

"So you want to stay single and don't encourage your sexual partners to become attached," she deduced.

"Yes," Lorn agreed.

She looked at Brody. "Is that breaking any rules?"

He shook his head.

"Good. We've established he's just a man who isn't into intimacy with lovers because he doesn't want to encourage them, and that's not a crime. Let's move on and get over that, alright? He's not looking for a mate." She stared at Velder. "Is having a mate one of the requirements to being a clan leader?"

"No, but taking a mate would be a good idea."

426

"Ideas are wonderful...but not a requirement." She addressed Lorn. "You look young. I know that can be tricky with VampLycans since you don't seem to age, but are you really old?"

"No."

"Let's cut the crap then. He's young, single, and not ready to take a mate. I'm sure that will change in time. Do you want to lead your clan? That's the most important question and it hasn't even been asked."

"It will cause difficulties."

Bat sat again. "What kind?"

Lorn mused for a bit, seeming to consider his words. "My father is loyal to Decker."

"Are you?" Bat took a sip of wine.

"No. I hate the bastard."

That was promising. "Do you want to start a war with other clans?"

"No." Lorn scowled. "We're all VampLycans and shouldn't fight amongst ourselves."

"Bingo—we have a winner." Bat leaned forward, gazing at Velder. "Isn't that what matters most? Peace between the clans? He wants that."

Velder cleared his throat. "Lorn, would you be willing to take over your clan?"

"I'd have to kill my father. He won't allow it any other way. That would break my mother's heart, and she'd probably die soon after." Lorn's voice lowered. "I've stayed with the clan to protect the weaker members, not for any other reason." He sat back in his chair and grimly regarded Velder. "You're asking me to destroy my family. There's also no

427

guarantee Decker won't return. He kills his enemies. I'd be condemning the people I've protected to a death sentence, including my brother. Decker and his enforcers would murder everyone I care about, out of spite."

A loud noise came from the roof and everyone looked up. The men leapt from their seats, knocking over chairs. Bat heard distinctive footsteps across the roof and then a thump from just outside. All gazes turned toward the front door. It opened and a hulk of a man entered.

"Shit," Bat gasped.

Rock guy had arrived. There was no doubt who he was. The huge black wings tucked behind his back couldn't be denied as he came through the doorway. He had short black hair, a handsome face, and wore arm bands with metal plates from wrist to elbow. Bat also noticed his shirt was missing—and he had a seriously muscled chest and arms.

"Lord Aveoth." Velder didn't seem pleased. "You're late."

"I was listening. Which of you is Lorn?"

The blond stepped forward. "I am."

"I'm your guarantee. Decker is *mine*."

Bat winced at the tone Aveoth's voice dropped to. It was almost painfully deep and loud. His gaze shifted to her suddenly and they stared at each other. His eyes were a brilliant blue but they seemed to shimmer, the color of them changing as she watched.

Kraven moved closer and wrapped an arm around her waist as he tugged her against his side. "This is my mate."

"Batina."

Aveoth knew her name. She wasn't sure if she should be frightened by that or not.

He tore his gaze from her to study Kraven. "Relax, my old friend. I would never kill you over a woman—even her. Though I admit to a little envy." He looked back at Bat. "Continue what you were doing. I like the sound of your voice and hate bullshit as well. Males love to posture. My time is limited and I need to return home. Let us determine the outcome of this meeting and we'll go from there."

Rock guy was scary, she decided. A chill went down her spine. He'd given her an order and she definitely felt inclined to follow it. She gripped Kraven to keep him close while she took a few seconds to find her composure and focus on the task at hand. Her hold on Kraven eased and she put a little space between them, going into professional mode. Her mate allowed it but he stayed close.

"Lorn?"

He returned to his spot at the table. "What?"

"You heard Lord Aveoth." *Don't call him rock guy. Please don't slip.* She feared the GarLycan didn't have a sense of humor. She could sense it. "Decker is his. I'll assume that means he won't be our problem anymore."

"I'll find him and end his miserable life," Aveoth clarified.

Bat swallowed hard. She believed rock guy meant every word. "Decker won't be returning to your clan. Someone needs to take charge. It's obviously going to be a tough decision for you to make, one that comes with grave consequences. I'm sorry for that."

"I need time to think about it." Lorn faced Velder. "Give me a few days to assess the situation at home. There will be infighting if I step up.

429

That's a given. I also need to consult with my brother, Lavos. I can't agree to challenge for leadership without his support."

"That's understandable." Velder sighed. "I am truly regretful for your situation but things can't remain the same. Some of your members have requested to move into other territories and become parts of our clans. That could leave only Decker supporters there, and we can't have that. They could start trouble for us all. Do you understand?"

Lorn nodded. "I do."

Bat wasn't exactly certain what that meant.

Kraven cleared it up for her. "We'd have to go in and make certain they weren't a threat any longer."

"You'd have to kill them?"

Kraven nodded.

Bat stared at Lorn. He looked miserable, and she felt pity for him. A lot rested on his shoulders. People were going to die, either way. Lorn would have to weed out the bad himself or the other clans would do it for him.

"Some will be too afraid to leave. They've lived in fear of Decker for far too long. That would mean you'd take out innocents in the process." Lorn's expression hardened. "I'll get back to you in a few days. Please give me that time."

"It's yours." Velder nodded. "Decker is on the run. We can wait. I'll temporarily halt permission for any of your clan to join ours."

"We will too," Wen announced. "I'll talk to my clan leader."

"So will I," Brody agreed.

"I have an enemy to hunt." Lord Aveoth bowed slightly. "We'll talk in a few days." He spun, leaving the way he'd come, closing the door behind him.

The dinner broke up fast, the two enforcers from the other clans and Lorn leaving. Bat expected her new father-in-law to rant at her for interceding once only family remained, but he surprised her.

"Batina."

She lifted her chin, staring at the man who looked a lot like Kraven. "Yes?"

"Lord Aveoth was correct. Males love to posture. You got to the heart of the matter and pinpointed the important details. Thank you. It could have been a long night otherwise."

"None of my furniture got broken during a fight this time. I appreciate that." Crayla grinned. "That's a first when the clans come together. The food distracts them for only so long but once it's eaten, they tend to throw a few punches."

Velder brushed a kiss on his wife's cheek. "We'll have her come when Lorn returns."

"Great. I'm the clan bullshitter but Bat gets to be the clan peacekeeper."

Bat frowned at her sister. "What?"

Dusti rolled her eyes. "Nothing. You did good. That would have been one brawl I didn't want to see go down."

"We're going home." Kraven snagged Bat's hand. "Good night."

431

Bat followed him out of the house and they walked to his cabin. It still irritated her that he refused to lock the door unless they were home, and even then he'd told her it was only to keep people from walking in and disturbing them.

Once inside, he pulled her into his arms and chuckled. "You shocked them."

"Are you mad?"

"No. The enforcers tried to pick a fight with Lorn over petty issues. We don't know him but *they* seem to. I had wondered why they were so resistant to him. He visits their clans when he's in heat. You made them reveal that fact."

"They were being assholes to Lorn."

"We're protective of our women. It would piss us off too if he came here and didn't leave a good impression with someone who agreed to share his heat."

"He just doesn't want a mate. Did you cuddle the women you slept with?"

He shook his head. "I'm not answering that. I love you. *You're* the most important woman in my life. The past doesn't matter."

She agreed. "I don't really want the details. I love you too."

"Aveoth will find Decker and kill him. I'll get you back to L.A. as soon as that happens."

Bat stared into his eyes. "I was thinking about that…"

"Decker talked the Vampire Council into putting a bounty on you, and the Lycans are aware of it too." Kraven's mood darkened. "Aveoth is a

432

good hunter. It won't take long, but we're not returning to L.A. until Decker is dead. I'd do anything for you but your safety comes foremost."

She chewed on her bottom lip. "I'm not asking you to take me home. To be honest...I'm okay with staying here for a while."

His mouth dropped open and she could see she'd stunned him.

"I'm not saying I'm ready to apply for a driver's license or sell my condo just yet, but your people need help. It was like watching a bunch of brooding teenagers trying to have an important discussion but their hormones were getting in the way. You need a clearheaded negotiator to keep them on track when they have sit-downs. I'm familiar with politics. You've got four governments, pretty much, that are trying to work together as a whole. Five, counting the GarLycans. And we're not even sure if Lorn will head his clan. That means other candidates might be in the running. It could take some time to sort this mess out. I need to learn your laws and regulations so I understand things better before the clans meet up again, but how hard can that be?"

He gaped at her.

"Close your mouth, sweetheart. I love a challenge. I need to get a look at your constitution or whatever you use."

He took a deep breath. "They aren't written down but I could explain everything to you."

"That's a good start. That way I won't have to ask what's allowed and what isn't."

"What are you saying?"

"Part of my job is settling disputes. There's a lot of negotiation that happens behind closed doors. Not every case goes to court." Her excitement grew the more she considered the possibilities. "You said there's tension between the clans, especially between Decker's and Aveoth's. Five parties need to sit down on a regular basis and come to terms."

"You want to be a part of that?"

"I do." She grinned and wrapped her arms around his neck to pull him closer. "I really do. It's the perfect solution."

He still appeared stunned.

"We'll get to stay here longer with your family and my sister. I haven't had time off in forever. It won't exactly be a vacation and I won't be paid. Pro bono is fine, and I won't technically be an attorney. I'm not licensed in this state. I could be though. I'll have to check into what I need to do about that. I'm certain someone here will need one, what with the way you guys love to fight."

Kraven grinned wide. *I love you.*

"I love you too."

His body turned rigid.

"What's wrong?"

"I didn't say that aloud."

"Yes you did. I heard it."

He sealed his lips firmly. *I love your ass, too. It's mine!*

Bat heard him but he wasn't talking. His voice sounded inside her head. It was her turn to gape at him.

"Our bond's in place. Try thinking at me."

"I don't know how."

"Try, Hellion. Just focus on me and think something."

This is freaking me out.

He laughed. "I know but it's part of being VampLycan mates. It's normal."

Shit! He heard me.

"I did. I do." He scooped her up into his arms. *I hope the physical bond is in place. We're about to find out.*

"What does that mean?" She clung to him.

He placed her on his bed and began to strip. "Amazing sex. Get naked, Hellion."

Her hands trembled as she removed her shoes and twisted on the bed to take off her clothes. "We're going to fight a lot if you can read my thoughts."

"We'll adjust to having private thoughts and open ones. Trust me."

I do.

He grinned. *Good.*

This is still freaking me out.

"We'll stop talking then. Only feel." He stepped closer to the bed and wiggled his finger. "Come here."

She went to him.

He reached out and pulled until she rose to her knees, facing him. "Open your mind, focus on me, and suck on my nipple."

"What are we doing?"

"It's a test to see if you can feel what I do. Try it, Bat."

She licked her lips, gripped his bared hips, and leaned in. Her mouth fastened over his nipple and she gently sucked. She used her tongue to play with him.

A moan tore from her when her own nipple throbbed and she jerked back, startled.

"You felt it, didn't you? How good it feels to have your mouth on me?" Excitement thickened his voice.

"Is that what that was?"

He nodded. "Keep your mind wide open." He backed up a little and separated them. "Close your eyes and lay down."

Bat followed his directions.

"Relax."

She tried. She forced her muscles to go lax and just lay flat on the bed. His fingers lightly ran down her stomach, lower, and Kraven gently touched her clit. She spread her legs wider to give him better access. His fingers brushed over the sensitive nub, rubbing back and forth. Bat moaned. It felt good but there was...a strangeness to it, for some reason.

She opened her eyes—and gasped.

He wasn't on the bed with her or even within reach. He stood in the exact same spot but he was cupping his erect cock with one of his hands, brushing his thumb over the crown. He released himself.

"We're linked. You ready, Hellion? You're about to learn firsthand why mates don't ever want someone else. Nothing can come close to what we're about to do together." He climbed on the bed with her and took possession of her mouth.

Desire and heat swamped Bat. It burned her up. She clutched at Kraven, trying to pull him closer. She couldn't get enough of him. She felt her own nails digging into her skin, despite actually clawing at *his* back. She ran her fingers lower to the curve of his ass, moaning. She twisted her head away from his lips.

"Fuck me now," she demanded. "I need you inside me."

"I know."

He adjusted his hips. She was ready, wet and needy as his cock rubbed against her spread pussy. He entered her with one swift thrust and Bat cried out, wrapping her legs around his waist. She lifted them a little higher almost immediately, realizing it made it easier for him to move when she did. He fucked her fast and hard. His powerful body pinned her to the bed, and sheer ecstasy inundated her.

Bat screamed out as a climax hit. She wasn't certain if he'd sent them over the edge or she had, but they were experiencing it together. She could sense his love for her, how much she meant to him, and incredible pleasure.

Fear came next. It was all too intense. Too much...

It's okay, baby. I've got you.

His voice inside her head made her focus on him. It helped.

"I'm right here," he rasped next to her ear. "I'm never letting you go. Don't be afraid."

Tears filled her eyes.

Kraven lifted his head, peering at her.

"I know, Hellion. You're wide open to me right now. I'm never going to hurt you."

She knew that. Knew for certain now. He'd rather die than do anything that would break her heart or put a wedge between them.

This is mating. It's two becoming one. Don't be afraid. There's no fear here. It's just us, together. It's beautiful, isn't it?

Yes.

Tears shone in his eyes but he smiled. *You act so tough but you're brimming with emotions. See? I'm feeling them too. You're my hellion and I love you.*

I think I'll die without you.

It won't ever happen. You're stuck with me.

Promise?

Kraven nodded. *I always keep my word.*

A sense of peace settled inside Bat. She believed him. Loving someone had been considered a weakness to her for so long...but not anymore. Kraven had changed everything about her life and made it better.

Her job in L.A. didn't matter. The man holding her did.

"You can have both," he rasped. "We'll make it work and find a way."

"We will."

438

50307702R00262

Made in the USA
Lexington, KY
10 March 2016